USA TODAY bestselling autho
London, England. She is marri
sons—which gives her rather t
insight into the male psyche—and also works as a
film journalist. She adores her job, which involves
getting swept up in a world of high emotion, sensual
excitement, funny and feisty women, sexy and
tortured men and glamorous locations where laundry
doesn't exist. Once she turns off her computer she
often does chores—usually involving laundry!

Canadian **Dani Collins** knew in high school
that she wanted to write romance for a living.
Twenty-five years later, after marrying her high
school sweetheart, having two kids with him,
working at several generic office jobs and
submitting countless manuscripts, she got
The Call. Her first Mills & Boon novel won the
Reviewers' Choice Award for Best First in Series
from *RT Book Reviews*. She now works in her own
office, writing romance.

STOLEN FOR HIS DESERT THRONE

HEIDI RICE

A BABY TO MAKE HER HIS BRIDE

DANI COLLINS

MILLS & BOON

First published in Great Britain 2023
by Mills & Boon, an imprint of HarperCollins*Publishers* Ltd,
1 London Bridge Street, London, SE1 9GF

www.harpercollins.co.uk

HarperCollins*Publishers*, Macken House, 39/40 Mayor Street Upper,
Dublin 1, D01 C9W8, Ireland

ISBN: 978-0-263-30674-3

04/23

MIX
Paper | Supporting
responsible forestry
FSC™ C007454

This book is produced from independently certified FSC™ paper to ensure responsible forest management.
For more information visit: www.harpercollins.co.uk/green.

Printed and Bound in the UK using 100% Renewable Electricity at CPI Group (UK) Ltd, Croydon, CR0 4YY

STOLEN FOR HIS DESERT THRONE

HEIDI RICE

MILLS & BOON

To all my wonderful readers,
with a special shout out to Carmen,
who first put the idea of doing a 'second generation'
story with Kaliah as the heroine into my head.

If you enjoyed Kamal and Kaliah's story,
then check out the other available stories
linked to the Khan family:

Carrying the Sheikh's Baby

Claimed for the Desert Prince's Heir

Innocent's Desert Wedding Contract

Banished Prince to Desert Boss

CHAPTER ONE

CROWN PRINCE KAMAL ZOKAN, the soon-to-be-crowned King of the Zokari tribal lands, stood in the paddock at Narabia's famed annual horse-racing pageant and scowled as he recalled the meeting the day before with Uttram Aziz, the head of his tribal elders.

The minarets of his neighbour Sheikh Zane Ali Nawari Khan's lavish Golden Palace glittered like jewels in the morning sunshine behind the high stone walls surrounding the stable yards and race arena as flags of every nation fluttered in the breeze and a string of thoroughbred Arabian horses gathered at the starting line. But Kamal could appreciate none of it.

Damn Uttram Aziz. Damn his attempts to defy me at every turn. And, most of all, damn his latest attempt to stop me from claiming my throne.

Adrenaline pumped through Kamal's system as the anger and resentment which had been burning under his breastbone since yesterday's meeting refused to release its stranglehold on his throat.

'It is the law, Kamal. You would know this already if you had a more cultured past. You must be married before the crowning ceremony next month or you will forfeit the throne.'

Born an outcast boy, he had fought his way from nothing to become Zokar's youngest army colonel, and now—after amassing a fortune by having invested in the country's fledging mineral industry—he was on the verge of becoming its king. The previous Sheikh had died without heirs two months ago and had named Kamal as his successor.

Kamal had no doubt the Sheikh's decision had been based on expediency. Zokar needed inward investment and Kamal was a successful businessman who had also proved himself a leader of men. Kamal had hesitated at first but, once he had decided to take the throne, Aziz and his followers had attempted to thwart him at every turn. And this latest ultimatum had only frustrated him more. How did they come up with this stuff?

Kamal could not have felt more out of place if he had tried, forced to attend Khan's lavish annual event in search of a damned bride. And not just any bride. A royal bride whom, Aziz had stated, would make up for Kamal's lack of breeding and sophistication...

He swallowed, all but choking on his fury. He didn't need breeding, or sophistication, to be a strong ruler and a good king. He was smart, ambitious and determined to obtain the investment Zokar needed to bring its infrastructure into the twenty-first century. He had already invested a small fortune of his own money to that end. But the more conservative elements of the country's ruling elite—represented by Aziz and his acolytes—insisted on putting barriers in his way. Every time Kamal scaled one, there would be another, and he was sick of it.

He glanced up at the royal box where Khan and his brother Prince Raif of the Kholadi people and their families stood with the other local rulers. Kamal shuddered, having escaped from the official greeting ceremony earlier with some excuse about joining his men in the stable yards—where he felt a great deal more comfortable—to watch the main race.

He had respect for Khan. He knew the man had worked hard to develop his kingdom after his father's harsh rule—and Khan had been quick to offer his support when Kamal had been named as successor to the Zokari throne. It was an endorsement Kamal was embarrassed to admit he had needed to smooth his path with the rest of Zokar's tribal elders. Luckily, neither Khan nor his brother Raif had recognised Kamal from their previous meeting fifteen years ago.

But Kamal still remembered the sickening humiliation of that day as if it were yesterday—when he had been a malnourished boy serving the royal party and Khan and his entourage had arrived for a state visit. Kamal had lingered, gathering the dishes as slowly as he could, fascinated by the pride in the powerful sheikh's voice as Khan had introduced his heir—his five-year-old daughter, Crown Princess Kaliah—to the Zokari Elders.

Unfortunately, Kamal had been so intent on eavesdropping on the conversation he hadn't spotted the pillow strewn across his path. He had tripped and dropped the dishes. The crash of breaking porcelain had made every eye turn on him.

Shame washed over him again at the memory of the striking blue of Princess Kaliah Khan's eyes as they had glowed with pity for him. He'd begun gathering the broken pieces, his pride burning, when his employer, Hamid, had appeared, apologising profusely for Kamal's clumsiness, and had proceeded to beat him with his belt.

The vicious swipe had stung like the devil—because the wounds from Kamal's previous beating had yet to fully heal—but not nearly as much as his pride when he'd heard the golden child's impassioned plea to her father. 'Daddy, you must stop that man. He shouldn't hit that poor serving boy, it's not right.'

Poor serving boy?

Khan had intervened, of course, and Hamid had been reprimanded for his behaviour. But the memory of that long-ago encounter still stung. Which was precisely why Kamal had not wanted to come to this event. Being in Khan's debt was bad enough, but the humiliation if he recognised him would be far worse.

At least the Crown Princess was not present in the royal box. The last thing he needed right now was to meet that spoilt, entitled child again—even if she would now be twenty or thereabouts—and risk her recognising him. Although that seemed unlikely. He was six-foot-four now, and twenty-nine years old, even if he felt a great deal older in life experience.

The cool evening air whipped at his skin and the crowd noise increased as the horses took their places behind the starting rope. He swallowed, the fury finally releasing its stranglehold. The rage and pain he had been subjected to as a child had stood him in good stead to ensure he never gave up, and never gave in, before he got what he wanted. Which was why he would scale this latest hurdle and return to Zokar with a willing bride in time to claim the throne once and for all.

His lips twisted in a bitter smile. Hell, he might even consider Kaliah Khan for the position, if she had learned some humility in the intervening years…although he suspected that was doubtful, given her reputation in the region as a wild child.

'Prince Kamal, the Race of Kings is about to start. His Divine Majesty and his wife Queen Catherine would like to welcome you to the royal box with the other heads of state.'

Kamal turned to find one of Khan's many advisers wearing a helpful smile on his weathered face.

'I shall watch the race from here,' he said, knowing he would need more time to prepare for the ordeal of having to socialise at the event scheduled for after the race. Khan and his wife had been welcoming earlier, and surprisingly easy going, but Kamal wasn't a man who knew how to make small talk. Nor did he wish to learn.

The adviser bowed. 'Of course, whatever you wish, Your Highness.'

Kamal turned as the man disappeared back into the crowd, just as a series of shouts came from the paddock. He frowned as a new horse and rider broke into the arena, galloping towards the starting line. The horse was smaller than most of the others, a mare, not a gelding. Kamal couldn't help staring, not just at the horse—whose midnight coat gleamed in the spotlights—but at the rider, who was tall for a jockey but impossibly slender. The way he held himself was spellbinding, so graceful and perfectly attuned with the magnificent horse.

The gun sounded as the new arrival was still racing to join the starting line. The field leapt forward en masse while the trailing horse accelerated as if it had been fired from the gun. The jockey's head was bent low over the powerful beast, his body as one with the animal as its legs ate up the ground.

The crowd went wild, the late horse providing added drama as it flew towards the rest of the field. Kamal's throat clogged as excitement powered through his veins. He had never been much into horse racing—leisure activities were not a part of his life—but even he could admire the poetry of the horse's motion and feel the swell of exhilaration as

the horse and rider shot round the first turn without breaking stride, hugging the fence to gain ground on the field.

On the back straight, the horse powered into the lead.
But, as the field raced back towards them, the mystery jockey's cap snapped off. Long dark hair fanned out, and Kamal
noticed the way the rider's silks flattened in the wind over
small, firm breasts.

A woman. What the hell?

As the horse and rider flew past, Kamal got a better look
at the jockey's fierce expression—and sensed the effort it
was taking for her to stay on the horse.

Fear careered through him.

The horse's speed was completely unchecked. The animal was going too fast, its hooves pounding hard, its flanks
sweating with the effort. Was the girl controlling the horse,
or was she merely trying to cling onto its back?

That little fool.

Kamal shoved his way through the busy arena stables
and leapt onto the nearest saddled horse. Grabbing the reins,
he ignored the shouts from the stable hand who had been
leading the horse to its stall and charged towards the arena.

The crowds parted to let him through as he galloped towards the track, his mind berating the foolhardy girl even
as the fear continued to streak through his body.

The horse was coming down the back straight again as
Kamal reached the track. The slender rider was bent so
low over the mare now it was clear she had exhausted herself. Adrenaline and something that felt uncomfortably like
arousal shot through Kamal as her wild hair flowed around
her features, while her slight body clung for dear life to the
still accelerating horse.

Kamal spurred his mount onto the track ahead of the

runaway mare as it took the turn—determined to rescue the idiot girl before she broke her foolish neck.

'Come on, girl, we've got this.' Excitement barrelled through Kaliah Khan's exhausted body.

We're going to win. And I will finally prove I'm not a total screw-up.

She clung to the reins and kept her body low over Ashreen's neck, urging her on, aware of all the muscles straining to stay on the horse as they careered around the track. She needed this victory to prove to her family, to prove to Narabia's establishment and to prove to herself she had what it took to win in a man's world.

But most of all to prove to that creep Colin, the guy she'd thought she was falling in love at Cambridge, he'd been wrong to call her a 'frigid bitch'.

Her anger was like an aphrodisiac, turning the fear and danger into exhilaration—and adding much-needed fuel to her flagging stamina. It was as if they were flying. Perhaps if she hadn't been so determined to win she might have controlled the horse more, but it was too late now—Ashreen had scented victory too.

Suddenly an unknown rider on a huge white stallion swerved onto the track ahead of her.

'Who the...?' Liah gasped.

Where had *he* come from? And what was he doing right in front of her?

The horse, much bigger than her mare, picked up speed and moved into her lane, keeping pace with Ashreen's strides. The man was a huge black shadow on the white horse, large and forbidding, powerful and overwhelming.

Liah's shattered mind imagined a Horseman of the Apocalypse come to collect her and take her to hell.

'Get out of the way!' she screamed, but her demand was whipped away on the wind. Her tired arms weighed several tons—all she could do was cling on, her body too weary to manoeuvre Ashreen away from the encroaching rider.

Ashreen lifted her nose, scenting the other animal, and for a split-second Liah was sure the mare would rear, but instead she slowed, almost as if she was intimidated by the huge stallion too.

'No, Ashreen!' Liah shouted. The finish line was just a few hundred metres away. But, before she could get the horse to accelerate again, the rider came alongside her. His hard, angular face was partially covered by a beard, but she could see the fierce concentration in his eyes and the spark of furious temper.

What the heck did he have to be angry about? She was the one getting pushed out of a race she'd been about to win.

'Let go of the reins,' he shouted. 'I'll lift you off her.'

'Are you mad?' she yelled back, but her fingers loosened instinctively.

The air expelled from her lungs in a rush as a hard forearm wrapped around her midriff and she became airborne, plucked from the saddle like a rag doll.

She heard the thunder of Ashreen's hooves as the mare bolted away towards the finish line, leaving her behind. She grunted in shock as she found herself dumped face-down over the rider's saddle. Her stomach slapped down on thighs hard with muscle and she caught a lungful of his scent— spice, musk and clean soap. His robe wrapped around them both as the mighty horse reared. But Liah didn't even have a chance to scream before the horse bowed to its rider's commands and its hooves crashed back to earth, giving her stomach another painful jolt against those rock-solid thighs.

His hand remained firm on her back, keeping her in place

as he steered the horse across the track, bringing them to a stop inches from the fence.

The crowd erupted, waving and cheering, as if the whole thing had been planned for their entertainment. Nausea boiled in Liah's stomach, her mind reeling as the giddy adrenaline rush slammed into a wave of shock and fury.

What had just happened? And who was this mad man? Because he'd nearly killed them both…and, more importantly—he'd just lost her the race. Every part of her body throbbed with pain. But what hurt most of all was her pride.

The rest of the field raced past them as the man dragged her up to seat her across his lap so she could see his face. Dark brows flattened over piercing golden eyes which looked weirdly familiar. Had she seen this man before? Because those amber eyes struck something in her memory from long ago.

But nothing else about him seemed familiar. And she was immediately struck by the thought that, if she had met him before, she would not have forgotten him.

He was huge, all hard, lean muscle, a brutal scar slashed down his left cheek creating a raised line through the stubble on his jaw. The fierce intensity as his gaze raked over her made the harsh planes and angles of his sun-weathered features look even more dramatic.

He wasn't what she would call handsome, his dark, raw-boned face far too intimidating and defiantly masculine for that, but he was breath-taking.

And hot.

Liah stifled the idiotic thought as unhelpful heat joined the bubble of nausea in her belly.

'You are not hurt?' he asked, his rough, heavily accented voice echoing in her chest—and triggering the pulse of something rich and fluid in her sore abdomen.

The question jolted her out of her trance—and drop-kicked her back into reality.

She pushed against his controlling arm. 'Of course I'm not hurt,' she said, her voice coming out on an annoying squeak. She gathered another breath. 'No thanks to you, you idiot. What on earth were you thinking, grabbing me like that? You could have broken both our necks.'

His dark brows lowered and anger sparked, turning the rich amber in his gaze to a flaming gold. 'I saved your life, you ungrateful little fool,' he snapped, his voice rigid with condescension.

Liah's temper burned through the last of her shock and misplaced awe.

'Are—are you deranged?' she spluttered, barely able to contain her incredulity at the arrogant statement. 'I was about to win.'

'The horse was out of control,' he said. 'And you were too weak to manage it.'

Weak? Weak!

She heard it then, the note of masculine disdain she had been battling from some quarters all her life, despite the unstinting support of her parents and Narabia's ruling council.

She swept the mane of unruly hair out of her eyes. 'I get it, you decided to rescue me when I didn't need rescuing because I'm a weak and feeble woman, right?' She glared at him with enough force to immolate lead.

Unfortunately, it had no appreciable effect. He didn't even have the decency to flinch before giving her an insulting once-over—which, infuriatingly, had that inappropriate shaft of heat returning.

'You are a woman?' He sneered, the rhetorical question dripping with sarcasm. 'This is hard to tell when you are dressed like a boy. And behave like a spoilt brat.'

Her temper shot straight to boiling point without passing go. She sucked in an agonising breath of outrage, the urge to punch the contemptuous look off his face so strong she had to force herself to breathe through the fury.

She had never struck another human being in her entire life and she did not plan to start now. Especially as his rough-hewn jaw looked so solid, it would probably break all her fingers if she tried. But it was a major battle to keep her tightly balled fists by her sides.

She broke eye contact first, but then the brutal humiliation returned full force as she spotted her father striding towards them through the crowd. Her mother followed, looking concerned. As the crowd parted for their sheikh, it occurred to Liah the spectators—the people she was one day supposed to govern—had been listening to every word of her exchange with the man holding her on his lap.

Terrific. How on earth am I going to regain any semblance of respect after this?

'Let me down,' she insisted, pushing at his controlling arm. She did not want to face her father's wrath while sitting on this man's lap. Her pride had already taken a direct hit, thanks to him. But, instead of releasing her, the jerk's muscular forearm tightened, keeping her in place with embarrassing ease.

Wrestling with him would only make it worse, so she was still stuck on his horse when her father reached them. She spotted the tight muscle in her father's jaw ticking like a demented metronome—a sure sign she had gone too far and was in serious trouble. She only prayed he would not break his golden rule and chastise her in public.

Her mother touched her father's arm and murmured something to him.

Liah felt the air in her lungs release as her father drew

himself back from the edge—her mother had always been able to work miracles on her father's temper. But his gaze flicked over her with enough derision to make her shudder before he addressed the man behind her.

'Prince Kamal, my wife and I can only thank you for rescuing my daughter,' he said, his voice clipped and curt.

Prince? This guy was a prince? *Seriously?* A prince of where? He looked—and had behaved—more like a bandit.

'He didn't rescue...' she began, but her father simply lifted his hand.

'Don't,' he said, the single word loaded with enough barely leashed fury to silence her instantly. 'Go and change into your outfit for tonight's reception, Kaliah,' he said, his tone going from chilled to freezing. 'And we can discuss this...' he paused, the muscle ticking over time '...this *situation* later, once I have had a chance to thank the prince properly.'

Which was clearly code for, *Get to the palace before I lose my cool once and for all.*

She bit her lip to stop the passionate defence of her actions spewing out of her mouth as impotent fury boiled in her sore stomach. If this jerk hadn't 'rescued' her, she would have won the race and her father would have understood why she had risked her personal safety. Instead of which, she just looked like even more of a monumental screw-up.

'I would,' she managed at last. 'Except he won't let me off his horse.'

'Perhaps if you had asked me politely,' the bandit prince interjected, 'I would have considered it, Your Highness.'

She spotted the mocking twinkle in his golden eyes and the twitch of his hard lips.

Indignation blind-sided her. *The rat.* He was actually enjoying this, getting off on making a fool of her in front of her father, her mother and all their subjects.

She forced herself not to rise to the bait. Everyone was still watching, and she would be the bigger person now if it killed her…which, judging from the pain in her chest as she struggled to breathe past her fury, might actually happen.

'Please, Mighty Prince Kamal,' she said, fluttering her eyelashes as if she were the simpering idiot he obviously took her for. 'Could you let me off your horse?'

Before I punch you.

The amusement in his eyes flared. A strange tingling sensation ran riot over her tired, sore body, waking up parts of her anatomy she did not want awakened and making her far too aware of the rock-hewn thighs beneath her bottom.

What on earth was that even about? Because she already couldn't stand this man and she'd only just met him.

Without another word, his muscular forearm released its hold on her stomach. She jumped down from the horse with as much dignity as she could possibly muster while her temper was still boiling and her legs had turned to mush. Everyone—her father included—was watching her as if she were a naughty child now instead of a princess.

Locking her knees, she forced her chin up and began her walk of shame. But, as she made her way through the parted crowd towards the palace, she could feel the Jerk Prince's mocking grin following her. Awareness rioted over her skin at the sudden thought of his fierce amber gaze sinking to her backside.

What the heck?

Her walk of shame turned into the seventh circle of hell as she bit into her lip hard enough to taste blood.

CHAPTER TWO

'DAD, YOU CANNOT be serious? The man is an arrogant, sexist jerk—who basically robbed me and Ashreen of the victory we've been training for for months. I don't want to spend ten seconds in his company let alone the whole evening as his personal tour guide.' Liah stared at her father, trying to keep the pleading note out of her voice.

But the punishment he had devised was too much. Even for him. She'd actually rather die than shepherd Prince Kamal around tonight's reception. Especially as he'd probably use the opportunity to be even more of an overbearing ass.

Her father's eyes narrowed as he looked up from his desk. 'Which is precisely why I want you to do it,' he said, being about as flexible as a lump of rock.

'But I—'

'Enough of the *I*!' He cut her off. 'Not everything is about you, Liah. This is the first time Prince Kamal has ventured out of Zokar after being named as the heir to the throne. He seemed ill at ease in the royal box earlier. He's ruling a country that is one of our nearest neighbours—and he has a background which hasn't prepared him for events like tonight's.'

What background? The question popped into Liah's head. She shoved it right back out again. She wasn't interested in the man or his background.

'As the Crown Princess, it is your job to make him feel welcome,' her father added.

Liah's belly tightened into a knot at the disappointment in her father's tone, which struck at all her insecurities.

Her father was a brilliant ruler who had dedicated his life to Narabia. He and her mother had been instrumental in helping to evolve the country's culture and traditions in the last twenty years so everyone had access to education and health care. Declaring their daughter as heir to the throne, when Liah had been their first born, instead of waiting for a son, had been an important part of that. But how did she tell them both, when they had always had such faith in her, that she had no faith in herself?

She didn't want to let Narabia or them down but, while she agreed with her father one hundred percent that a woman could rule the country just as well as a man, deep down she wasn't convinced she was that woman.

Her parents had always ruled her brothers and her as they ruled the kingdom—by consent. They'd allowed Liah to spend her childhood summers in Kildare, at her cousins' stud farm, because of her love of horses. And had allowed her to study in the US and the UK when she'd asked.

The problem was, she had always been impulsive and headstrong…and she couldn't seem to change that part of her nature, not even for them, no matter how hard she tried.

She sighed, trying not to let the creeping feeling of inadequacy show. If there was one thing she'd rather die than lose, it was her father's respect.

'Fine, I'll do it,' she conceded. 'But I'm only doing it because you've asked me to. I still think Prince Kamal is a jerk and that I did not need rescuing.'

'I know.' Her father's lips quirked, creating a crack in his stern expression. He masked it instantly, but the knot in her belly loosened. She knew she exasperated him a lot of the time. They exasperated each other, probably because they were so alike. But she also knew he loved her, fiercely and without compromise. And that would never change, no matter how many times she screwed up.

Thank goodness.

'You're an exceptional horsewoman, Liah,' her father added. 'And, maybe if your mother and I had known you'd been working with Ashreen ever since you returned from college, we wouldn't have both shaved several years off our lives watching you shoot round that track as if you had wings…'

She heard the pride in his voice, which had always been there, ever since she'd been a little girl and he'd believed she could do anything if she put her mind to it. 'But if you ever do anything like that again,' he continued, thrusting his fingers through his thick dark hair, the strands of grey at the temples making him look even more distinguished than he had when she'd been a child, 'I may have to ground you for the rest of your life.'

'Point taken.' She huffed out a laugh. It was an empty threat. They both knew it. But she could hear his anxiety.

Okay, she owed him one.

'I promise I'll be the perfect hostess with Prince Kamal this evening.' *Aka Prince Rat.* 'And I'll do my absolute best not to tell him what an ass he is,' she added, which, in all honesty, would require every molecule of self-restraint she possessed.

Kamal heard the knock on the door and swore under his breath as he stared at the scrap of black cloth hanging limply around his neck. It would probably be one of Khan's staff waiting to escort him to the event downstairs.

The event he did not wish to attend—at all.

The black tuxedo trousers and fitted white shirt had been expertly tailored to fit his muscular frame, but still he felt like a fraud. He was not used to formal western evening wear, much preferring the loose robes of the desert. But he knew he needed to become accustomed to such things for the European trade tour he had planned as a precursor to his coronation. Assuming, of course, he could find himself a convenient bride.

He scowled at his reflection in the floor-length mirror. At least the trousers and shirt had been straightforward. The tie, though, had completely confounded him. Khan's wife had offered to supply him with someone to help him dress, but he had declined, thinking the concept absurd—he had been dressing himself for as long as he could remember. Now he wished he had not been so hasty.

The knock sounded again.

He marched through the suite of rooms to the door, the last of his patience evaporating.

He swung open the heavy oak door. 'Yes?'

The vicious spear of lust he had been suppressing all evening—ever since Princess Kaliah had been wriggling on his lap—shot back into his groin.

Her. Again. This time not dressed as a jockey but as a princess. A nearly naked princess.

A stunning red satin creation draped down to her ankles, but had a plunging neckline and a slit up one side which highlighted her modest cleavage and mile-long legs, while the jewelled shoulder-straps appeared flimsy enough to snap at any minute. His gaze swept over her, from the artfully arranged curls piled on top of her head to the peak of painted toes in heeled sandals.

She cleared her throat and his gaze jerked to her face.

Her sapphire eyes had been enhanced by some kind of glittery, smoky stuff, while her full lips glistened in the dim lighting of the palace's courtyard, making them look even more kissable.

'Prince Kamal, I presume?' she began, her voice a little breathless.

He knew how she felt. He had not been expecting her—and especially not dressed like *this*. She certainly did not look like a boy any more. Not that she ever really had.

'What do you want?' he asked more rudely than he had intended. But she had him at a disadvantage, the uncomfortable awareness from earlier now turbo-charged, and he did not like it.

If he had briefly entertained the idea Princess Kaliah might be a possible candidate to become his queen, he had dismissed the thought as soon as he had realised who was the rider he had rescued.

As much as he had enjoyed getting some payback for the long-ago humiliation he had suffered at her hands—and watching her ice blue irises turn to hot steel while she'd attempted to struggle out of his lap—he had also realised the princess's reputation as a wild child had been well-earned. Kaliah Khan was clearly completely undisciplined, headstrong and spoilt. He needed a queen who would do as he told her, who would respect his authority and be a good role model, not an unruly girl who seemed to have no control over her behaviour whatsoever.

So proposing to her was out.

His gaze raked over the revealing dress again. Not only was her reckless behaviour a problem but he also doubted she was a virgin. She was far too confident and aware of her sexual allure. And, while he didn't much care for the double standard required of him in his position, he had no intention of offering for a woman who was not untouched. He was not about to give Uttram Aziz and the other more conservative elders a chance to reject his bride on a technicality.

He could see the spark of temper in her eyes now, but she masked it—mostly—before she replied, her voice an annoyingly husky purr. 'My father requested that I escort you to the reception and introduce you to the other guests.'

So she was here under duress. It figured.

'Requested or demanded?' he asked.

Surely she had no wish to accompany him any more than he wished to have her as his guide? He had enjoyed baiting her earlier. But the payback he had wanted had now been fulfilled.

As she had left the arena, haughty fury emanating from each regal stride, he had been unable to unglue his gaze from her pert backside. Which was problematic, because he had already dismissed her as a prospect for marriage.

He also recalled now how she had felt on his lap, her back rigid, her breasts rising and falling in an erratic rhythm beneath the jockey silks, her wild hair clinging to the graceful line of her neck, and also recalled the scent of her—the musty spice of subtle perfume and female sweat, all but addictive.

And now here she was again, looking stunning. The unwanted heat settled back in his groin on cue.

Kaliah Khan—and her strident beauty—was a distraction he did not need while he looked for a biddable woman to propose to this weekend.

She sent him a flat look and placed a clenched fist on her hip, making the gown's fabric skim her cleavage in a way that had his mouth watering involuntarily.

'Demanded, actually,' she replied, her brutal honesty gaining his grudging respect. 'But I'm willing to overlook your ruining my chances of winning the race.' She bit the words off, her temper making those pure blue eyes sparkle like the jewels in her intricately beaded hair. 'So I can help you out tonight. My father says you don't know anyone, that you're not used to this kind of event, and he wants you to feel welcomed and at ease.'

His back stiffened. He could hear only irritation in her tone at her father's demand, rather than condescension, but he had spent enough of his life being looked down on to detect it nonetheless.

Having spent twenty minutes wrestling with the idiotic piece of fabric around his neck, he was not about to be bested by this spoilt young woman.

'Tell His Divine Majesty that I appreciate it,' he said, making it very clear he did not appreciate it. 'But I do not require the help of someone who believes herself above me.'

He stepped back, intending to shut the door, glad to have the last word and expecting her to be glad she would not have to spend the night in his company. But, to his surprise, she slapped her hand against the heavy oak. The irritation had left her eyes to be replaced by what could only be described as curiosity.

'Wait—what gave you the impression I think I'm above you?' she asked, the question apparently a genuine one.

Because you were born royal. And I was born a nobody.

He cut off the errant thought ruthlessly. The accident of his birth did not make him beneath any man...or any woman.

Feeling annoyed and exposed, he propped his shoulder against the door frame, crossed his arms over his chest and glared at her.

'Is this not the case?' he asked, determined to regain the high ground. 'When we met earlier, you did not speak to me with respect.'

To his surprise, instead of saying what he had expected—that of course she was better than him—a line appeared between her brows and her gaze softened, making the deep blue glow with something that looked oddly like embarrassment.

'Well, to be fair, you didn't exactly talk to me with much respect either,' she said. Before he could counter her observation, she added, 'That said, I was angry with you earlier for rescuing me when I didn't need rescuing. But, if I gave you the impression I was angry at you for some other reason, I apologise. Believe me, I don't think I'm above anyone. And, at the moment, my father would certainly agree with me on that score.'

He straightened from the door frame, so surprised by the candid comment and what sounded like genuine regret that he was momentarily disconcerted.

Surely it had to be a trick?

But somehow, he couldn't seem to throw her artless apology back in her face. Because it was the first he had ever received from someone of her status. The pulse of emotion in his chest was ruthlessly quashed, though. Sentimentality had no place in his life. And he certainly did not *require* an apology from her or anyone else. He had stopped caring what people thought of him a long time ago.

'If you are genuinely sorry, perhaps you could show me how to deal with this.' He flicked the offending tie. Maybe she could be useful after all. 'Do you know what is supposed to be done with such a pointless thing?'

She nodded, clearly willing to accept the uncomfortable truce. Then, to his surprise, she sashayed past him into the suite of rooms. The swish of her skirt sent a waft of the subtle, refreshing perfume through his system again…and gave him a disturbing view of her naked back. The damned gown plunged down to the curve of her backside, and his gaze snagged on the round orbs again, which looked like two ripe plums ready to be plucked.

He forced his gaze to her flushed face as she swung round to face him.

'Okay, you'd better close the door,' she said, the guileless look in her eyes suggesting she had no idea how that request would make the heat pulse in his groin. 'I'm not exactly an expert myself on bow-ties, but I've helped out my younger brothers a few times, so I'll give it my best shot.'

He found himself closing the door against all his better instincts. But, as she reached up on tiptoe to grasp the two ends of fabric, he tensed. 'What are you doing?' he growled, his voice a rusty purr.

Good God, was she trying to unman him?

She stood so close, the gown brushed his legs and he could see the outer edges of her breasts. Was she even wearing a bra? How did her breasts remain inside the gown—surely they could fall out at any moment?

Her gaze rose to his, her golden skin darkening as she blushed. Her blue eyes were guileless—but also round with curiosity. 'Tying your bow-tie,' she said. 'What did you think I was going to do—ravage you?'

Liah cursed the loaded question as soon as it left her lips.

Why did she always have to say exactly what she thought? And what on earth had she been thinking, strolling so casually into this man's suite? Because, now she was standing in the large lavishly furnished living area, alone with him, it felt far too…dangerous.

She stepped back, aware of the dark intensity in his gaze and the heat emanating off his muscular frame.

She'd been instantly overwhelmed as soon as he'd flung

open his door with that harsh look on his hard, angular features. Which was of course why she'd begun babbling inanely—and trying to assert herself.

She hadn't expected him to open his own door. And certainly had not been prepared for the sight of him in dress trousers and a fitted white shirt, the dark hair on his chest visible through the expensive linen. The untied bow-tie draped casually around his neck, the small nick on his chin where he must have cut himself shaving and the delicious aroma of sandalwood soap and clean male had only added to the strange sense of intimacy and sensory overload.

As his gaze had raked over her—with ruthless entitlement—she'd suddenly felt naked, her dress choice ill-advised, to say the least.

She loved the designer gown, adoring the way it draped over her slender curves and made her look less boyish—but she felt a bit too much of a woman right now.

A woman this man could probably devour in a heartbeat if he chose...

Not that she wanted him to. Not at all, she told herself staunchly, even if her knees felt a lot less solid than usual and as though a hot, heavy rock had dropped into her abdomen and started to glow.

He was still staring at her. But, instead of answering her beyond stupid question, he simply inclined his head slightly.

'No,' he said. 'Proceed,' he added, like a man who was used to giving orders and having them obeyed.

So much for her father's assertion that Prince Kamal was uncomfortable about his role, because to her he seemed to be a natural born ruler.

She was forced to step closer to him again.

The strong brown column of his throat flexed as he swallowed. Inappropriate moisture flooded her panties as she slipped her fingers under his collar to hook the top button on his dress shirt.

He huffed.

'Is everything okay?' she asked, feeling oddly as if she were trying to calm a highly strung stallion, a wild one that could stamp her to dust at any moment.

His golden gaze met hers. 'It feels as if I am being strangled.'

'Sorry,' she murmured. 'It's necessary to have the collar buttoned to tie the bow-tie.'

He nodded, but she could see in his eyes he was unimpressed.

Lifting on tiptoes, she grasped the ends of the tie, cursing her trembling fingers, her curiosity piqued again. The way it had been moments before when he had accused her of disrespecting him with that jaded, deliberately unconcerned look on his face, as if he was used to such treatment. A million questions rose to the surface of her brain, questions she knew she shouldn't indulge, but even so…

Why had he never worn a tuxedo and bow-tie before? How had he gained the throne of Zokar? What *was* his background—the background her father had referred to as not having prepared him for events like the one which had already started downstairs? Where had he got that scar? And why did his golden gaze seem somehow familiar?

She chewed her lip to stop the intrusive questions coming out of her mouth and concentrated on tying his bow-tie while preventing her knuckles from brushing against the warm skin of his throat.

One thing was for sure—doing this service for her two youngest brothers, Kasim and Rohaan, was nowhere near as nerve-racking, even though neither one of them could stand still for more than a nanosecond.

After several endless minutes of torture, she managed to arrange the bow-tie into some semblance of order.

'There, that's it, I think,' she said, dropping her hands and scooting back.

She glanced up to find him watching her. His golden gaze was assessing, focussed and full of something hot and intense—which for once did not look like animosity.

A wave of warmth spread up her neck, making her far too aware she had only the stick-on bra cups under her dress to stop her puppies falling out of the daring gown.

'How does it feel?' she asked, determined to break the strange spell.

He touched the tie, shifted it slightly then stretched his neck. 'Uncomfortable.'

'You've never worn one before?' The question popped out.

His jaw tightened. Had she offended him again?

But his gaze remained direct as he gave a curt shake of his head.

'There was no need for such nonsense in the Zokari army,' he explained.

There was distain in his tone, but she found his reply refreshingly blunt. An appreciative laugh burst out of her mouth.

'Just be glad you don't have to do this in ridiculous foot-wear too,' she said, extending her leg to show him her four-inch heels.

His gaze roamed over her thigh and down to her ankle, blazing a trail along her flesh.

'Elegant,' he murmured.

The gruff compliment reverberated through her torso as his gaze finally arrived back at her face.

She hastily draped the satin back over her leg.

Good grief, Liah, why not give him an eyeful of all your charms?

She couldn't prevent the shudder as the heat centred in her core.

He lifted a black tailored jacket off the back of a chair, slipped it on then did up one of the buttons, completing the devastating effect.

He really did look spectacular, his dark skin and rugged features as striking as they were intimidating. The formal wear only seemed to enhance his raw masculinity, the aura of command which clung to him. Whatever his background, it was clear he was a man used to commanding men…and no doubt women too.

But not this woman. You're your own woman, Liah. Remember that.

She squeezed her thighs together, determined to ignore the insistent pulse that had centred between them.

Then, to her surprise, he offered her his elbow. 'Let's get this over with before the foolish thing strangles me.'

Another chuckle escaped her lips. But the hot blast of appreciation in his gaze as she touched his muscular forearm and felt it tense beneath the expensive fabric choked the laugh off in her throat.

CHAPTER THREE

SHE IS FASCINATING. And I want her

Kamal found himself staring again at the young woman beside him, who was chatting with considerable authority about her horse Ashreen to the Queen of Zafar, an Irish woman who he understood was a cousin of the royal family by marriage and owned a world-renowned racing stud in Kildare.

Princess Kaliah's passion for the subject of horses and racing was evident in the way her eyes gleamed, and her tawny skin literally glowed with enthusiasm.

She had remained by his side throughout the evening, introducing him to everyone and talking with depth and knowledge on a variety of topics, both trivial and complex. She had made an effort to involve him in these conversations—and for once he had not found her interventions condescending or annoying. In truth, she had beguiled him.

He knew she was being so attentive to please her father, but to his surprise she had not shirked the responsibility as soon as she could. Instead, she appeared to be working overtime to put him at his ease.

Good luck with that.

How could he be at ease when he kept catching her intoxicating scent, and while tantalising glimpses of her unfettered breasts, moving against the line of her gown, and her toned thigh every time she walked, was driving him insane.

Would it really be so wrong to seduce her before I start searching for a suitable wife?

The errant thought made the slow burn in his gut flare.

Probably not a good idea. For all her wild-child ways, Kaliah Khan was a future queen. The sort of woman who would have expectations he could not fulfil.

Although, to his surprise this evening, she had been forthright—including him in the joke, rather than attempting to make him the butt of it.

As much as he still wanted to resent the reckless young woman who had railed at him at the race track, he was finding it harder and harder not to notice her passionate response to him.

Women had always been straightforward to him—a means of slaking his physical needs, but little else. He had never conducted an in-depth conversation with any of the women he had slept with, because all he had ever needed was confirmation that they were happy to tumble into his bed for the night.

Kaliah Khan, though, was an enigma. Her obvious interest in him was both captivating but also somehow unclear—the woman had been reckless enough to ride a virtually wild horse at breakneck speed, so her reticence now made no sense to him.

Hence the intriguing mystery she represented.

He had seen the flush of awareness back in his suite, and had suspected the decision to help him with the bow-tie had been a means of flirting with him. Perhaps even to tease him, the casual brush of her fingers on his throat enough to tie his guts in knots for the rest of the evening. But he sensed innocence, rather than calculation, every time he caught her watching him.

She liked what she saw too, but had remained business-like since leaving his suite.

But, the more she attempted to hide her attraction, the more he found himself wanting to force her to acknowledge it.

Again, not wise. As she was the wrong woman, at the wrong time, in the wrong place.

Perhaps there remained some of that invisible serving boy still inside him who would never have been good enough for a woman like her—making the desire to bed her all the more fierce.

He could have any woman he wanted now. But tonight there was only one woman he wished to have. He'd enjoyed watching her interact with the many pointless people at this reception, but it was past time to show her he could see her interest in him and that he returned it.

They only had tonight to see where this chemistry might take them, before he would have to spend the rest of the weekend looking for a wife.

'It was lovely to meet you, Prince Kamal.' The Queen of Zafar broke off her discussion with Kaliah to address him directly. 'I do hope you will consider visiting us in Kildare when you are in Ireland on the trade tour,' she added.

He nodded, surprised she knew about the tour, which he had only finalised a week ago.

'Thank you for the invitation,' he said, making no commitments. The need to find himself a wife had to be his first priority or there would be no tour.

Resentment at the thought of his predicament tightened his throat, as Queen Orla left them.

Princess Kaliah turned to him, her gaze probing. 'Why

didn't you accept her invitation?' she asked, the question abrupt and intrusive. 'Orla and Karim are an important power couple in the region, and they also have a high profile in Europe.'

He bristled at the suggestion he could not navigate the social commitments of a king. The surge of heat, which had been tormenting him every time he looked at her, only intensified his resentment. He should not have stayed by her side all evening but should have been acquainting himself with the more suitable women here he was required to seduce.

'And this is your business how, exactly?' he snapped, his frustration building as her breasts pressed against the edge of her gown, and he imagined drawing the fabric aside so he could finally look his fill.

She blinked, her skin flushing. 'Are you naturally surly, or is it just me?' she asked, the bold question tempered by the vulnerability in her eyes.

She masked it quickly, but even so it made the heat ignite. He wanted her, and she wanted him. Why deny this attraction, when it would be simple enough to feed?

He stepped closer, touched a knuckle under her chin and felt her gratifying shudder of response. 'It is most definitely just you, Kaliah.'

Her eyes widened, then darkened with awareness. The heat in his groin throbbed.

She didn't say anything. He let out a rough chuckle. Was she trying to be demure?

He swept his thumb across her bottom lip, then let his hand drop. He would never pressure her physically. But he went after what he wanted. And tonight he wanted her.

'Perhaps we could go somewhere less public to discuss it?' he suggested.

The vivid blush on her cheeks heightened. He had been too blunt. But he was damned if he would pretend to be someone he was not—a man with finesse and fancy manners.

As he waited for her response, transparent emotions skittered across her expressive features—shock, indignation and then a vivid, vibrant curiosity. The heat in his groin swelled against the confines of his suit trousers. Why did the fact she was so transparent only make her more alluring to him?

But, just when he was convinced she would tell him to get lost, her answer came out on a throaty purr. 'Okay.'

He threaded his fingers through hers and led her through the throng of people. As his grip tightened, he forced himself not to walk too quickly. But as they made their way through the large palace atrium and into a quieter courtyard, where a fountain surrounded by tropical blooms gave the dry desert night the sultry scent of flowers, his heartbeat accelerated.

The crowds of guests melted away as they reached the staircase to the private terrace where his suite of rooms was situated. He made himself take the steps one at a time, although the desire to lift her into his arms was all but overwhelming. Especially as the sound of her harsh breathing matched the vicious pump of his pulse.

Perhaps he should say something to put her at her ease. But he had never been a man for pointless conversation, especially now, when the desire that had been kept at bay so ruthlessly all evening was ready to burst its bounds.

He wished to make this good for both of them. And for that to happen he needed to concentrate on keeping his hunger in check before he got her naked.

So he remained silent and led her into the night.

* * *

You need to stop this madness, Liah, before it's too late. You don't even know this man. You're not even sure you like him.

Even as she struggled to keep up with Kamal's forceful strides, the hum of conversation and music fading as he led her through the dark corridors towards his suite, Liah couldn't seem to stop the buzz of attraction sinking deep into her sex.

Where had that insistent throb come from that had made her so brutally aware of this man? Even though he had been silent, bordering on rude, all evening. He'd barely spoken to any of the people she had introduced him to. He'd made no real effort to enter into the sort of polite conversations that were a requisite of these events.

She had wondered more than once what he was thinking behind those fathomless eyes. Was he judging her—judging all of them? It was clear he thought the whole event frivolous and—even though she would normally have agreed with him—she had found herself wanting to defend her way of life.

She should have left him to his own devices hours ago because almost as soon as they had arrived at the reception it had been clear that, although Prince Kamal knew virtually no one here, he didn't need her help to smooth his path because he had no desire to fit in.

But his apparent disdain had done nothing to dispel the deep pulsing need that she now realised had been tormenting her ever since he had plucked her off Ashreen and draped her over his lap without even breaking a sweat.

Since when had she been attracted to overbearing, arrogant men? All her previous boyfriends had been intellectual, bordering on nerdy. Was that why they had never excited her the way this hard, unknowable man did?

She gathered her breath as they finally reached his suite. He released her hand to open the door, then stood on the threshold, his large frame even more imposing in the moonlight.

She should make her excuses and leave.

She'd always been impulsive, but what was she doing, allowing Kamal Zokan to drag her to his room like a possession?

What are you doing, Liah? However exciting he is, even you can't be this reckless!

But, as she tried to think of a diplomatic way out, the silence pressed in upon her, trapping the words in her throat behind the great big ball of reckless lust and intoxicating energy.

Her body didn't feel like her own any more. She felt enthralled, spellbound, driven to do dangerous things. And it was intoxicating. He hadn't said a word ever since they had left the reception. But then, she hadn't really expected him to. Even from their brief acquaintance, she already knew he was a man who preferred action to words.

'If you have changed your mind, I will escort you back to the reception,' he said at last.

She should be relieved. But something about the fact he had sensed her indecision—when she would never have suspected he had a sensitive bone in his body—called to the reckless gene that had made her do stupid things her entire life.

Especially when his expression, so full of hunger moments before, became shuttered and a cynical smile tilted his lips.

'After all, I cannot offer you more than one night,' he added.

The words—so arrogant, so full of amused indifference—called to that rebellious streak like a red rag waved before a charging bull.

He was expecting her to chicken out.

The bastard.

The hot, fluid throb of arousal was joined by the fierce pulse of adrenaline.

'What makes you think I *want* more than one night?' she shot back.

Why was she fighting this need, this hunger?

Something about this man made her want him more than she had ever wanted any other man. But surely this was just chemistry, pheromones? Maybe it didn't even have that much to do with him. Maybe it was merely the frustration of Colin's cruel betrayal finally coming home to roost. She wasn't frigid, and now she would prove it.

One night would suit her just fine. She wanted to know what it felt like to have wild, untamed, no-holds-barred sex with a man who wanted the same thing. And nothing more. There could never be more between them. Their pasts, their futures, their goals, desires and ambitions could not be more different.

A man like Prince Kamal would never touch her heart.

'Because you are a woman, and sometimes a woman cannot tell the difference between sex and emotion,' he supplied, clearly not realising her question had been rhetorical.

Liah gasped, momentarily speechless.

Of all the chauvinistic…!

The adrenaline surged. She grabbed his lapels and yanked his face down to hers, determined to show him who was boss.

'It's lucky I'm not your average woman, then,' she snapped.

The fierce, unfettered need in his gaze turned the deep amber to a fiery gold. 'Good,' he replied.

Then his lips slanted across hers in a shockingly possessive kiss. Need fired through her system as his tongue drove into her mouth, demanding entry. Her lips opened for him, instinctively, need throbbing into erogenous zones she'd never realised she had as he feasted on her as if he owned her.

His hands roamed over her naked back where the gown plunged and he tugged her into his body. The solid, unyielding strength of him made her writhe against him, the riot of sensations too fierce, too full.

She heard her own sharp intake of breath as he explored the recesses of her mouth, commanding, devastating, as the pulsing sensation centred at her core. The weight that had tormented her all night became jammed between her thighs, growing to impossible proportions and making the ache painful—even as she kissed him back with equal fervour.

He ripped his mouth away, his large, callused palms rising to grasp her cheeks, to angle her head for better access, then he sunk into her again.

Their tongues tangled in a battle of need and desire, as much argument as acquiescence, each trying to gain the upper hand.

When they were finally forced to part again, to catch their breaths, she could feel the thick ridge of his erection pressing into her belly.

'Be aware, no matter how good this is, it can only be for tonight,' he rasped, his hand resting on her cheek as he brushed the curls behind her ear. 'I cannot commit to more.'

The arrogant jerk.

'Well, then, it's good I'm only interested in you for your body, pal,' she shot back, determined to prove she would never mistake endorphins for love.

Instead of being offended as she had intended, though, he simply laughed, the rumbling chuckle gruff with approval.

'Yes, it will be very good,' he replied. Before she could get even more indignant, he scooped her up into his arms and strode into the suite.

He carried her through the living area into the master bedroom. A full moon gave the lavish Moorish furnishings a luminous glow. Her breathing accelerated as he set her down beside the huge king-size bed. With its colourful silk cushions piled high on one end, and the intricate screens that shielded them from the night gilded by moonlight, the setting seemed fanciful and romantic.

She gulped down a ragged breath.

Not romantic. This was a transaction of passion—nothing more, nothing less.

But as he turned her body towards the open terrace doors, then unpicked the jewelled pins from her hair before drawing the heavy mass to one side and kissing her nape, his callused hands almost reverent, her breath got trapped in her lungs.

She could see the gardens below the balcony. Fountains and exotic plants made the space an enchanted oasis—or so she'd dreamed as a child while she'd roamed the palace grounds with her brother William, pretending to be a fairy queen. The dim lights of the old women's quarters in the distance and the dark windows of her family's private suites on the opposite terrace, where her two younger brothers were probably asleep, made something hard and scary lodge in her gut. What had happened to those long-ago dreams of finding love and romance she'd once had within these walls—a passion for the ages, like the one her parents shared?

The sudden fear that the step she was taking tonight

wasn't as small or insignificant as she wanted it to be assailed her as Kamal's lips left her neck and she heard him take off his jacket and dump it on the chair beside her.

You're not a little girl any more, and you haven't been for a while. It's past time to become a woman.

His thumb rubbed against the hammering pulse at her collarbone. 'Is there a problem?'

She jolted at the gruff and far too perceptive question.

Could he sense her hesitation, her fear? Not of him, but of what this night might mean, even though she didn't want it to mean anything other than a chance to finally find out what all the fuss was about.

She spun round—to find him watching her with the hunger undimmed in his eyes, an unreadable expression on his face.

He was so close. He'd not only lost the jacket but the bow-tie too and had unbuttoned the confining collar she knew he hated while she had been taking her daft trip down memory lane. His thick hair stuck up in haphazard rows, as if he'd run impatient fingers through it while she'd stood and romanticised this moment like a fool.

A new layer of stubble had grown over his jaw in just a few hours, making him look like a pirate or a bandit. But it was the gleam in his eyes that seemed to yank at her heart and sink deep into her abdomen—compelling, exciting, dangerous.

'There's no problem,' she said, determined to believe it.

This was just a virgin's jitters.

'You are sure?' he said, his voice so low she could barely hear it.

'Yes, absolutely,' she replied with a certainty she didn't feel but was determined to make herself believe.

This was just sex, not a relationship. She didn't have to

care about the fairy tales she'd made up as a little girl in the enchanted garden below them.

And she certainly didn't have to imagine the man she had envisioned falling in love with one day—a man who would be strong but tender, fiercely intelligent, commanding and determined, but also kind and patient. Because Prince Kamal was not that man, nor would he ever be.

The only thing that mattered now was tonight.

She stretched on tiptoes to unbutton his shirt the rest of the way. Her fingers trembled, her movements frantic and clumsy. But, as she finally reached the bottom and tugged the cotton out of his cummerbund to reveal the ridges of his six-pack, his large hand captured her fingers, preventing her from caressing the golden skin.

Her head jerked up, panic joining the fierce need.

'What?' she asked, scared he was going to stop her. Had he guessed how inexperienced she was?

He tugged her fingers to his lips and kissed the tips. The gesture was almost tender, until he sucked one finger into his mouth, and what had been strangely sweet became devastatingly erotic, the drawing sensation echoing painfully in her sex.

At last he released her hand to lift her hair from her neck and press those marauding lips to the pulse at her throat. He licked and suckled, sending brutal sensation pounding down.

'There is no rush,' he whispered with gruff amusement. 'We have all night.'

Was he laughing at her? She wanted to be indignant, annoyed. But it was hard to be anything but desperate when with deliberate purpose he parted the plunging V of her gown's neckline to reveal her breasts to his burning gaze.

His brow furrowed as he skimmed a thumb under the swollen flesh. 'What is this?'

She glanced down and realised the problem—the flesh-coloured discs which covered her breasts, making them look weird. Heat mottled the skin across her collarbone.

'Um, my bra. It's a stick-on.'

'Ingenious,' he murmured as he circled the rubberised discs. 'Does it hurt to remove them?'

She huffed out a strained laugh. *Awkward, much?* 'No.'

He brushed his thumb across the peak of her breast, the nipple distending beneath its shield.

She sucked in a breath. She could see his amusement, but also the fierce passion that hadn't dimmed.

'May I remove them?' he asked.

Speech deserted her at the bold request. She'd never quite envisioned her first seduction being this awkward, or this hot.

'Yes,' she managed.

To her astonishment, he sunk to his knees which, because of his height, brought his head level with her breasts. For several pregnant seconds, he studied the design. Then he slipped his fingernail under the gel-like substance and peeled it back with infinite care.

She grasped his broad shoulders, the prickling sensation made unbearably erotic by his concentration. His wide shoulders bunched beneath the shirt, but then he threw away the stick-on and licked across the nipple.

The rush of feeling as the tip engorged was like nothing she had ever felt before. The nipple, already tender, swelled and throbbed as he lathed the peak, his large hands capturing her hips to hold her steady for the delicious torment.

A cool breeze brushed across her tender flesh as he leaned back on his heels then proceeded to peel away the other bra cup. Again, he played with the exposed nipple with his tongue, making darts of brutal sensation arrow into her sex. At last, he captured the swollen peak between his lips and suckled hard.

Her body bowed forward, her fingers sinking into his hair as heady, insistent desire fanned out from her breast and blazed a trail through all her erogenous zones.

She was weak, panting, barely able to stand, when he finally released her from the exquisite torture. He stood to ease the gown over her hips until she was standing before him in nothing more than her lacy thong.

She folded an arm across her breasts, every one of her senses heightened, aware of the slick moisture dampening her panties.

'Do not hide yourself from me,' he said, the comment part-request but mostly demand. To her surprise, she released her arm on his command.

Her back arched as she lifted her breasts. She wanted him to see all of her. Wanted to experience the rush of exhilaration as he thumbed the nipple, his breath gushing out on a grunt of need.

'It's your turn,' she managed, suddenly desperate to see him too, to touch, tempt and devour him the way he had done to her.

His head lifted, but then he lowered it to concentrate on unzipping his trousers.

Power surged through her and she had the strangest sense of a man, who took orders from no one, taking orders from her.

He kicked off his shoes and dragged off his trousers and boxer shorts together.

Suddenly he stood before her, naked except for the open shirt that he hadn't removed. She wanted to demand he lose that too, but all she could do was shiver uncontrollably as she devoured the sight of him—magnificent and strange, his big, perfectly formed body gilded by moonlight. Dark curls of hair bloomed around his nipples, defining the heavy slabs of his pectoral muscles, then trailed into a thin line to bisect his abdominal muscles. His obliques stood out, arrowing down to his groin, and the bush of dark hair did nothing to disguise the thrusting erection.

She drew in a staggered breath, feeling light-headed.

Oh. My.

The column of his sex stood upright, bending towards his belly button. She'd never seen a man's naked penis before, and certainly not one so magnificently erect, but she was sure very few could compare to the length and girth of this one.

Her throat dried, even as the moisture flooded between her thighs. She should have been panicked—how on earth was all of that going to fit inside her?—but somehow all she felt was a heady charge at the sight of him, so hard, so ready, just for her.

'Can I…can I touch it?' she stammered, her voice low with awe.

His eyebrows shot up his forehead and then he laughed. 'Of course,' he said, his tone more than a little incredulous.

Humiliation flared and she wanted to bite off her own tongue.

Way to go, Liah—why not make it totally obvious you're a virgin?

As if she needed to make him any more big-headed. She swallowed down the pulse of embarrassment.

It doesn't matter what he thinks…you will never see him again after tonight.

Reaching out, she traced her fingertip down the thick length.

He groaned as the long column seemed to bend to her

touch. Heat scoured her insides, but this time it had nothing to do with mortification and everything to do with excitement. She wrapped her fingers around him, marvelling at the way the flesh felt so soft and yet so solid. His breathing accelerated, and his abdominal muscles tensed as he stood, stoic and unmoving, and let her explore.

A bead of moisture appeared at the tip, fascinating her even more. She rubbed her thumb across the straining head, using the viscous liquid to ease her grip as she stroked the velvet length.

He made a guttural sound. The power surged as he swelled and throbbed in her hand.

But, just as the empty ache in her core became unbearable, her need reaching fever pitch at the thought of seeing him lose control, he grasped her wrist and pulled her fingers away.

'Enough,' he murmured, his tone no longer mocking. 'Do you wish to unman me?' he asked, the question raw.

She smiled. 'Yes?'

He laughed. The rough chuckle was like a balm to her soul. Her heart swelled at the weird, disconnected thought that, for all his arrogance and even chauvinism, this man had no problem seeing her as an equal. He enjoyed the challenge, the battle for supremacy between them, as much as she did. He didn't think less of her for wanting to best him, he actually thought more.

But, before she had a chance to contemplate that bizarre revelation—which surely had to be the endorphins talking?—he scooped her into his arms again to carry her to the bed.

He tossed her onto the wide mattress as if she weighed nothing.

'You little witch,' he murmured as he joined her on the

bed, his big body looming over hers. 'Two can play at that game.'

She scrambled backwards, but he grasped her ankle to draw her towards him. Cradling her hips, he knelt between her legs then cupped her bottom to bring her throbbing centre towards his marauding mouth.

She squirmed, as shocked as she was exhilarated.

Was he actually going to kiss her...*there*...?

He parted her folds with his thumbs then blew softly across the heated flesh, which did nothing whatsoever to cool the vicious heat.

'Yes... Please.' She didn't even recognise the guttural plea as her own until her gaze met the vivid amber of his eyes, the wicked intent in them as intoxicating as the desperate need making her pulse points throb and the slick flesh between her legs swell.

He breathed in, then groaned. 'You smell so delicious. I may have to feast on you all night.'

He was teasing her, but the playful words seemed part-promise, part-threat.

Before she could come up with a counter claim, he licked across the swollen folds. Her hips bucked involuntarily, almost throwing him off, the sensation so raw, so real, her whole body seemed concentrated on that one melting spot.

He held her firmly and continued to probe and swirl, finding the very heart of her desire and ruthlessly exploiting it. She sobbed, the sounds crude and elemental as she sank back on the bed and gave herself over to the brutal passion, the devastating need.

The coil tightened like a vice, her body becoming one raw, throbbing bundle of sensation centred on the devastating play of his tongue as she bucked and writhed against his hold.

Then he captured the swollen nub at last and suckled hard.

The vicious climax slammed into her, bursting into a thousand glittering shards. She came down slowly, aware of him licking her through the last of the brutal orgasm, her body shuddering in the wake of something so shattering, she wasn't sure she would ever feel her extremities again.

'Please, I can't...' She touched his hair and felt the silken waves beneath her fingers.

He stopped abruptly and rose above her.

She watched in a daze, her mind blown, as he leaned over her and produced a small foil packet from the bedside table.

He rolled it on the thick erection, so distended now it looked even more overwhelming than it had before. But somehow the sight only made the empty ache at her core more desperate to be filled.

He cradled her hips in shaky palms. The spurt of power, at the knowledge he wasn't as steady or controlled as he appeared, was a welcome relief. Maybe she had lost the battle, but she had not lost the war. Yet.

He probed, finding the slick heart of her, then pressed forward in one smooth, devastating thrust.

She gasped and flinched, gripping the hard muscles of his shoulders under his shirt. He felt immense between her legs, the pulse of pleasure dimming to become sharp and discordant.

He stopped abruptly, holding still inside her. 'Are you all right? You are very tight,' he added, the concern in his voice calling to a place deep inside her.

She shook her head, the pain easing as she adjusted to his size.

'No, don't stop,' she said, surprising herself a little. She didn't want him to stop. Didn't want him to withdraw. Yes, he was overwhelming, but the pleasure was already returning, sensation building—her body eager to endure anything to enjoy another shattering release.

Her fingers glided over his shoulders, feeling strange ridges...what were those?...as she loosened her grip to let him sink the rest of the way into her.

'I want all of you,' she murmured in the darkness.

The words should have been merely sexual, but he jolted, and something flickered into his eyes—something surprised but also wary.

He eased out, then pressed back. She groaned as he rolled his hips, easing the tight, stretched feeling by incremental degrees.

The pleasure rippled, sparkled, bubbling up from her centre again.

'Good?' he asked.

'Yes, very good,' she said, and he groaned.

At last, he was buried inside her to the hilt. Raw emotion blindsided her at how gentle, how careful, he had been. The exquisite pleasure pulsed as her body tightened around his, massaging his thick length. She doubted she would orgasm like this but, even as she resigned herself, he pulled out to thrust back, adjusting the angle.

Shocking sensation rolled through her as he rubbed a spot she hadn't known existed. She sobbed, the desperate sound echoing around the room. The pleasure built again, so raw, so elemental, too much and not enough, as his movements became more forceful, more demanding. Her hands slipped on his sweat-slicked shoulders, feeling those confusing ridges again as she braced for the ruthlessly deep stroking, each thrust taking her higher, further, but never quite taking her over.

She clung to him, aware of every sight, every sound, every sensation, and aware of nothing except the power of his body and that deep, internal caress swelling the wave of release.

Suddenly he took one hand from her hip and delved where their bodies joined, rubbing his thumb over her clitoris.

'Come for me now, Kaliah,' he ordered.

The cataclysmic wave crashed over her at last, as if at his command.

He stiffened above her, his shout of fulfilment matching her fierce cries. The wave swept her over that high wide peak until she found herself tumbling into a hot vat of stunning pleasure, impossible bliss. Her heart hammered her chest wall so hard, she was surprised he couldn't feel it as he dropped on top of her, following her into the bottomless abyss.

She clasped him to her breast, blinking back tears as stunning afterglow enveloped her.

She could feel his heart beating for several precious, beautiful moments as she absorbed the shocking intensity of their joining. And it occurred to her that for all his flaws—and she was sure she didn't even know the half of them—Kamal Zokan had made her first time magnificent.

But then he lifted off her, withdrawing slowly as she released him with difficulty.

He rolled away from her onto his back. 'That was good, yes?' he said.

'Yes,' she replied, stupidly touched he would ask.

Get a grip, Liah. It's just sex, remember? Sex and chemistry. Really spectacular chemistry.

Which had to be why she couldn't stem the surge of joy and gratitude making her throat close and her heart hurt.

His large hand landed on her thigh, his thumb caressing the bare skin in a lazily possessive manner that only made her heart thunder harder.

A renewed jolt of pleasure shot through her exhausted flesh, despite the soreness at her core.

Down, girl.

She shifted, ready to pull away from his touch. But then he rolled towards her and tucked her body into the lee of his. She could feel the thick length, still semi-firm, pressed into her bottom. His breathing slowed to an even rhythm as his arms wrapped around her waist.

Her heart jolted and swelled, disturbing her even more.

Prince Kamal's a snuggler... Who would have guessed?

'Sleep now.' His deep voice rumbled against her back. 'Then we can go again when I am recovered.'

Her heart jolted. But, instead of feeling indignant at his arrogance, and the assumption she would stay in his arms all night without being asked, all she felt was the stupid pulse of gratitude that he would want her.

His breathing deepened behind her, his arm becoming heavier as he relaxed into sleep.

She lay staring at the full moon through the latticed window, breathing in the potent perfume of night jasmine from the garden below—which had enchanted her as a girl and flavoured all those foolish dreams—and tried to gather her shattered wits. But the perfume of the night garden was masked by the even more compelling scent of sex, sweat and him.

She forced herself to ignore the painful squeeze in her ribs as she became aware of the soreness between her legs. She couldn't stay, and certainly didn't want to risk another session or she might mistake the pain in her ribs for something other than endorphins.

But, even so, when she finally managed to tug herself out of his arms she couldn't quite make herself believe that what had happened between them meant nothing.

She dressed furtively in the moonlight, then rushed through the shadowy palace corridors back to the safety of her own rooms, while the ache in her chest refused to ease.

And as she washed the scent of him from her body, far too aware of all the places where he had touched and caressed her, she couldn't seem to wash away the fear she had lost an important part of herself.

CHAPTER FOUR

LIAH WOKE AS the knocking in her head became real.

She groaned, every single spot Kamal had explored last night aching in unison.

'Who is it?' she shouted. And what time was it? Because bright daylight was shining through the screen on her terrace.

Damn, she must have over-slept. A lot.

'It is Aisha, Highness,' came the reply, from one of her mother's private secretaries. 'Their Majesties ask that you join them in the Sheikh's private study as soon as possible.'

That was weird—she only ever got called to her dad's study on official business or when she'd screwed up.

'Okay, do you know what this is about?' Liah asked, sitting up and clasping her sheet to her tender breasts as Aisha popped her head around the bed-chamber door.

'I am not at liberty to say, Your Highness,' the usually level-headed woman said as she flushed a deep red. 'But they require your presence as soon as possible...'

Heat burned in Liah's cheeks. Had her parents spotted Kamal and her high-tailing it out of the reception last night?

Even as the mortification threatened to engulf her, she dismissed the idea. This was just her guilty conscience talking, because she'd left his room last night without saying goodbye.

She was a grown woman. While her father might dress her down for risking her neck on what he thought was an untrained horse, her parents would never judge her for her personal choices.

Even so, the heated blush refused to subside.

After Aisha had disappeared, Liah flung off the sheet and shot across the room, ignoring the discomfort between her thighs. Whatever this was about, she needed to get it out the way before she could flee to the Aleaza Oasis, the special place where she always went when she needed a time-out from palace life.

Not *flee*, she corrected herself, locating an outfit while simultaneously trying to tame her epic bed-hair. She wasn't fleeing the palace, or Prince Kamal. She was simply taking a break for three days, while her one-night lover returned to his own kingdom, so she could lock the disturbing intimacy they had shared last night into a box marked 'no biggie'.

Twenty minutes later, as she tapped on her father's study door, she was still struggling to get the stupid blush under control.

'Come in, Liah,' her father called.

Stepping into the room, she spotted her father seated at his desk and her mother standing behind him, her vivid chestnut eyes rich with...*what was that?*

Because her mother was wearing the sort of concerned expression Liah remembered from her childhood, when she'd done something reckless, or dangerous...or both.

Her gaze darted to her dad. But he didn't look mad, he looked concerned too.

'Liah, sit down. We have a situation we need to discuss,' her father said, his voice so grave she began to panic.

But then another far too familiar voice rumbled from

behind her. 'There is no discussion necessary, Your Majesty. We must be married. The Crown Princess was a virgin when we slept together last night. It is the honourable course, and also the responsibility of every sheikh, to offer marriage to any woman whose virginity he takes. Is this not written in the Law of Marriage of the Sheikhs?'

The humiliating blush napalmed Liah's cheeks as she swung round and her horrified gaze landed on the man she hadn't spotted sitting behind the door.

His tall, indomitable frame rose like a phoenix from the ashes of her memory—or more like a dragon from its lair—incinerating the last of her composure in the process as he strode towards her.

Conflicting emotions charged through her system at warp speed—shock, embarrassment, mortification but worse was the wave of something rich and fluid as all the sore, tender spots began to throb.

But then she registered his grim expression. He looked even less pleased to see her than she was to see him—which, on the scale of not being pleased was on a par with getting kicked in the gut by Ashreen. Then his outrageous proposal registered and the choking rage rose up her throat like acid.

He'd told her parents about their one-night stand—their *private, secret, never-to-be-repeated* one-night stand—and the fact she had been a virgin... And now he expected her to *marry* him because of some arcane law.

She spluttered. The only thing shocking her more than Kamal's unbelievable gall was the fact her head hadn't exploded.

Then the outrage spewed out of her mouth, like lava erupting from a volcano.

'Are you completely and utterly nuts?'

* * *

Kamal clenched his fists so hard, he could feel his finger-nails cutting into his palms as he battled the desire to grab the infuriating woman in front of him and throw her over his lap so he could give her the spanking she so richly deserved.

He had never laid a hand on a woman without her consent in his entire life—and certainly not in anger—but right now he could feel every fibre of his being straining to maintain the cast-iron control he had acquired, after a childhood of abuse and an adulthood of having every one of his desires and ambitions questioned and judged.

He would not lose his temper, or his civility. But it was a hard-fought battle. Harder than any of the many others he had fought in his twenty-nine years. She had left him in the night, without a word, like a thief. But, worse, she had not told him of her virgin state.

'Do you deny I am your first lover?' he asked, to be absolutely sure he had not jumped to the wrong conclusion when he had awoken, heavily erect and aching to sink inside her again, to find the bed beside him empty and speckles of blood on the sheets, probably evidence of her virgin state.

The vivid blush on her face darkened and her breasts rose and fell beneath the fitted T-shirt she wore with jeans and boots which displayed her slender frame far too effectively.

'That is absolutely none of your business,' she said.

Which was not a denial.

He was right—she *had* been a virgin—which meant she had put them both in an impossible position for which there was only one solution. This wayward, reckless, infuriating woman would have to become his wife.

His honour demanded it, as a man and a prince. And so did hers as a member of Narabia's royal family.

The Law of Marriage of the Sheikhs was an important

responsibility for every ruling male in all the kingdoms of the region. If a man in his position took a woman's virginity, he was compelled to offer marriage. He had been taught as much during the lessons on Zokari cultural traditions and institutions he had been required to take to prepare him for the throne.

Kamal's eyes narrowed. 'Do you think the Law of Marriage does not apply to me because I was not born of royal blood?' he sneered, his anger starting to strangle him.

Was that it? Had she believed she could deceive him about her virgin state because he had no right to his throne?

'*What?* No, of course not.' Her eyebrows lifted, the blush becoming radioactive. 'I just don't give a toss about such a stupid, archaic tradition.'

'You think tradition and culture is stupid?' He raised his voice, the desire to spank her so all-consuming now, his palms began to itch. 'You dishonour your family, your country and yourself with this attitude, and you also dishonour me. You will become my wife now or—'

'There's no way on Earth I would become your wife under any circumstances,' she interrupted him. *Again.* 'You're an arrogant, overbearing—'

'Okay, *enough*!' The shout from her father had them both turning to see the Sheikh stand and stride around his desk. 'Stop yelling, the both of you, and sit down.'

Kamal straightened, having completely forgotten Sheikh Zane Ali and his wife were in the room the minute their wayward daughter had appeared.

But the brief spurt of shame was swiftly quashed. This situation was not of his making, and he refused to be placated or dismissed by anyone. Not even a man as powerful and well-respected as the Narabian Sheikh. He might be embarrassed the man and his wife had witnessed their unseemly spat, but he planned to marry their daughter and they would have to get used to it, as well as her.

He had requested a meeting with the Sheikh this morning and had told him of last night's development—after finally getting over his own fury with the shoddy way Kaliah Khan had treated him, enough to think coherently, at least. When he had formally requested the man's daughter's hand in marriage, Zane Khan had not reacted the way he had expected.

Instead of seeing marriage as the only solution, he had seemed circumspect, and had insisted on calling in the Crown Princess to 'discuss' the situation. There was no discussion Kamal could imagine that would change the facts, and he did not like the way the man was looking at them both now, as if this was some kind of lovers' quarrel which needed to be handled instead of an extremely damaging diplomatic incident.

He took a moment to breathe through his anger—which meant keeping his eyes off the woman beside him and focussing on her father.

He did not take orders from Zane Khan or any man, and he would not be thwarted on this. But, at the same time, he was in the man's home. And he did not wish to make an enemy of Khan, or risk him withdrawing his endorsement, not unless he absolutely had to.

'I will not sit until we have an agreement on this,' he said, deliberately leaving off the honorific.

'If you think you're getting me to agree to marry you...' Kaliah began, but her father simply lifted his hand.

'Liah, just sit down, damn it,' he said, weary resignation in his voice. 'And stop making things worse.'

'But, Dad, you can't be seriously entertaining any of this?' she said, a high, desperate note entering her voice.

Kamal stared at them both, confused by the familiarity with which she addressed her father. He had noticed it before, after the race, and he couldn't help but be astonished by it.

He had no understanding of how families worked, having never had one of his own, but surely it could not be right that she would talk to her Sheikh with such disrespect? Although, somehow, Kaliah Khan's wilful behaviour did not surprise him. It seemed the woman had no respect for anything—not the culture and traditions which had bound their region for centuries, and certainly not him or the gravity of what they had shared the previous night.

Her audacious behaviour only annoyed him more. Did she actually believe he *wanted* to marry her? As much as he might need a wife, and as much as he had enjoyed the sex, he was not a fool. Their chemistry was explosive, that was certainly true. But the intensity of their physical connection had also disturbed him. The fact he'd been her first only disturbed him more.

How could she have been so enchanting, so alluring? How could his climax have been so…he breathed, trying to prevent the bolt of desire journeying any further south… overwhelming when she had been so inexperienced? How could she have had him clinging to his control? And where had that damned possessive streak come from, which had blindsided him as soon as he'd seen the flecks of blood?

He was good at sex. He had learned how to pleasure women as a young soldier. Pasha—his first lover—had been in her thirties and a widow. She had been patient and kind with him and had taught him well. And, until last night, he had always enjoyed using his skill to bring a woman to orgasm before he found his own release.

But, with Kaliah Khan, patient enjoyment had become

desperate need. It had almost killed him to hold back. If he had interpreted her odd mix of boldness and shyness for what it was last night, he would have stopped before it was too late if she'd asked him to. But seeing her again, feeling the vicious surge of desire all over again, only made him realise how hard that would have been...when it should have been easy.

How could he still want her so desperately? Enough even to want to marry her on one level, although he knew she was the precise opposite of the sort of woman he should make his queen.

He needed a partner, a woman who could respect him and look up to him—despite his past—a woman who was mature, responsible and most of all willing to listen and learn. And it was clear, from this morning's display of hubris, entitlement and reckless disregard for everything except herself, that Kaliah Khan was not that woman.

'Please, Prince Kamal, perhaps if you sit down...if you *both* sit down...' the Queen said, sending her daughter a pointed look, 'We could all discuss this like rational adults.'

He frowned. Was Queen Catherine implying *he* was not behaving like an adult? Before his temper could spike again, though, he registered the beseeching look in the older woman's warm chestnut eyes and his temper defused a little...

He forced himself to walk stiffly back to his chair and sit down. He waited, aware of Kaliah's rigid stance, the temper bristling off her as she continued to stand and glare at both her parents. He felt an odd ripple of sympathy. Apparently, she did not enjoy being trapped any more than he did. Even if it was all her own fault.

At last, she trudged over to the chair opposite her father's desk—the chair furthest from his own, he noted—and sat. He ignored her petty show of defiance.

Her desires made no difference now. Surely she would have to bend to her father's will and honour the traditions she had been born into, whether she wished it or not? They both would.

Her father returned to his desk and sat behind it. Steepling his fingers, he directed his gaze at his daughter and asked quietly, 'Is it true, Liah? Did you sleep with Prince Kamal last night and were you a virgin?'

'Dad!' Kaliah leapt back out of her chair. 'You're not seriously asking me that question?' she cried. 'What I do in my private life is none of...'

Khan put up a placating hand to interrupt her latest disrespectful diatribe. 'Okay, okay, Liah. Calm down. I'm just trying to establish the facts, that's all.'

It was obvious from the pained look on the Sheikh's face, though, that he knew what Kamal had told him was the truth, because his daughter had yet to deny it.

Kamal sat rigidly in his chair, ignoring the confusion and the fury bubbling like acid under his breastbone. Not to mention the low-grade arousal that was always there when he was within two feet of Zane Khan's unruly daughter.

He waited for Khan to state the obvious—that a marriage would have to be arranged—but, instead of doing so, Khan turned to Kamal, his expression strained but resolute.

Kamal didn't like that look one bit because he had seen it many times before. In the face of Uttram Aziz when he had announced Kamal would have to marry to secure the throne. In the face of his commanding officer, during his first desert campaign, when he had been ordered to take his troops into bandit country with no cover, and only himself and four of his men had come out alive. In the face of Hamid, when his employer had unwound his belt to give him another brutal beating—unlike the staff at the orphanage, or his first drill sergeant when he had entered the Zo-kari army, Hamid had been a bully who'd enjoyed exploiting the power he'd held over that defenceless boy.

He also remembered that look from his earliest mem-ory—when a tall man had told him to be a good boy then walked away, leaving him on the steps of the orphanage. He hated that look because he knew it meant only one thing—he was about to get shafted.

'Here's the thing, Prince Kamal,' the Sheikh said with an apologetic note in his voice, despite the determination in his eyes. 'While the Law of Marriage of the Sheikhs is an honourable tradition, meant to protect women—and I can totally understand why you, as a conscientious and clearly honourable man, would want to adhere to it—in Narabia it's not something we would insist upon any more, unless both parties are one hundred percent amenable.'

Kamal's anger rose in his chest, but he kept his gaze on Khan and refused to let any of the emotions churning in his gut—everything from indignation to fury—show. Because that would just give this man the upper hand.

'What does this mean, exactly?' he asked, determined to make Khan spell it out.

'That you have no obligation to marry my daughter just because you took her virginity last night,' he said. 'It's fairly clear from what my wife and I have just witnessed that there's no love lost between the two of you,' the man con-tinued, the tinge of paternal condescension making the fire in Kamal's gut burn. 'And I very much doubt you wish to be shackled to Liah any more than she wishes to be shack-led to you.'

'Gee, thanks, Dad,' Kaliah muttered, but Kamal could hear the relief in her tone and wanted to punch a wall.

They were telling him his honour, his country's honour,

did not matter. And he could not accept that. But, worse, they were suggesting the responsibility he now felt for Kaliah was of no significance too.

Khan let out a deep sigh, then grasped the hand his wife had laid on his shoulder while he'd spoken.

Something about that gesture, the visceral connection between this man and his wife—supportive, generous and fierce—only made Kamal feel more alone. And more isolated.

The fire leapt in his gut. Damn them. He didn't need anyone's support. He had always survived on his own.

'So, basically, I think we can all just pretend this never happened. And the details of last night's…' Khan cleared his throat uncomfortably '…last night's events will never leave this room, so no one's honour need be challenged. You've fulfilled your obligation by coming here and proposing, Kamal, and I appreciate it. But I'm not about to require you to marry a woman you don't love,' he finished.

Love? What on earth was the man talking about? An emotion as fickle, fanciful and foolish as love had no bearing on any of this. And Kamal certainly did not require love. Not from anyone. He never had and he never would. He had himself—that was all he required.

'I hope you will stay for the rest of the weekend?' Khan added. 'As our honoured guest.'

Kamal had no intention of staying after being insulted so comprehensively. But he needed time to think before he made his next move. He had come to Khan this morning expecting this to be fairly straightforward. Clearly the man was even more indulgent of his wayward daughter than Kamal had realised. But he would find a solution once he could unknot his brain enough to think clearly.

'As you wish.' Kamal stood, too furious to say more or

even to look at the woman who was the cause of this disaster. His pride was burning, but what was far worse was the way the pain in his gut had morphed into the gruelling hollow ache he remembered so well from much of his adolescence—every time he'd faced another rejection, another put down, another cruel dismissal, because he'd never been strong enough, never brave enough, never important enough to matter.

He gave a shallow bow and strode out of the room.

He was not that sad, rejected boy any longer.

And he would prove it by showing Kaliah Khan that Crown Prince Kamal Zokan was good enough for any woman. And certainly one as wild, spoilt and wilful as Narabia's future queen.

CHAPTER FIVE

LIAH SWIPED THE angry tear from her cheek as she spurred Ashreen over the rocky escarpment. She glanced over her shoulder in the gathering dusk. The minarets of the Golden Palace had disappeared behind the mountain ridge.

The crushing weight that had been sitting on her chest ever since she had been ambushed by Prince Kamal in her father's study finally lifted a little. But, as she tugged on the reins to slow Ashreen before they headed down the rocky slope to the oasis, the knots in her gut refused to ease.

She'd never been more humiliated in her whole entire life than she had been that morning. And that was saying something for someone who seemed so adept at screwing up on a regular basis.

She'd trudged back to her room, packed a small bag and had waited—while regretting every single wrong, foolish decision that had led to the worse mistake she'd ever made last night by deciding to sleep with that man. No one had come to ask her to attend any of the day's events, and she knew why. She suspected her parents were keen to keep her away from Kamal—and stave off a diplomatic incident.

As soon as the sun had dipped towards the horizon, making the weather cool enough to ride out to the oasis, she had sneaked down to the stables, saddled Ashreen and escaped, leaving a note with one of the stable hands to deliver to Malik, her father's head of household. She didn't want her parents to worry, but at the same time she very much doubted they'd be sad to see the back of her right now.

Another tear leaked out. She pushed it away, knowing she had no right to be upset. These were tears of self-pity.

Why can't you ever get any single thing right?

She tried to re-gather some of her anger towards Kamal and his outrageous demands, which had managed to sustain at least a little of her pride and self-worth during that awful meeting. But the scalding anger had died hours ago…and all she felt towards him now was a vague feeling of misery.

Because she couldn't get the image out of her head of his face as her father had informed him there would be no marriage. For once he had been completely transparent. And, while the foremost emotion had definitely been fury, what she'd also seen was confusion and something that had looked uncomfortably like shame.

As much as she wanted to hate him, she could see she was the one who had been thoughtless and selfish. She'd used him to lose her virginity.

She flushed as the memory of his lips, his tongue and his teeth on her flowed through her again. She could still feel the slow glide of his callused palms owning every inch of her body, making her beg and moan, setting off fires that had finally overwhelmed her completely when his hard, thick length had pressed relentlessly but so carefully into her tender flesh. And she'd surrendered the last of herself to him.

Heat pulsed and throbbed in the sore spots that still troubled her after last night. Why hadn't it even occurred to her that there would be emotional repercussions, not just for her, but for him too?

The truth was, she'd totally forgotten about that silly

old law, but why hadn't she figured out that Kamal would consider taking her virginity something he would have to atone for?

On one level, the whole concept of him insisting on marriage was totally nuts. But she knew nothing about him—how he'd come to the throne, the mysterious 'background' her father had alluded to—and she hadn't bothered to ask.

Typical Liah. Just dive in head-first, do what feels good and don't bother considering anyone else's feelings or responsibilities.

Shame flooded through her as she spotted the oasis in the distance.

The iridescent pool of water, fed by a spring that flowed over limestone rocks, shimmered in the twilight as night fell. The grove of palms, shrubs and desert blooms provided much-needed shade from the bitter desert sun in the day time. The luxury encampment—several tents and a corral—was kept well-stocked and regularly checked by her father's staff to ensure her family could escape here when necessary. And it was also a good bolt hole for unwary travellers who got lost in the regions vast and unforgiving landscape.

As she released her hold on Ashreen, the horse broke into a canter, having scented the fresh water. But somehow the place which had always fortified and liberated her as a teenager, a place where she knew she could be one hundred percent herself, felt less of a well-earned escape this evening…and more like a coward's hideout. Even this oasis couldn't change the fact she would never be the woman her family needed her to be.

Not a queen. Not a mature woman. But a spoilt child.

After dismounting, she tugged off the saddle and the rest of the tack, her arms aching. As she rubbed the horse down, and fed and watered her before attending to her own needs, she tried to rationalise away the weight still crushing her ribs.

She hadn't slept well last night. Maybe she just needed a few days here to get over this feeling of ennui and hopelessness? Once Kamal left the palace and returned to Zokar, she would surely be able to make amends for her latest disaster?

But the memory of the disappointment in both her parents' faces made her stomach tangle into a tight knot of regret. Far worse, though, was the memory of the look in Kamal Zokan's eyes when he'd walked out of her father's study—angry and intense but also guarded and wary and, for a moment, beaten down.

Way to go, Liah. The undisputed Queen of Monumental Screw-Ups.

After she had bathed off the trail dust in the cool spring water and lit the torches to keep any unwanted visitors away, she collapsed into the tent and stared at the sturdy poles and embroidered fabrics above her head.

She'd never really considered herself fit to be Queen of Narabia, but now she'd proved it beyond a doubt. Not just to her parents, but to a man who—as much as she wanted never to see or think of him again—she had a bad feeling had left an imprint on her body and soul she might never be able to forget.

As dawn fired across the horizon, Kamal galloped towards the rocky ridge which marked the edge of the Narabian desert, his destination the Azeala Oasis. He had managed to bribe the location out of one of the palace staff as the place where Kaliah Khan might be hiding.

The little coward.

The low-grade fury which had been riding him for over twenty-four hours—ever since Zane Khan had informed him oh, so casually that his honour meant nothing—now felt like a boulder jammed in his throat that he couldn't dislodge.

He'd attended all the foolish events laid on for the guests yesterday, hoping to corner Kaliah Khan in person and inform her that, whatever her father had said, he would not let her off the hook so easily.

So what if the news of their night together never left the Golden Palace? He would know what he had done—what *they* had done. What it felt like to feel her swollen flesh stretching to receive him…to take a man's body for the first time.

Shame, fury and a weird sense of possessiveness engulfed him again. The deed was done. And it couldn't be undone. Plus, he needed to find a wife this weekend. And, however unsuitable she was, she would have to be the one. Because he'd been so preoccupied with her, he hadn't had the headspace, or frankly the inclination, to pursue anyone else.

He hit the top of the ridge and tugged on Asad's reins to survey the land below him.

The morning light illuminated the encampment and the oasis below. The sunrise turned the water to a flaming orange to match the flicker of torches which had burned down during the night.

Was she really here alone, as the stable hand had suggested? Surely it was not safe for her to stay in such a place without an armed guard? He circled round, approaching the encampment from behind, and spotted in the corral the thoroughbred horse she had been riding in the race, munching on its feed-bag.

The mare's ears pricked up as Asad approached.

Kamal patted his stallion's neck to stop him alerting Kaliah to their presence before he was ready.

Dismounting in silence, he draped the reins over the corral railing, then unhooked the bridle so Asad could get a well-earned drink. But he didn't remove the saddle. They could not stay here for their discussion. He'd noticed a weather alert this morning for the whole region, signalling the possibility of sandstorms this afternoon.

The storms were rare, but could be dangerous, especially in such an exposed position. And, anyway, he did not want their conversation interrupted by the need to flee back to the palace. He wanted her on his own turf—where he could get the answers he sought out of her without any interference. The choking fury closed around his throat again.

She had used him and then discarded him—he understood that now—because he was not of royal blood.

He yanked off his keffiyeh and dunked his head in the water trough. The cool water washed away the sweat but did little to cool the anger and frustration that had been building ever since he had woken yesterday morning, the need for her still pounding through his system.

A need which hadn't really abated in the last twenty-four hours, even though she had rejected him.

Perhaps he ought to wait for her to wake up but, as he strode towards the main tent, he discarded the idea. They'd gone past politeness a long time ago. And he would be damned if he'd treat her like some rare, exotic bird when he'd been inside her, when her fingernails had dug into the scars on his back as she'd clung to him and the heady sobs of her climax, the sweet scent of her arousal, had driven him into a frenzy.

This has nothing to do with your honour, or the Law of Marriage of the Sheikhs, or even your need to find a convenient bride. Stop kidding yourself. This is much more basic and elemental than that.

The thought echoed in his head as his groin throbbed and the choking fury was joined by the feeling he hated and thought he had conquered long ago—of shame, of vulnerability, of yearning, the longing for something he knew he could never have, could never deserve.

He cut it off. *Again.*

He had fought long and hard to leave that child behind and become a man of standing, of huge wealth, importance and position. And he was not about to let some reckless virgin make him feel like that rejected boy again, however desirable she was, however royal her heritage.

The irony that she had made him feel this way once before, when she'd been five and he fourteen, didn't escape him as he ripped open the tent flap.

'Kaliah, it is Prince Kamal,' he announced as he stepped into the cool, shadowy interior. 'If you think you can run from me and our responsibilities, you are wrong. You have five minutes to clothe yourself.'

It took several seconds for his eyes to adjust to the light. But, several minutes later, she had yet to come out of the bedroom—or even reply to his perfectly reasonable demand.

To hell with this.

He strode across the lavishly furnished space. 'Time's up!' he shouted, and marched through the curtains guarding the bed chamber.

As his gaze slanted over her empty unmade bed, and a lung full of her spicy, sultry, spellbinding scent fired through his system, his temper charged back.

He marched out of the tent, the last threads of his control fraying.

When he finally located her, it would be nothing short of a miracle if he managed to prevent himself from flinging her across his knee and spanking her.

Liah sighed as the spring water gushed from the rocks and doused her in glorious cold. It was already warm, and would be scorching later, but she had a solar-powered generator here to keep the living quarters cool.

Her skin tingled and pulsed, alive and still far too sensitive from her night of debauchery. She would have to return to the palace tomorrow—her father's steward had contacted her on the satellite phone twenty minutes ago to tell her of the threat of sandstorms. Their data were suggesting she should be okay, but her father was insisting she return home or he would send out the guard to bring her back.

After all the trouble she'd caused in the last few days, she knew she'd have to comply. At least Malik had also told her Prince Kamal and his men had departed for Zokar that morning, so she didn't have to hide out any longer.

She tilted her face into the flow and let the invigorating stream sluice down her body.

You're not hiding from him. You're simply giving him time to make a dignified departure.

She turned to tiptoe back across the rocks, her drenched T-shirt and panties making her aware of places still tender from his forceful caresses.

But, as she stepped away from the splashing water, a deep, husky sound, like someone clearing their throat, reverberated in her chest. Her head snapped up so fast, she almost got whiplash.

Him?

Heat and panic fired through her system, swiftly followed by shock. And a strange out-of-body sensation which made her sure she had to be imaging the tall, dark shape of the man who had occupied her thoughts for two solid days standing by the water's edge. His muscular arms were folded across his broad chest and his long legs were akimbo, encased in dusty jeans and riding boots, as if he were braced for action. The short black robe he wore to stave off the heat caught on the breeze and swirled around him, making him look like an avenging angel... Or, rather, an avenging devil.

She stared, utterly transfixed, as the heat continued to ripple through her over-sensitised body... Perhaps she'd got more sun than she'd thought on the ride here yesterday. Her worst nightmare could not possibly be here, standing on the shore of *her* secret oasis, his dark gaze roaming over her features then sinking down to examine her breasts with insolent entitlement.

Her nipples chose that precise moment to swell and elongate, poking against the wet T-shirt like two Exocet missiles. And making her brutally aware of the fact she was not wearing a bra. She folded her arms over her breasts.

Don't freak out. He's a mirage—he has to be. This is all in your head, and your guilty conscience.

But then the devastating illusion spoke. The brutal command in his voice was far too familiar as his searing gaze shot her body temperature into the danger zone.

'Get out of the water, Your Highness,' he said, the honorific dripping with contempt. 'We have a long ride ahead of us to get to the safety of the Zokari gorge before the sandstorms hit.'

She pressed her forearms into the yearning flesh of her cleavage to stop it throbbing, and tried to give him her *No way, José* glare, which she reserved for her younger brothers when they were being particularly annoying.

Unfortunately, her glare lacked the usual searing effect, the shiver of sensation, the aching swelling in her breasts and the tender spot between her thighs all throbbing in time to her erratic pulse.

Am I losing it? I must be.

'W-what are you doing here?' she managed, still hoping he wasn't really here at all and this was all some kind of lurid, erotic nightmare.

'Saving you from a sandstorm and ensuring you become my wife—not necessarily in that order,' he barked.

Okay, so either she *had* lost the plot, or he had.

'You have ten minutes to get dressed and pack what you need while I prepare the horses for our journey,' he continued, as if he were the lord of all he surveyed and she his subordinate.

Her rebellious spirit finally kicked in. *Think again, buster.*

'I'm not going anywhere with you,' she declared, still shivering, still aching, the dread starting to engulf her.

'This is not a negotiation,' he said, his tone tight with strained patience. 'If you will not keep yourself and your horse safe, I will do it for you. You now have nine minutes.' So saying, he turned and marched back through the palm trees, leaving her shivering, shaking and swearing profusely at his departing back.

Fine, she'd get dressed—because being virtually naked while she confronted him was not a good plan—and then she would tell him where he could stick his rescue and his ludicrous notions of marriage. *Again.*

'Read my lips—I am not going with you. The data suggests the sandstorm will not hit until tomorrow at the earliest, by which time I intend to be safely back at the palace.' The flush of colour on Kaliah Khan's face and her obstinate stance, not to mention the loose robe she had donned to stay cool in the sun, was not doing a damn thing to calm Kamal's temper. Nor was the image of her exactly eight-point-five minutes ago with her pert nipples visible through the clinging fabric of her soaked T-shirt.

He had found her at the pond all but naked, her slender curves only accentuated by the drenched cotton. And, when she'd turned to him, he had become fixated on the plump flesh beneath. Her large, puckered areolas had been clearly visible and had only become more pronounced as he had stared, imagining them hardening beneath his tongue.

The sight had made his erection painful, which would make the six-hour ride they had ahead of them to get to safety even more fun. The sexual frustration had only added to his fury. How could she take such risks, to bathe as good as naked in the middle of the desert? There were few bandits in the region now, but anyone could have come across her.

'Get on your horse or I will put you on mine,' he snarled, clenching his jaw so hard he was amazed he did not crack a tooth.

Modern weather data could be useful, but it often lied. He could already smell the tinge of sulphur on the air, could feel the first tendrils of wind and see the dark red rim around the sun, now fully risen above the horizon. He would always trust his own instincts first and his gut was telling him they needed to leave now. But he would be damned if he would explain any of that to her. She did not respect him, or his instincts, so he refused to pander to her tantrum.

The woman continued to glare at him, stubborn, infuriating and proud.

'No,' she hissed.

The single forceful word snapped the last ragged thread on his patience and self-control.

She shrieked as he reached for her and began to kick, gouge and shout angry words he had never before heard come from the mouth of a woman. But he ignored her struggles, her protests, and ducked to avoid the worst of her slaps and punches—he was a trained fighter, forged in the fires of battle, and no mere slip of a woman would be able to best him, however strong her anger.

Clasping her around the waist, he threw her over one shoulder and marched across the corral as she struggled. He dumped her onto the powerful stallion's back.

Asad's head jerked sharply. Kaliah's scream was followed by more swear words as she grasped the horse's mane to prevent herself from falling. It kept her hands conveniently busy as he unhooked the reins from the post and mounted behind her. His aching groin bumped against her backside as he banded a controlling hand around her waist to draw her securely into his lap.

The horse reared, unfamiliar with the double weight, but Kamal controlled him easily with his knees. He felt the jolt going through her slender body, her teeth clicking as Asad's front hooves landed back on the parched earth.

'You…you bastard!' She gasped, but she sounded less angry now and more stunned.

He doubted anyone had ever sought to tame her before him, and he did not kid himself he had won. But her efforts were feeble now as she tried to prise his arm loose, her whole body shaking with the effort it was costing her to fight his far superior strength.

The scratches on his arm and his cheek stung as he spurred the stallion, who had been bred for endurance, into a gallop, whistling to ensure her mare, who he had already untied and saddled, followed them.

Kaliah shouted more obscenities at him, continuing to struggle and scratch but, as they galloped further from her camp towards the mountainous border region, he could feel the fight draining out of her. The struggle to stay on the powerful horse eventually became too much, even for her prodigious temper.

He slowed after an hour, knowing the punishing pace was not good for the horses in the rising heat, any more than it was good for his unruly passenger.

She sat stiffly against him, her body rigid with tension even though he could feel how exhausted she was, her ragged breaths making her breasts heave against his controlling arm.

Her silence seemed even more deafening than her earlier shrieks of protest.

But he didn't care. She could sulk all she wanted. He would have her where he wanted her now. The Zokari gorge would provide a natural shelter from the storms, and he had a lavish, well-stocked encampment there which he used to get away when the pressures of his new position became too much. So they would have peace and privacy for the conversation they needed to have.

He would make her understand he refused to be treated with such contempt. But, more than that, he would show her he was not a man who could be dismissed and discarded.

She still wanted him. He knew that much. And, once she had admitted as much, he would show her how a marriage between them could benefit them both.

'My father will kill you when he finds out what you've done,' she said finally, on a husky breath of outrage. 'You have just made a formidable enemy. I hope you realise that.'

'Your father will thank me,' he said, not disturbed by her threat. Khan would be furious, but he had only himself to blame for raising such a wayward, unruly child. And if this meant a stand-off between them, so be it. He would not back down again. 'For teaching you what it means to be a queen,' he continued. 'It is time you learned to observe the responsibilities that your position demands, instead of behaving like a wild girl who can do anything she wishes without consequence.'

She remained silent and rigid. An hour later, she began to sink into exhaustion, her body slumping against his despite her best efforts to hold herself apart from him.

A spurt of admiration went through him, despite the trouble she had caused him and the torn skin still smarting on his cheeks and forearm.

For all her wild ways, Kaliah Khan was a fighter.

She had fallen into a fitful sleep, her back resting against his chest, by the time they reached the entrance to the gorge, the rock faces shielding them from the worst of the heat.

He directed Asad up the rocky slopes, over the parched riverbed and into the trees. When they finally reached his encampment, she was too shattered even to lift her head. He carried her into one of the bedroom tents and laid her down on the pile of cushions. She rolled away from him—no doubt deliberately.

He waited until her disdainful shoulder lifted and fell in a steady rhythm again, then strode from the tent to prepare food and tend to the horses. And to clean the scratches on his face.

When she awoke, they would eat, then he would insist she trim her nails. And after that he would leave her alone. Even if it killed him.

Eventually, she would have to come to him—for they would remain here as long as it took for her to see reason.

But as he took the saddles off Asad, then Ashreen, fed and watered them both then cleaned their hooves and gave them a rub down, fatigue began to drag at him too. The adrenaline rush of the journey and the tussle beforehand had subsided to be replaced by a strange sense of uneasiness.

He had never physically manhandled a woman in his life. And, although he had only done what was necessary to bring her to safety and protect her from herself, the unsettling feeling lodged in his gut. Finding meat and a selection of vegetables in the camp's cold storage, he began preparing a stew for their supper—as the memory of her voice, sharp with resentment and anger but also tinged with hopelessness, pushed at a place he thought he had sealed off long ago.

The place where he had locked the deep sense of injustice which had nearly destroyed him as a boy, when he had been beaten, abused and told he had no right to make choices of his own by that bastard Hamid.

It is not the same.

He sprinkled flour on the meat and set it in the pan over the campfire.

Kaliah Khan has led a privileged, charmed life. She has never had to fight, never had to endure the contempt and disrespect of others. She has always been loved, cherished and indulged. It will do her no harm to be shown she can't have everything her own way all the time.

But as he watched the stew bubble, and threw in a few herbs and spices, he found himself dwelling on her refusal to look at him, even to speak to him. And the feel of her, so wary, so guarded, so tense and fragile, in his arms.

He was not good at interpreting other people's emotions

because he had never had the luxury of examining his own. And he saw no purpose in regretting actions already taken.

But as the sun sank beneath the cliffs above them and the air chilled, his simple plan to rescue Kaliah, to bring her here and then set about showing her a marriage between them was destined and necessary, didn't seem quite so simple any more.

CHAPTER SIX

LIAH JERKED AWAKE, groggy, sore and angry. It took her several moments though to remember why she was not in her own tent at the Aleaza Oasis…and then the memories flooded back. Kamal's shocking appearance at the pool, the battle to stop him from putting her onto his horse. She'd screamed, kicked, punched and struggled against his hold with every ounce of strength she'd possessed. But he'd subdued her with disturbing ease, and an even more disturbing indifference to her rage.

He'd thrown her over his shoulder, dumped her on his horse—which had nearly thrown her in the process—and swung up behind her, his hard chest pressed against her back like a brick wall, banded one unyielding arm across her midriff and then galloped away with her without a thought to her feelings, her needs, her wishes or desires.

He had treated her like a disobedient child. Maybe he'd been careful not to hurt her and had in no way fought back against her tirade. But so what? She was a grown woman who had the right to make her own decisions. And he'd ignored that.

He's kidnapped me.

She shuddered. She had no idea where she even was. He'd mentioned something about a gorge. Were they in Zokar?

What if he tried to force her into an arranged marriage? How the heck would she stop him?

Panic bumped against her breastbone as she raced through every possible scenario, each one scarier and more horrifying than the last. She breathed through it, her head starting to ache with the struggle to remain calm, focussed and decisive.

Zokar might not be as developed as her father's kingdom, but it was not unsophisticated. Just like that of Narabia, the economy had thrived in the last twenty years after the decision to mine its vast mineral wealth and it had begun to open itself to the world.

She thought of Kamal, dressed in a tuxedo at the Race of Kings reception. And later, in his bed-chamber, as he had stroked her to orgasm with a care and attention she had not expected. He was not an uncivilised man, however badly he had behaved this morning.

She had to believe that.

Her head continued to ache, along with every other part of her anatomy after their never-ending ride.

Stop panicking and start thinking, Liah. Because you're the only one who can get yourself out of this mess.

But as she glared at the ceiling of the unfamiliar tent, and the circular hole in the top used to allow cooling air into the space, it was hard to keep the fury at bay when it replaced the panic. Shooting stars flared across the inky blue above, a flash of brightness which instantly flickered and died. Unlike her temper, which was liable to blaze for a long time to come.

Stolen!

There was no other term for what he had done to her. Because she had not gone with him willingly—and she had certainly made that crystal clear in every way she could.

Perhaps he'd convinced himself he was rescuing her from a possible sandstorm. Kidnapping her for her own good, or some such nonsense. But they both knew that was just an excuse. And a pathetic one at that.

The storm wasn't due to hit until tomorrow—and, even if it had hit today, she would have been fine. She'd seen the storms before, maybe not in an encampment, but the desert tribes survived them so why shouldn't she?

Rolling over, she forced herself out of the bed, found the facilities at the back of the chamber and washed the trail dust off her face.

He'd left her clothed, at least, although her riding robe was now filthy and sweaty. In the outer chamber she found the bag she'd packed intending to head back to the palace. She dressed quickly in a pair of loose trousers and a T-shirt, then caught the scent of something rich, spicy and delicious.

Her stomach growled like that of a starving lion.

The realisation she hadn't eaten since the night before did not help control her fury because that was Kamal's fault too. But she hesitated before charging out of the tent to demand to be fed and then returned to the Golden Palace, ASAP.

For once, you need to be strategic.

Having a temper tantrum now would just give Kamal another excuse to treat her like an unruly kid. She took several deep breaths which, while they didn't do much to control her fury, did manage to stop her from marching out all guns blazing and giving the man who had kidnapped her yet more reasons to be a self-righteous jerk.

She lifted the tent flap slowly, to survey her surroundings.

She spotted Kamal instantly, crouched by the camp fire about ten feet away. His handsome features looked even harsher and more unreadable in the orange glow of the firelight.

Handsome? When did you start thinking he was handsome? He's not handsome—he's a flipping kidnapper.

But even so she felt the familiar flicker of reaction as she studied him.

'Know your enemy' was something she'd read in books, but it felt remarkably appropriate now if she were to have any chance of getting out of this mess without ending up unintentionally married, or triggering an international incident between Narabia and its nearest neighbour.

As much as her first instinct was to flee the first chance she got later tonight, saddle up Ashreen while Kamal slept, find her own way back to Narabia and her family and forget this had ever happened, she could already see that course of action was fraught with danger.

She didn't know where she was. She had no means of navigation. And, despite having a first from Cambridge in the politics and history of the Nazar Desert kingdoms—which encompassed Narabia, Zafar, Zokar and the surrounding land—she had absolutely no experience of life in the desert, apart from the occasional overnight stay in the luxury accommodation supplied by her father.

She could die, lost out in the desert alone. And even she wasn't reckless and impulsive enough to put her life in danger—no matter how mad she was right now—which meant she would have to find a way to reason with the man who had kidnapped her. A man who seemed about as reasonable as a force-ten hurricane.

He didn't look her way, although she knew he had sensed her watching him from the way his stubbly jaw clenched.

She took the opportunity to study him, unobserved. The first thing she noticed was the way he was squatting on his haunches. It looked uncomfortable. But she'd seen her uncle Raif, the ruler of the Kholadi tribe, sit the same way whenever he was with his tribesmen. He'd once told her it was the most comfortable way to sit if you wanted to stay cool.

Did Kamal's stance provide some clues to his mysterious past? Strangely, despite her fury with him and the way he had treated her, her curiosity hadn't abated in the slightest. But maybe that was a good thing, because it might help her to figure out a way to persuade him what he'd done was abhorrent. And, given his arrogance, she suspected she was going to have an uphill battle persuading him anything he did was not okay. She wasn't sure she'd be able to talk to him tonight without losing her temper, though. She was still too angry with him.

Her stomach chose that moment to growl so loudly, she suspected it could probably be heard back at the Golden Palace.

His gaze shifted to hers, the intensity in his eyes ripping through her hard-won composure to the girl beneath who had always refused to bow to any man—even her father most of the time.

And she respected and loved her dad.

Prince Kamal, not so much.

He stood, lifting off his haunches to his full height. He wore an open shirt and a pair of loose-fitting riding trousers, but his feet and head were bare and his hair was wet.

'You must eat,' he said, in that commanding voice which made it clear this wasn't a suggestion, it was an order.

Part of her—a very large part of her—wanted to tell him to get lost. But she was starving, the stew smelled delicious and there seemed no point in starting another argument until she was at least well-nourished enough to withstand the shudder of awareness playing havoc with her heart rate.

What is that even about?

So she strolled to the fireside, sat on one of the rocks and sent him a level look that she hoped conveyed how furious she was with him—as well as the fact that, just because she needed to eat before her stomach turned inside out, she had not forgiven him in any way, shape or form.

To her astonishment, he seemed to get the message, because he served up a generous helping of the stew and handed it to her without another word.

Their fingers touched as she took the bowl. She jerked her hand back, shocked by the visceral sensation that flared through her system.

Her gaze rose to his to find him watching her with the same dark intensity she remembered from their first night. He didn't smile, didn't really react at all. Though somehow she knew, in that patient, unreadable expression, he had felt the brutal awareness too but he was just better at controlling his reaction to it.

Great.

The vulnerability she had tried so hard to hide seeped into every corner of her being alongside the unwanted and uncontrollable reaction to the simple touch.

She tried not to bolt down the stew but, apart from the fact she was starving and it was delicious, she was suddenly desperate to get back to the relative safety of her tent. To regroup and start figuring out a strategy—not just to get him to take her back to her family, but how to handle the traitorous arousal.

After everything he'd done, how could she still desire him? Was this Stockholm Syndrome? A result of the stress of the last two days, ever since she'd sneaked out of his bed in the middle of the night?

But, as she sat beside him in the firelight, her body continued to yearn for his touch. And it occurred to her getting out of this mess was going to be much harder than she had assumed. Because he still seemed to have a strange command over her body, which she had no control over whatsoever, despite the appalling way he'd behaved.

And that could be bad. In fact, it could be very, very bad. Because it was that same visceral reaction that had helped get her into this enormous mess in the first place. And she suspected he knew how to use it against her. So getting to know him better was fraught with all sorts of risks she hadn't even considered.

What if her curiosity about him—that odd feeling of connection, of sympathy for the battles she suspected he had fought for so much of his life—brought an intimacy she also couldn't control?

Oh, boy, I'm so screwed—and not in a good way.

Leaving the last few bites of the stew, because her appetite had suddenly deserted her, Liah dumped the bowl and spoon in a water vat he had placed beside the fire then got up and marched to her tent without another word.

He didn't stop her.

Perhaps he was expecting her to thank him, maybe even to offer to wash up. Well, he could forget both. She was here against her will, and she did not plan to have another conversation with him until he had apologised and offered to take her home.

Refusing to engage with him, and this enforced campout, was her least worst option. Or rather the only strategy she'd come up with so far.

As she tied up the tent flap to make it crystal-clear she did not want a visit from him tonight—or any night—her fingers shook. Because she had a bad feeling Prince Kamal might well be the most stubborn, intractable and taciturn person she had ever met. And that meant their stand-off could last a very long time.

Way to go, Liah. This is turning into your most epic screw-up ever.

CHAPTER SEVEN

YOU'RE GONNA NEED a new strategy.

Waking up on the morning of day three of her enforced camp-out, Liah finally admitted the silent treatment was not working. She'd spent approximately forty-eight hours giving Kamal the cold shoulder and he didn't even seem to have noticed, let alone tried to communicate.

She'd assumed he'd eventually come to her, if only to demand she do her fair share around the camp. She'd had a whole speech ready and waiting for that moment, which she had edited and re-edited in her head about five thousand times—explaining in words of one syllable exactly why what he had done was wrong and what the consequences of his actions would be if he didn't return her to Narabia pronto.

But he'd outsmarted her, because they'd barely exchanged three words in the last three days, and she was about to burst with frustration.

Instead of demanding she help out, or even bringing up the question of their first night and his demand they marry, he had been stoic and uncommunicative. All the while he'd taken care of the horses, cooked their meals, cleaned up and then disappeared for most of the day on his stallion.

She'd taken Ashreen out for an exploratory ride the day before while he'd been away—hoping against hope that maybe she wasn't as far from Narabia as she'd thought. But, after an hour-long ride to the end of the gorge, she'd scanned the desert plane beyond that they must have traversed during the long ride to get here with a pair of binoculars she had found in the camp's supply tent. The terrain was rugged and inhospitable, and she hadn't been able to locate a single familiar landmark or rock formation.

Forced to return to the camp, she had expected Kamal at least to say something about her decision to venture out without his permission. She'd almost hoped he would be mad at her so she could finally force him to confront the seething atmosphere simmering between them—and deliver her damn speech. But he had simply stared at her. For a split second she had thought she saw relief in his eyes, but she was sure she must have imagined it when, saying nothing, he had handed her a plate of the fried meat and rice he had been eating, and then returned his attention to his own meal.

She glared at the open hole in her tent roof, the morning sun sprinkling the bedchamber's lavish furnishings with a golden glow, as her anger built at his apparent indifference to her whereabouts yesterday.

Who was giving whom the silent treatment here? Because it seemed that, after two long days and nights, he was winning the damned sulk-off she had started, which just infuriated her even more.

How on earth was she supposed to deal with a man who was so flipping contrary? What exactly did he even want from her? Why had he brought her here, if not to try and coerce her into marriage?

Throwing off the fine linen sheets, she marched to the wash basin to cool down. As she sluiced the water over her face and chest, she ignored the low-grade hum that had been pulsing over her skin ever since Kamal had discovered her bathing at Aleaza four days before. The low-grade hum that flared every time she spotted him in the camp, or woke up hot, sweaty and unbearably aroused every night troubled by erotic dreams...

Curtailing her wash so as not to encourage the hum, she strode to her pack and pulled out the last of her clean clothing. *Terrific.* She didn't even have clean panties for tomorrow, when she had no doubt at all they would probably still be here, busy avoiding each other like a couple of grumpy teenagers.

Her father would surely be looking for her by now. She needed to inform him where she was. And for that she would have to speak to Kamal.

First things first—you need clean panties before you figure out a whole new strategy to get Prince Hard Head to see the error of his ways.

She knew there was a water source nearby—she was pretty sure Kamal used it to bathe. She'd avoided it herself. She did not want to give him another chance to find her in a compromising position.

The hot spot between her thighs throbbed on cue at the memory of the last time he'd caught her bathing.

After dressing in her jeans and T-shirt, she strode out of the tent to find the camp empty and no sign of Asad or Kamal anywhere. He must have gone on his daily ride.

As she grabbed the pile of dirty clothing, her temper simmered at the thought of all the freedom he enjoyed that she did not. She could wash the clothes through, while coming up with a new strategy to finally deliver her speech without compromising her autonomy or giving him any hints about the stupid hum!

After checking on Ashreen, who she discovered had already been fed, watered and exercised by Kamal that morning, she headed through the ferns and palms that surrounded the camp, following the thin trickle of water in the nearby riverbed until she caught the sound of running water—and the scent of jasmine and desert sorrel.

As the trail took her deeper into the gorge, its red walls towering over her, the rocks turned to sand and the stream widened.

The splashing sound became louder as she finally passed through the last of the trees and found a sandy cove that surrounded a wide, deep pool of iridescent blue.

The splashing noise came from an impressive thirty-foot waterfall that tumbled into a pool at the far end of the gorge. She took a moment to take in the stunning beauty of the natural pond, the urge to strip off and dive into the cool blue all but unbearable.

This pool was much larger and more dramatic than the pond at Aleaza, lapping against the inland beach on one side and the base of the red rock-cliffs on the other.

But, just as she debated stripping off for a quick dip, she heard a nicker. Kamal's horse walked through the trees at the other end of the beach. The magnificent stallion wasn't wearing a saddle or bridle as it dipped its head and drank thirstily at the water's edge. The sheen of sweat on its rump and flanks suggested the horse had been ridden hard—and apparently bareback—not long before.

Is Kamal here too?

She should go back to the camp. But somehow she couldn't seem to turn and retreat, her thundering heartbeat sinking deep into her abdomen.

Then Kamal's dark head surged out of the water ten feet away. She eased back into the shelter of the trees, spellbound as she watched him swim in fast, efficient strokes towards the waterfall. The glimpse of tight buns had her heart jamming into her throat and sinking down to throb painfully between her thighs.

He's naked.

Her gaze remained glued to him as he ploughed through the water towards a rocky outcrop beneath the falls.

Go back now, before he spots you and the hum becomes completely unbearable.

But she couldn't move, couldn't even detach her gaze, as he planted strong hands onto the lichen-covered rocks and levered his strong body out of the water.

Her avid gaze trailed up long hair-dusted legs roped with muscle and over the smooth, paler rounded orbs of his exceptional gluts. But then her eyes widened and her heart slammed into her chest wall as her gaze reached his back.

The breath she hadn't realised she'd had trapped in her lungs gushed out on a shocked gasp, then the pulsing ache charged up from her core and wrapped around her ribs in a vice. The copper-brown skin, so muscular and strong, was marred by a criss-cross of scars, so many scars.

'Oh, no,' she whispered as the backs of her eyelids burned.

Even from this distance she could see the raised marks clearly. The ragged strips covered the whole of his back, stretching from the broad ridge of his shoulder blades all the way down to the base of his spine. She stared, her breath clogging in her lungs, recalling the strange ridges she'd felt when she'd clung to him as he thrust into her. Ridges she'd been curious about but had never seen because of the shirt he'd Insisted on wearing.

He reached up to slick back his hair and step into the stream of water pounding down from the fissure in the rock wall. The torn flesh on his back flexed and stretched.

These were old scars which had healed long ago. But,

even so, she couldn't swallow down the well of sympathy building under her breastbone at the evidence of the violence and abuse this hard, indomitable man had once endured.

Knowing exactly how strong he was now—thanks to her own first-hand experience—she knew no one could have done this to him as an adult.

Was that why he hadn't removed his shirt during their night together?

The wrenching in her chest became worse.

Kamal was a proud man. She'd convinced herself he was too proud—willing to ignore her wishes, and even his own, to satisfy some arcane tradition, some stupid sense of honour. She swallowed to ease the thickness in her throat and the thundering pain in her ribs. It occurred to her his pride, his determination to do the right thing after he'd taken her virginity, might have nothing to do with tradition, honour or even his new position as a desert prince and everything to do with the boy who had once been so brutally beaten. Was that the real reason his pride meant so much to him?

She retreated into the undergrowth—suddenly feeling like the worse kind of voyeur—and retraced her steps along the rocky path back to the camp, the bundle of dirty clothing forgotten in her arms. Her heart continued to pulse at her throat but, instead of fading, the thickness in her throat became raw and jagged as one of her earliest memories flickered at the edges of her consciousness. An encounter she remembered from long ago, when she'd been a little girl, and she had made eye contact with a serving boy while on a diplomatic visit to Zokar with her father and her uncle Raif.

She had never forgotten that boy—although he hadn't seemed like a boy to her then, because he'd been so much older than her. But, as she recalled him now, she realised he could only have been a teenager, tall, wiry and way too thin, and no match for the brute who had appeared from no-where and attacked him when he had dropped a few plates.

She could still hear the hideous thud of the belt slicing through flesh, the man's angry shouts and the boy's strange grunts as he had lifted his arms to stave off the attack. Could still hear her cries of distress as she had begged her father to intervene—and stop the awful punishment. And she could still see her father leaping up to grab the man's arm and prevent him from hitting the boy again.

Recalling that terrifying incident, and how her father had reprimanded that horrid man and spoken quietly with the boy to ensure he was okay, her love and respect for her father swelled.

But the swell of respect and affection for her father was nothing compared to the surge of distress and pity she still felt for that boy...

And her shock at the look in his eyes when his gaze had connected with hers that day. She could still picture his face as clearly now as if that incident had been yesterday, not fifteen years ago—the sallow skin, the high cheek-bones hollowed out by malnutrition and the deep amber of his eyes sparking with anger, resentment and fierce pride. But what had shocked her most of all was the lack of tears, even though she'd been able to see blood seeping through the worn fabric of his shirt.

She blinked furiously, aware of the sting behind her eyes again.

From the first moment she had met Kamal something about him had seemed strangely familiar. And now she knew what it was. His eyes were the same deep amber as that boy's eyes, and they'd had the exact same expression in them, four days ago in her father's study, when he had demanded marriage and had been told no.

As night fell over the gorge, Kamal led Asad along the trail back to the encampment, his skin bristling from his second cold swim of the day, after yet another hard ride through the canyon to try and alleviate at least some of the sexual frustration that had been threatening to blow his careful plans to have Kaliah come to him for three endless days now... And even more endless nights.

How much longer is she going to ignore me and the incessant heat between us?

The heat he'd been able to see in the flush of her skin as she'd sat across the fire from him and eaten the food he had made for her wearing a sour, angry expression on her face.

He had spent the last two days venturing further and further away from the camp on Asad so he would not have to spend time close to her. And had forced himself to trust she would not try to leave again after he had tracked her to the edge of the canyon yesterday. He had been prepared to follow her into the desert, if she tried to cross the deadly terrain. But, as he had watched her through the spyglass while she'd assessed the desert beyond the gorge, he had seen her shoulders slump and the defeated look on her face.

Pride had risen in his chest alongside the ever-present frustration. Kaliah Khan might be impulsive and reckless—and far too captivating—with a temper that could put an unbroken stallion to shame but she was not a fool.

Even so, when he had left the camp today, determined not to return until nightfall—for his own stress levels as much as hers—the fear she would do something reckless had not helped to control the unsettled feeling that was now a permanent fixture in his gut.

Last night he had stopped himself from touching her, from goading her, from demanding to know what the hell she had been thinking, believing she could survive in the desert alone. Not just because he wanted her to feel less of a prisoner but also because he could not trust himself not to go too far. The desire to glide his fingers over the swell of her breasts, pluck those responsive nipples, nibble across her collarbone and make her beg was something he was becoming increasingly concerned was liable to drive him wild.

He huffed out a breath, the heat pumping back into his groin.

Damn. Stop thinking about the scent and texture of her skin and the soft sobs which drove you mad on that one night with her in your arms or you will need yet another cold swim.

Asad snorted as they entered the camp. Kamal tied him alongside Ashreen in the corral. He patted the mare's back, surprised to see new feed had been added to her bag and the stall had recently been mucked out.

A small smile creased his lips.

Finally. Kaliah was relenting. Surely this had to be a sign she had decided to stop sulking? Perhaps tonight he would be able to coax her back into his bed and prove to her that a marriage between them would have some benefits.

Although the need to persuade her to marry him felt a lot less urgent than it had three days ago. His concerns now almost exclusively centred on the need to get her back into his arms and for her to forgive him for the high-handed way he had got her here.

He frowned as he rubbed down the stallion, poured fresh grain into its feed bag and replenished the water in the corral's trough. Not that he needed to be forgiven. He had done what was necessary for her safety as well as his future. Was it his fault she still had some growing up to do?

He stopped abruptly though as he walked out of the corral, surprise swiftly followed by the pulse of longing.

Kaliah sat beside a newly built fire, the simple outfit of jeans, boots and a T-shirt doing nothing to disguise her long legs and small but perfectly formed breasts. Her tawny skin—glided by the firelight and the gathering twilight—glowed with health and vitality.

The heat surged in his groin and he let out a harsh grunt. So much for the long day spent away from her, and the cold swims. Her head swung round and their gazes locked. He smelt it then, the aroma of cooked meat and spices.

Had she made supper for them both?

Something he did not really understand pressed against his ribs. He had many chefs at the palace in Zokar who could conjure up the most delicious dishes. And then there were the servants at his home in the foothills of the tribal lands. He had employed them primarily to cook for him. Because he had gone to bed hungry so many nights as a boy, he had promised himself one day he would always be able to afford to have the best food, the richest food, whenever he wanted it.

But no one had ever cooked for him before now, without being paid to do so. And he certainly had not expected such domesticity from Kaliah, when she probably still hated his guts.

He took in another lungful of the spicy aroma. In truth, he was also astonished she knew how to make a meal in the desert—perhaps she wasn't as pampered as he had assumed.

She stood as he approached the fire and tucked her hands into the back pockets of her jeans in a nervous gesture which made the worn cotton stretch over her breasts.

He studied her face, expecting to see anger. Her expression was flushed and wary, but there was no fury in the crystal blue.

'I figured it was my turn to make us supper,' she offered, surprising him even more.

He nodded. 'It smells good.' He forced the words out past the dryness in his throat, aware that this was the first conversation they had had without rancour since their first night.

Her tongue flicked out to lick across her bottom lip, the gesture one of nerves. But still he felt the shock of arousal. The tension ramped right back up again, but this time it was as exhilarating as it was frustrating.

'Take a seat,' she said, gesturing towards a place on the other side of the campfire. 'And I'll serve you a bowl, so you can tell me if it tastes good too.'

He didn't want to sit so far away from her. But the truce—after so much animosity—felt too fragile to test, so he did as she asked.

It occurred to him, as he hunkered down and watched her intently while she ladled a generous helping into one of the earthenware bowls, he had never shied away from rancour or animosity before. He was used to fighting for what he wanted and was more than prepared to meet fire with fire, confident in his ability to do whatever was necessary to win.

But he'd used brute force to get her here four days ago. And for once the process had left him with doubts he had never experienced before. Doubts not so much about the result—he would never have left her alone with a sandstorm forecast—but rather the method. He was still convinced it had been necessary, but could he have used more finesse, more subtlety? Did he even know how?

He had never been a particularly erudite man. And he had no experience of flattering or cajoling women, especially women who required more than what he could offer them in bed. But the fact he had taken her choices away from her had left him feeling oddly unsure every time she had glared at him as if she wished to peel his skin from his bones.

Her virginity had disturbed him greatly once he had discovered it—for the simple reason he had convinced himself it would mean they must marry. But, over the last three days, something else about her virgin state had begun to disturb him a great deal more. Why had she chosen him as her first lover? Why had she trusted him with something so precious, when they were virtual strangers?

And had he done enough to deserve that trust? The thought that he must have done only concerned him even more. Because her trust felt like something precious he had earned unwittingly, and then discarded far too easily the next morning in her father's office with his demand for marriage... And which he had ultimately broken beyond repair with his decision to take her from her homeland.

He took the bowl from her, absorbing the ripple of reaction as their fingers brushed.

She scooted back around the campfire to sit on her allocated rock, rubbing her palms against her jeans. He dipped his head and concentrated on digging his spoon into the fragrant stew to hide the smile curving his lips.

Why was he complicating this? Desire was the reason she had chosen him—the chemistry they shared had been obvious from the start. The only difference was she had no experience of such a connection. No ability to deny it.

But you've never felt a connection this kinetic and all-

consuming either. And you have a great deal more experi-
ence than she does.

The smile died as he shovelled a spoonful of stew into
his mouth and the rich, earthy flavours burst on his tongue.

Stop over-thinking this. She is precious. But this rela-
tionship is about sex, first and foremost, and necessity.

He spent the next five minutes eating, letting the heady
flavours fill his belly and ignoring the tender space that
had opened inside his chest at the thought she had made
this meal especially for them. For him.

Kaliah Khan was no fool, and as he finished off the stew,
scraping the last of the gravy from the bowl, it occurred to
him what this truce was really about.

It was a bribe—pure and simple. But her wish to barter
was something he could use. Because communication was
always better than silence when it came to negotiations.

With his belly pleasantly full, and the flicker of firelight
making his skin pulse and glow, he dumped the empty
bowl into the water vat he kept by the fire and stretched
out his legs.

Their gazes connected again and he let the desire charge
through his system unchecked as his gaze roamed over her.

'That tasted as good as it smelled,' he murmured, his
voice husky with hunger of a different kind.

'I'm glad,' she said.

He searched for calculation in her eyes but saw none. Perhaps she was warming to him. Good—it would save time
if she had finally accepted a marriage between them would
not be such a terrible thing. If there was a way for them to
both get what they needed, he intended to find it. Tonight.

'So tell me, Your Highness,' he murmured, feeling confident about his approach for the first time in days. 'Is there
anything you would like from me in return?'

* * *

Liah saw the hot light in Kamal's eyes and the promise of pleasure only he had ever fulfilled. Need ricocheted through her over-sensitised body. She was playing with fire now. She got that, because a relaxed and self-satisfied Kamal Zokan was even more dangerous than a furious or dictatorial one.

Who knew?

But, even so, she couldn't stop the question she had been waiting to ask him ever since that morning from bursting out of her mouth.

'Why didn't you tell me we had met before when we were children?'

He stiffened and straightened against the rock, no longer smug. But the guarded look in his eyes, and the wary tension which made the muscle in his jaw jump, told her all she needed to know. She had been right. The man who would soon be King of Zokar and that abused serving boy were one and the same person.

His gaze became hooded. 'I do not know what you refer to,' he said evasively, but the defensive tone only confirmed her suspicions.

Her father had told her Kamal had an unusual background for a prince, but she'd had no idea he had managed to gain the throne after such a tough start.

Apparently he seemed determined to hide the fact, though. But why?

She huffed out a breath, the nuclear blush from that morning's realisation heating her skin all over again as he studied her intently. She was going to have to reveal why she had recognised him all of a sudden.

Terrific.

She swallowed past the dryness in her throat then blurted out the truth.

'I went to the pool this morning to wash out some of my clothes. But you were already there...bathing.'

His gaze narrowed, the feral light in his eyes making the heat flare at her core. But with it came the flicker of shame.

'You...you had your back to me,' she added.

The muscle in his jaw twitched as he clenched his teeth. 'You spied on me?'

She broke eye contact. 'Yes, I guess I did. And I'm sorry.' She forced her gaze back to his despite the guilt prickling over her skin. 'Something about you always seemed familiar, ever since we first met at the track.'

She gulped down the blockage in her throat as he simply stared at her, his expression deliberately blank. 'But I couldn't put my finger on it. Probably because I'd met you so long ago. But when I saw the scars on your back, it all came back to me. That afternoon during our state visit to Zokar. The serving boy who was so brutally punished by his employer for such a minor infraction. The violence shocked me at the time, probably because I'd led a rather sheltered life.' She was babbling now, but she couldn't seem to stop, her heart in her throat as he stared at her, the blank expression making the ache in her stomach so much worse.

What must it have been like to be treated with such casual cruelty? How had he survived it? Had there been no one to protect him? What had happened to his parents?

'I had nightmares for years afterwards about that incident,' she continued, suddenly desperate to get a reaction out of him, or at least an acknowledgment. 'But one thing I never forgot was that boy's bravery. His refusal to be bowed. He seemed so fierce and proud to me.' She took in a deep breath and let it out slowly. 'Why didn't you tell me that boy was you?'

Did he despise her, resent her, because she had led such

a pampered life compared to him? In some ways she would understand that. Was that why he had ignored her for the last four days? She felt embarrassed now that she hadn't offered to help out around the camp and had left him to do all the work. At the time it hadn't been a status thing—not at all—it had been a temper thing. But she could see how it might have seemed very different to him.

Her parents had always told her brothers and her that their heritage and wealth did not make them better than anyone else. That the role of royalty was one of dignity, service and duty. But she'd screwed up with Kamal—behaving like the spoilt brat he'd accused her of being without intending to—right from the first moment she'd met him… And suddenly she wanted to take all that back, to start over, to prove to him she'd never thought she was better than him. And had certainly never believed she was too good to marry him. If anything, the opposite was true. She had always been a screw-up and now this proved it.

'I would never have thought less of you,' she continued, probably sinking even further into the ginormous hole she'd already dug for herself, but unable to stop digging. 'For being that boy. I hope you believe me.'

Kamal stared at the earnest expression on Kaliah's face, her compassion worn like a badge of honour. It triggered a strange warmth in his chest he had never felt before. And frankly didn't want to feel.

But as the miasma of conflicting emotions boiled in his gut—shock, anger, pain, humiliation—he had no idea how to respond to her.

A part of him wanted to continue to deny he was the boy she remembered. Because it made him feel brutally exposed in a way he hadn't felt since he'd been that boy. No one knew the whole truth of his origins, not even the tribal elders. *Especially* not Aziz. If they did, his early life—as an orphan, a mere serving boy—might be used as another reason to deny him the throne.

What sickened him the most was the thought of her seeing the scars he had kept hidden for so long. But what shocked him was that, instead of thinking less of him, she appeared to think more of him. Was this some kind of weird fetish she had, to befriend the downtrodden? Or simply a clever trick to gain his confidence and cooperation?

But, even as he tried to galvanise his temper, he couldn't make himself believe there was anything calculating or condescending about her declaration. Her expression was far too forthright, and more open than he had ever seen it, and her words rang with an integrity that seemed genuine.

He stood, agitated and disturbed. He walked round the fire, then clasped her wrist to tug her off her rock until she stood toe to toe with him. The dark compassion in her eyes didn't falter as she searched his face—still looking for answers, still trying to see that valiant boy who was long gone.

He cupped her cheek and dragged his thumb across her lips, unable to resist for a moment longer the temptation to touch her again that had been driving him for days.

She jolted, her gaze flaring with awareness now, as well as the deep compassion that was doing strange things to his stomach muscles.

Desire flared, potent and provocative, providing a handy escape from the raw emotion in her eyes.

'I did not tell you because that boy died a long time ago,' he said, his voice gruff with an emotion he didn't want to feel.

Her eyes widened and it occurred to him he had just revealed something to her he had never revealed to another living soul. Hamid had died not long after he had joined the army and, after he had resigned his commission and made the investments which had made him a wealthy man, he had erased his past. He'd literally had all the records of his apprenticeship and his early life at the orphanage in Zultan destroyed.

'Did he?' she whispered, the approval in her gaze making his insides clench with a longing he hadn't felt in many years—to matter to someone other than himself. She covered his hand with hers, her gaze rich with a fierce emotion he did not understand.

He didn't want to be that boy. That boy might have appeared fierce and proud, but in reality he had been weak and pathetic. He had allowed himself to be beaten and abused, had made the mistake of wanting someone to care for him.

'I'm not sure he did, Kamal,' she said.

The betraying glow in his chest spread through his system but he braced against it.

He hated that she still saw that boy. And that she might understand him in ways that boy would once have yearned to be understood, but which the man knew were fundamental weaknesses.

He breathed in her scent—that intoxicating aroma of fresh water, salty sweat and the sweet musk of feminine arousal.

He threaded his fingers into her hair, clasping the back of her skull to lift her face to his.

'Do not mistake me for that boy, or I will have to prove I am very much a man,' he murmured against her lips.

Arousal flared, turning the crystal-blue of her irises to black. She shivered, her reaction like that of a wild horse ready to be tamed.

Anticipation surged, turning the threatening warmth to scorching heat.

Then her lips parted in an instinctive sign of her surrender. It was all the invitation he needed to slant his lips across hers and plunder.

CHAPTER EIGHT

LIAH OPENED HER mouth as Kamal's tongue thrust within—commanding, devastating but also desperate. She let the giddy ache build, pressed her body to the hard unforgiving contours of his and absorbed the thrill of connection, of yearning. And ignored the small voice in her head telling her to be careful.

She needed this, needed him…because he needed her too. She could feel it in the rasp of his breathing as his tongue delved and possessed. She grasped his shirt in handfuls to drag him closer as his callused palms roamed down her back then cupped her backside, making her brutally aware of the ridge in his pants.

He lifted her into his arms, dragging his mouth from hers. 'Wrap your legs around my waist.'

She did as he demanded without an argument, surrendering to the madness. He marched them through the camp site towards his own tent. Firelight flickered in his dark eyes as she continued to kiss him—pressing her lips to the scar on his cheek, his stubborn chin, the fierce frown on his forehead.

Perhaps she should have been worried about what this all meant for them both—especially after what had happened the last time she'd made love to this man. But this didn't feel like a surrender, it felt like a meeting of equals.

Whipping away the tent flap, he headed across the luxurious space, drenched in moonlight. Starlight sparkled through the hole in the tent roof, magical and romantic. Her breath hitched at the strange beauty of the setting. But the enchantment faded, becoming more urgent, more elemental, as he placed her on her feet beside his bed.

He ripped open his shirt, flung it away then got to work on his trousers.

'Undress, Kaliah.'

The harsh command made her shudder, but again she followed his orders, tugging off her T-shirt, slipping off her boots and jeans and scrambling out of her underwear—until they stood naked, only inches apart.

His chest looked even more magnificent than she remembered it, but as she curved her fingers over one broad shoulder she touched the ridges on his back. He shuddered, his gaze intensifying—the flash of vulnerability so vivid for a moment, her chest tightened, even as need shuddered to her core.

Her heart expanded, her breathing laboured, as she drew her fingers down his chest, brushing over the flat nipples, trailing through the thin line of hair which bisected his abs, until she got to the thicket at his groin.

He let her explore, standing stoically as he allowed her to touch, tempt and tantalise. She discovered other scars—a small one across his left pec, another mark slanting over his ribs, one more that grazed his obliques. How could she have been so preoccupied in her own pleasure not to have noticed them before?

Her heart pulsed harder. So much pain, so much suffering. She absorbed the evidence of the hard life he had led, all the damage he had endured.

His erection stood out, long and thick, the swollen head shiny with his need.

She glided her fingernail over the tip and he groaned as the strident flesh leapt towards her touch.

Excited, exhilarated, she swallowed past the dryness in her throat, suddenly desperate for the taste of him, desperate to show him she could appreciate everything he was—the man as much as the boy.

She sunk to her knees in an act of reverence and supplication. But as she looked up and saw him staring down at her—the flare of passion in his gaze as surprised as it was intent—her own power surged.

'Kaliah,' he moaned. 'You undo me.'

Taking him in her hand, she wrapped her fingers around the thick girth then licked him from root to tip.

He groaned, the sound so low, guttural and tortured it felt as if it had been dragged from the depths of his soul. The salty taste of him thrilled her, and the power became intoxicating as she kissed and caressed the erection with her tongue, her teeth, her lips—finding how to make him moan, how to make him ache, the way he had once done to her.

At last, she opened her lips as wide as she could and sucked him into her mouth. He grasped her head, his whole body trembling with need now, his hips moving as he stroked his length into her mouth.

She lapped up every sweet sensation, every shuddering grunt. But suddenly his fingers dug into her hair to drag her back.

'No more, or I will lose myself...' He groaned.

Taking her arms, he yanked her back to her feet, then plundered her mouth again.

Could he taste himself on her? The thought was so erotic, the swell of power became all but unbearable.

They fell onto the bed together, a tangle of limbs, a battle to hold, to taste, to touch every inch of flesh.

He kissed her breasts, stroked her sex, as she continued to caress him wherever she could reach.

He reared back, then flipped her onto her belly to drag up her hips and position her on all fours. She jolted as the huge head of his erection nudged at her entrance from behind.

'You are so wet for me, Kaliah,' he said, the pride like a benediction. He dragged the erection through her swollen folds, rubbing, teasing. She quivered, bracing for the devastating thrust, but it didn't come. She bucked as his erection nudged her swollen clitoris—the touch almost enough to send her over. But then he withdrew.

'Tell me you want all of me,' he demanded. And somehow she knew he spoke of that battered boy as well as the indomitable man.

'Yes… Yes, I do…' She groaned, so desperate now she couldn't breathe.

At last he pressed within, the all-consuming thrust forcing her forward, but he held her firmly as he anchored himself to the hilt.

She could feel him everywhere. Her body clamped down on the thick intrusion. She felt impaled, possessed, conquered. Her chest heaved, the power still there but somehow rawer, more carnal, more basic.

Then he began to move, rolling his hips, drawing out of her, pressing back, forcing her to take every vital inch. His chest pressed against her back, his hands cupping her breasts to hold her steady for the ruthless, relentless thrusts.

She sobbed and begged…for him to go faster, harder, to take her all the way. But he kept the same steady pace, each slow, devastating thrust taking her further to that edge, but building her higher, until she was sure she couldn't take any more.

'Please... I can't bear it!' she cried, the pleasure so intense now it robbed her of breath, of power, until all that remained was the throbbing bundle of fraying nerves, the endless yearning.

'Yes, you can, you must,' he commanded, his voice as wild as her own.

She reached down to touch herself, to end the torment, but he grasped her wrist, preventing her. Then he touched her there, where she needed him the most, sweeping over the yearning point with brutal accuracy.

The coil inside her cinched tight and then released in a rush. The pleasure soared and shattered—so sharp, so hot—burning up from her core and sweeping through her body like a comet.

She massaged the thick erection as the searing orgasm pulsed through every nerve-ending, every pulse point, exploding into a conflagration so bright, so bold, she felt the touch of it in every recess of her heart, her soul.

He pumped into her, his shout matching her cries as his seed flooded her womb. And she let herself fall.

Kamal groaned and rolled off the woman beneath him. The chemistry was still incendiary between them—maybe too incendiary.

Nothing could have prepared him for the sight of her, on her knees before him, taking him into her mouth. For the feel of her lips as they'd closed around him.

His heart jolted at the memory. Her gaze as she had stared up at him had been so strong, so determined—every inch a queen—and yet also so full of that fierce compassion, it had nearly unmanned him.

She sat up beside him with her back to him, then shifted away, as if she were about to leave his bed.

'Don't go...' he said, grasping her arm, the words harsher—and more needy—than he had intended.

She glanced over her shoulder, then sent him a guarded, almost shy smile that made his heart thunder against his ribs. 'Okay,' she murmured, settling back into his arms.

He gathered her close, deciding not to question the urge to hold her—an urge he had only ever had with her. After all, he intended to make this woman his wife and soon. He had shown her precious little tenderness so far... Perhaps it was time for him to dig deep and find that part of himself he had discarded to survive.

He felt strangely content as he cradled her back against his chest and pressed his face into the fragrant curls that haloed around her head.

But, before long, the liquid weight pooled again in his groin, making him harden against her bottom.

'Don't get any ideas, buster,' she said, her voice sleepy. 'You've exhausted me.'

He let out a gruff chuckle—enjoying the way she always stood her ground.

'Ignore it,' he said. 'I have no control over my reaction to you,' he added, surprised—and a little concerned—to release it was the truth, and another first with her.

He gathered her wild curls in his fist to place a kiss on her nape. She shuddered in response, and a fierce sense of possessiveness flowed through his veins.

'I did not use protection,' he said. 'Will this be a problem?' he asked, even though it would not be a problem for him. If she were to become pregnant, it would only help his cause. The thought of her slender body heavy with his child sent an erotic charge through him that felt completely disconnected from his desire to make her his queen.

'Are you healthy?' she asked with a directness that surprised him all over again.

He caressed her neck with his thumb, tracing the graceful line down to her shoulder, unable to stop touching her. Perhaps he should be offended, but somehow he found her bluntness refreshing and beguiling instead. Was that the afterglow too?

'Yes, I am healthy. I have never taken a woman without protection before now,' he admitted, realising this was yet another first. He traced his fingers down her side, then settled his hand over her flat stomach, imagining a child—*his* child—growing there.

Fierce pride joined the possessiveness.

Children had always been an abstraction before now. He had accepted he would have to provide heirs as part of his responsibilities to the Zokari throne, but the thought of Kaliah Khan having his son—or daughter—made it seem so much more real. And something he found impossibly arousing.

She would be his then. Always.

'My concern is only about a possible pregnancy,' he added, wrestling the conversation back to where he wished it to be. He'd always intended to use protection. The explosive passion in the moment had ensured no thinking had been done at all. But now the chance of a pregnancy seemed fortuitous. And a golden opportunity for him to press his case.

She sighed, then threaded her fingers through his to draw his hand away from her belly. 'There's no need to worry. I'm on the pill.'

Disappointment flooded him, and he frowned.

'Why is this so?' he asked, something hot and uncomfortable piercing his happy glow. 'When I am your first lover?'

She stiffened in his arms and glanced over her shoulder. The indignation in her eyes contradicted the blush on her cheeks somewhat.

'I'm fairly sure that's none of your business, Kamal,' she said.

Of course, it is my business. You are to be my wife.

He bit down on the thought. It was too soon to press her on this. Then she added blithely, 'But, just for the record, you weren't my first lover.'

Okay, this is too much.

'How is this so when we both know you were a virgin?' he demanded. Was she playing games with him again, trying to pretend she had not been untouched?

'Again, not your business,' she said, pulling out of his arms and scooting off the bed. 'I think I should return to my own tent. This was obviously a mistake.'

She scooped her T-shirt off the floor, tugging it over her head.

He jumped up to snag her wrist before she could run from him again.

Her eyes widened as her gaze shifted to the strident erection that he could not disguise. The vivid blush flared across her collarbone as her eyes met his.

'I'm not sleeping with you again, Kamal,' she said. 'So you can just get that idea right out of your head.'

'I told you to ignore that,' he shot back. 'I would never force myself on a woman,' he added, his own temper rising. 'But I wish you to tell me—if I am not your first lover, what did you do with the others?'

The jealousy blindsided him, making the words spill out, and reminding him painfully of that boy who had always needed validation, approval, when it had never been forthcoming.

'Did you get on your knees before them too? Did you make them ache, the way you made me ache?'

Liah twisted her wrist out of Kamal's grasp and glared back at him. But her fury was tempered by her panic. Kamal Zokan was formidable—and even more annoyingly hot—when he was being a possessive, macho jerk. His chest heaved with indignation—and he was apparently completely unembarrassed by his nakedness and that strident erection.

What the hell?

The truth was, she'd never got past kissing any of the boyfriends she'd had in school and college. She'd gone on the pill six months ago when it had looked as though she and Colin were getting serious, until she'd overheard him talking to one of his friends about her.

'She's a frigid bitch, but she's gorgeous, and she's going to be a queen one day. So I'm more than prepared to suffer for the cause.'

Maybe he had been joking, but the joke had been on her. She'd thought he liked her, for herself. That he found her exciting and interesting. But he'd been manipulating her all along, and laughing at her, because of who she was—and what he could get out of her. It had sickened her and upset her. How could she have trusted such an idiot? They'd been going out for four weeks and she'd never guessed that he was like all the other men and boys she had dated, only interested in her because she had status and wealth that they craved.

What had hurt most of all was that Colin had never even excited her that much, but she'd been willing to go all the way with him to discover if there could be more.

With Kamal, though, it had always been different. There hadn't really been much thought to any of it. She'd been swept away on a tidal wave of yearning, and so had he. Or at least that's what she'd assumed.

But now, once again, she was unsure of herself. She'd thrown herself at him tonight, believing they had made a connection when she'd recognised the boy behind the man. Someone vulnerable who had struggled with their position in the world, something she could relate to. But now she wasn't so sure, because he looked every inch the desert prince again. A man who took what he wanted and wasn't interested in intimacy or emotions.

One thing she did have to thank Colin for, though, was the fact she was using contraception, because until Kamal had mentioned, oh, so casually, that he hadn't suited up, she hadn't even considered the possibility of an unplanned pregnancy. She had been way too steeped in afterglow and had become stupidly sentimental about the feel of his strong arms cradling her—even the press of that enthusiastic erection against her bottom—to worry about anything other than when she was going to get her next endorphin fix.

But she'd come crashing back to earth, with a vengeance. Because he was looking at her as if he owned her, and as if he had a right to expect an in-depth history of her sex life. Something she had absolutely no intention of giving him, because it would make her look and feel pathetic. They wouldn't be equals any more. But had that been an illusion too—the power she'd thought she'd wielded?

What had she been thinking, giving in to him again? His outrageous questions though, deserved an equally outrageous answer.

'If you're asking me whether I've had oral sex before,' she said, slapping a hand on her hip and trying to look a lot more experienced than she actually was, 'I'll let you figure that out for yourself.'

She'd loved kissing him, touching him, caressing him. She was proud of the fact she had made him ache. But he'd made her feel cheap and used now. He'd taken all the power away from her. And she hated him for it.

She swung round, planning to march out of the tent, glad she'd got in the final word. But he leaped forward, grasped her arms from behind and wrapped his strong body around hers. Suddenly she was trapped, sensations she couldn't control streaking through her again.

'Let me go,' she murmured, trying to struggle free, the tears she refused to shed making her throat hurt.

'I am sorry, Kaliah.' The gruff apology shocked her—almost as much as the feel of his arms softening and then releasing her. 'I was jealous. It is a new experience for me.'

She gulped in several raw breaths, the emotion still pressing against her chest but, when she turned to see the haunted look in his eyes, she was stunned.

He cradled her cheek in his palm, the calluses rasping against her skin. She should pull back. They were having an argument, and he still had that possessive gleam in his eyes. But she couldn't seem to draw away from his touch, or deny the thundering of her heartbeat. No man had ever looked at her like that before, with such intensity.

'I know you have not done such a thing for another man,' he said.

She blinked, trying to push her temper back to the fore. 'How do you know that? Wasn't I any good at it?' she demanded, feeling insecure again, and hating it.

Colin had called her frigid. And, as much as she'd hated him for it, she had always been a little scared it might be true.

But Kamal simply laughed, the chuckle releasing the

tension that crackled around them. 'You are far *too* good at it. Which is why I am honoured you chose me to experiment with.'

She could deny it, of course. Pretend she had experience she didn't. But her throat closed on the lie as she braced against the warm glow in her chest, the stupid sense of validation. She didn't need this man's approval. So why did it mean so much?

His thumb glided down to capture her chin and lift her face to his. 'Am I wrong?' he asked, his tone coaxing now.

She looked away from him, the gentle question making her throat tight again. She blinked furiously, unsure about why she was becoming so emotional.

'Why does it matter?' she replied, feeling weary and defeated. 'It's not as if I'm *your* first, now, is it?' she added, the indignation brewing again.

'This is true,' he said, making her feel even more deflated. But then he slipped his finger into her hair and hooked the unruly curls behind her ear, forcing her to look at him again. 'But you are very different from the other women I have been with.'

'How?' she asked, hating the neediness in her voice, but wanting to know.

'I cannot really explain it,' he said. 'We have exceptional chemistry, but also...' He paused, as if he were searching for the right words. 'You are my first too in many ways.'

He frowned, and she suspected he had said more than he had intended to. The warmth spread in her chest, but she pushed it away, not quite able to believe he meant it. Was he trying to flatter and cajole her? He had always seemed like a very blunt man, but she knew he still wanted to marry her, so there was that.

'Is it because I will one day be Queen of Narabia?' she asked, deciding to put him on the spot.

Was he like all the others? Attracted first and foremost to her status, wanting her for *what* she would be one day, not who she was now? She felt the dart of pain in her stomach, knowing that somehow it would be so much worse if Kamal was like the rest.

His brows shot up his forehead, the puzzled expression on his face making relief course through her, and then he laughed. 'You are already a queen, Kaliah. The Queen of Trouble.'

A chuckle burst out of her mouth at the outrageous statement. But something about the playful smile on his lips— something she already knew was rare, because he was an extremely serious man most of the time—made her heart bounce.

'Fair point,' she said.

He laughed again, the rough, rusty sound impossibly beguiling, then reached out and captured her hand in his. 'Come back to bed. I promise I will not ask you any more questions. Let us lie together. I wish to have you in my arms when I wake tomorrow,' he said, the flirtatious light in his eyes another surprise, but no less compelling. 'And you robbed me of this on our first night.'

She knew she shouldn't encourage any more intimacy between them, but she couldn't find the will to object when he led her back towards the bed.

Now they were actually talking again, she would have to press him about contacting her father first thing tomorrow. She should explain to him the danger he was putting himself in if her father discovered he had kidnapped her.

But as she climbed into the bed with him, and allowed him to tuck her against his chest and hold her, contentment settled over her. She could feel his heart thumping against her back in heavy thuds, feel the still firm erection nestled against her bottom—and the feeling of connection she had never shared with another man overwhelmed her.

It was an illusion, of course, a result of the fact he had been her first. But it felt good to know she wasn't the only one who had been altered by their encounter. She doubted she could ever be friends with this man, but as she drifted into a deep, exhausted sleep—her body tingling insistently in all the places he had touched and caressed—it felt as if sex wasn't the only thing that connected them.

Kamal saw her in a way no other man ever had. Not just as a sexual being, but also as an equal, different from the other women he had known, in the same way he was so different from the men she had known.

And that felt important…and precious. Somehow.

CHAPTER NINE

WHEN LIAH JERKED awake the next morning, she found the bed empty beside her and the sound of distant rumbling in the air.

Was a thunderstorm coming? And where was Kamal?

She dressed hastily in the clothes scattered around his bed chamber and rushed out of the tent, her heart pumping double time when she spotted Kamal standing with his back to her, staring down the gorge.

The rush of euphoria turned to panic as she realised the rumbling was the sound of horses' hooves echoing off the canyon's walls.

She reached Kamal's side just as her father appeared, galloping towards them on his stallion Zufar, leading a column of at least fifty men.

She grasped Kamal's arm. 'Let me speak to him, Kamal,' she said urgently over the noise of the approaching army. 'This could get awkward.'

Kamal's brows furrowed. 'I am not afraid of your father, Kaliah,' he said, placing his hand over hers. The touch of his palm sent sensation skittering.

She tugged her hand out from under his—the possessive gleam in his eyes not helping with her anxiety attack.

Terrific—just what I need. My endorphins playing tricks

on me when I need to come up with a plan—fast—to save Kamal from the consequences of his actions.

He'd brought her here against her will, but she knew now he wasn't a bad man, just an impulsive, impetuous one who tended to act first and think later.

She took a step away from him, just as her father leapt off the powerful stallion and strode towards them.

'Liah, thank God! You're safe,' he said, then dragged her into his arms.

She clasped him around the waist and let herself be held, aware of the shudders wracking his tall, lean body.

When he drew back at last, and held her at arm's length, she was shocked by the worn, weary expression on his face.

Her father was her rock—a man who never faltered, never lost his cool…at least not completely. But his hands were shaking as he clasped her upper arms, the look in his eyes one of utter relief.

'You're not hurt?' he asked, his voice breaking.

Guilt seared her insides. She'd known he would be concerned she hadn't returned sooner from the oasis, but she hadn't expected him to be quite this frantic.

'No, I'm fine. I'm sorry I didn't come home sooner…' She swallowed, trying to explain why she was in Zokar— and had been for four long days. Although she was a little surprised her father hadn't already confronted Kamal. 'There's no mobile phone service here, so we weren't able to let you know where we were,' she said lamely.

He cradled her cheek, then to her surprise let out a wry laugh. 'It's okay, Liah, I'm not mad, just incredibly grateful you survived.'

Survived? It was her turn to frown. *Survived what, exactly?*

Before she could even formulate the question, her surprise turned to astonishment when her father turned to Kamal and clasped his arm, before shaking his hand vigorously. 'Thank you for saving my daughter. My family and Narabia are for ever in your debt.'

Kamal nodded, apparently completely unfazed by the conversation. 'There is no debt to be paid. It was my honour to protect Kaliah.'

I'm sorry—what now?

She'd expected her father to be furious, to demand to know what the heck Kamal had done, bringing her to the gorge—and keeping her here against her will. And, while she had been more than prepared to lie on his behalf, to protect him from any repercussions, now that Kamal and her were, well, friends of a sort, her father's decision to completely absolve him was a little aggravating, frankly.

'Excuse me, but what exactly did he rescue me from this time?' she asked, testily, interrupting the developing bromance.

Her father's eyebrows hitched up his forehead, then he frowned. 'The sandstorms, of course,' he said, looking at her now with something less than extreme relief. 'Four major storms converged on the region the afternoon after you headed to the oasis—we had to declare a national emergency. Your mother has been coordinating relief efforts in Narabia while I've been searching for you. Nearly half of Raif's tribal lands were hit. Two people died in Zafar from sand inhalation when it swept through there, and it buried the encampment at Aleaza. I thought you were under it, until we received word that Prince Kamal had made a detour *en route* back to Zokar to check on you.'

He thrust his fingers through his hair, his drawn face making the guilt sweep through Liah again—this time on steroids.

Good grief. Kamal really had rescued her this time by insisting they leave the oasis. And she'd had no idea. Sandstorms were very rarely deadly, but she would have been alone and completely unprepared in the middle of what sounded like the worst storms for a generation. No wonder her father had been so frantic. He had to be exhausted too.

'I'm so sorry,' she said, horrified at her own selfishness. Her father had been trying to find her, when he would have wanted to be in Narabia to coordinate relief efforts himself. Could she actually have screwed up any more comprehensively than this? *Doubtful.* 'Is everyone okay in Narabia?' she asked. They were her people, people she was one day supposed to rule, and yet she'd let them down again by going AWOL. And she'd had no idea.

Nausea joined the lump of shame forming in her throat. Her father had told her a week ago that not everything was about her. Perhaps it was past time she stopped thinking about herself—stopped panicking about how she would ever be good enough to be a queen and actually began behaving like one.

'The repair bill is going to be enormous, but no one was badly hurt, which is the only thing that matters,' he said.

'Dad, I'm so, so sorry.' She flung her arms around his waist again, buried her head against his sturdy chest and breathed in his familiar scent—leather and horses. The tears lodged in her throat like boulders.

He wrapped his arms around her, so solid, so strong, so dependable.

'Hey, Liah, it's okay,' he said as he kissed her hair, in a way she remembered him having done so many times before, ever since she'd been a little girl when he'd always praised her out of all proportion to her achievements. 'We've found you and you're okay, that's the main thing,' he finished as he gave her a final squeeze.

She pulled back, swallowing furiously to contain the emotion pushing against her chest.

Kamal stood stoically beside them, saying nothing. But she spotted the confusion in his gaze before he could mask it. And it made her feel so much worse.

She had always had her father's approval, her family's unconditional love and support, even when she'd done nothing to earn it. While Kamal had had no one to protect him from that awful man who had beaten him. Everything he had, he'd had to fight for, while she had never had to fight for anything.

She'd fought her destiny for so long, even resented the fact she, and not her brothers, would one day be expected to rule Narabia. It was way past time she stepped up to the plate and began to earn at least some of her father's respect.

So when her father frowned, his gaze going back and forth between the two of them, she decided she would do anything necessary now not to make this situation worse.

'Just out of interest, Kamal, why *didn't* you return my daughter to the Golden Palace several days ago?' he asked, his gaze probing now as his euphoria at finding Kaliah began to fade.

As grateful as her father had been to Kamal moments ago, Zane Khan was no one's fool. She could see his sharp mind shifting into gear. He had to be recalling the acrimonious way she had spoken about Kamal five days ago— and her determination to have nothing to do with him, or his proposal of marriage.

Uh-oh.

While her father was her greatest cheerleader, he was also her biggest defender and protector. She knew a part of him still considered her his little girl—despite all the evidence to the contrary in the past week—and all his gratitude towards Kamal would dry up in a nanosecond if he thought the neighbouring prince had taken advantage of her or the situation.

Think, Liah, think. Time to finally put your fledgling diplomatic skills to the test.

She needed to come up with a way to defuse the growing tension—a white lie that would adequately explain why they had apparently made no attempt to return to civilisation after surviving the storm. Something appropriate and suitably innocuous that didn't involve her telling her father the truth…that she'd spent last night in Kamal's bed. But then heat flared across her collarbone, making her brain stall completely, just as Kamal spoke.

'I did not return her because Kaliah is going to become my wife,' he said, managing to torch all her good intentions in one fell swoop. 'We slept together last night and she may be carrying my heir,' he finished, throwing petrol on the fire and turning an awkward situation into a raging inferno.

Kamal heard Kaliah's horrified gasp beside him. Her father's eyes narrowed as his blue eyes—so much like his daughter's—became chips of ice.

Kamal lifted his chin, more than ready to stand his ground. Khan was a powerful man, both in the Nazar region and the wider world, and Kamal could see he was not happy about this development.

But he'd be damned if he would bow to any man—especially on his own land. He had stopped bowing and scraping and being ready to settle for scraps as a boy of sixteen, when he had finally escaped from Hamid and enlisted in the Zokari army. Maybe he was not of noble birth, but that did not make him a lesser man than Zane Khan. And he was more than happy to prove it to Khan and the small army he had brought with him.

'You did *what*?' the Sheikh snarled with barely leashed fury—the fierce gratitude of moments ago apparently obliterated by Kamal's statement of facts.

So be it.

The man's gratitude had made him uncomfortable anyway. After all, he considered it *his* duty to keep Kaliah safe now, not her father's.

'You heard me,' Kamal shot back.

'Kamal, stop it!' Kaliah cried, pushing between the two of them and bracing her hands against his chest. 'Please, just stop talking, you're making this so much worse.'

'I will not stop talking. I am telling the truth,' he said.

'Just for the record, did my daughter have a choice in any of this?' Khan shouted.

'Are you accusing me of rape?' Kamal demanded, as his own temper incinerated the last of his control and his fingers tightened into fists.

The Sheikh's men dismounted to circle them, ready to intervene if Khan requested it. Kamal's temper flared, the tension on a knife-edge.

He was outnumbered and outflanked. But the fury strangling him refused to subside.

For many years, all he had had was his honour. And Khan had just questioned it. *More* than questioned it.

'Dad, it's okay, I had a choice!' Kaliah's frantic cries finally pierced through the hot rage rushing in Kamal's ears. 'What happened last night was one hundred percent consensual. Kamal would never do something like that.'

Khan's gaze jerked to his daughter, although the fury

still vibrated through his body. And Khan's men were still watching, ready to do as their sheikh demanded.

But all Kamal could see in that moment was Kaliah.

Her fierce defence of him sent shockwaves through his body. He had not expected it. He would never have believed it would matter so much to him but somehow it did.

'You don't need to defend him, Liah,' her father said, clasping her arms, searching his daughter's face again to see if she was hurt, the way he had when he had first arrived. 'If he took advantage of you, or kept you here against your will, that's on him—not you. And he will pay the consequences. And you're certainly not obliged to marry him, even if you are pregnant right now, I hope you know that.'

Kaliah's gaze shifted from her father's face to Kamal's. And what he saw in her gaze had the shockwaves turning into something harsher and even more disturbing—releasing a depth of emotion he had never felt before, touching that open wound in his stomach he thought he had cauterised so long ago. The wound that had always been there when he'd been a boy, every time Hamid had taken a belt to him, or he recalled the hazy memories of the man who had left him sitting on the steps of the orphanage as a young child. A man he had convinced himself in the years since must have been his father. The father who hadn't wanted him.

Kaliah looked so strong in that moment, but the wary knowledge in her gaze spoke volumes.

He braced, prepared for her to tell her father the truth— that he *had* brought her here against her will. That he had kept her here without offering to return her so he could persuade her—by whatever means necessary—to marry him. They had slept together last night because their chemistry was off the charts, but how much of a choice had she really had when he was so much more experienced than she was?

Shame seeped through the layer of fury.

But when she spoke her words only shocked him more and sent furious longing through him which he could not control.

'Dad, Kamal's not lying,' she said, her voice trembling. 'He asked me again and I accepted. We're engaged to be married.'

CHAPTER TEN

'I DO NOT recall asking you to marry me again, nor do I recall you accepting my proposal, so why did you say this to your father?'

Kaliah swung round at Kamal's question.

Even in the shadowy interior of her tent she could see the frown on his face. He had his arms crossed over his chest and looked even more formidable than usual—which was saying something.

She sighed.

Great—just what I need. Another hot-tempered alpha male to placate.

She stopped stuffing the last of her belongings into the saddle bags she'd packed nearly a week ago, intending to escape from this man. A man she'd just spent half an hour trying to persuade her extremely sceptical father she was desperately in love with.

Thank goodness her father had finally agreed to let her travel to Zokar to make an official announcement about their 'engagement'. After feeding and watering their horses, her father and his men were now on their way back to the Golden Palace.

Diplomatic crisis averted.

Apart from the six-foot-four-inch crisis standing in front of her now, brooding magnificently.

Kamal had remained silent and watchful throughout her conversation with her father. But thankfully he had not contradicted her—nor had he intervened when she had insisted they needed to travel to Zokar to announce their engagement. Given his penchant for throwing petrol on any given situation, with his infuriating need to take charge of everything, she considered that a minor miracle in itself.

She had hoped Kamal's silence meant he had figured out she was lying through her teeth so they could avoid their little tryst in the desert leading to a major diplomatic rift between Narabia and Zokar, and that he was on board with her plan...

From the deep suspicion in his eyes, though, apparently not.

She dumped the saddle bag at his feet.

'Isn't it obvious?' she said, her own temper flaring. Seriously? What the heck had he been playing at, goading her father like that when he'd been outnumbered fifty to one—did the man have a death wish?

'Not to me,' he shot back.

'I was saving you, Kamal. My father was on the verge of withdrawing his support for your monarchy,' she snapped. 'You saved my hide at the oasis, so I was returning the favour.'

He tensed, the offended look in his eyes only making her more furious. So that was the deal? He was allowed to save her but she wasn't allowed to save him? *Figured.*

'So, it is a lie, then?' He sounded outraged. 'You do not intend to marry me?'

'Of course not—we'd probably end up killing each other within a week. Then both our sacrifices would be for nothing,' she said, letting every inch of her frustration show. Not just with Kamal, but also with her father, who frankly hadn't exactly covered himself in glory with his refusal to believe her for thirty frustrating minutes—while she had waxed lyrical about how much in love with Kamal she was, having known him for precisely six days.

She'd never been more humiliated in her life. But, as she crouched down to buckle the straps on her saddle bags with more force than was strictly necessary—while steadfastly ignoring Kamal, who was still glaring at her with that smouldering look of disapproval—she decided she had only herself to blame.

She'd got into this situation by making a ton of stupid decisions and it was her job to get herself—and Kamal, who appeared to be his own worst enemy—out of it. Perhaps the solution she'd come up with—faking an engagement between them until her father backed off—wasn't the best solution, but it was the best one she'd been able to conjure up on the spur of the moment before all hell broke loose.

'You expect us to travel to Zokar and announce an official engagement between us, but you have no intention of marrying me?' Kamal's words were laced outrage.

She let out a heavy sigh, her already knotted stomach twisting tighter, before she stood and faced him.

'I know it's not ideal, Kamal. But I had visions of the two of you coming to blows, which wouldn't exactly have been great for diplomatic relations, now, would it? I was scared, okay, and I was trying to defuse a situation which you managed to torch with that daft comment about me being pregnant. I told you I was on the pill—there is zero chance of me being pregnant and you know it.'

'Your father is not a fool,' he said, choosing to ignore her last cogent point. 'He would not have destroyed diplomatic relations with a neighbouring state over such a thing.'

'You don't know my dad,' she replied wearily. How could

Kamal be so obtuse about this? But then she recalled that boy, fierce and proud but also so alone. Had he ever even had a father? Was that why he was so clueless about how family dynamics worked?

'My father's a strong ruler, and a good one—he's also a brilliant diplomat. But his family and his children mean everything to him. There's nothing he wouldn't do to protect us, to the point of being completely irrational if we are threatened in any way,' she continued. 'And I've never seen him quite so strung out. Plus, my mum wasn't here to help defuse the situation. So I did not want to take the risk, okay?'

The tell-tale muscle in Kamal's jaw twitched. 'I told you I was not scared of your father,' he said, completely missing the point. 'Did you think I needed you to tell lies on my behalf? Because I did not. It is not your place. I can protect myself. I always have and I always will. I have no need to rely on others to protect me.'

She simply stared at him, aware of the fierce pride bristling around him like a force field. Part of her wanted to shout at him. To get it through his thick skull she'd been trying to help him, not hurt him. But she could hear the confusion in his voice, right behind the fierce determination always to be self-sufficient, and recalled the hideous scars on his back.

Kamal's pride was clearly the only thing that had got him through the abuse he had suffered in childhood and had made him into the man he had become. Thick-headed, for sure, arrogant, autocratic, ruthless and everything in between. But also honourable and honest.

Plus, this man had saved her life with his pig-headedness. So there was that.

She heaved another sigh and tried to dredge up what was left of her flagging patience.

Hello again, newfound diplomacy skills.

'I'm sorry if I've put you in an awkward position,' she managed. 'But it really doesn't have to be that awkward. We certainly don't have to go through with the whole official engagement thing. I just wanted to get my dad to leave before anything bad happened to you. Or him,' she added hastily, the admission sounding somehow too intimate, too presumptuous.

His brows lowered still further. 'You were worried about me?' He sounded genuinely stunned. And her heart cracked at the thought of that boy who had only ever had himself.

'Precisely,' she said, willing to admit that much if it would get Kamal to see she had never meant to insult him or trap him—perish the thought. 'But we really don't have to announce anything at all. We could just spend a couple of days together in Zokar, while my dad calms down in Narabia. Then I'll go home. Tell him we broke it off after all. That it was all just a silly infatuation on my part.' Which would make her look like even more of a romantic imbecile in her father's eyes.

But then maybe that was a good thing. Her father had always had far too much faith in her. Perhaps it was high time she began to downgrade his expectations and made him see she wasn't queen material.

Although, the thought of him losing his faith in her only depressed her more. Because, if this afternoon had taught her one thing, it was that she didn't have to be such a screw-up all the time. If she could start putting her duty and her responsibilities ahead of her impulsiveness, her recklessness and her own selfish choices, the way she had this afternoon, maybe there would be hope for her after all.

Kamal shook his head. 'This is not a solution.'

'Why not?' Liah asked, confused by the stubborn look

on Kamal's face. She'd just offered him a way out of this mess, why wasn't he taking it?

'Our honour requires that we go through with the engagement now.'

Oh, for...

She pursed her lips to stop herself losing her patience again. Because it didn't help anything, especially not with Kamal, who only became more impossible when confronted. They were both hot heads, so one of them had to figure out how to back down gracefully... And, on this occasion, apparently it was going to have to be her.

'I don't think it does,' she said wearily. 'But, if you think it's necessary, I'm happy to go ahead with the announcement. After all, I was the one who suggested it. Then we can figure out a way to break off the engagement without arousing any suspicion at a later date.'

Perhaps this was another penance she deserved. A fair price to pay for the sense of entitlement she had never even realised she had relied upon her whole life. She hadn't considered Kamal's pride when he had first proposed marriage. She had far too easily dismissed the importance of his honour to him. Because her pride had never been questioned. Because her status—as the eldest child of the Narabian Sheikh—had never been in any doubt.

And, really, would it be so terrible to spend a few weeks posing as Kamal Zokan's fiancée, given that there were so many things about him she found fascinating?

Her skin flushed as his gaze gleamed with a purpose she recognised. Because he'd looked at her the same way last night before he'd kissed her so hungrily in the firelight.

He cupped her cheek, his voice becoming huskier as his thumb cruised over her bottom lip. 'Don't look so worried,' he murmured. 'There will be some very pleasurable benefits to our arrangement.'

She nodded. 'I know.'

Which was precisely the problem.

She was still drawn to this man, far too much. Even though their association so far—and that explosive chemistry—had caused them both nothing but trouble.

But somehow, as they prepared the horses and packed the rest of their belongings to travel to Zokar and announce their fake engagement, she convinced herself this arrangement would work.

Perhaps it was time she indulged the side of her nature which she had denied for so long, and which Kamal had triggered without even trying. Surely giving in to this chemistry would eventually wear it out? And, when they broke off their engagement in a couple of weeks' time, a month at the most, her father would have got over his anger with Kamal and she would have established a good working relationship—of a sort—with the ruler of Narabia's nearest neighbour.

It was all good.

Totally. All. Good.

After the primitive luxury of the camp, Liah couldn't help gawping as they galloped towards the prince's palace on the outskirts of the sprawling town of Zultan—Zokar's main city.

She didn't know what she'd expected, but certainly nothing this magnificent. Flanked on two sides by the red rocks of Zokar's mountain range, the palace had been built around a huge oasis. After being ushered inside the walls by an honour guard, they rode through an avenue of palm trees and exotic flowers planted beside an intricate series of fountains and waterways.

Liah's breath stalled again as the main palace buildings appeared, built into the rock wall of the canyon. Constructed in the Ottoman style, the stunning structure stood five storeys high, an intricate collection of domes, towers, minarets, arches, balconies and covered walkways—with decorative wooden ramparts that hailed the expertise of ancient craftsman and jewelled mosaic tiling that glittered in the sunshine.

She had no idea what she had expected, but certainly nothing this sophisticated or stunning. She realised she had never seen this place when she had accompanied her father on the state visit all those years ago. They had instead been accommodated in a tented encampment out on the plains. When had this palace been constructed? Because it looked at least as old as Narabia's Golden Palace, and equally as lavish.

The decision to fake an engagement with the new Crown Prince suddenly felt a great deal more complicated. Especially when a group of staff gathered to greet them as they rode through the palace's main domed arch and arrived in a smaller courtyard. A beautiful fountain stood as its focal point, the gold figurine in the centre shimmering as water spouted from its mouth and sparkled like rare gems in the sun.

A line of dignitaries appeared in full ceremonial garb, clearly having assembled to welcome their soon-to-be-crowned king.

Liah knew all about pomp and circumstance, having grown up a sheikh's daughter, but even so she stared wide-eyed as Kamal was greeted with great deference by men she suspected must be the ruling elders he had mentioned on the ride, when explaining to her how they would have to present the engagement.

'There will be expectations—just let me handle it,' he'd said with his usual authority.

After the scene at the camp with her father, she had been way too stressed to worry too much about what that might mean, until Kamal jumped down from his horse then marched towards her to help her off Ashreen.

She slipped down into his arms, shocked by the oddly proprietary gesture as he stared into her eyes, towering over her, and held her around the waist. Was he going to kiss her in front of all these people?

Her lips tingled, as her gaze dropped of its own accord to those firm, sensual lips that quirked now with a rueful smile.

'Do you wish me to stake my claim on you, Kaliah?' he murmured, his voice a husky purr full of amused arrogance.

'No, of course not,' she mumbled, jerking her head up and trying to tug herself out of his embrace. But he held her firmly, stopping her from retreating, the mocking light in his eyes suggesting he knew exactly how off-balance she was.

'We don't need to be quite *that* convincing,' she added breathlessly.

'Don't we?' he said, the amusement dropping from his expression.

Then, to her stunned surprise, he dropped his head to press his forehead to hers and breathed in, the gesture some-how even more intimate than a kiss. Suddenly everyone else faded away until it was just the two of them, cocooned in the rare chemistry which seemed to shimmer in the air around them like the glittering light on the palace's mosaic tiling.

Her heart pounded so hard, she was surprised it didn't

beat right out of her chest as his callused palm settled on her cheek and then slid down to cup the back of her neck.

'We cannot sleep together at the palace unless we are wed,' he said, his voice so low only she could hear him. 'Tradition demands I show my future queen the ultimate respect.'

She nodded. 'Okay.'

That's probably a good thing. Surely sex—especially the kind of sex we have—would only complicate this situation more? I need to start weaning myself off this man now.

But even as she tried to persuade herself this new development was for the best, disappointment rippled through her system and weighed down the hollow ache in her stomach. Then his thumb caressed the hammering pulse point in her neck. She sighed before she could stop herself and he chuckled.

'Do not worry. I embark on a European trade tour tomorrow. You will come with me as my fiancée.'

What?

The information registered, delivered—as per usual—not as a question but a command. Even, so she struggled to get her mind to engage while the tantalising scent of him filled her senses.

'For…for how long?' she managed, knowing she should object. A European trade tour had not been part of their agreement. And surely presenting herself as his fiancée on the world stage would only make things that much trickier when they called it off?

'Ten days,' he said, then skimmed his thumb across her lips, pressing down on her bottom lip and making the ache so much worse. 'I will insist we have adjoining suites. And no one will dare question our activities after the official business is conducted.'

'But…what then?' she murmured.

'Then we return to Zokar,' he said.

Ten days to indulge this insatiable passion before they went their separate ways?

Should she? Could she? Surely such an arrangement would be playing with fire? Hadn't she already been scorched enough?

She tried to open her mouth to clarify exactly what her official duties would entail. And to get a more robust commitment out of him regarding the parameters of their fake arrangement. For example, how long did he envision them lying about the engagement once they returned to Zokar?

But she couldn't seem to speak past the lump of anticipation and excitement forming in her throat…and making her panties damp with need at the thought of being so close to him for ten days. Having the chance not just to sleep with him every night, but to spend time with him in his role as the soon-to-be King of Zokar.

Perhaps she needed this. Perhaps they both did, to finally burn away whatever it was that had drawn them together so forcefully. Theirs had never been more than a physical connection. That was what she needed to remember. Why shouldn't they indulge it? After ten days, they would be more than ready to part, and her fascination with him would be over.

So she simply nodded. 'I guess I can do that,' she said, even though she knew full well he hadn't really asked her. He had told her.

His arrogance was something else they could work on in their ten days together, she thought ruefully as he dropped his caressing thumb to clasp her hand in his and lead her to the ruling elders, who were still hovering nearby, waiting patiently for their little *tête-á-tête* to end.

As they marched round the fountain together, Liah pushed her unruly hair back from her face, wishing she had at least had a chance to wash before making these introductions.

It doesn't matter, remember? You're not his real fiancée.

'Gentlemen, I present my future wife,' Kamal announced, the thick pride in his voice not sounding all that false. Who knew the man was such a persuasive actor? 'And the future Queen of Zokar, Crown Princess Kaliah Khan of Narabia.'

The men dropped into low bows, some of them even kneeling before her and genuflecting, a custom that had been done away with in Narabia during her father's rule.

But, as the ruling elders greeted her formally and congratulated her profusely on her new role, with a deference which made her feel like a total fraud, Liah could see the stunned shock on everyone's faces but Kamal's.

She knew just how they felt, because as Ashreen was led away by the palace grooms, and she was spirited away by a trio of new personal assistants and shown to a lavishly furnished suite of rooms in the women's quarters—where she was to spend the next twenty-four hours being 'prepared' for her first official engagement as Prince Kamal's bride-to-be—her fake engagement didn't feel at all fake any more.

CHAPTER ELEVEN

One week later

'LIAH, IT'S SO marvellous to see you here.'

Liah spun round at the familiar voice to see her old Cambridge University acquaintance, Clara Turnbull, approaching her through the throng of people gathered in the ornate rose garden of the Zokari embassy in London's Mayfair. The torchlight gleamed off the woman's elaborate blonde chignon.

Liah's heart sank and the nerves in her stomach twisted.

The daughter of a British investment banker, Clara had been one of Colin's friends, not hers, but it didn't surprise Liah in the slightest to see the woman at the exclusive gathering being given in Kamal's honour by the Zokari ambassador.

She forced herself to smile and accept the obligatory air kisses. 'Clara, why am I not surprised to see you here?' she managed, trying not to let the nerves that had besieged her for the last week show.

She was used to being at lavish diplomatic gatherings like this one, where champagne and diplomacy flowed freely and important relationships were forged between nations under the guise of small talk. After all, she'd been brought up in this rarefied world and she knew how it worked.

Unlike Kamal. She had been watching him all evening on the other side of the garden, looking tense and irritated in his formal suit, after he had been whisked away from her side as soon as their engagement had been lavishly toasted.

Her heart pulsed with sympathy for him.

One of the many things she had discovered about Kamal in the past week was that he hated small talk, almost as much as he hated wearing a suit, because he saw no need to fit in. And he didn't drink alcohol, so he couldn't even use its effects to relax as he was paraded round like a prize—something she also knew he hated.

She wondered if he had really factored in what his position would entail when he had worked so hard to achieve it. Because during the whirlwind activities of the past week—as they'd done a whistle-stop tour of the commerce capitals of Europe, attending a series of equally lavish events, then tearing each other's clothes off as soon as they were alone each evening—she had seen the toll it had taken on his patience and control.

She knew from the conversations they had late at night, after they'd made mad, frantic love—his ferocious need for her as intoxicating as listening to the plans for his country she had never expected him to share with her—that all he had ever really wanted was to see Zokar thrive. And to evolve the more traditional customs which he felt held the country back from achieving its full potential.

Even though his was mostly a ceremonial position, she knew he'd spent his own money, not just restoring the prince's palace to its former glory but also investing in Zokar's ageing infrastructure, its education and health system. He understood very well the importance of attracting more investment to the region, but what he didn't understand—and, she had discovered in the last week, had no aptitude for whatsoever—was how to be diplomatic. To pretend to be one of the ruling elite. The fact Kamal did not consider himself one of *them*, and had no desire to pretend otherwise, didn't help either.

'Darling, I heard you were going to be here with your princely new desert hottie, and I could not resist angling for an invitation,' Clara supplied, sending her an arch look which made Liah want to punch the woman on the nose.

Desert hottie? What the actual...?

'Kamal's not a piece of meat, Clara, he's incredibly intelligent and erudite.' Something else Liah had discovered more about in the past week. 'And he's also the heir presumptive to a vast and extremely prosperous desert kingdom. Not to mention a successful businessman.'

She felt the little trickle of shame which had assailed her more than once over the past seven days. Hadn't she herself objectified Kamal once, even considered him unsophisticated? But her first impression had finally come crashing down all the way during their tour. He was blunt, yes, and had no time for the insincere niceties used in the name of diplomacy. But that was because he did not suffer fools and dealt with everyone with the same honesty and integrity—no matter their station in life.

She'd been there to smooth his path, and it had flattered her when he had seemed grateful for her presence. She'd loved the thought he needed her there, that he genuinely valued her input and expertise. Who knew she had more diplomatic skills than she'd ever realised?

They'd been feted in Italy, having toured a series of vineyards and olive farms, where the minerals which Kamal's company had discovered in the dry river beds of the Zokar foothills were proving so effective as a natural insecticide. They'd also received a lavish welcome in France, where they had toured a series of factories and wineries, and where a reception had been held in their honour amid the Baroque splendour of the Palace of Versailles.

Kamal had conversed in faltering but functional French with a host of dignitaries and businessmen about the investment potential for them in Zokar's vast mineral wealth. But he had been more than happy to let her handle the more detailed conversations because she was fluent in the language. Not to mention all the small talk necessary to finesse a commitment out of cagey investors and politicians.

They wanted what Kamal had to sell and he knew it, which was why he had no patience with attempts to finesse a better deal out of Zokar. But he had relied on her to soothe ruffled feathers. They actually made a good team, out of bed as well as in it.

'Don't be insulted, honey,' Clara said in a mocking tone that couldn't help but be insulting. 'I'm sure he's very smart but, more to the point, he's got a raw charisma which I bet makes the down time between diplomatic engagements very rewarding.'

Liah stiffened, not liking the woman's tone at all. As if Kamal really were a piece of meat.

'No wonder you dumped Colin—if you had this hunk waiting in the wings to propose,' Clara continued, apparently oblivious to Liah's rising indignation. 'Or was this an arranged marriage?' she continued. 'If so, you lucked out, being forced to marry *him*.' She finished, her openly lascivious gaze devouring Kamal as she made typically ill-informed assumptions about the culture and traditions of Liah's home region.

'I'm not being forced to marry anyone.' Liah glared, the fact she wasn't actually going to marry Kamal at all not stopping her from wanting to defend their union.

'Oh my, so it's a love match?'

Clara's mocking gaze shocked Liah for a moment. What was going on here? Did Clara have some kind of axe to grind?

'That was fast. I thought you only broke up with Colin a few months ago?'

'It was six months ago, actually, and Colin and I were never that serious.'

'Yes, I know,' Lara said, her tone becoming laser-sharp as her gaze raked over Liah. 'You do know he was sleeping with me at uni while waiting for the Crown Princess to finally get off her pedestal?'

'W-what?' The word came out on a shocked gasp. She'd known Colin was a jerk and had got over his betrayal long ago. He'd used her, and she was pathetically grateful now she had never slept with him. But something about the fact she had been stupid enough to ever consider sleeping with him made her feel ashamed now. And like an idiot.

What a shallow fool she'd been, believing his lies and flattery. Thinking he cared for her when he never had. Had everyone known he was using her, except herself?

'He always insisted you were frigid, but I guess that was just his pride talking. From the way your new guy looks at you, it's pretty obvious you're keeping him well satisfied.' Clara's chuckle seemed bitter somehow, but behind it was a sadness that defused Liah's anger until all that was left was pity...and the humiliating pulse of heat at the thought of exactly how well-satisfied Kamal was keeping her.

Was she using him too? Because she was enjoying pretending to be his fiancée a bit too much. The engagement didn't feel like a lie any more—at least, not completely—ever since they had arrived in Europe and he had been happy to rely on her, to defer to her whenever his natural brusqueness created waves. And then there were the nights when he had come to her suite or dragged her into his and ravaged her with the same power and passion he had used ever since that first night. As if everything about her fascinated and excited him.

And her response to him was equally as ravenous.

How did he know just how to taste her, to touch her, to caress and cajole her, to make her beg for more? Only last night he had thrust into her from behind as he'd caressed her in the shower, turning her body into a mass of molten sensations.

She had become obsessed with him, that much was obvious. Obsessed not just with what he could do to her body, but how he could make her feel. As if she was being worshipped on the one hand, but in charge of her own pleasure on the other. He challenged her, provoked her at every turn, demanding more than she had ever thought she would be willing or even capable of giving... But he also enjoyed it when she challenged and provoked him too. He wasn't afraid of her recklessness, wasn't scared of her demands, because he could be equally as ruthless and demanding.

They were equals in the best sense of the word.

'Colin was a jerk,' Liah said softly, knowing how true that was now. Colin hadn't been a man—he had been a spoilt, entitled boy. Kamal, on the other hand, had been a man from a very young age, too young an age in many ways. But he'd turned all his disadvantages into advantages, his powerlessness into strength, and he wielded it with a dignity and integrity that most people in his position could only dream of.

'We're both lucky to be rid of him,' she added. Although she could barely remember Colin any more. The heartache he'd once caused her felt little more than an irritating ripple now compared to everything she had begun to feel for Kamal.

Clara nodded, toasting her with her champagne glass. 'Ain't that the truth?' she said, then downed the contents in one go. 'I always wanted to hate you, you know,' she went on, surprising Liah with her candour. 'But, FYI, you didn't miss a thing with Colin. He was as selfish in bed as he was out of it.' So saying, she melted into the crowd just as a large hand landed on Liah's waist.

'Who is that woman? And what did she say to you?' Kamal stared down at her, his eyes flashing with barely concealed fury.

'It's nothing, Kamal, I'm fine,' she said, stupidly touched he seemed so angry on her behalf and also oddly exhilarated by the protective look in his eyes—and the fact he must have spotted her distress from the other side of the garden and come charging to her rescue. Why didn't that possessive tone bother her any more?

'Clara's someone I knew at Cambridge,' she added.

He lifted his hand to skim a callused thumb down her cheek. She shivered, as always far too aware of the slightest touch. His hand landed on her collarbone, both intimate and somehow protective, his gaze riveted to hers as that dangerous thumb continued to rub her pulse point. 'I do not like her. She has made you unhappy.'

'I'm fine,' she repeated, aware of the other guests staring.

A camera flashed nearby as the official photographer took their picture. The photos would be in all the papers tomorrow—because, much to her consternation, in the last week she and Kamal and their whirlwind romance had become a favourite subject of the celebrity media all over Europe. For once she didn't feel like a total fraud, though.

'Honestly, she just reminded me how glad I am I'm no longer at uni.'

He nodded. 'Who is Colin?' he asked, his tone lowering.

Uh-oh, so he'd heard some of their conversation. Liah
stiffened, the probing look in his eyes making the shame
and humiliation return.

'He's nobody,' she said truthfully. Because Colin meant
nothing to her now, and he never really had. To think she
had once tried to kid herself she could love a man like that,
when what she felt for the man in front of her was so much
more intense after only a couple of weeks in his company.

She was drawn to Kamal even though his arrogance was
as infuriating as his dominant, taciturn nature. The sexual
connection between them was so tangible, so fierce, she
could feel herself getting moist—her body already preparing to accept his—while they were at an event crowded
with people.

But the connection she and Kamal shared had become
so much more than that. He respected her, even as he challenged her. He needed her, more than even her family. Why
did that suddenly seem so much more seductive than his
incendiary ability to make her climax on demand?

'Is he the fool who did not take your virginity when he
had the chance?' he asked.

Oh, for the love of...

Fire leapt into her cheeks as her skin became hot. 'Kamal,
how about we don't talk about this here?'

She'd never considered herself to be shy, but something
about the way he was looking at her, with both rich appreciation and grim determination, made her feel brutally exposed.

He nodded. Then gripped her hand and proceeded to
drag her through the crowd towards the gated entrance to
the garden and the steps back into the embassy.

'Kamal, where are you going? We're the guests of honour tonight and the event's not finished.'

'It is for us.' He threw the words over his shoulder, the autocratic reply unbearably compelling. 'I wish to know why that woman upset you, and if we cannot talk here, we will do it in private.'

The last thing she wanted to do was talk about Clara and Colin. Short of creating a scene, though, she didn't have much of a choice. But as he marched through the crowd, ignoring anyone who tried to waylay them, she found her heart ricocheting into her throat. When had she begun to find his arrogance so compelling?

The Zokari ambassador approached them. Kamal ignored him too and ploughed on to the exit as Liah threw a few parting pleasantries over her shoulder... From the indulgent smiles and shocked expression on the faces of many of the guests, most of them probably assumed he was marching her off to seduce her.

Dignified, much?

Leaving the scent of roses, the chill of the evening air and the flicker of torchlight behind them, Kamal strode into the embassy and along the darkened corridors of the empty residence to lead her up the stairs to their adjoining suites.

'For goodness' sake, Kamal. Every single person there will think we've run off to have sex. And our sudden exit is bound to be reported in tomorrow's press,' she said breathlessly, trying desperately to sound reasonable. And to actually care what anyone else thought, while her insides were in turmoil and the pulse point in her sex was about to explode if he didn't touch her soon. *Very* soon.

Since when had she begun to find his ruthlessness, his dictatorial behaviour, so arousing? After taking the stairs two at a time, trying to keep up with his long strides—not easy in four-inch heels—she struggled to catch her breath, desperate to control the deep pulse of yearning which felt like so much more than desire.

Leading her into his room, Kamal slammed the door behind them and swung her round to face him. Her back in the plunging gown touched the cool wood of the door. But that wasn't the reason she shivered as he tucked a knuckle under her chin and tipped her face up to meet his gaze.

'This Colin, he is the man you *wished* to take your virginity?' he asked, his voice rough with something that sounded oddly like regret, his amber eyes dark and intense, but also full of an emotion which matched her own.

Why did she feel as if she were at the centre of a gathering storm? A storm she couldn't control but had no desire to escape.

'*What?* No!' she said, struggling to get a grip on the conversation when everything inside her was yearning for... It wasn't sex...or not *just* sex. When had she begun to want more? To need more? They'd only been together a couple of weeks. And yet the connection between them had begun to feel so strong, so important, ever since their night together in the encampment—maybe even before that. How could they have built something so vivid, so all-consuming, so quickly? How could this stark, stern, unknowable man feel like her soul mate?

'But he is the reason you will not marry me. Yes?' Kamal demanded, his gaze filled with the same yearning as her own.

'No, Kamal.' She touched his cheek, shocked to see the flash of intense longing in his gaze.

Was this more for him too? Why hadn't she seen it before now?

'Why, then, will you not make this engagement real?'

he demanded, his voice raw with desperation. 'If it is not him, who is it?'

'It's too soon, Kamal,' she said weakly. 'We hardly know each other,' she murmured, trying to cling to practical considerations, but even those felt like lies now, pale, cowardly excuses.

'You know more of me, more of my past, than anyone alive,' he said, so simply her heart ached for him. He moved his head to bite into the swell of flesh under her thumb, the soft nip sending sensation shooting through her body. A sob of desire issued from her lips. He pressed a hand over hers, to kiss the tender flesh, then turned to her again, trapping her in that smouldering gaze.

'I know all the ways to make you ache, to make you beg. We are a team, Liah. We could rule together, both Narabia and Zokar. With you by my side, I feel whole for the first time in my life.'

Her heart hammered her chest wall as his urgent words, the fierce yearning in his voice and the approval in his eyes struck down all the insecurities she had lived with for so long.

She had always been terrified of one day taking the Narabian throne, terrified of trying to live up to her father's and mother's legacy. But it suddenly occurred to her, they had not done it alone. What if Kamal was right? What if they could rule together too, bind their two countries?

But, as her heart thundered against her ribs and her pulse raced, she knew such practical considerations had nothing to do with the emotions battering her as she looked into those dark eyes and saw a man she wanted with every part of herself.

I don't just desire him. I don't just want to rule with him by my side... I love him. For who he is...who he has made himself...against all the odds. And because I know he could love me too. Not just the princess I am, the queen I will be one day, but who I am inside—the reckless, impulsive, insecure me, with all my imperfections. All my flaws.

Because Kamal had seen every one of those flaws in the short time they'd known each other and he still wanted to marry her.

He sank his face into her hair and kissed her neck, exploiting the spot where her pulse hammered—the place he knew would drive her wild.

He grasped her waist, tugging her against the immense ridge in his trousers—the evidence of how much he wanted her, how much he needed her—and turned the storm of emotion into a tsunami in her chest.

I love him. How can it be too soon?

Hadn't her own parents married each other after only a few weeks? she reasoned frantically, as she heard the zip of her gown releasing. He shoved the satin sheath down and unhooked her bra to free her breasts with ruthless efficiency.

She stood before him, naked now except for the thin swatch of lace covering her molten sex.

His tempestuous gaze roamed over her quivering flesh, then he moaned and bent to capture one turgid nipple in voracious lips. She shuddered, shocked by the sensation shimmering down as he tugged, nipped, suckled—first one swollen peak then the other. Her breath came out in ragged pants as she threaded her fingers into his silky hair, dragging him closer. She arched her back, forcing her breast into his mouth to ease the torment, desperate to satisfy the need.

He dragged himself back to throw off his jacket and rip off the shirt and tie. Buttons popped, the desire in his eyes flaring.

Then, to her astonishment, he sank to his knees, pressing his face to the apex of her thighs and drew in an unsteady breath.

'You smell so sweet to me, Kaliah...' He groaned as she clasped his head.

Then he lifted one of her legs over his shoulder, forcing her back against the door, exposing her molten sex completely. She shivered, vulnerable and yet so sure. Ripping aside the soaked gusset of her panties, he swept his tongue into the slick folds.

She cried out, her head bumping the door, her whole body on fire now as he licked at the stiff nub...too much and yet not enough.

She groaned, the sensations merging, the vice at her core cinching tight, and tighter still 'Please, Kamal, please...'

He glanced up at her, ceasing the exquisite torture, leaving her wanting, waiting, desperate. His gaze locked on her face, dark with demand and desperation. 'Say you will marry me, Kaliah. Say you will become my queen?'

'Okay.' The word was released in a staggered rush, the emotion like a wave barrelling towards her. So right, so true. 'Yes, I'll marry you. I love you, Kamal.'

He went still. And for one bright, beautiful moment she thought he would say it too. Surely, he must feel it too? But, instead of saying the words, he nodded then lurched to his feet, dislodging her leg.

She stood, shuddering, naked, vulnerable, as she watched him release the huge erection from his trousers. Lifting her easily in his arms, he lowered her, impaling her on the thick girth.

She groaned, the stretched feeling one she recognised as she struggled to adjust to his size. But this time it felt so much more overwhelming.

He hadn't said it. But did that really matter? she thought vaguely, her mind dazed, her emotions so raw. He would say it soon, when he was ready.

The pleasure built again with startling speed as he began to move, massaging that tender spot inside her he had exploited so many times before. But this time the pleasure was harsher, swifter, more devastating. She could hold none of herself back from him and the brutal onslaught.

She clung to his heavily muscled shoulders as she tried to find purchase, to find her equilibrium again. But, as her fingers brushed over the tell-tale ridges he had let no one see but her, she found herself torn adrift, with only him to centre her.

Her sobs echoed off the lavish antique furniture, the bright lights of the city outside nothing more than a haze as her vision blurred. His harsh grunts matched the rhythmic thuds of her back hitting the door as she soared into another dimension. Not just her body, but her mind, her soul and every part of her heart.

The pleasure burst in fast, vicious waves, rolling through her, barrelling over her, shooting her into the abyss. She slumped against him, her face buried against his neck, her chest imploding, her heart shattering, as he shouted out his own release.

As the afterglow washed through her, she wrapped limp arms around his neck—his length still firm, still there inside her—and held him tight.

Even if he didn't love her yet, she loved him enough for both of them. And they would work this out together. Agreeing to marry Kamal for real was madness, on one level, but it felt so right, so perfect, on another as he carried her into his bed chamber, laid her on the king-sized bed then draped the covers over her.

She gathered the rest of her strength to lift up on her elbows as she watched him finish undressing in the moonlight then climb in beside her.

'Shouldn't I head back to my own room?' she asked. They never spent the whole night together in case their staff caught them in the morning.

But he simply grunted, yanking her into his embrace. 'No,' he said as she rested her head on his broad shoulder, loving the feel of his strong arms around her. 'You are mine now, always,' he said with typical possessiveness.

She smiled as she drifted into a deep sleep.

And you're mine, Kamal. Even if you don't know it yet.

'I love you, Kamal.'

The whispered words echoed in Kamal's head as he stared at the grandiose moulding on the ceiling of the London embassy's master bedroom, listened to the soft snores of the woman in his arms and tried to think past the raw emotion crushing his ribs like a boulder.

Kaliah's declaration was not something he wanted, not something he knew what to do with. Not something he even understood. But he couldn't seem to deny the deep feeling of satisfaction—even stronger than when she had agreed to marry him—when she had said those words to him.

The hope in her eyes, though, had stunned him more. How could she be so open, so trusting, so sure?

He frowned, his heartbeat accelerating to reverberate in the quiet room.

When she had first suggested this fake engagement to appease her father, he had been furious. He did not need a fake queen, damn it, he needed a real one. And he did not require her protection, nor did he require her pity. But he had been forced to resign himself to the subterfuge. Not least because he knew he was not ready, *yet*, to let her go. They still had unfinished business.

Plus, a part of him had marvelled at her intelligence and her bravery, not only in standing up to her father, but also standing up to him when Khan had arrived at the encampment.

That she had seen his scars and had not been repulsed had also had a profound effect on him—even if it was one he had refused to truly acknowledge up until now. But he admitted now, as his breathing finally evened out and his mind blurred, that enough of that brutalised boy remained to want to wallow in her approval.

The purpose of bringing her with him to Europe had been to finally put this need, this constant longing, to rest. But, each night he took her, the need only increased—her instant and enthusiastic response to him only fuelling the desire like dry grass in the path of a wildfire.

He wanted her, all the damned time. But worse was the discovery of how much easier it would be to negotiate this new world he had entered with her by his side. He had expected her to condescend to him, to perhaps even be disgusted at his lack of diplomacy, his intense dislike of the games politicians played. But instead she had encouraged and supported him. Not only did he not speak any of the western languages with any skill apart from English, but he was a man used to plain speaking, to giving orders and having them obeyed, which meant dealing with bureaucrats, politicians and diplomats was nothing short of excruciating.

But, every time he'd become frustrated or irritated, she had stepped in to help. Not only that, but she had listened with interest when he had spoken of his plans for Zokar.

Not just listened, but encouraged.

And slowly, as the need built each night, and having her

by his side each day became more of a necessity, a thought had begun to form in his head...

He wanted Kaliah Khan to become his queen—for real. But even so he had hesitated. He'd had no desire to ask her for her hand and be rejected again... Because now it would have hurt so much more than just his pride.

And so he had side-lined the thought. Until he had seen her face fall while talking to that woman at the reception tonight, and as he'd got close enough to hear the mention of another man's name.

Anger had hit first. Who was this woman who had hurt her? But worse had been the spurt of jealousy and fear. As he had dragged her up to their suite, he hadn't been able to think past it.

She'd responded to him as she always did, with fierce desire, genuine hunger and complete honesty, and suddenly he had needed to make this commitment real. To ensure he didn't lose her.

When she had told him she loved him, he had been humbled and shocked.

But most of all he had been scared.

Because as he had claimed her, pouring his seed into the tight clasp of her body, wanting to imprint himself on every part of her, to brand her as his always, to seal the bargain they had made, he knew he would never be able to let her go...

CHAPTER TWELVE

'DAD? I'M SO glad you called. I take it you and Mum got the official invitation to our wedding this weekend?' Liah said down the phone, her heart galloping at the sound of her father's voice.

'Yes, we received it by special messenger this morning, Liah,' he said, his tone grave.

She clutched the handset. His voice sounded so familiar and yet somehow so far away, her heart hurt as she stared at the water trickling down from the fountain in the court-yard of the palace's bridal suite in Zokar.

'I know you've always been impulsive, sweetheart,' he added. 'But surely this is a little fast, even for you?'

I know, right?

She swallowed the reply and the lump of panic that had been there for two days.

She and Kamal had only arrived back from London forty-eight hours ago, and she'd been more than a little stunned to realise plans were already in place for their wedding in less than four days' time. She'd assumed she would have more time…a lot more time…to adjust to the reality of the situation. And the fact she'd hardly had a chance to see Kamal since they'd returned, let alone speak to him, hadn't exactly helped ease her anxiety about the speed of the wedding.

She'd missed him, not just at night, but during the day too. She understood tradition demanded they remain separate now until the ceremony was conducted before sharing a bed in the palace. But why did everything have to be so rushed?

Ultimately, though, she had forced herself not to panic. Surely, these were normal wedding jitters? She'd made a solid commitment to Kamal in London. And her feelings for him had only increased during the last of their official assignments and the journey home.

Kamal had been protective of her, and possessive. And she knew he hated this enforced separation as much as she did. He'd said as much when the plans for the whirlwind wedding had been revealed—and her short period of isolation had begun.

'There is nothing I want more than to make you my wife, Kaliah, as soon as possible. Is this not what you want too?'

The intense emotion in his voice had made her nod before he'd left her at the door to her new quarters two days ago. Yes, it was all a bit fast, even for her, but she had no qualms about her decision. Not only was she looking forward to being with Kamal, she was also excited about her future role as Queen of Zokar. She had been given full command of hiring her own staff—and defining her own duties—but, more than that, Kamal had informed her through his executive assistant that, once they were wed, he would relinquish any claim to the Narabian throne.

She didn't want to relay any of her concerns about the speed of the marriage to her father, though. Because it would feel like a betrayal of Kamal, and the new phase of her life they would embark on together when she became Queen of Zokar.

'Well, you know me, I never do anything by halves.' She

let out a laugh, which only felt slightly forced. 'I hope you'll all be able to come to the ceremony. Raif and Kasia have already confirmed they can attend with their oldest four,' she said, the nerves knotting in her stomach. 'And we're hoping Karim and Orla will be able to make it too, as they're in Zafar at the moment instead of Kildare. Unfortunately, Dane said Jamilla can't come, as she has some big event in Manhattan she can't shift,' she added, mentioning Karim's half-brother, a nightclub entrepreneur, and his wife, who ran a charitable foundation in New York. 'But Dane's coming with their three-year-old twins. By the way, why are there so many sets of twins in our family?' she added, her laugh sounding manic now even to her own ears as her father remained suspiciously silent. 'Seriously, I should probably be concerned.'

'Take a breath, Liah,' her father said, his voice finally stopping the stream of inane information.

'You are coming, aren't you?' she managed, the desperation in her voice impossible to hide.

'Of course,' he said.

'Thank God!' she blurted out. 'And William and Kasim and Rohaan?' she added, suddenly knowing she needed her brothers there too, to ground her. Unshed tears scraped at her throat. She missed them all so much.

'Yes, they'll be coming too.'

She blinked to hold back the traitorous emotion making her chest feel tight.

Why did she feel unsteady, so unsure? This was silly. She'd agreed to this marriage. She loved Kamal. But the thought of seeing her father, her mother and the whole of her family made it all seem more real and that much more overwhelming.

'You don't have to go through with this if you're not ready, Liah,' her father said gently.

The words didn't even register at first, but when they did the strange combination of uncertainty and anxiety pressing on her chest morphed into something even more disturbing—panic. 'But…but I am ready,' she said.

'Are you sure, honey?' he said again, sounding concerned.

And suddenly she was a little girl again, with his strong arms around her as he held her on the saddle of her first pony, and as he let go, telling her not to go too fast over the jumps. Of course, she had gone too fast, and she'd fallen and broken her arm in the process. He'd raced to her side, picked her up and cradled her on his lap until the palace medical team had arrived. But he'd never chastised her. And neither had her mother.

They'd always stood by her, even when she'd made stupid mistakes.

But this isn't a mistake. It can't be.

'I know he needs to get married before his coronation ceremony next week or he risks losing his throne,' her father added. 'But you shouldn't feel pressured into agreeing to this marriage if you're not one hundred percent sure.'

'Sorry, what?' she said, her voice a squeak of distress.

Had she heard that correctly? Surely she couldn't have?

'You didn't know?' Her father swore, the ugly, angry word making nausea well in Liah's gut.

Had Kamal lied to her? Why hadn't he told her he needed a wife to secure his throne? Was that why he'd asked her to make this engagement real, why the wedding had been scheduled so quickly? Had he used her, the same way Colin had used her?

He never said he loved you. And now you know why.

The bleak thought had the nausea bubbling under her

breastbone. The hollow weight in her stomach was worse, because it was a feeling she remembered when she'd overheard Colin's making fun of her to his friends. But this time the weight was so much heavier...

Because she'd never loved Colin. Had never felt for him even a tiny part of what she felt for Kamal.

'Liah, I'm coming to get you,' her father snapped, sounding furious, and more than a little irrational. But something about his anger, the fiery temper, helped to calm her own panic—a bit. 'No way in hell are you marrying a man who can't be honest with you about something so funda—'

'Dad, it's okay, I knew.' She forced out the lie, determined to defuse the situation and give herself time to think.

There had to be a reason why Kamal hadn't told her all the details. Perhaps he had been scared to tell her, in case she changed her mind, scared to trust her.

That wasn't good. If they were going to have a life together, they had to learn to trust each other implicitly. And he should have given her all the facts. But she refused to assume the worst. She knew he needed her, wanted her, that he saw in her things she hadn't even seen in herself until a few weeks ago.

It can't be a lie.

He'd made her stronger. His approval had done so much more to build confidence in her ability to be a good queen, a strong role model and an equal partner to him.

Don't throw all that away over a stupid misunderstanding.

'He damn well better have,' her father said, his US accent more pronounced.

'Listen, Dad, I need to go, there's so much to organise still,' she said, ending the call as swiftly as she could—much to her father's consternation.

But this wasn't his problem to solve, it was hers.

She needed to have a serious talk with her groom, the man who had essentially been avoiding her for two whole days.

She stuffed the phone into her jeans pocket.

A little of her old bravado returned to quell the panic churning in her gut as she headed across the courtyard towards the suite of rooms she had been forbidden to enter until the marriage was officially consummated.

Sod tradition. I need to see him now.

'But there is no need to relinquish your claim to the Narabian throne, Your Highness. As the husband of Princess Kaliah, you have the right to become their king and unite our two kingdoms...'

'Stop talking, Uttram.' Kamal scowled at the lead council elder. He'd expected this intervention but he wasn't going to budge. It was about time the guy learned he was in charge of his own destiny. 'We are not having this conversation. My decision is final. I will not take her heritage from her.'

Because I have already taken enough.

Uttram stared back at him, clearly trying to think of a new approach, when a commotion outside the room had them all turning.

Kamal's heart rammed his chest as his bride-to-be strode into the room in jeans and a loose-fitting shirt which draped over her lithe physique.

Awareness and exhilaration surged as he crossed the room, stupidly pleased to see her. The last two nights had been torture without her in his arms. But worse had been how much he'd missed her counsel, her input, as he'd been forced to make decisions about their marriage alone.

He'd also had far too much time to consider the years ahead.

How has she come to mean so much, in such a short space of time?

'Kaliah, what is it?' he asked, concerned by the emotion in her eyes.

'Kamal, we need to talk.' Her gaze flashed to the elders behind him, who Kamal could already hear whispering about the break with tradition her appearance had caused. 'In private,' she added pointedly.

'Leave us.' He threw the command over his shoulder, unable to take his eyes off Kaliah—the strange expression in her eyes, wary but also full of hope, starting to concern him.

The majority of the elders filed out while continuing to whisper in hushed tones, except Uttram. 'Your Highness, it is not appropriate that you speak to—'

'Leave us!' he shouted, his patience with the man at an end. Bowing obsequiously, the man finally left them alone.

The silence was oppressive. He could hear her ragged breathing and the thunder of his own heartbeat as he dragged in a greedy lungful of her scent. Desire pooled in his groin. But worse was the desperation, the yearning, which he had spent the last forty-eight hours trying to deny.

Why could he not control his need for this woman, not just in bed, but out of it too? The sight of her excited him in so many ways—but not all of them were sexual.

She tugged her arms free of his grip and stepped back. He plunged his empty hands into his pockets.

Folding her arms over her waist, her gaze sharpened.

'Why didn't you tell me you needed this marriage to happen now to secure your throne?'

He stiffened. He could hear only confusion in her tone, not accusation or distress, but even so the guilt lodged in his chest.

'Because it was not relevant,' he said.

Her brow furrowed. 'That's nonsense, Kamal. Of course it's relevant, that's why the ceremony is happening this weekend and not six months from now, isn't it? Admit it.'

Of course, she was right about that, but admitting as much seemed pointless, and fraught with complications, so he changed tack. 'It is not relevant, because I would have wished for this marriage anyway,' he said, knowing it was the truth. 'You are everything I want and need as my queen.'

Instead of placating her, though, his declaration only seemed to disturb her, the expression on her face turning from confusion to consternation.

'As your queen?' she queried, searching his face, as if looking for something. 'What about as a woman?'

The hammer thuds of his heart dimmed a little. This question at least was very simple to answer. A slow smile spread as his gaze dipped to take in her high breasts and the flutter of her pulse in her collarbone. His mouth watered at the thought of kissing her there.

'As a woman, I want you very much,' he said. He lifted his hand from his pocket to wrap it around her arm and tug her against him, making her aware of the burgeoning erection. 'Do you wish me to prove it to you?'

Her breath released in a rush, her eyes darkening. He could scent her arousal, and the powerful desire surged. She was his, she would always be his. Their chemistry was so strong, neither one of them could deny it.

But as he bent his head, intending to suckle the place on her neck he knew would make her melt, she braced her palms against his chest.

'Stop it, Kamal. I'm not talking about sex. I'm talking about love.'

'What?' he murmured, shocked by the deep yearning in her eyes, and the shimmer of hope.

He had seen it once before, when she had told him she loved him two days ago and had waited for his reply. Just as then, it struck fear into his heart.

He released her abruptly.

He couldn't have this conversation—not now, not yet— because he had no answer that would satisfy her. But nor did he wish to lie or make her promises he could not fulfil.

'I want to know, what do you really feel for me?' She said the words carefully, gently, without an ounce of entitlement but with a grim determination that told him there would be no ducking the truth a second time. 'Not as a queen, or as a…' the flush spread across her collarbone '…a—a sexual partner. I want to know if you love me, even a little bit. The way I love you.'

He stepped back to lean against his desk, studying her as he thrust his hands back into his pockets, contemplating what the hell to say. Her beautiful face was so expressive, so open, so transparent. It was one of the things he adored about her. But right now that devastating combination of hope and fear was crucifying him.

'It's not a difficult question, Kamal,' she said, her gaze so intense now—looking for something he knew he could not give her—that the fear returned. 'Why is it so hard for you to answer it?'

Lie. Tell her what she wants to hear. Your throne depends on it.

The voice in his head demanded what he should say. The voice he had relied on as a boy to survive. The voice which had pushed him for so long to do and say whatever it took to get what he wanted, what he needed, to prosper and achieve his goals… But he could not get the necessary words out past the boulder of guilt and remorse growing in his throat.

He had lied before when he'd needed to… But he could

not lie to her any more than he could fight off the pain in his chest at the sight of her distress.

Tugging his hand from his pocket, he brushed a thumb down the side of her face, needing to touch her, to feel that connection he could not put into words as he told her the truth.

'You are a romantic, Kaliah,' he said softly. *Because you can afford to be*, he thought silently. 'But love is simply a word,' he added. 'It means nothing tangible, nor is it something I require. Commitment is all that matters. Commitment and honesty.' He rested his hand on her shoulder, rubbing his thumb across the frantic pulse, willing her to understand, the pain in his chest increasing at the despair in her eyes. 'I wish you to be my wife, my queen. I wish you to have my children. To rule by my side. Is that not enough?'

'I see,' she whispered, her voice calm, but the expression in her eyes somehow broken. 'Thank you for being honest with me.'

He nodded. But, instead of feeling satisfaction at her measured response, his pulse continued to rage, the pain refusing to ease.

She blinked as a single tear spilled over her lid. The pain gathered, becoming all but unbearable. But he braced against it and the sudden urge to drag her into his arms, to make love to her and tell her anything and everything she wanted to hear to make her love him still.

It was better that she knew the truth about what he was capable of—and what he was not. Better that she accepted it.

Even so, as she swiped the drop away with a shaky fist and walked away from him, he could not shake the devastating feeling that enveloped him... Or the suspicion he might just have lost something more precious than the Zokari throne, and infinitely more rare than the perfect queen.

* * *

He forced himself not to dwell on it, not to allow foolish sensibilities to derail him during the sleepless night that followed, as the picture of her devastated expression, the depth of feeling in her eyes, woke him from nightmares.

But the whole fragile house of cards came crashing down the next morning when one of his advisers dashed into his bed chamber to deliver the news that the Crown Princess had left Zokar under cover of darkness with the assistance of one of her staff. And handed him a note.

I'm so sorry, Kamal. I can't marry you knowing there is no prospect you will ever love me. Love isn't just a word. Not to me. It's everything.

I hope you don't lose your throne because of this, when I know what a good king you will be.

Kaliah xx

Agony broke open in his chest, but right beneath it was rage. She had dared to leave him. How could she have loved him and then left him to forfeit his throne? Scrunching up the note, he threw it across the room.

But the vicious anger drained away almost as quickly as it had come and the tearing agony remained, leaving him raw, shaky and…for the first time in his life…defeated.

He had lost everything…and he had no idea how to get it back.

CHAPTER THIRTEEN

'I LOVE HIM, but he doesn't love me. He doesn't even *want* to love me…' Liah scrubbed the tears off her cheeks, the skin smarting after all the tears she had already shed as soon as she'd arrived home—and her mother had wrapped her arms around her.

It had been a long, arduous journey overnight through the desert in the SUV she'd managed to liberate from the palace with help from her lady's maid, Maya. She was utterly exhausted now, not just from the physical toll of the eight-hour drive over the rough unforgiving terrain, but also from the emotional devastation Kamal had caused when she had confronted him about his motives…and he'd given her nothing.

She'd been such a fool to think he loved her. That he wanted her for herself, and not simply to keep his throne. What hurt more, though, was the thought that even up to the moment when he'd gone utterly still…staring at her after her question about his feelings had dropped into that awful, heavy silence and he'd said nothing for the longest time… she'd had so much hope. Hope that she'd misread the situation. That it had simply been a mistake. That she'd judged him too quickly. That he'd chosen her because he believed in her, because he believed in *them*. Not because he simply needed a convenient bride.

But then it had all come crashing down.

'You're a romantic, Kaliah.'

The derogatory note in his voice had hurt immeasurably. Because in it she'd heard that cruel judgement she remembered from the day he'd plucked her off her horse at the Race of Kings. And she had finally realised that, despite everything they had done together, everything they had shared, he still viewed her on some level as a privileged brat.

She'd had parents who loved her, who supported her, who cared what she did and who respected her judgement—who hadn't abandoned her and forced her to do everything alone. But was she supposed to prove her worth because she hadn't suffered as he had, hadn't had to overcome anything like the same obstacles, for the rest of her life?

Far worse than his judgement about her strength of character—which he had clearly decided would never be as strong as his—had been the shuttered look in his eyes when he'd told her all he wanted was a wife, a queen. Not a soul mate, not a kindred spirit, not someone to share his heart with—only his throne. And then she'd understood he would always hold a part of himself back...

She gulped in a breath, the wrenching sobs making her chest hurt as her mother held her tight and consoled her.

'Shh, Liah, you need to breathe,' her mother murmured against her hair, her calming scent so familiar.

Liah sucked in a breath past the constriction in her throat, gulped in air and tried to even her breathing. At last, the storm began to pass. Until the wrenching sobs turned to hiccups.

'You need to tell me exactly what he said, sweetheart,' her mother said, her warm caramel-coloured eyes so full of compassion and understanding, Liah struggled to hold down another round of sobs.

'H-he… H-he said love was just a word. Th-that it didn't *mean* anything.' Even now, sixteen hours later, the ignorance of such a statement made her chest hurt. 'Th-that he just wanted a wife and a queen and a mother to his children.'

The surge of indignation fortified her a little—enough to finally pull herself out of her mother's arms and sit up on the couch in the Queen's study. 'Can you believe it?' she added. 'L-like I'm some sort of royal brood mare. Seriously, Mum, can you imagine if Daddy had ever said something like that to you? It's so cruel and so chauvinist.'

Her mother sent her an easy smile Liah didn't understand. How exactly was her having her heart ground to dust even remotely amusing?

'Actually, Liah,' her mother said, her voice gentle, but that enigmatic smile still in place, 'It sounds very much like what your father *did* say to me when he first demanded I marry him.'

Liah blinked, astonished by her mother's confession. 'He *demanded* you marry him?' *What the heck?* 'You're not serious?'

Surely her mother had to be exaggerating, or joking? Or simply trying to make her feel better about Kamal's cruelty?

Her parents were a great love match, a wonderful partnership. Everyone said so. And she'd seen how good they were together every day of her life. Of course, they had the occasional argument, some of which got pretty heated, because they were both strong-willed people in their own way, but they would never deliberately hurt each other—the way Kamal had so callously hurt her.

But her mother didn't look as if she was joking. In fact, that annoying smile broadened as she cupped Liah's cheek and pushed the wet strands of her hair back from her face. 'I should probably come clean at this point and admit we only got married originally because I was pregnant with you.'

'W-what?' Liah's strangled reply bounced off the walls of the quiet office. 'But…that… That can't be true. You both adore each other.'

'We didn't always adore each other, Kaliah. Nor did we understand each other,' her mother said softly as Liah's stunned shock turned to incomprehension. 'The truth is, there were a lot of ups and downs in the early years,' her mother added, her tone warm with reminiscence, as if she were reciting a funny anecdote—instead of rewriting the whole history of Liah's childhood.

'In fact, I ran away from him too because I was so upset with him. But one thing I always knew was that he was a good man… A pushy, overbearing, dictatorial and arrogant one at times, but still a good man.'

'But…how did you get past a forced marriage?' Liah said, still so shocked she could hardly talk.

'Oh, it wasn't forced, more expedient,' her mother said, touching Liah's arm gently before the smile turned a bit wicked. 'And your father has always been super-hot, so he was very persuasive.'

'Eww, Mum, stop! I do not need that picture in my head,' Liah muttered, feeling like a teenager again, catching her parents necking enthusiastically when they were supposed to be totally asexual.

But something about the whole conversation had started to ease the fierce, stabbing pain under her breastbone that had been there ever since her showdown with Kamal.

'I still don't understand how you got past having to get married because of me,' she said, her curiosity getting the better of her.

'Well,' her mother replied, considering. 'Firstly, we discovered a lot of things about each other. For example, I discovered the extent of the abuse he had suffered,' her mother added, her expression sobering.

Liah knew her grandfather, the previous Sheikh of Narabia, had been a cruel ruler and a worse father—she knew he had kidnapped her father as a teenager from his mother in LA and had also disowned her uncle Raif when his mother had died in childbirth. But, because Sheikh Abdullah had died before Liah had been born, and her father had never spoken of him, she'd never really considered what that had all really meant.

Her mother continued. 'I discovered, because of his father's abuse and his mother's neglect, Zane had been forced to protect his feelings at all costs. Letting me in was incredibly painful for him, something it took me a while to appreciate.'

'That's so sad,' Liah murmured, her heart breaking for both of them.

'Yes, but the point is we figured it out. Eventually.' Her mother laughed, the soft, musical sound making Liah's sore heart pound. Her mother gripped Liah's hands and rubbed her thumbs across the skin. 'People can heal, Liah, but only if they want to enough, and if they are given the tools and space to do so.'

Liah met her mother's gaze, feeling oddly ashamed. Had she simplified and romanticised everything? Made too many demands on Kamal? She'd run away from him and as a result he might lose his throne. She'd thought he was judging her, but had she given enough consideration to what he had been through in his life before he had ever met her?

'From everything you've told me about Kamal, and the things he said to you, he sounds quite similar to your father in those early days,' her mother said softly. 'I'm not saying you should marry him, not even to help him keep his throne—that's not a reason to marry anyone. And your father is absolutely right, he should have told you the situation from the outset. But maybe you shouldn't write him off completely. It's obvious that, despite everything Kamal's said and done and the things he hasn't done or said, you still love him… What you have to ask yourself now is, do you want to throw those feelings away, or is it worth working on them with him? Because, make no mistake, marriage and relationships are hard work, especially the ones that last.'

She sighed. 'Love really is just a word, you know, he's right about that. It's what's behind it that matters. I can't tell you the number of times I've wanted to strangle your father because he was obtuse, or hot-headed or uncommunicative… But I never stopped wanting to do the work. And neither did he.'

Liah felt hope bubble in her chest again. But this time it felt so much more painful.

'But I'm not sure Kamal does want to do the work,' she said, still desperately unsure. Maybe she had been naïve, maybe she had over-simplified things, but how much evidence did she really have that Kamal saw her as more than a means to an end? 'He told me he didn't require love.'

Catherine nodded. 'It sounds to me like he's terrified.'

'Kamal? Are you joking?' Liah spluttered. 'He's even more overbearing and intimidating than Dad. I don't think he's ever been scared of anything in his life.'

'Are you certain of that?' her mother said, her gaze probing.

And suddenly Liah recalled the flicker of shame in his eyes when she had mentioned his scars. Was there still some of that boy inside him, who had been taught from such an early age he would always be alone, that he wasn't worthy of love, that he would never be cherished?

What if her mother was right and it wasn't that he couldn't love her…it was that he was terrified of loving anyone? Of trusting anyone to love him?

'Oh, no, I may have made a terrible mistake,' she murmured, the bubble of hope becoming a balloon.

Just as a confident smile tilted her mother's lips, Kaliah's aunt Kasia—the Princess of the Kholadi tribe—burst into the chamber, holding the hands of her two-year-old twins, Khalid and Sami. 'Liah, you need to come to Zane's study. Someone just arrived by helicopter and Zane's having a tough time preventing him from charging through the palace in search of you.'

'Kamal?' Liah murmured, that bubble of hope pressing against her larynx.

'If he's six and a half foot, and even more scarily intense than my husband when he's freaking out about me getting pregnant again, then that would be the guy,' Kasia replied with an easy smile. It was a running joke in the family—given Kasia and Raif had had three sets of twin births—that Raif was not in a good place whenever his petite wife became pregnant.

Liah rushed past her aunt and her cousins, unable to think about anything but the painful pressure in her chest. It didn't take her long to catch the sound of her father and her fiancé shouting at each other. She followed the commotion, pushing her way through the palace staff who had amassed by the door to the study, clearly eavesdropping. She burst into her father's study to see Kamal and her father going head to head.

She'd thought she would never see him again. Why had it not occurred to her until this moment, as he stood glaring at her father, his robes swirling around his long legs, his stance rigid, that it was the thought of *never* seeing him again which had hurt most of all?

'Kamal?' she gasped, breathless and stupidly euphoric.

He swung round, his gaze bright but also awash with pain. 'Kaliah, you must come back to me,' he rasped. He looked distraught, she realised, as she crossed the room towards him. His stance was so rigid, his eyes shadowed and so intense. This wasn't arrogance, this was fear. Just as her mother had said.

'You'll do no such damn thing, Liah,' her father interceded. 'This bastard has no right to—'

'Dad, stop talking!' She cut off her father's tirade, unable to detach her gaze from the man in front of her, the man she loved.

'What the...?' her father began.

'Dad, please, this isn't your business,' she said, finally managing to stop staring at the man who had come to mean so much to her in such a short space of time. 'Kamal and I need to talk in private.'

'How can it not be my business?' her dad demanded, temper replaced with confusion. 'He made you cry.'

Her heart swelled at the distress in her father's tone, symbolic of the unconditional love she had taken for granted her whole life.

Kamal has never had that kind of support. Don't underestimate how tough it is for him to let his guard down. To trust his feelings, as well as yours.

She nodded at her father. 'I know, but I can handle this now.'

Her father's gaze flicked from Kamal to her, and she could see he didn't want to leave her alone. But then her mother approached and took his arm.

'Give it up, Zane,' her mum said, placing a tender kiss on his jaw as she tugged him out of the room. 'She's not our little girl any more. She's her own woman. And she's got this.'

As the door closed behind her parents, Liah felt the balloon in her chest swell to impossible proportions. But she made herself swallow it down.

She could see the emotion on his face, knew that much more was going on than she had assumed. But one thing still held true—she had to stand her ground now, more than ever, for them both.

He stepped towards her and lifted his thumb, brushing it down the sore skin on her cheek, irritated by too many tears, tears he had caused.

'I am sorry, Kaliah. I did not mean to make you cry.'

She blinked, touched by the simplicity of the statement and the abject misery in his face. 'I know.'

'Why then did you run from me?' he asked, as if he really didn't know.

But she could see in his eyes, he did know. So she chose not to answer that question.

'I can't come back to you, Kamal. I won't. Not until you give me a good enough reason.'

He swore softly and stepped away, thrusting impatient fingers through his hair. She could see the flash of frustration, of temper even, but beneath it was the fear. It was so clear and vivid to her now, she was amazed she hadn't seen it before.

Or perhaps he had always just been really good at hiding it from her—from everyone.

Her heart lifted a little more, the hope expanding again. That he couldn't hide it from her any more was definitely progress, of a sort.

He marched across the room and clasped his hands behind his back, staring out of the domed window at the Golden Palace's gardens and the high walls bathed in sunshine.

But something about that rigid stance—the tremor in his legs, the bunched muscles in his shoulders—made her see the darkness within. A darkness from which she could feel him struggling to break free. When he finally spoke, his voice a strained monotone, she sensed the battle he waged, even as she willed him to win.

'You asked me to love you,' Kamal said, feeling so broken inside, so needy, he was surprised his guts hadn't spilled out onto the priceless Afghan carpet on Zane Khan's study floor.

If he hadn't been so terrified, he would have been humiliated beyond bearing. But grovelling—even exposing all these horrifying new emotions—didn't seem so insurmountable any more if it would bring her back to him.

'But I don't even understand what that means,' he whispered, mortified by the rawness in his throat, the soreness behind his eyes. 'My earliest memory…before Hamid, before the orphanage…' he gulped, the memory still so painful '…is of the man who left me there. I think he must have been my father. But he did not love me. He cannot have done or he would not have left me. And if he could not… how can anyone?'

His father had left him. And he hadn't come back. He could have been a good boy, a better boy, but his father had never given him the chance to make amends for whatever he had done.

He had never cried, not since he'd been a little boy and he had begged for his father to return. Only to find all the tears in the world would not change what was.

But he had to strain every sinew now not to release the futile tears again as he waited for Kaliah's response to his confession.

He heard her footsteps, and braced himself for the pain of her leaving him again, but then her arms wrapped around his waist from behind and she pressed her face into his spine.

He slumped, the relief coursing through his body so immense, he was surprised he could still remain upright.

'It's okay, Kamal,' she said softly, her voice like a balm to that little boy, as well as the man he had become. 'You don't have to understand love—you don't even have to say you love me yet. All you have to do is let me know you need me. We can work everything else out as we go.'

He turned, clasped her shoulders and dug his fingers into her upper arms to lift her face to his. The tears glinting in her eyes crucified him, even as the tears he could not shed tore at his own heart. 'Really? This is all you require? How can it be enough?'

He wanted to believe her, wanted more than anything to pick her up and carry her to the nearest bed chamber so he could claim her, brand her as his for all eternity. But how could what he had given ever really be enough when she had given so much more?

A small smile creased her lips as she placed a trembling palm against his cheek. 'Because I love you, Kamal,' she said so simply, he felt his heart break open inside his chest and all the fear and confusion bleed out. 'I love your strength and your arrogance and your determination to protect me, and your desperate need never to show a weakness except to me.'

He covered her palm, absorbing the certainty in her words. She meant it. He could see that now with every fibre of his being.

He had no idea what he had done to deserve this, to deserve her, but he would not question it again—ever.

'And I think you love me too,' she added with a confidence, an arrogance, he had always adored, perhaps because it was more than a match for his own. 'You just don't know it yet. That's all.'

His heart exploded with joy as he lifted her off her feet then captured her mouth with his. The kiss was fierce, furious, but also tender.

A long time later, when they were finally forced to come up for air, she wiggled out of his arms and grasped his hand.

'Come on—we probably need to get back to Zokar ASAP,' she said, attempting to tug him towards the door. 'We've got a wedding to plan and time is running out.'

He smiled as he resisted, charmed by her urgency. 'There is no need,' he said simply. 'The wedding is cancelled.'

'What?' Her eyebrows launched up her forehead, charming him even more. 'But what about your throne? Oh, my God...' She began to tug on his hand even harder. He remained firm. 'Kamal, stop messing about. For goodness' sake, we have to un-cancel the wedding. Pronto.'

'Shh, Kaliah.' He actually laughed, her frantic expression only making him adore her more. She would always have his back. Why had he not realised how much he needed that support from her until now? 'It's okay. We are not un-cancelling anything.'

'But the elders? The law? You have to be married to...'

'No, I do not,' he said, cradling her cheeks, loving the feel of her soft skin, the intoxicating scent of her. A scent he had become addicted to the first time he had inhaled it. 'If the elders choose another man to rule Zokar on this foolish technicality, that is on them.'

'You can't mean that!' she said, still sounding frantic.

'I do mean it,' he assured her, knowing he spoke the absolute truth. 'I will not jump through hoops for their benefit. You are too important to me. Our marriage is too important to me to rush into it before you are ready.'

'But I am ready now—totally. What difference does a few extra days or weeks make if it means you can keep...?'

He pressed his finger to her lips to silence her panic. 'Do you not understand, Kaliah? It was never about that.' He sighed, the relief that he was finally able to be honest with himself, as well as her, almost palpable. 'I wished to rush you into marriage because I was scared of losing you. I see that now. The marriage ultimatum, the throne, was just a convenient excuse.' He shrugged. 'If they are foolish enough to discard me because of their asinine demands, then they are the idiots. Because I am by far the best man to be their king.'

'True.' Her lips quirked as the panic finally died, to be replaced by amusement and the same joy exploding in his heart. 'And you've also found the best woman to be their queen.'

'Also true.' He grinned, boosting her into his arms so he could take his own sweet time ravaging her lips.

Maybe the elders—especially Uttram and his followers—would see how good Kaliah and him would be as Zokar's rulers, maybe they would not. But, as she gripped his scalp and sunk into the kiss, the joy streaking through his body became turbo-charged.

Because the only kingdom he really *had* to rule now—and always—was the kingdom of Kaliah Khan's heart.

EPILOGUE

'YOU WERE SPECTACULAR TODAY, Kaliah. I am so proud to have you as my wife, my partner, my queen.'

Liah sighed as Kamal's lips brushed her nape. She covered the hands he pressed into her stomach with her own. Her heart beat a giddy tattoo in her chest, as it had been doing all day—ever since she had stood before a crowd of people she loved and respected and had declared her loyalty to this strong, commanding man and his kingdom, while he'd declared his loyalty to hers.

She blinked furiously as he kissed the pulse point in her neck, which always made her ache, and stared down at the enchanted garden in the Golden Palace's courtyard where she had once dreamed of finding a prince to love.

A watery smile lifted her lips. Today's ceremony had been part of the week-long wedding celebrations that had started five days ago in Zokar, not just to make their marriage official but also to link their two kingdoms, as Kaliah had taken her place beside Kamal on his country's throne and they'd been declared joint heirs to her parents' throne in Narabia.

The ceremony had been over six months in the making, with Kamal—intractable man that he was—insisting he did not want to stake a claim to her father's throne. In the end, she'd had to make him see that she had no desire to lead Narabia without him when the time came. But the good news was, her father and mother didn't look as if they were about to relinquish the throne any time soon, the recollection of their proud, happy smiles this afternoon making the emotion swell in her throat.

'What are you thinking?' Kamal murmured as he turned her in his arms.

She smiled, reaching up to place her palms on the rough stubble that had grown on his cheeks during the long day of official engagements. 'That I'm ridiculously proud to finally have you as my husband,' she said, lifting up on tiptoes to press her lips to his.

His hands grasped her waist in her beaded gown as he bent to take her mouth in a firm, possessive kiss. Need sparked and throbbed in her belly, right beside the flicker of excitement and anticipation at the news she had waited five interminable days to give him.

They'd been too tired and busy for her to find the right time ever since she had taken the test—the schedule of engagements and ceremonies to celebrate their union in both kingdoms nothing short of punishing. And, anyway, she'd wanted to wait until she was at the Golden Palace, in her childhood home—where all her dreams of love and romance had begun.

Kamal was nothing like the man she'd envisioned falling in love with one day. He was far too forthright and demanding, far too intense and masculine, far too vivid and vibrant... He made the Prince Charming of her daydreams seem pale, insubstantial and, frankly, exceedingly dull in comparison.

'Good,' he announced with a possessive huff, before scooping her into his arms. 'Because now I intend to get you out of that dress which has been driving me wild all evening and make you my queen in the only way that counts.'

She laughed as he marched into their bed chamber but, as he placed her beside the bed and set about divesting her of said gown, she clasped his hands. 'Wait, Kamal.'

'What? Why?' he asked, his impatient frown only making her love him more. She hoped that fierce need would never dim...

'I have something to tell you...' She hesitated as her heart throbbed into her throat.

He cradled her face in one callused palm, his thumb brushing away the tear that slipped down her cheek.

'What is it, Kaliah?' he asked, that flash of fear something she hoped to erase completely one day.

She swallowed, the emotion all but choking her.

She'd planned this moment so carefully over the last five days—exactly what she would say and how she would say it—but it all suddenly seemed like too much. They were entering another brand-new phase of their lives together, after only having just embarked on the last one and, as much as she knew Kamal wanted this, she wasn't sure if he wanted it right now.

'Whatever it is, we will fix it together,' he said, still stroking her cheek, his face a mask of confusion now, and determination...and love.

Oh, for goodness' sake, Liah, just say it. You're scaring him.

'I'm pregnant!' she blurted out with a great deal less finesse than she had planned.

His eyes widened with shock, and then his gaze darted down to her stomach.

'You...? Y-you are having our child?' His expression was filled with awe as his gaze met hers.

She nodded, her stomach bouncing as he pressed a hand to where their baby grew.

'I found out on Monday. I guess my contraception must have failed when I had that bout of food poisoning last month...' She began to babble. 'I know we didn't plan it just yet, and it's going to be a lot to take on with all our new responsibilities, and the US trade tour next...'

'Shh...' he said then, to her astonishment, he sunk to his knees and pressed his cheek to her belly as his arms wrapped around her hips.

She stroked his silky hair, feeling the tremble of fierce emotion.

'Kamal, is everything okay?' she asked, her voice thick with tears now.

He looked up at her at last, his gaze dark and intense — and so full of joy, she had to wipe away the tears now streaming down her cheeks.

'Yes, everything is much, much better than okay,' he said.

Then he surged to his feet, lifted her into his arms and swung her around with a whoop of triumph.

Her laughter joined his deep chuckles as he set her back on her feet at last...and the fierce joy spread like wildfire in her heart.

* * * * *

A BABY TO MAKE
HER HIS BRIDE

DANI COLLINS

MILLS & BOON

To Doug, who has been my sounding board
through this whole series, cheerleading me
through the rough patches and celebrating with me
when I finished each one. Thank you for
your profoundly endless patience. I love you.

CHAPTER ONE

VIENNA WAVERLY PARKED outside the house she owned but had never seen.

Her brother, Hunter, had bought it a month ago, in the most bizarre way.

"Can I use your numbered shell to buy a house without telling you why?" he had asked. "It's nothing criminal, I swear."

"I didn't think it would be, but I thought you were dissolving those." They each had a shell company that Hunter had set up to protect their assets while they'd been in litigation with their stepmother.

"I will, but this came up," he had said.

"What did?" Vienna liked to think she and her brother were close, but it was more accurate to say they were close—adjacent. Kitty-corner. They always had the other's back, but they also kept things from each other, usually in an effort to protect. She loved Hunter to bits and would do anything for him, but this had been a very odd favor.

"It's fifty years old," he had continued in his brisk, close-the-deal manner. "Off-grid, upgraded with solar and water filtration. Great location. The current owners run it as a vacation rental, so it's furnished and in good repair. I'll take it offline, though. There won't be any maintenance or management to worry about. I'll cover all the fees and taxes and explain why I want it in a few months. Then you can do whatever you want with it. Until then, you can't mention this to anyone, not even Neal."

She had barely been talking to her soon-to-be ex-husband, so that had been an easy promise to make.

"Does Amelia know about it?"

"I'll tell her." Hunter had left a distinct pause. "When the time is right."

He had only been married five or six weeks at that point, to a woman who had kept secrets of her own—including the fact that she'd had Hunter's baby. There'd been a massive scandal over the revelation, including his last-minute cancellation of his wedding to one of Vienna's best friends.

Since then, Hunter and Amelia had seemed to be falling for each other. If he was hiding something this big from his new bride, however, that was a huge red flag.

"I need your answer now, Vi," he'd prodded.

"That's really all you're going to tell me?"

"Yes."

Since there were also things she wasn't ready to tell him, she had felt obliged to trust him even though he was leaving her in the dark. "All right. Yes. Go ahead."

"Thank you." He'd sounded relieved. "I wouldn't do it if it wasn't important."

"I know."

She would not have leaned on Hunter's executive assistant to get here without any trace appearing in her own accounts if it hadn't been important, either. She would eventually reimburse all the expenses for her two chartered flights, her company credit card and her temporary phone on the Wave-Com account, but dropping off-grid was exactly what she needed right now.

When she had landed in Nanaimo, on British Columbia's Vancouver Island, a company-leased SUV had awaited her with a full tank of gas and all the groceries she would need. She hadn't told Hunter's PA where she was going, but had asked him to forward her new number to Hunter so he would have it when he needed it.

When the proverbial poop hit the propeller, was what she had meant.

That would happen shortly after Neal was served his divorce papers. Vienna's PR team was cued up with instructions to go on the offensive at that point, with statements that the divorce was a fait accompli.

Never in her life had she been such a sneaky, cutthroat person, but her requests for a quiet, uncontested divorce had been met with faux hurt, promises they could continue trying for a baby, and subtle threats about going to the press with a tell-all about the Waverlys.

That had been last year, when Hunter had been steeped in that ugly court case with Irina, their stepmother. Vienna hadn't wanted to add to his stress with her own drama, so she had simply asked Neal for space. She began spending all her time at their apartment in Toronto while he remained in Calgary, where he was Wave-Com's VP of Sales. She had quietly changed her driver's license, redirected her mail and opened a separate bank account. As long as she maintained the illusion that they were happily married, making herself available for Neal's work engagements and inviting him to a handful of her family appearances, Neal hadn't cared.

She *told* people they were separated, though. Not a lot of people, but solid character witnesses for when the time came.

Nevertheless, she knew Neal would play the victim and say this had come out of the blue. He would claim he wanted to reconcile. There was too much money at stake for him to go quietly. Too much cachet in being Hunter Waverly's brother-in-law.

This story would be yet another gold mine for the clickbait sites, but scandal was unavoidable. That was what Vienna had come to accept. The best she could do was exactly what she'd done. She had waited until Hunter had left with Amelia on a belated honeymoon so the blast radius wouldn't scorch them too badly.

Now she was taking cover herself to ride out the fallout. The address on the conveyancing documents had brought her to Tofino, one of the soggiest places in Canada, located where the western edge of the country dropped into the brine of the Pacific Ocean.

Neal didn't know this house existed. Only her lawyer knew where she had gone.

Soon, she promised herself. Soon she would be divested of the worst mistake of her life. She would be free to do what *she* wanted.

With a sigh of relief, she stepped from the SUV. After the long drive across the island, her body thanked her for the stretch. Her nostrils drank in the cool fragrance of cedar and pine and fir. The chatter of squirrels hidden in their boughs was cheerfully deafening, drowning out the rush of the ocean against a shoreline she couldn't see.

She left everything in the vehicle, wanting to see inside first. It was supposed to have solar power and a well so she assumed she would have functioning electricity and plumbing, but she had a propane camp stove and a large jerry can of water just in case.

The tall, skinny house had probably been avant-garde in its time, built over the edge of an embankment like this. A narrow wooden walkway, reminiscent of a draw-bridge, took her from the graveled driveway to a pair of entry doors flanked by stained glass windows.

She would bet anything that sunshine had not broken through these panels in at least a decade. Nature had closed in around the structure, giving it a distinct "forgotten castle swallowed by brambles" vibe, complete with a moat of empty air between the wraparound veranda and the tree trunks that stood sentry a few feet away.

Maybe a tree house was a better comparison. Either way, she was in love. The siding might be weathered gray, and she imagined the roof was more moss than shingles, but she understood what it was like to be neglected for years, yet still hold potential. This was the perfect place for a dejected princess to shake off the spell she'd been under and awaken into her new life.

The paperwork promised that the keypad on the door had been returned to its factory setting, which was four zeroes, but when she punched that in, it didn't work.

Annoyed, she walked around to where another small bridge connected a side door to the garage. Both of those doors were locked, so she continued to the back.

Here the deck opened into a massive outdoor lounge and dining area with a barbecue built for crowds. The expansive view of the ocean over the treetops stopped her in her tracks.

Wow. Thank you, Hunter.

She took a few deep breaths, grounding herself in the moment so she would remember it, then turned to the two sets of sliding doors interspersed with three wide picture windows.

Clean windows, she noted with a shiver of premonition. It struck her that the deck was swept clean of needles, the furniture was all right side up with the blue-and-yellow-striped cushions in place. The barbecue was uncovered.

Wait a minute. Was that door *open*? The screen was closed, but the glass behind it was wide open.

Her heart tripped as she scraped the screen out of her way and saw that yes, she was able to walk right in.

She expected—hoped?—to see water damage on the floor. That would mean that the previous owners or a property agent had irresponsibly forgotten to lock up properly, but no, it was clean as a whistle in here. Everything was in good order.

With her heart battering her rib cage, she took in that there had been updates carried out over the years. The floors were not the dreaded shag carpet or yellowed linoleum. There was a bright blue-and-black mat that she stepped on as she called out, "Hello?"

She was every idiotic woman who had gone down to the basement in a horror movie, but a more rational side of her mind was telling her some vacation renters had been given faulty information.

Was she even in the right house?

"Hello? Is anyone here?"

The floor plan was an open concept arranged around a massive river stone chimney. On her right, the kitchen had been given a complete makeover with Shaker-style white cupboards and granite countertops. The oval dining table was antique oak, the sitting room furnishings out of fashion but in good repair.

Her gaze lurched back to the wooden bowl on the table. That fruit was real! Two green bananas, an orange and a bright red apple with a sticker on it.

Through the open tread stairs that rose from the back of the sitting room, she could see a desk in the window near the front door. There was a laptop on it, closed, but plugged in with a coffee mug beside it.

Someone was definitely here!

In fact, steps inside the pantry began to creak under the weight of someone climbing them.

Snakes began to writhe in her middle as her morbid gaze stared into the open door of the pantry. This was *her* house, but she wasn't an idiot. She turned to leave the way she'd come in.

"Who are you?" The rumble of a deep, unfriendly voice behind her lifted the hairs on the back of her neck.

She turned back and found not a scruffy squatter, but a fit, well-kept thirtysomething in a gray T-shirt and gym shorts, one who radiated the dangerous energy of a gathering storm.

Her senses were *accosted* by lake-blue eyes that pierced so far into her soul she shivered. His jaw was clean-shaven and looked hard as iron. The glower he wore was even harder. His legs were planted like hundred-year-old oak trees.

He looked her up and down as though she were a squirrel he'd have to shoo out with a broom. His thick brows went up, demanding she answer.

Habits of a lifetime had her wanting to make an apology and slink away. *I'm nobody.* Confrontation had never worked out for her, but she had to start standing up for herself. She wasn't actually in the wrong here, even though he was making her feel that way.

"Who are *you*?" She kept her tone polite, but chilly. "This is my house."

"No, it's not." His confidence was so absolute, it caused uncertainty to roll in her abdomen, instantly putting her on the defensive.

"I can show you the proof on my phone—" She looked to her hands and found only a key fob. She'd left her phone in the car, but, "This is 1183 Bayview Drive. That was the number on the post at the end of the drive." She pointed in that direction.

His thick brows crashed together.

Ha. She was relieved to have scored a point for once in her life. See? She was not always wrong.

"Kindly explain why you're in my house," she repeated.

His eyes narrowed further. "Vienna?"

Her heart lurched. She'd come here hoping not to be recognized.

Jasper Lindor was about to start his daily workout in the basement when he heard someone try the keypad on the front door. He had changed the code when he arrived here, but a contract killer wasn't likely to try a legal entry anyway. Nor was law enforcement.

He listened to a single pair of light footsteps follow the wraparound deck to check the side door then move to the deck at the back.

Had someone found him or was this person lost? Either

way, he was annoyed. He was in the middle of placing a thousand dominoes with delicate precision. He needed another month before he could tip the first one and knock them all down. He didn't want that jeopardized.

When he heard the screen door scrape and the call of a female voice, he let out a hacked-off sigh.

She wasn't trying to hide her presence, so Jasper didn't, either. He came up the stairs to the inside of the pantry only to find her leaving.

She had a spectacular ass. That was his first base impression. Snug jeans cupped a beautiful heart-shaped rump. Her sleeveless top exposed arms that were toned and tanned. Her long hair hung loose to the middle of her back. The brunette color held ash-blond highlights, the sort that pricey salons dispensed. All of her gleamed with the polish only money could buy.

Real estate agent? He should have let her leave, but recent betrayals had made him into the suspicious sort. Had she planted something while she was here?

"Who are you?" he demanded as he swept the rooms with his gaze.

She turned around and— Damn, she was lovely.

His guts twisted as he took in the wavy hair framing wide cheekbones and a flawless complexion. Beneath her peaked brows, her gray-green eyes took him in. Her narrow chin came up.

"Who are *you*?" She gave off an aloof, condescending air, the kind that still had the power to needle him all these years later, when he was no longer the broke teenager standing in a grocery store parking lot. "This is my house."

"No, it's not." He knew who owned this house, but

even as she rattled off the house number, his brain made the outlandish connection to the handful of photos he'd seen online.

"Vienna?"

She stiffened. Confusion shifted in her eyes as she tried to place him. Wariness.

"Did Hunter send you?" His thoughts belatedly leaped to his sister and her new baby. "Did something happen?"

"*I'm* asking the questions," she insisted in a haughty way that grated. Her jaw lifted a notch so she was looking down her nose at him. "Who are you? This house is supposed to be empty." She faltered as though mentally reviewing whatever data she'd been given. "At least, Hunter said it wouldn't be used for vacation rentals anymore. Does he know you're here?"

"Yes." Jasper grew cautious himself. He wasn't reassured to learn his intruder was Hunter's sister. She seemed genuinely surprised the house was occupied and didn't seem to know who he was, but she could still ruin his plans.

"Do you work for him? Who are you?" she demanded.

"You really don't know?"

"Would I ask if I did?" Her knuckles were white where she fisted her hands at her sides.

Interesting. She wasn't as full of lofty self-assurance as she was trying to seem.

He gave his clean jaw a rub. Keeping his beard off was a nuisance, but he was relieved to know that it had changed his appearance enough from his own dated online photos that she didn't recognize him.

"Tell me first why you're here. Are you with anyone? Your husband?" She had one, he recalled with a flick of his gaze toward the windows that looked onto the driveway. "Someone else?" he added with a twist of his lips.

A flash of indignation crossed her expression. She didn't like being called unfaithful. Something more vulnerable followed—perhaps a realization that she was alone with a stranger because she lifted her chin and spoke with bold dishonesty.

"My husband is right behind me. You should definitely leave before he gets here."

"Don't lie to me, Vienna," he said wearily. "I hate liars." He really did.

"Well, I dislike people who pretend they know me when they don't. Are you going to tell me who you are and what you're doing in my house?"

"Your house." He ran his tongue over his teeth, still judging that a fib.

She took fresh issue and stood taller.

She was on the tall side for a woman, with a figure that was willowy but indisputably feminine. Pretty. So damned pretty. He couldn't help noticing even though she was very married.

Beauty on the outside didn't mean beauty on the inside, he reminded himself starkly.

But the fact that she hadn't known he was here, and didn't recognize him, told him she wasn't working for REM-Ex.

"I'm Jasper Lindor, Amelia's brother."

She seemed to stop breathing. She stood so still only her lashes quivered as her gaze bounced from his hairline to his gym shoes.

"Do you have proof?" she asked shakily. "Amelia was

told you were dead. Hunter wouldn't keep something like this from her."

"She knows I'm alive. So does our father. I've seen them." Once. It had been too short a visit, both heartening and heartbreaking. "I'm not ready to go public on the reasons for my disappearance, so Hunter let me stay here."

She tucked in her chin. Her brow crinkled as she tried to decide whether to believe him.

If trust was a two-way street, they were both circling the block, unwilling to turn onto it.

"My passport is upstairs." Worse for wear after all this time, but he'd managed to hang on to it. "Shall I get it?"

"No. I see the resemblance," she murmured, her gaze traveling over his features with a thoroughness that made his chest itch. She cocked her head, relaxing a little. Her tone warmed. "Is this why Hunter was so strange about buying this property? I had no idea you were alive or staying here. That must have been such a relief for your family to learn you were okay."

"Okay" was a stretch. He barely slept. He was haunted by the death of his friend and couldn't help feeling threatened by a woman who posed as much physical danger as a knitted blanket.

None of that could be erased or fixed, but he was taking steps to achieve some justice. It all hinged on keeping that fact he was alive, and back in Canada, under wraps a little longer.

"Why are you here?" he asked bluntly.

She sobered. A flash of injury in her eyes was quickly screened by her lashes. Her mouth pursed.

"Seeking some 'me' time."

"And you picked this house? Out of all the houses your

family owns?" He didn't know exactly how many there were, but he would bet there were several condos, cottages and cabins to choose from.

"I'm allowed to come to a house that *I* own."

From what he'd read—and he'd read very little about her because she hadn't seemed relevant to his situation—Vienna had struck him as the quintessential vapid heiress: feckless and superficial. She was always pictured in the most classically perfect clothing, wearing the same meaningless smile whether attending a fundraiser or an award banquet or her brother's canceled wedding. She didn't have a job, didn't have kids, and somehow kept her head above water despite a habit of flooding proverbial toilets.

"Well, this house is occupied. I want to be alone, too." He tilted a flat smile at her. "That's why no one knows I'm here."

"I wouldn't have come if I'd known," she said in a burst of defensiveness. She folded her arms and glanced over her shoulder to the SUV in the driveway. "I can't go anywhere else, though. Someone will recognize me. The gulls will flock in."

"Gulls?"

"Paparazzi." She curled her lip in rueful disgust. "I'm embarking on the latest mile of the Waverly Walk of Shame: *divorce.*" She lifted her brows facetiously to emphasize what a disgrace that was in some eyes.

All he heard was *paparazzi*, "You're bringing reporters to my doorstep?" His blood pressure shot up to pound behind his eyeballs. *"Come on, lady."*

She jerked her head back, eyes brightening.

"It's not *your* doorstep. It's *mine,*" she reminded snippily. "And no, I took precautions. No one knows I'm here. That SUV is leased by Wave-Com. I have a burner phone like some kind of drug lord and my PR team use a secure chatroom. I went to a lot of effort to insulate myself—and Hunter, and Amelia, and Peyton—from what will be a feeding frenzy. I refuse to stand in the pillory anyway, just because my presence here is inconvenient for you. This is my house. I'm staying right here."

Fighting for control over your own life was terrifying. Jasper was a very intimidating man, crossing his arms so those mountains he called shoulders seemed to bunch even higher.

Hunter wouldn't be helping him if he was dangerous, she reassured herself. In fact, Hunter had sworn this house wasn't being used for anything criminal. Jasper wasn't a fugitive evading justice, just a really imposing recluse who was annoyed because his privacy had been invaded.

"We're adults," she pointed out, trying for a more conciliatory tone, but she could feel the strain in her voice. "Family."

She offered a welcoming smile, genuinely happy to meet Amelia's brother, but for some reason their gazes clashed like steel on steel, sparking and hot. Her throat felt scorched.

His glower rejected her overture and his disapproval rolled toward her like a fugue, seeping into the heart of her insecurities.

Not you. You're not wanted. Get lost.

She resisted giving in, refusing to run like a coward. It was *her* house.

She waved at the wide rooms around them.

"I'm sure we can make this work. We both seem to be motivated to keep our presence here quiet." She certainly was. "It seems like a big enough place that we should be able to share it without getting in each other's way. I brought my own groceries."

One dark brow lifted, unimpressed.

"I'm only staying a week." Once the initial shock wave passed, she would fly to Europe to attend a wedding. "I have to be seen in public at least once before Hunter and Amelia get back. I'll surface in Toronto so they won't be inundated at their home in Vancouver." Hopefully. "I have a *plan*. This isn't my first time in the goat rodeo of bad publicity."

He snorted.

"I won't even make noise! I brought my art things." So she could finally work on her own projects, rather than curating finished pieces for others. "Are you really going to refuse to let me stay here?"

"I can't, can I?" His voice dripped sarcasm. *"Mi casa es tu casa."*

CHAPTER TWO

WHAT A GRUMP.

Vienna walked outside to collect her bag and exhaled a huge sigh of bottled-up tension. Was she out of her mind to stay? His attitude was pretty much her worst nightmare, having grown up with her stepmother radiating that same pained tolerance.

It's my house, she reminded herself.

But she really should start communicating more frankly with her brother. He'd been going through a lot with his new marriage and new baby, so she hadn't wanted to be a bother. She *never* wanted to be a bother, but nearly everyone treated her as though she was.

She needed to grow up and grow a pair. She knew that. She needed to stop worrying about what other people thought of her and go after what she wanted without shame or guilt.

She had come this far on that journey already, hadn't she? This was not the time to let her courage fail her.

Yet, when she walked back in to face Jasper's judgmental gaze, and the sensation that he saw all her flaws clear as day, it took everything in her to say, "I'll take one of the guest rooms. Don't worry about moving out of the big one."

His snort as she sailed under his nose suggested he was not worried at all, but she held her head high as she took her suitcase up the stairs.

She set it down in a bedroom that was adjoined to another through a Jack and Jill bathroom. A brief exploration showed her a reading nook on the landing then she peeked into the primary suite where the blue-and-yellow decor was fresh and bright. The room was dominated by a pillow-topped king-size mattress in what looked to be a waterbed frame built of massive timbers. Light poured in through the glass doors to a balcony with a limitless view of the ocean.

Aside from a bookmarked spy thriller on the night table and a flannel shirt hanging over the back of a chair, the room looked unoccupied.

Amelia had always made Jasper sound so human. Her stories were always mixed with distress that he was missing, but now Vienna thought about it, Amelia's mood had lightened recently. Vienna had thought it was more to do with how well she and Hunter had been getting along, and the honeymoon to the South Pacific that they had impulsively planned, but now she thought perhaps the switch had happened when Amelia had learned her brother was alive.

For Amelia's sake, Vienna was thrilled that Jasper had survived his disappearance, but he certainly wasn't anything like the doting brother Amelia had described. He seemed embittered and gruff. Hard.

Maybe that's just how he feels about *you*.

Stop it. She had been to therapy. She knew self-defeating thinking when it rang in her head.

Actually, that ringing was the door chime. He was

going in and out while she was lingering up here, avoiding him.

She made herself go back downstairs and found Jasper had brought in most of her groceries.

"*How* long are you staying?" he asked, and set down the insulated box holding meat and dairy.

"I like to cook and knew I'd have time."

The reality of sharing a house with him caused her stomach to pitch. She had never been so aware of a man. Not in this way. She'd suffered the friction of a difficult marriage where more went unsaid than was ever acknowledged aloud. Simply being a woman meant she'd endured the company of men who made a woman feel unsafe, but that wasn't why she felt so uncomfortable right now.

Physically, she sensed no danger from Jasper. Emotionally? His unfriendliness stepped right on her old bruises. She was right back to feeling that every word or deed could be a giant misstep while she felt obliged to get along because their siblings were married.

Don't make waves, Vienna.

It had always been her job to make everyone else feel comfortable, no matter what it cost her. She fell back on that habit as he came back with the jerrican of water.

"I was planning to make halibut tonight. There's enough for two."

He put the jerrican down in a corner on the floor. His casual strength was mesmerizing, but the way he eyed her as if looking for a catch kept a wall of antagonism between them.

"I thought we were going to stay out of each other's

way." He picked up the little sack of fair-trade coffee beans and tucked it into a cupboard.

"We're—" She didn't dare call them family again. "In-laws. We should get to know each other." Maybe then she would quit feeling like she was walking on hot coals.

"I know who you are, Vienna," he said pithily.

"Really? How?" She prickled under his laser-sharp stare, feeling painfully transparent yet affronted. How could he possibly know anything about her when she had no inkling herself? She had lost any sense of self years ago. "Online trolls, I suppose?" She was instantly stinging with the poison of false reports. "I'll disregard what your sister has said about you, then, and believe everything *I've* read."

She hadn't read much. Amelia had insisted he wasn't the kind of person to walk away from a job or get someone killed, but that was what he'd been accused of. And maybe Vienna ought to give more credence to that, because the warning that flashed in his gaze was down-right lethal.

All he said, however, was, "Touché."

His acceptance of her remark did nothing to alleviate the uncomfortable tension in her belly. She didn't care whether he approved of her. She didn't.

She shouldn't.

She went back to stowing items in the refrigerator.

"I thought this said 'pastille' and you'd brought a huge box of candy." He was holding her brand-new case of *plein air* colors. "You're a pastel artist?"

When she overcame her imposter syndrome enough to call herself any kind of artist, yes, but her whole body wanted to fold in on itself that he was touching her things. It was as if he was looking straight into her and it *hurt*.

"Sculpture," she joked past the suffocating sensations. She crossed to take the box from his hands and tuck it away with her pads and colored pencils, moving the whole lots to the far end of the dining room table. "The hammer and chisel won't bother you, will it?"

"Not while my heavy metal is playing."

He cocked a brow that said, *I can play that game too.*

"I'll pull your car in." He picked up her key fob and exited out the side door, the one that led to the garage.

She let out another pent-up breath and was finishing the groceries when he returned.

"Is there a path to the beach?" she asked. "I'd like to walk off my travel."

And get away from these oppressive undercurrents.

"I'll take you. It's overgrown. You might get lost."

Terrific.

It was August, so the ground was dry and the air warm, but there was coolness in the shadows beneath the boughs of the trees that spoke of old growth and time measured in centuries.

Jasper walked this path every day. It was easy enough to follow, but it would be just like a city girl to wander into the ferns and get disoriented. The last thing he needed right now was to have his *sister-in-law* lost in the woods.

Why did that word bother him so much? They were related by marriage. That was a true fact and, someday soon, he would regain his old life. He would visit his sister and her baby and would cross paths with Vienna and her husband—

No. She was divorcing. That was why she was here. She was taking cover while it was announced. The gossip sites did love a celebrity breakup, but she wasn't a celebrity in the league of an American pop star. How bad could it be? From what he'd read…

Huh. She'd put him in his place on that one, hadn't she? He'd been subjected to false reports himself, so he had some sympathy on that front.

"What did she say?" he asked over his shoulder.

"Who?" Her voice was farther behind him than he'd realized.

He had spent half his life off-grid, so ducking branches or stepping over roots was as easy as a flat sidewalk for him. He stopped and watched her pick her way carefully down a short drop, clinging to a sapling. She paused to drink in the moss-laden branches around them, expression serene and all the more appealing for that softness.

"My sister," he clarified, yanking his thoughts from where they shouldn't go. "You said you would disregard what she had said about me and believe what you'd read online."

"Oh. Um. I don't know. That everything online was wrong," she said wryly. "That you looked after her when your mom passed and taught her to drive. Things like that. She said you probably would have killed Hunter with your bare hands if you'd been around when she turned up pregnant." She chuckled dryly, but he thought he caught a glimpse of agony in her expression before she blinked and looked curiously to where a crow was cawing in the trees.

"It sounds as though our father was prepared to do that when he showed up at Hunter's wedding." The fact Jasper hadn't been there for Amelia, and had instead caused her and their father untold distress, was a continuous knife of guilt in his belly.

"Tobias was pretty livid," she agreed, smile oddly wistful. "I think it's nice that you're so close, though. It makes me envious."

"You and Hunter aren't close?"

"Not in the same way. Our upbringing was very different from yours."

"Wow." He would go ahead and believe his first impression of her, if that was how she talked. If the opinion of people like her mattered to him, he would point out that his net worth was in the same neighborhood as hers.

"Not because of means," she said, cross and defensive. "Our father remarried. Hunter was tapped to take over the family business and it's not exactly a dry cleaning outlet. He was busy with that so we had a very different upbringing from *each other*."

"You don't work for Wave-Com?" It was a national communications conglomerate. There had to be room for her.

"No. My—Neal does. He's the VP of Sales and Marketing."

Her ex, he presumed.

"I couldn't believe who Amelia married," he admitted and started walking again, still astonished his sister was married at all.

He'd been in a remote village on a tributary of the Bío-Bío River, tanned deeply enough to pass for a local when a stranger had come looking for the Canadian who was reputed to be staying in the area.

I'm working for your sister's husband. You can trust me, he had said to Jasper in Spanish.

Like hell. Jasper had impatiently waved him away, sending him downstream.

The next day, the man had come back with a story from Amelia's childhood that Jasper genuinely believed she wouldn't share with anyone except someone she trusted. By then, he'd been gone more than a year. A year in which he'd made very little headway, despite constant efforts to raise investigations in Chile. Along with causing a painful loss, REM-Ex had cut him off from more than his family and his resources. He had lost his reputation and very identity.

It had been a gamble to trust that stranger, but he had reasoned that his dad and sister already believed he was dead. He had climbed aboard the private jet and read up on his sister's husband while flying back to Toronto.

"Hunter was about to marry someone else," he recalled. "That doesn't exactly sound like a love match for Amelia." That was eating at him, even though Amelia had seemed happy when he'd seen her.

"Hunter wouldn't have let it get that far if he'd known about Peyton," Vienna insisted behind him. "Eden has since married someone else, too. It all worked out for the best."

"It certainly worked out for me," he said ironically. "I got a free flight back to Canada, but I can't help worrying she married him for my sake."

Jasper pulled his own weight. He solved his own problems. People came to *him* for solutions. He didn't rely on others. It galled him that his sister had had to come to his rescue and he couldn't help wondering what it might have cost her.

"They married for Peyton's sake," Vienna assured him. "It was bumpy at first, but I've never seen Hunter as relaxed as he is around Amelia and Peyton. I don't know what kind of father I thought he would be. Ours was…"

He stopped again, turning to see her cheeks were hollow, her mouth pensive.

"What?" he prompted.

She shrugged it off. "Hunter has always been very supportive and concerned about my welfare, but he's different with them. He's very open and loving, more so than I've ever seen him. It's cute." Her expression softened, then brightened. "Oh!"

She brushed past him to where the trees opened onto the beach.

"I was starting to think the climb back up wouldn't be worth wherever it was you were taking me, but this is beautiful!"

She shaded her eyes as she scanned the cove formed by an arm of treed land extending outward to the south. Ahead, a small island with exactly three trees stood in the water. It was just far enough away that it remained unreachable on foot even when the tide was out. The sky was an intense blue, the sun glittering off the green water, illuminating the foam of the incoming waves. The sand was granite-gray and littered with kelp, utterly empty of human occupation.

The wind dragged at her hair and pressed her clothes to her front. He would have pegged her for a white sand, all-inclusive beach type, not so much raw nature, but she was entranced.

A sense of accord settled over him. He was a loner and had become very proprietary about this small stretch of paradise, but if he had to share it, he was glad it was with someone who appreciated it.

She glanced at him and caught him staring at her. Her carefree joy faltered into uncertainty.

He looked away, rebuking himself. *Not her.* For many reasons.

"There's a hotel around that outcrop. I walk this direction." He began negotiating the thick fence of gnarled driftwood thrown up on the beach by eons of wind and waves.

Tension filled the silence between them as they walked across the untouched sand.

Vienna told herself it was the breeze playing in her hair, snapping it against her face, that made her feel so sensitized. She was an artist, naturally affected by tangy, earthy aromas. That was why she wanted to take off her shoes, so she could feel the shifting temperatures in the sand. That was why her eye wanted to watch the sunshine paint itself over the planes of his body and the angles of his face.

It had nothing to do with that moment when they had come onto the beach, when she had suddenly felt noticed. *Seen.*

Most people only saw a curated version of her. She engineered it that way. She hid behind layers of perfect manners and pretty clothes, flawless makeup and carefully styled hair, protecting her thoughts and feelings with whatever image she thought they wanted to see. She was the Wave-Com Heiress or Neal Briggs's Wife. Hunter Waverly's sister or Peyton's Auntie Vienna. She hated that she had to put up all these fronts. It was exhausting, but the nakedness of being herself was worse.

The wildness of the empty beach had called her out of her shell, though. For those vibrating seconds, she'd simply existed as part of the world. She was alive and unstoppable and beautiful *because* of the marks that flotsam and time had left upon her.

Then she realized Jasper had been studying her in her unguarded moment.

How would he use it against her? How would he hurt and diminish her?

"I'll save that for another day," she said when they reached a creek that cut a wide swath across the sand. They couldn't cross it without getting soaked to their knees, so they started back.

She surreptitiously looked at him as he walked in long, powerful strides beside her. His gaze moved constantly, ignoring the beauty of a champagne-like splash of a wave on a rock, or the majestic soaring of an eagle on an updraft. His watchfulness was unsettling, his rigidity adding to her tension.

"How long have you been here?"

"A month."

Before that, he'd been missing for a year. If Amelia hadn't learned she was pregnant, she would have gone to Chile to find him. She had rightfully smelled something fishy in the fact that Jasper's employers had claimed he was dead, but refused to pay out his life insurance.

"You're protecting your family by staying under the radar," she realized.

His gaze raked her. "That's one reason, yes."

"Am *I* in danger?" She touched her chest.

"Not if no one knows we're here," he drawled.

"Only my lawyer, I swear." She held up her hand as if taking an oath. "Hunter doesn't even know what I'm doing, obviously. Otherwise, he would have told me this was not the place to ride things out."

"He doesn't know you're getting a divorce? Why not?"

She'd been afraid he would talk her out of it.

"Call me old-fashioned, but I thought my husband should be the first to know," she said ironically. "Once he receives the papers, I'll tell Hunter."

"Your *husband* doesn't know?" Jasper choked on a humorless laugh. "That's cold."

She lurched to a halt.

"You know *nothing* about my life." *She* was the cold one? Right now, sure, her voice was as frigid as the tundra during an ice age. Her heart had plunged to the bottom of a canister of liquid nitrogen, but Neal was the one incapable of basic human warmth. That was why she was walking away from her marriage and the bleak future he offered her.

Jasper stopped two paces ahead of her.

She willed her hot eyes not to well with tears of rage or, worse, the humiliation that had been such a constant companion all these years. But the deep, horrible suspicion that maybe she was to blame for the lack of love from her husband was always there, ready to choke her.

"You're right." Jasper's cheek ticked. "I was out of

line. Your reasons for divorce and how you go about it are none of my business."

Her jaw almost fell to the sand. She really was going to cry now, because at no point in her marriage had her husband ever offered anything close to that sort of personal accountability. It was always, *Don't be ridiculous, Vienna. What about* my *feelings?*

Fearful she would break down completely, she ducked her head and walked past Jasper without another word.

Ah, hell. He'd handled that poorly, hadn't he?

Women were more vulnerable than men. They were vulnerable *to* men. He knew that. Even the trophy wives he wanted to lump her in with, the ones who seemed happy to use their looks to feather their nests, were physically smaller than men. They were objectified and subjected to sexism.

For all he knew, Vienna's marriage had been abusive. He had no right to pass judgment on how or why she had chosen to leave it.

He was trying to hold Vienna at a distance, though. Trying to dismiss her as avaricious and manipulative so he wouldn't admire things like how she moved with the grace of a gymnast.

They had reached the obstacle course of driftwood between the beach and the forest. She stepped atop a log and balanced her way along, shifting to the next and the next as she worked her way up the beach. She didn't look back once, which told him how much he had annoyed her.

He followed, brooding, watching for the path back to the house in case she missed it.

They were almost there when she gave a sideways

leap to a log that had been sanded by wind and waves to a smooth, slippery finish. Her foot shot out from under her and she waved her arms, about to topple onto a pile of broken driftwood.

Jasper reacted without thought, leaping to catch her into the front of his body, giving her that extra moment to find her balance again.

It was seconds—less than five—that he held her, but the feel of her slender back and the firmness of that gorgeous ass pressing into his groin left him branded by her shape.

At best, he expected a grudging thank-you, but when he released her and she looked back at him, her expression was startled and defenseless. Her gaze traveled over him as though she was seeing him for the first time. As though she was seeing through his clothes and touching his skin. Or wanted to.

There was such earthy, sexual awareness in her eyes, such wonder when she lifted her gaze to meet his, that it struck him as a delicious punch in the stomach.

He was experienced enough to know when a woman had decided he struck her fancy. He was man enough to consider it when one did. Everything about her appealed to him. Her flowing hair glinted with sunlight. Her soft mouth and naked lips were shiny and receptive. Kissable.

Damn, but he wanted to taste that mouth. Her curves enticed his palms to gather and stroke and something intangible within her called him to a brighter place, drawing him like a flame in the night. Beckoning.

It's not infidelity if she's divorced, the devil on his shoulder pointed out.

It could happen. *They* could.

Theoretically, he corrected dryly, as she blushed with mortification and jumped to the sand, hurrying up the path to the house.

That was probably for the best. An affair with her was a terrible idea.

CHAPTER THREE

VIENNA HAD ALWAYS found an escape in art. Her only true memory of her mother's life was the funeral when she'd been laid to rest. Not even the service, but the aftermath, when a well-meaning aunt had handed her a coloring book and some crayons.

While family and guests had condoled in drab colors, speaking in heavy, somber tones around her, she had scribbled sunset orange and aquamarine against patches of vibrant violet and dusty denim. Hunter had patiently read the labels to her until she knew their names by sight, not yet able to read them herself.

She still reached for colors and patterns when she was agitated—electric lemon and fern green, smooth lines and pleasing balance. It was more than an effort to create order when her life was out of control. It was about taking something difficult and messy and finding the good in it. The beauty.

Given what she'd been through in her lifetime, she ought to be a heralded artist with several showings under her belt by now. Sadly, she had not dropped everything and picked up her sketch pad every time she was overlooked by her father or humiliated by her stepmother or disappointed by her husband. More often than not, she had channeled her emotional energy into creating a better Vienna. Her insecure self had always reasoned that she was the thing that needed work, otherwise all of those people would have treated her better.

Thus, she had learned to use a makeup palette so she appeared prettier. She had learned to accessorize a couture dress with the right designer handbag and custom jewelry. She could arrange flowers and host the perfect party and recover from whatever farce her stepmother turned an occasion into. She had learned to decorate a home so people would think her life within it was magazine perfect even when it was the farthest thing from it.

She didn't know how to gloss over what had happened on the beach, though.

Her foot had slipped. She hadn't been paying attention because she'd already been disconcerted by that man in a hundred different ways and when he'd caught her close, something had happened to her. Her skin had come alive. She'd felt so sensitized that she'd practically felt the whorls in his fingerprints against the bare skin of her arm. A sweeping sensation had flown through her, like a breeze that picked up all the brittle leaves within her, wafting them away.

The libido that had never been very strong, and which had sunk into a veritable coma through her marriage, had awakened in a blunt rush. Her lungs had gulped for air as if she'd been underwater for too long. Polarities in her blood had aligned to point at him.

He had released her, but slowly, ensuring she had her balance.

She hadn't.

Her whole world had tilted on its axis.

It had hit her that not being married meant the wide chest of a man wasn't something to admire objectively as an artist. It was something that could be attractive in a more physical sense. A carnal sense.

She didn't have carnal feelings, but he was so close, and the memory of that strong wall imprinted on her so tangibly, the memory of wanting to splay her hands across his pecs and feel him. Explore.

This welling of sensuality was so new, it had felt like a spell. As she looked up at him for an explanation, she'd been mesmerized by the glints of molten silver in his blue eyes.

Her heart had flipped over. The charged air between them shimmered, making colors more vivid, the sound of the waves more lush. When his gaze dropped to her mouth, he'd left a sensation there sharp as a bee sting.

This is desire, she had realized through her haze.

Ironically, she recognized it because she'd never felt anything like it before. She had always been convinced that movies and books exaggerated the basic physiology of arousal, but this flood of heat and awareness was exactly as had been described. A fire had been lit within her, one that softened her knees and made her throat feel tight and held her trapped firmly in the moment.

She wanted things in those charged seconds. Explicit things. His mouth. His touch. The right to touch him back and the knowledge of how his voice sounded when he was aroused. She wanted to know how he smelled and how his body would feel against hers. She wanted his weight upon her and the sensation of him thrusting inside her.

The corner of his mouth had curled with anticipation,

sending a fresh spear of white heat into the pit of her stomach.

Panic had then clogged her throat. *He knows, he knows!*

She had turned away, hurrying back here to the house, but there was no escape. She could try to get lost in Caribbean blue and prairie yellow and arctic white, but he would catch up to her eventually.

She sat on the deck off the kitchen, barricaded behind one of her new sketch pads and a fresh box of colored pencils. When she heard him come in through the door to the basement she wanted to die. Crushes were for thirteen-year-olds, not a woman finally taking the wheel of her own life.

He didn't come upstairs right away, though, and she recollected the weights she'd seen in the basement. She had a feeling she had interrupted his workout when she arrived so, when she realized he was staying down there, she relaxed and became more intentional in what she was doing.

Her goal this trip was to work on a portrait of Peyton for Hunter and Amelia. For now, she got to know her colors and paper by calling up different photos of objects that she'd loaded onto a digital picture frame specifically for this purpose.

She was soon immersed in layers of color, playing with pressure and line thickness, only to be yanked from her concentration when she heard the shower come on upstairs.

He was naked up there?

Don't think about it.

She did, though. She clenched her eyes shut, trying not to, but her artist's imagination conjured a vivid image of suds tracking through Jasper's chest hair, down his abdomen and into the crease between his thigh and—

Nope.

But now she was back to dwelling on how obvious she'd been on the beach. She wanted to duck her head into her arms and sob with embarrassment. It had been bad enough when he had acknowledged that he was judging her unfairly. That had pulled the rug out from under her, but then she'd let him see how astonished she was by her own ability to *feel*. How gauche!

The worst part was, now that those stupid feelings had been awakened, they sat under her skin like fresh tattoos, hot and livid and undeniable. She would never be able to hide them again.

The shower cut off.

She frantically swiped through her photos, trying to find something to distract her. There. Her neighbor's cocker spaniel. She forced herself to concentrate on rendering the rippled hair of his square ears and his adorable head tilt of curiosity.

It was so challenging to set those small curved strokes of caramel fur that she lost track of where she was. When the door into the house rolled open beside her, she was startled into gasping and sitting up straight, disoriented by her surroundings.

"I'm starting dinner," he said. "Would you like a glass of wine?"

"You're cooking?" His words didn't make sense. Neither did his impassive expression. Wasn't he going to laugh at her with his eyes and make her feel small for overreacting?

"Unless you prefer raw fish, but I'm no sushi chef. I

wouldn't risk it if I were you." The corner of his mouth tilted with self-deprecation.

"No…um. Thank you. Yes, please, to the wine."

She was so taken aback that she had barely gathered her thoughts, let alone her supplies, before he returned with straw-colored wine in a stemless glass. He set it on the table within her reach and turned away to start the barbecue.

"Would you like help?" she offered.

"No. You're busy."

She glanced at her sketch, catching herself before she dismissed it as unimportant. If it was important to *her*, then it was important. Or so her therapist had stressed.

Her page and pencils held little interest for her when she could watch him move with economical efficiency, though.

"What do you do while you're here?" she asked when he came back out to set the fish on the grill. "I don't mean that as a criticism," she hurried to add. "I saw your laptop, so I assume some kind of remote work?"

"That depends on how you define work." He closed the lid on the barbecue and twisted off the cap of the bottle of beer he'd brought outside for himself. "Some of it is research and reports that will serve me once I've cleared my name and can resume my life. I've been compiling evidence and putting other things in place toward that goal. Mostly I'm waiting for a certain someone to come home from international waters, so he can be arrested and held accountable."

"Who?"

"Orlin Caulfield. President of REM-Ex. If he catches

wind that I'm out of Chile and coming after him, he'll stay where he can't be touched."

"What did he do?" She hadn't liked asking Amelia too many questions about Jasper since it had always been such a painful topic for her.

He took a pull off his beer and stared into the trees, his profile like granite. The silence went on so long she decided he wasn't going to answer and looked down to her work again.

"He started by hiring me under false pretenses. Then he got my interpreter killed and has been trying to hold me responsible for it." His features flexed with anguish.

"In Chile? I'm so sorry. Was—" He? She? Did it matter if his interpreter was a man or a woman? A lover or a friend? It was obviously very painful for him. "That's tragic."

"It is." The lines of grief in his face made her hurt for him. Did he blame himself, even though he wasn't responsible? "Saqui was helping me work with the Mapuche. That's how I learned how much environmental damage was already being done by REM-Ex. I had been hired to ride point on a new project, but I raised concerns over what I'd heard and went to see the valley for myself. That's why they claim I walked away from my job site, but I was trying to help the company get ahead of a crisis. I was writing a plan for cleaning up their mess, but their response was 'What mess?'"

"The corruption was coming from inside the house?"

"Exactly. The landslide that killed Saqui was deliberate. Someone set off a charge. I want to believe they were only trying to hide their crime, not commit murder, but either way Saqui was killed." He ran his hand down his face, clearly still tortured by it.

She wanted to get up and walk over to hug him; she felt his pain so deeply, but there was an invisible wall around him, firmly holding her off.

"I was supposed to be there with him." The lines in his face flexed with fresh anguish. "I'd gone into town to email photographs and a report on what I'd seen. Saqui wanted to stay and make more notes. The site was miles away from town, but I know what it sounds like when dynamite drops half a mountain. Emergency crews went out, but they blocked the road and wouldn't let me see it for myself. I went to Saqui's family, hoping he'd turn up there."

He hadn't, obviously. Vienna felt so sick for him. So very sorry.

"REM-Ex called to tell them Saqui had been caught in the rubble and said I was responsible. They said if I wasn't buried with him, I would be arrested for negligence and manslaughter. They didn't realize I was sitting in their kitchen."

"You didn't set off the charge!" she cried.

"No. And I don't run away from my problems," he asserted tightly. "But if that's how they were playing, I couldn't risk arrest. How the hell could I clear my name from a jail cell?"

"So you pretended you had died, too?"

"Not by choice. The first few days I was in the bush, avoiding arrest, but I gave everything I had to Saqui's sister. She took it to the papers, but REM-Ex quashed it, saying it was a hoax. They said I couldn't have written it because I was dead. That was a genius move because it allowed them to cancel my documents and flag my passport if I tried to cross a border or fly. I hated that Dad and Amelia believed I was dead, but given REM-Ex had already killed Saqui, I thought it was safer for them. I didn't think this would drag on for a *year.*"

Vienna had been denigrated in many ways, but never accused of a crime. She couldn't imagine how he'd felt at that level of persecution.

"What did you do? Where did you go?"

"Saqui's family want justice for his death as much as I do. I stayed with some of his relatives, helping on their farm while we tried to get the police to investigate, but REM-Ex has deep pockets. They papered the country in a smear campaign, even pinning their environmental crimes on me, things that happened before I had ever set foot in that country! Thanks to being dead, I was locked out of my accounts and I was afraid to use them anyway. What if someone traced me? I didn't want to put Saqui's family at risk. Or Dad and Amelia. I couldn't afford to underestimate what REM-Ex would do because, even if Saqui's death was an accident, they obviously don't want it coming to light that they caused it. I make a far tidier scapegoat."

"But now you can finally get Orlin What's-his-name arrested? How?"

"The rest of my plans are classified," he said grimly. "No offense, Vienna, but I don't want you screwing up my one chance to catch the bastard who's trying to frame me."

"None taken," she lied, and dropped her gaze to Bowser's red collar.

Jasper woke at 2 a.m. Hard.

It was basic biology that celibacy and a nearby woman would put him in this state, so he ignored it. It wasn't as if she'd done anything to encourage it. Over dinner, they'd talked about incidentals—the climate in Chile and the latest season of a series they had both binged.

He'd been trying to mentally step back after talking about Saqui. Vienna's earnest sympathy had unsealed the door on his anger and grief and he couldn't help feeling she had slipped through in the same breach. It was disturbing enough he'd sought distance after dinner, plugging in his earbuds and checking on his ghost purchases of REM-Ex shares.

Perhaps she'd felt the same need to shore up because she'd gone upstairs and only come down once for a cup of tea before bed.

Not seeing her hadn't meant he wasn't aware of her. She had stayed in his thoughts when he went to bed. It should have been a welcome change from replaying old conversations with Saqui, trying to rewrite history, but he'd only tossed and turned with restless arousal.

When he did drift off, she was right there in his dreams, stepping into his arms instead of running away.

What was it about this woman? He went long stretches without female company. Hell, he had lived alone—often in the wilderness—for weeks at a time. He preferred it that way. Coming from a close-knit family didn't mean he was a pack animal. At heart, he was a lone wolf.

Which wasn't to say he didn't have relationships. They just died on the vine because of the work he'd chosen. Most people who married did so because they wanted to spend time with that person, not live alone, waiting for them to come home.

Besides, he wasn't ready to let anyone in. Saqui had been the first close friendship he'd had in a long time and

Jasper hadn't really had a choice. It had been Saqui's nature to draw people out and make jokes and bring them home to eat with his family.

He'd been young and ambitious and eager to learn everything Jasper could teach him. Jasper had seen himself in Saqui and couldn't stop hating himself for hiring him, inadvertently pulling him into something that had wound up costing him his life. The guilt at not seeing the danger, and not insisting Saqui come to town with him that last, dark day, was unrelenting.

But of all the unique minerals he'd picked up over the years, none had been a crystal ball.

Logically, he knew he hadn't caused Saqui's death, but his self-blame had gone off the scale as REM-Ex had tied his hands against revealing what had really happened. Saqui's family hadn't had any resources to seek justice on their own. They were humble farmers who'd been kept afloat with Saqui's financial help. The best that Jasper could do for them was help them navigate getting a life insurance payment—which had taken forever because it had been bought through Jasper's company and he was "dead."

The Melillas hadn't wanted money anyway. They wanted their son back. Seeing how devastated they were, and how much they missed him, ate holes in Jasper's soul.

This was the real reason he pursued a solitary life. Grief was horrific. Better to hold himself back from risking such crippling pain.

A creak in a floorboard had him lifting his head to see a faint bar of light appear beneath his door. Was that a quiet knock?

He threw back the covers and pulled his shorts over his briefs.

When he opened the door, the hallway was empty. He glanced to where the lamp glowed in the reading nook.

Vienna looked up from where she knelt before the low bookshelf. She stilled and so did he. Neither of them seemed to breathe.

The yellow light and her buttercup nightgown wrapped her in gold. He dragged his gaze from the lace that plunged between her breasts and the gathered silk that cradled the swells so lovingly.

"What are you doing?" He had to clear a thickness from his throat.

"I couldn't sleep and saw these earlier." She held up one of the historical romances.

Goodness, what could be the cause of both of them suffering sleeplessness, he wondered facetiously, even as he imagined dropping one of those strings off her shoulder and pressing his mouth to her luminous skin.

"I knew I wasn't going to turn on my phone while I was away, but I forgot to bring any books." She absently tucked her hair behind her ear as she dipped her head to read the back.

Let me, he thought, imagining the feel of that stud in her lobe against his tongue.

"The vampire one is decent." He leaned his shoulder against the wall. "The duke is dry. The pirate is filthy." In a good way.

"Oh?" The way she brightened with interest and promptly shoved the duke back on the shelf in favor of the sea blue cover of the erotic swashbuckler was adorable. "I didn't expect you would read romance."

"I don't sleep well. I've read everything in this house, trying to nod off. There's a board book in the basement about a hungry caterpillar that almost worked, but the ending got too exciting."

She chuckled and rose. "I'm pretty sure I read that one back when I was learning to read."

Her nightgown only went to the tops of her thighs. He bit back a groan.

"I'm sorry about the insomnia." Her concerned gaze was a fresh hit of pillowy softness. "Is it stress? Because of all you've been through?"

"Yeah." He was exhausted by it. Bone-deep tired. The desire to ask for solace with her was profound.

"I'll try not to get up in the night and disturb you, then."

Heh. Good luck with that, he thought as she went back into her room and closed the door.

CHAPTER FOUR

TAKING THE SEXY book was a huge mistake.

Vienna was already struggling against her attraction to Jasper. That was why she hadn't been able to sleep. She'd been thinking very wrong things about him even before she'd knelt outside his door like a concubine.

Her torrid thoughts had been made even more libidinous by a few chapters of the book he had recommended. Why did it feel like an erotic love letter to know he had read these provocative scenes and knew she was reading them now?

Soon, she had to set it aside because all she could imagine was Jasper holding *her* captive. He coerced her into performing ribald acts to prolong her life, making her kneel on the cushion he provided when he opened his breeches. She then succumbed to his strength when he overwhelmed her and pressed her onto her elbows and knees so he could cover her and thrust into her for as long as he liked…

She buried a groan of lust into her pillow, giving up on sleep entirely once light broke through the crack in her curtains.

She was outside on the deck, doing her best to metaphorically scribble over her lascivious fantasies when he yanked her out of her trance again.

"More coffee?"

"Oh!" Her jolt came less from being startled, and more from excitement. Thrill at having him near again.

He stood behind the door screen holding the carafe, impassive and polite.

This behavior of hers was so mortifying!

She belatedly tilted her empty cup. "Yes, please."

He slid the screen open and came to pour.

"Help yourself to the quiche," she invited, trying to ignore the slope of his tanned shoulders beneath the torn-off sleeves of his white T-shirt and the frayed hem of his cutoff jeans, but those thigh muscles. The fine hairs on the back of his flat wrist. His Adam's apple. Why did he have to be *so much*?

"Thanks."

He took the carafe back to the kitchen and returned with his own mug and a slice of the quiche she had made. He settled into a chair across from her, squinting against the bright, overcast sky.

"You really focus when you work, don't you?" His gaze flickered to the wide sketchbook she held.

"It's why my grades weren't the best in school. I would start doodling and, next thing I knew, everyone was turning in a quiz and all I had was a caricature of the class gerbil."

"That's not caricature. Is it Peyton?"

He had seen what she was working on? She started to tilt the pad into her chest, always protective of her work. Now that she thought about it, the urge to hide what she was doing probably had its roots in grade school, when she had got in so much trouble for drawing.

"I guess you haven't seen much of her." That thought broke her heart. She looked at the page she had filled with different profiles and expressions of a baby who was sheer perfection. Cuddling her wiggly body was the purest joy Vienna had ever experienced.

"I held her for a few minutes the one time." There was a note in his voice that was hard to place. Wistful? Homesick?

Vienna impulsively tore the page from her pad and offered it. "Since you don't have any photos of her."

He started to take it, then chucked his chin at her. "Sign it first."

To her eternal chagrin, she blushed. It wasn't good enough to *sign*, but she scrawled her name on the bottom.

"Thank you." He took it and spent way more time studying it than made her comfortable. She was about to start making excuses about how hard it was to capture the sparkle in Peyton's eye, when he asked, "Do you sell your work?"

"No," she scoffed. "I didn't even finish my art degree."

"Art isn't engineering. You don't need a diploma before you're allowed to get paid for it," he said dryly. "Especially not when you're this talented."

Talent was highly subjective.

"I haven't spent much time on it since I dropped out. Pursuing art felt... I don't know. Useless." She picked at the bits of paper that had been left behind in the spiral ring that bound the pad. "I was due to start my third year when I got engaged and everyone said, 'What will you do with an art degree? Why bother?' So I quit."

"Hunter said that?"

"No. He was the only one encouraging me to stick with it, but I thought Neal and I would start our family right away so it made sense to focus on my marriage. Or so I thought. I was twenty. What can you expect?" she joked, trying to hide how much it still pained her that she'd quit for him. For a life that had been a pantomime of things she wanted, but false and farcical at its core.

"How long were you married?"

"Six years." She could have left it there, but she was tired of maintaining an illusion that she had been in love. "It was more of a merger than a marriage." She darted a look at him, expecting him to judge her again.

He only held his expression of polite interest.

"I'm not business-minded. Not like Hunter. Our father didn't really want me there anyway. He was all about the boys' club and father-son legacy. He was pretty sexist." Horribly sexist, actually. His attitude had been that women were good for a handful of things, most of them involving the way they were plumbed. "I thought if I married to benefit the business, Dad would be happy."

"He wasn't?"

"Not particularly. But I should have known better. I should have listened to Hunter and stayed in school. He already had a connection with Dad, though. I didn't, but I wanted one. The thing I failed to realize was that *Dad* didn't want one. Not with me." It took everything she had to keep her voice even, but the unsteadiness was there, deep in her chest. "That's what I meant yesterday, when I said we'd had different upbringings."

He blinked in a small flinch, as though he couldn't imagine his father behaving so callously.

"And you don't have kids. Do you? I only mean, I didn't see anything online that suggested you had."

"No. No kids." The topic was still raw enough to catch in her throat. "Which I know people will say is a blessing once they hear we're divorced. No children were harmed by the breakdown of this marriage," she said with bitter humor. "It doesn't feel like a blessing, though."

"I stepped on a nerve. You wanted a family," he acknowledged grimly.

"I did. But I can't. I have what's called a hostile uterus."

"I've never heard of that."

"It means I can't get pregnant. Not without help." She spotted the striped, mousy shape of a chipmunk scampering in the branches of a nearby tree. She started to block it onto her page. "That worked for Neal because he didn't really want kids."

It was the first time she'd said that aloud, always keeping that hurtful truth unspoken so it sat pulsing and festering under her skin, insult to the injury of her fertility issues. It was the reason she had asked him for a divorce the first time.

"He told me he wanted a family before we married, but he's the kind of salesman who will tell you anything to close a deal." She exchanged pale ivory for almond, working fast before she lost sight of the small creature.

"After we married, he kept talking me into putting it off. 'Don't do it to make your father happy'," she quoted. "It would have made *me* happy, but mutual consent, right? Finally, he agreed to try, but a year and a half went by without success. I was devastated every month. He was relieved. I could tell."

She scratched honey and umber against the page.

"I wanted to try IVF, but he had a lot of excuses for why the timing wasn't right and he kept missing his appointments."

She didn't look at Jasper, not wanting to see his reaction. He was probably turned off by her oversharing or giving her a look of pity, but silence was one more thing she had endured for the good of Wave-Com. She was so tired of suffering in silence.

Maybe she just wanted to justify her divorce since she felt so guilty about giving up.

"I finally faced that it was better if I didn't have children with a man who didn't want them. At the time, Dad had just died and Hunter was going through a court case with our stepmother, so I didn't tell him that Neal and I were separated. I wanted to keep it out of the press anyway. I started taking curating jobs in Toronto and spent most of my time there. Neal didn't care." She reached for hickory.

"It must have felt very unfair that Amelia got pregnant so easily."

"Everything about pregnancy is unfair. Now, at least, I'll be able to find someone who wants what I want." Antique brass. "Maybe I'll do it on my own."

"Single parenting is hard."

She dropped her pencil.

"That's not the voice of experience," he said dryly, catching the pencil as it rolled across the table toward him. "Maybe it is a little." He offered it back to her.

"What do you mean?" she asked as she took the pencil.

"Dad worked shifts while I was growing up. Even when he was home, he was often sleeping off his graveyard rotation. Mom ran the show. She came across as strict, but it was necessity, especially when Amelia was little. We were solid middle-class, not struggling, but no frills, either. Dad had a union wage as a tradesman. Mom worked at the sewing shop, but she literally could not do it all, so I picked up groceries and learned to cook and walked Amelia to the dentist after school."

"How old were you when you lost her?" she asked gently.

"I was finishing high school. I had been accepted at UBC, but I couldn't leave and come all the way across the country. Dad still had to work. Amelia was eleven—not old enough to stay home alone at night—so I stayed and provided some half-assed parenting while I took courses at the local college until I could transfer to U of T."

"Geology?" she guessed.

"And geography and business. I left when Dad made foreman and started working steady days. I did a couple years in the oil patch, then the Yukon, working on my master's degree. REM-Ex like to paint me as some upstart they hired off the street, but I had been operating as a private consultant for five years by then, building my professional reputation. They don't get to take that away from me."

The deadly promise in his tone sent a shiver down her spine.

"But you were talking about your ex," he reminded. "You said yesterday that you still have to inform him? When does that happen?"

"Any day." The chipmunk was gone, so she filled in what she could from memory. "He's in and out of the office. It's a matter of the process server catching up to him."

"Will he contest it?"

"I don't see how he can. We've been separated a year. I'm agreeing to exactly what was in our prenup. And, look, I want to say I'm sorry," she blurted, lifting her gaze so he could see her remorse. "Now that I understand why you're here, I can see what a nuisance it is that I showed up. I didn't mean to jeopardize what you're doing, but this seemed like the only way. I tried to end it once and Neal threatened to make it really difficult. He'll probably still make it difficult, but this time I'm not asking him for a divorce. I'm telling him. I can't stay tied to him. I just can't." The despondency that encased her when she thought of it was absolute.

"I understand," he said quietly. "You don't have to apologize for that."

"Thank you." She started sliding her pencils back beneath their loops, but couldn't seem to make her fingers cooperate. She wound up clapping the top of the box over the loose pencils and rising. "I'm going for a walk."

It started to rain while she was changing. She put off her walk and read a couple more chapters of high-seas sex.

By the time the rain let up, she was in dire need of cooling off. Sheesh! Too bad she wasn't a petite ballerina of a woman like the heroine. Jasper was strong, but she didn't think he could brace her high on a wall with his bare hands on her butt while he stood with his head buried between her thighs.

She kind of wanted to find out, though.

"Jasper, I'm going down to the beach," she called as she trotted down the stairs.

"I'll come." He closed his laptop.

"You don't have to." She turned at the bottom of the stairs to face him at his desk. She felt as though her dirty thoughts were right there at the forefront of her mind, still warm on her cheeks. Could he see them? "I just want some exercise."

"Me, too." He rose and stretched his arms up. His gaze slid down her jeans in a way that caused the embers of desire sitting in her belly to flare hotter.

He was checking that she was dressed appropriately, for heaven's sake. That's *all*.

The temperature had dropped significantly from yesterday, now that the tail end of a rainstorm was pushing inland, drawing cool air through the wet trees. She hugged herself in her pullover as he locked the basement door behind them.

"This is a weird situation," she said as they started down the path. "I feel like we're strangers on a train, both waiting to arrive at a new place in our lives. I want to make conversation to pass the time, but we keep falling into really heavy topics."

"Where are you headed?" he asked with dark humor. "Freedom? I'm going all the way to revenge."

"Oof." That just made her feel melancholy. "What if we did meet on a train, though? And our destination was Edmonton and none of this other stuff was happening? What would you talk to me about?"

"Rocks. That's why I'm still single."

She had to chuckle at that. "Really? Well, good news. I don't know anything about rocks. Why did you decide to study them?"

"I don't even remember. Dinosaurs, I think. There was a school trip to a place not far from where we grew up that got me excited about fossils. Looking for those is like gambling. You only need to find one trilobite and you're hooked for life. I started learning how they were made and that led me into geodes and stalagmites and diamonds. Pretty soon I needed to know where every kind of rock came from."

"The universe?" she joked.

"Time," he replied. "And the power of nature. The fact I can stand here and hold something that existed millions of years ago fills me with awe." He stopped and pointed at the ground. "In some ways, it's beyond comprehension, but it also makes me realize how small I am. How little I matter."

"There is a strange comfort in that, isn't there?" she said, captured by that thought.

"What would you talk to me about?" he asked curiously.

"Oh, I wouldn't talk to you." She shook her head. "I'd be too scared."

He dipped his chin. "I admit I've been in a very salty mood lately, but none of this has happened." He flicked his hand toward the house. "Tell me about your relatives in Edmonton."

"What makes you think I have relatives in Edmonton?"

"It's not exactly a hotspot for tourism. Unless you're going there for work? That's why I went there."

"I don't know why I'm going." She hugged herself as even this silly game devolved into something more serious. "I've never taken the time to figure out who I am, so I can't tell you." Dear Lord, that sounded tragic.

"You're single?"

"On the train? Yes," she said firmly.

"Maybe you're visiting a lover." His eyelids drooped with speculation.

Her heart lurched. "I don't think so."

"Why not?"

Because then she couldn't talk to him on the way there. Not like this, with possibility beginning to sparkle on the air between them.

Was she imagining it?

She nervously licked her lips.

His narrowed gaze followed the tip of her tongue, making wanton urges seesaw in her stomach.

She nervously looked past him to where the path continued.

"We should talk about it," he said in a rumbling voice that was as low as a train car rattling over the tracks.

"What?" She flashed her attention back to his mouth and the way his lips shaped words. She pressed her folded arms to her middle, practically hunched into a ball of apprehension and yearning.

"About the fact that we're two people sharing a house, and whether that's all we'll share."

She opened her mouth, but her throat closed.

"That's not pressure or presumption on my part," he continued quietly. "Shake your head and we won't talk about it ever again."

She couldn't move. She was paralyzed with longing and fear of rejection.

For a few moments, there was only the drip of rain off the trees.

He stepped closer and watched his own finger as he scooped a tendril of hair that had fallen from her ponytail and tucked it behind her ear. His fingertip lingered on the shell of her ear, slowly tickling down to the hollow behind her earlobe and leaving a trail of fire against the side of her neck.

"*Is* it something you want to talk about?" he asked.

"I don't know how," she admitted in a strained whisper.

"Talk about? Or do?" The corner of his mouth dug in with humor while his finger traced her collarbone where it was exposed by the neckline of her pullover.

"D-do." Her eyelids fluttered at the sensation his barely-there touch was provoking. "I don't know how to be with anyone except—" She didn't want to say his name. Not right now. "I mean physically," she clarified, dying at how naked she felt. "Because I don't want to jump out of one commitment and into another, but I don't want to use you as a rebound."

"No?" All his fingers came into play as he caressed her throat. "I would love you to use the hell out of me right now."

She swallowed.

His hand cupped her throat, making her aware of how hard her pulse was pounding into his palm.

"What if it's awful? I don't want to sit across from you at Christmas dinner someday and remember how awkward this week was."

"It won't be."

"How do you know?"

Something perplexed and amused and patient sifted behind his eyes as he slid his hand to hook it behind her neck and slowly dipped his head. He barely grazed his mouth across hers, just enough to leave her lips buzzing with yearning.

Her eyelids fluttered closed and she reflexively took hold of the front of his sweatshirt, drawing him closer.

A rumble sounded. Thunder? No, it was a sound of satisfaction deep in his chest.

He continued to hold her for his lazy, teasing kisses. His mouth caught hers more deliberately. Once, twice...

She stopped breathing, aching with anticipation.

On the third pass, he shuffled his feet wider and set a heavy hand on her waist, fingers digging in. He slanted his head, unhurried while they found the right fit. She went up on her toes, increasing the pressure.

His arm went around her, then. He drew her tight against him. Secure. Then he devoured her until she was dizzy. Until she forgot that breathing was a thing and that anything beyond this seductive heat existed.

She stretched herself against him, curling her arm around his neck for balance, reveling in his hands moving over her back. Reveling in the thickness of his erection against her abdomen. She hadn't felt wanted in so long. Ever. Not really. But there was the proof. He wanted her.

She could have wept.

She kissed him back with abandon, falling into the bliss of it, distantly thinking, *This is how it's supposed to feel*.

Or not. With a rough growl, he twisted and set his arm against the rough trunk of a tree, then trapped her in the cage of it. While the exhale of the towering cedars soaked the air with their fragrance, his mouth came back to hers in a deep, lush kiss. His free hand slid over the pocket of her jeans, long fingers splayed across the cheek of her backside, wicked and thrillingly possessive as he lifted her leg, guiding her to crook her knee to his waist where he trapped it with his elbow.

Now his hips pinned hers and that fierce evidence of his desire was flush against where she was soft and yielding. He rocked in a deliberate rhythm that sent shots of gold outward to her fingertips.

This was how it was supposed to feel. Like she was ripe and ravenous and divine.

His mouth caught her wanton sobs and his tongue brushed hers. She sucked on it and speared her hands into his hair and lifted her hips into that relentless pressure that was driving her mad. Climax was always elusive for her, but she'd never been this aroused. She was so close that she trembled.

His heady kiss abruptly stopped, leaving her mouth feeling abandoned and bruised.

She dragged open her eyes, dazed, bracing for a hard clunk back to earth if she was in this alone, but he wore a flush of carnal hunger on his cheeks.

"Feeling awkward yet?" he asked in a voice roughened by lust and smugness.

"I've never felt like this in my life."

He sobered. "You should always feel like this."

A stab of inadequacy had her looking to the base of his throat.

His hot mouth swept down into the crook of her neck and he nuzzled his way back to her ear where he let her feel the edge of his teeth.

"Come back to the house with me. Let me keep making you feel like this," he whispered.

She nodded and let him draw her back up the hill.

CHAPTER FIVE

THEY ENTERED THROUGH the basement where they removed their muddy shoes. Jasper hung his wet sweatshirt
on a hook. Vienna did the same with her pullover, wa-
vered briefly, then opened her jeans. The seat was damp
from where he'd pressed her against the wet trunk of the
tree and probably stained by the moss.

He watched very closely as she peeled them off and
threw them onto the washer.

"Those are pretty." His touch was cooled by the outdoors,
so goose pimples rose on her skin as he grazed the lace
of her bikini-style undies across her hip and upper thigh.

"I—"

She sucked in her breath as the knuckles of his two
bent fingers brushed the emerald silk down the center in
a feather-light caress that made her throb.

"You do have trouble talking, don't you?" he teased
as he dragged his gaze up to hers.

All she could see was the wall of his chest and the sin-
ful tilt of his mouth and the promise in his eyes. With a
shade more pressure, he drew a firmer line in the silk.

"I—" She tried to remember what she had to say. "I
don't have condoms. I've had every test and I can't get
pregnant, but—"

"There are some in the en suite bathroom."

She suddenly whirled away from him and ran to the bottom of the stairs leading up to the kitchen.

When she stopped there and looked back, he was in the open door of the laundry room, hands braced on either side of it.

"It's like that, is it?" His voice was gritty enough to tighten her hand on the stair rail. "You'd better run, then, because I'm definitely going to eat you."

A small scream left her as she raced up the stairs and through the pantry, tossing a look behind her when she reached the kitchen.

His steps resounded with steady purpose, oozing confidence that he would overtake her.

It was a thrilling chase that had her doing something wild because she felt wild. Unfettered. There were no wrong answers today, not with him.

She skimmed the lace and silk down her legs and left them at the bottom of the stairs as she started up them.

He swore as he emerged from the pantry and spotted them.

She laughed, starting to run again, but she was looking back, so she stumbled on the stairs.

He was there to catch her, softening her landing, his strength so far outmatching hers that he turned her in a way that felt as though she did it herself. Perhaps she did. Either way, she was pressed onto her back on these see-through stairs and he was braced over her.

"I want you like nothing I've ever wanted," he told her.

The faint stubble on his chin burned as he stole a hard kiss.

"And I have *wanted*, Vienna. For the last year, I have

wanted a lot of things. All day and night, I made myself all sorts of promises if I could only get my life back. You, though... I didn't know I wanted you." His hand slid under her shirt, palming her breast through her bra while his teeth scraped the point of her chin.

"Then let's go upstairs," she urged. One stair tread was a sharp line in the middle of her back. Her foot found another so she could lift and arch, alleviating the discomfort, but he was still heavy upon her.

"What did I just tell you I was going to do?" He dragged the hem of her shirt up and slid down to kiss her stomach, then he warmed her mound with a hot breath.

She groaned and tried to bring her legs together, but he was having none of that. He set his teeth against her inner thigh in warning and shifted so he could hug her legs while he knelt on a lower tread.

"Jasper." It was darned close to the pirate fantasy and— "Oh..." she gasped, as his tongue took a long taste of her, leaving a damp stripe of yearning in its wake.

She suffered a flash of *I don't deserve this*. She was supposed to absorb pain, not accept selfish pleasure, but his palm slid up, capturing her breast again while he painted those licks of acute sensation into her center.

Maybe she would have pushed him away if he hadn't made such a noise of gratification, but he acted as though she was offering him something, instead of selfishly enjoying it. Her hands didn't know where to settle. She wound up grasping through the stairs above her to find the back edge of a step. Now she was secure and able to arch her back off the corner of the stair so there was nothing but pleasure as she offered herself, his to consume.

He feasted on her with unhurried purpose, as though

savoring her. As though the press of his finger into her was as much for his own pleasure as hers, despite the fact it made her flesh clench and quiver.

All her orgasms were self-induced. She had never been given one so generously, and suddenly she felt very vulnerable. Her thighs tried to close again, but one finger became two. The rhythm of his movement was slow and slick and drew her even closer to the edge of climax.

Her body moved of its own accord, hips lifting as she twisted in the agony of wanting him to keep pleasuring her this way while trying to maintain some semblance of herself. A bleak sense rose in her, warning that if she let herself go completely, he could break her.

The cracks and fissures were chasing her anyway, crumbling her ability to resist that final surrender. Her shivers became shudders. Her flesh clamped onto his intruding fingers and her orgasm accosted her with the force of a hurricane.

She rolled her hips as she rode out the buffeting waves, aware that the noises of abandon echoing off the rafters were coming from her, but she couldn't bite them back. This was too powerful to withstand. Too intense to bear.

Yet so very satisfying.

With her breaths still rattling her chest, she slowly relaxed.

He swept his tongue up to her still trembling abdomen, then pushed her bra cup out of the way and caught her nipple in his mouth. He lingered to draw on it, pulling forth fresh threads of need before he released it with a wet pop. Then he kissed her jaw and somehow gathered up her boneless body.

He carried her up the final stairs and into his bedroom. She was still dazed when he set her on the bed. In some belated reflex, she tugged the veil of her shirt down across the apex of her thighs.

His brow went up. The lazy heat in his expression banked. "Changing your mind?"

"No." She made herself release her shirt. "Shy."

She expected him to laugh at her. It was too late for bashfulness after that performance, but he only sent his gaze in a proprietary wander down her legs and back up to where her breasts lifted the front of her shirt.

"You have nothing to be shy about. I will happily relive that memory every time I use those stairs."

"That's what I'm afraid of."

"Why?" He slipped into the bathroom and came back with a box. He pulled a condom from it and left both on the nightstand, then popped the button on his jeans.

He was dismantling her defenses with no effort whatsoever. A kiss, a caress, a heavy-lidded look and a rumble of approval in his voice.

She had always been very good at keeping a wall between herself and other people. She offered tiny pieces of her thoughts and ambitions, her emotions and her deepest insecurities, but always on her own terms.

She was afraid she wouldn't be able to hold herself back from giving everything to him. Actually, she had just let go of far more inhibitions than she had expected to. He was shaking her to her very foundations.

She *should* change her mind, but he was stripping off his shirt and pushing his jeans down and off, taking his underwear at the same time. He straightened in all his masterfully formed glory.

A very primitive part of her admired him as he tore

open the condom and rolled it on. He was the epitome of a powerful, appealing mate, the kind who struck a sharp pang in her angry womb because it would never carry his baby. He would make beautiful babies and stick around to keep them fed while protecting them from lions and crocodiles, she just knew it.

As he came down over her, he seemed carved from golden heartwood, lovingly polished and hard, but deliciously alive.

"Still shy?" he asked as he nuzzled her temple. "Or can we lose this shirt?"

She touched his shoulder and he rolled away. She sat up and threw off her shirt, then unfastened her bra and dropped it off the edge of the bed, too.

When she sprawled herself over him, he drank in a long breath, chest lifting her while he ran his hands over her back, making her arch into him. Her legs fell open across his and she moved on him as they kissed, wanting the friction of his chest hair against her breasts.

"Bring those up to me." He cupped her bottom, urging her to rise and offer her nipples to his questing mouth.

It was blatant and again felt like a selfish move, but he seemed very happy to have her present herself this way and his attentions sent fresh arrows of need straight into her loins. She combed her fingers into his hair while he cupped and toyed with her breasts, drawing her nipples to sharp points until they were so sensitive she could hardly bear the texture of his tongue across them, but the ripple effects in her pelvis were worth it. Eager slickness gathered there until she felt hollow and lost. Until she needed the broad shape of him inside her. *Needed it.*

"Can we...?" She drew back, shifting backward and

straddling him, taking hold of his steely shape, squeezing and caressing, learning how to make his breath catch before she guided him where she needed him. *There*.

She knew he was watching her. She closed her eyes against the intimacy, but that only amplified the sensation of his broad presence invading her. She slowly—gratefully—impaled herself upon him.

Oh, that felt good.

His hands never stopped moving, tickling her thighs and shaping her hips, clasping her waist and cupping her breasts then sliding down so his thumbs could bracket where they were joined. He parted her outer folds, found the moisture where she was stretched around him and caressed it all around her inner tissues. He rolled his thumb across the knot of nerves that made her clench her inner muscles and an earthy cry of pleasure lodged itself in her throat.

She began to move on him, greedy for the friction and the plunge. He rolled his hips, meeting her each time she returned. He drove her relentlessly upward until her hands were slipping on his sweaty chest.

It's okay, she wanted to tell him. *It won't happen for me. Not like this. But you should let go.*

She couldn't speak, though. Flames of acute pleasure were licking upward through her, lashing and twisting and pulling at her. Then one strong hand clasped her hip and held her still on his thrusting hips.

She began to shake. Maybe she already was shaking, but when he slid his other hand between them and pressed his thumb firmly on that swollen knot of nerves, her vision went white. Lightning struck, making her sob.

He rolled his thumb and lightning exploded all around

her. Within her. Pleasure struck again and again with such ferocity that she didn't know if she could survive the storm. She didn't care. She was wind and rain and fire and light. She was shameless as she ground herself on him, greedy and unrestrained.

Then the world spun and he was atop her, thrusting powerfully. Whatever control he'd exerted until this point evaporated. Yet he didn't hurt her. He was near feral in his drive toward his own satisfaction. Ragged noises tore from his throat on each uneven thrust, but she only cried, "Yes. Yes." And when she opened her eyes to the lust suffusing his face, he was watching her. His teeth were bared, his hands clenched on her shoulder and hip, holding her still for his rough, animalistic claiming, but she was safe.

And wanted. *Needed*.

She had never felt so necessary. His focus told her she was his salvation and, impossibly, that knowledge caused a delicious wrenching inside her that brought her to the brink yet again.

She curled her nails against his ribs and begged, "Don't stop. Never stop."

His wordless noise was pure torture, but he kept thrusting. He didn't let go and didn't let up, not until her ragged breaths were broken by fresh cries and she was pulsing with the intense contractions of the joy he delivered so ruthlessly.

Only then did he bury himself deep and release his own shouts of triumph.

Jasper gathered his weight off her and gently pulled free, glad that Vienna kept her eyes closed because he needed a minute.

He needed a lifetime to process that. What the hell had just happened?

He rolled to the side of the bed where he discarded the condom in a wastebasket, then he fell onto his back.

Kissing her in the trees…he hadn't planned that. He had been very prepared for her to shoot him down when he floated the idea of them passing their time here with a pleasant hookup.

Maybe he had even hoped she *would* shoot him down. He loved sex, but he wasn't a horny teenager with no sense of consequence. Far from it. At that age, he had learned an indelible lesson on the responsibilities and consequences that could befall a man when he let his south pole do his thinking. As a result, he was very careful when he considered getting involved with a woman.

Getting involved with her wasn't the same as hooking up with a stranger. They would see each other again. Her concern about awkward dinners was legitimate.

But when she had asked, *What if it's awful?* he could have laughed. Their chemistry was obvious. Wasn't it?

One kiss. That was all he'd intended. He'd wanted to kiss her and show her their potential, but she had swiftly ignited, taking him right along with her into the conflagration.

That had been the most incredible sex of his life. Every point of contact with her had penetrated to his bones, awakening parts of him that had been asleep for years, long before he'd left for Chile. Places he had deliberately sanded off and forgotten about.

He hadn't expected that. He had expected physical fulfillment, obviously. Maybe a few of those awkward moments she'd been worried about since few couples got it right the first time. But that? He hadn't been able to make it up the stairs. Not without making a claim on her.

That was what had consumed him from their first kiss, though. He had never been the possessive type, but a primal need had compelled him to wipe out the memory of the previous *one* man in her life. Not for his ego. It had been more basic than that. He had needed her to be as deeply affected by him as he was by her.

Paradoxically, the more she gave herself up to him, the more he craved. Making her writhe and lose all inhibition had filled him with power and humble gratification. With hunger for more. The hunger was still there. Need. He wanted more.

What if it's awful?

What if it's unstoppable?

"I'm, um, going to go," she choked and sat up.

"Are you crying?" He sat up in a horrified lurch and caught her arm. "Did I *hurt* you?"

"No." Her feet swung off the side of the bed. She drew a pillow into her lap and hugged it. "I just feel so stupid."

"*Why?* Don't. That was really great sex, Vienna." Wasn't it? Had he been so lost in passion that he'd missed something?

"Yes, I know that, Jasper," she said with strident anguish. "And now I know how truly *awful* the sex was that I suffered through for *years*."

Ah, hell. He started to tell her he'd never experienced anything like this, either, but didn't think it would be any consolation for her. Her sorrow wasn't about the quality of their sex, but the broken dynamic of her previous relationship. The broken promises and her broken dreams.

"That wasn't on you," he reminded her.

"Yes, it was. I stayed with him! I asked him for it. I *begged* him to please make a baby with me." She hunched into the pillow and her shoulders began to shake.

He couldn't take it. He raked the covers down, then dragged her under them, spooning around her while she wept into her pillow.

Don't let him do this to you, he wanted to urge. But he only stroked her hair and pressed his mouth to her crown and held her tight.

Vienna woke alone, thank goodness. She was able to slip into her room for a quick shower.

Her skin felt every stinging drop while her cotton-headed brain formed only one thought. *What had she done?*

She didn't know how to process so much intimacy. Not just the nudity and the way she'd let Jasper touch her, or even the way she had regressed into some primitive form of herself. She had told him the worst, most miserable secret of her marriage and *cried* about it.

No one saw her cry. They denigrated her when she did.

Man up, Vienna, her father would say.

She can't take a joke, Irina would say with an eye roll.

Quit being so dramatic, Neal dismissed.

Even Hunter, with the best intentions, had always tried to fix things. *Don't cry. I'll talk to Dad.*

Jasper hadn't said anything like that. He had wrapped himself around her like a protective shell and let her drain the poison from her aching heart.

How was she supposed to come back from that sort of exposure? She couldn't! He would forever know how utterly tragic her mistakes were. How grossly she had misled herself and how pathetically she had debased herself to a man who wasn't worth it.

She had honestly believed she could have casual sex with Jasper because sex with Neal had been functional and detached. She had never loved him, not really. In the early days, when he'd been courting and charming her, she'd been infatuated and called it love. She had tried very hard to love him while trying to make their marriage work, but for a long time now, she hadn't even liked him.

As for Jasper, she didn't know what she felt. She didn't know him well enough to be sure her instinctual liking and trust were justified. She knew he valued the truth. He had principles. He was a generous lover and—this was what really made her nervous—he knew how good he could make her feel. That gave him power over her.

Remaining detached from him now would be impossible. Even as she winced in embarrassment at the memory of him taking her apart on the stairs, libidinous heat tracked back into her loins, pulsing a guilty throb where his mouth had been, wanting that again.

Stop, she begged her wicked, wanton brain.

She left the shower and dried off.

Outside, the rain had rolled back in, bringing an early dusk and a comforting patter on the roof. She dressed in three-quarter yoga tights and a cozy tunic, then made herself go downstairs.

He was cooking again. *Help.*

Why did he have to be so incredibly hot and so incredibly thoughtful? He was moving with his casual efficiency, muscles shifting beneath his jeans and a forest green Henley that looked soft enough that hugging him would make her sigh with contentment.

"Hi," she said sheepishly.

He sent her a look that was remote and inscrutable, making her heart unexpectedly swerve.

"Your divorce is in the national headlines." He reached for an empty wineglass and set it on the island. "Your phone has been ringing." He nodded at the table.

"Oh." Her stomach plummeted. She looked to where she'd left her phone with her art supplies.

"I thought you said it was off." He poured the crisp wine from yesterday into the glass and returned the bottle to the fridge.

"That's the new one," she murmured. It wasn't really a throwaway, either. It was a new-model smartphone that she had kept on and charged and *close* for this very reason. "If it's ringing, Hunter has the number. He'll want to talk to me."

This is it. It's done.

But it wasn't. Not really. She had miles to walk before it was finalized, but the bomb had been dropped. She stared at the phone with anticipation and dread.

"Are you going to tell him you're here?" Jasper sipped his own wine, expression impenetrable.

"Not if you don't want me to." She sat down on the far side of the table so her only backdrop would be the black windows behind her.

She drew a breath and collected herself, piling all her fears and misgivings behind a mask of *everything's fine*, then pressed the button.

Hunter answered on the first ring.

"—join you after I talk to her," he was saying before slamming his full attention through the screen and onto her. "Vi."

"Hi." She forced a bright smile. "What a gorgeous view." Blue-green water stretched behind him toward an island with a massive misshapen rock upon it. "How's the trip?"

"Great." He shrugged off the paradise that was Bora Bora, demanding, "Are you okay?"

"Of course." She was aware of Jasper blatantly eavesdropping and could hear him saying, *Don't lie, Vienna. I hate liars.*

"Vi." Hunter's frown scolded.

"I know. I'm sorry. I should have talked to you about it first so you weren't blindsided. Neal didn't want anyone to know we were separated, but he didn't want a divorce, either. This was the only way."

"Don't apologize. Tell me what you need from me." Hunter pitched his voice into a gruff gentleness she'd only heard once and very recently, when Peyton had bopped her brow against his chin and started to cry.

"That, actually." Vienna blinked, fighting the unsteadiness that accosted her vocal cords. "For you to tell me you're not disowning me." She tried to make it sound like she was joking, but the fear had been real. She bit her lip, unable to keep her chin from crinkling and revealing her distress.

"Never," he swore. "I'm worried about you, though. The press will come after you pretty hard and I'm not there—"

"No! This is why I did it while you were away, so you wouldn't be bothered by all of that. I'm handling it."

"You're never a bother, Vi," he insisted, in a way that abraded her nerves.

He wasn't trying to invalidate her feelings, but the net result was the same. She bit the corner of her mouth.

He looked disgruntled, as if he knew his abrupt words had stung and regretted it.

"Listen. I would be more upset if you stayed married to someone who was making you miserable." That was a nod to the person who was really to blame for how fragile her sense of self-esteem was.

Their father had stayed married to Irina despite constant scandals and affairs. She was the reason the Waverly name still went viral. She was finally out of their lives, though, remarried and living in Palm Springs, torturing some other hapless man and his family.

"Where are you?" Hunter asked. "Do you need extra security? What can I do from here?"

"Nothing. Really. The B-team will have been given my instructions. I'll check in with them shortly and I've already asked for a security detail when I head back to Toronto. For the moment, I'm perfectly fine."

"Don't go to Toronto. Stay with us. Or we could meet at the cabin. Are you in Calgary? I don't recognize what's behind you."

"I leave for Germany before you get back. Oh, you probably don't know. Quinn and Micah are getting married."

"Really." He took a moment to consider the news that Eden's best friend was marrying Eden's brother. "I could never figure those two out, but wish them well for me. Add our names to the gift."

She snorted. "I don't know if that's what the etiquette books advise, but okay."

Eden didn't seem to be holding a grudge against Amelia for destroying her wedding to Hunter, though. The one time Vienna had been able to catch up with her, Eden had sounded really happy that she had married Remy. The fact that Vienna had been invited to Micah's wedding told her Micah didn't blame her for Hunter's actions. Maybe Hunter and Amelia's well-wishes would be a nice gesture that would close out that episode once and for all.

"I'll release a statement of support right away," Hunter said, veering back to the business at hand. "Are you sure you don't want extra security right now? Where are you?" he asked again, clearly not letting it go.

"Can I keep it redacted for the moment?" She didn't glance at Jasper. "My lawyer knows where to find me if it becomes relevant. I don't trust this phone."

"This isn't a secure line, either," he grumbled, gaze lifting off screen. "And Amelia's waiting for me on the beach, so I should go. Call me for *anything*. You hear me?"

"I will. Give Amelia my love. And kisses for Peyton."

"She's covered in sand right now, so that's a big ask," he said dryly.

"I insist, then. And—" She hesitated, unable to remember the last time she'd told him this, but hearing how close Jasper and Amelia were made her wish for a better relationship with her brother. "I love you." She ran the words together.

He recovered quickly from his shock and offered a gruff, "Love you, too, Vi. I'm always behind you. I hope you know that."

"I do." She was even starting to believe it. "Bye."

CHAPTER SIX

VIENNA CLEARED HER throat after she ended the call, visibly moved by her brother's support.

Jasper brought her wine to her.

"Thanks," she murmured as she sipped.

"Did you really think he would object to your divorce?" He was still astonished by that.

"No?" She grimaced. "Hunter has never let me down, but he's deeply invested in the company, emotionally and financially. He fought hard to pry Irina's fingers off it and is still repairing the damage she did. I've always seen my role as support. I'm supposed to make things easier for him, not harder."

By staying married to a man who had lied to her about one of the basic building blocks of marriage...? Either you wanted children or you didn't. There was nothing wrong with either choice, but partners had to agree because there wasn't much room for compromise in a game changer like that.

"I should check in with my PR team. It's a secure connection, don't worry."

He waved at her to go ahead and went back to the lemon pesto chicken he was throwing together.

When he'd woken with her in his arms, he'd still been

reeling from how profoundly she was affecting him. He was a normal person who cared about people in an abstract sense. He wanted human rights for all and a clean planet and regularly gave to crowdfunding and emergency response charities and blood donation clinics. He would help an old lady cross a street, but the only people he really cared about—the people he would take a bullet for—were his father and sister. And niece, obviously. Saqui's family, too, he supposed.

He was starting to feel protective of Vienna, though, which didn't make sense given how recently he'd met her. He had been tempted to stay in bed with her, not simply for the sensation of her naked warmth snug against him, but because he wanted to *know* she was safe and warm and comforted.

Disturbed by that realization, he had slipped away and come downstairs, where his idle glance at the headlines had jolted him.

She hadn't been wrong to hide from the coverage. That had been his first thought. He'd been skeptical of the lengths she'd gone to, escaping to a secret home and having her husband served his papers in her absence. It had seemed like a lot of subterfuge for something that was fairly routine in this day and age.

Not for a Waverly, apparently. The headlines were disgustingly sensationalized, none of them flattering or empathetic to a woman who simply wanted to leave a bad relationship. Notably, her husband wasn't vilified. He was barely mentioned. No, she was the focus and it was all slanted to tear her down.

Appalling as those stories were, there had been a part of him that was relieved to see her divorce made public, given he'd left her sleeping in the bed they'd wrecked. It was that primitive possessiveness rising in him again.

She's not his. That man doesn't deserve her.

And you do? a cynical voice asked him, deep in his psyche.

A chill wafted through his chest and he dismissed it. Vienna had made clear that she wasn't looking for another committed relationship. He wasn't in a position to offer one, either, so this affair—light and temporary— was a win-win.

If his circumstances were different, though...

They weren't, he reminded himself. He was fighting to get his life back and she was clawing her way into a new one. The broader question was, would this affair continue now that she was facing all she did?

"No, I don't need to hear what they're saying," she said with a strained smile. "I can imagine."

"Okay, but the fact that no one's seen you is becoming a story of its own," a woman on-screen was saying. "My concern is that Mr. Briggs might dox you."

"Neal has no idea where I am," Vienna said confidently. "Continue with the statements about requesting privacy and release whatever Hunter sends you. I hate to wish anyone ill, but isn't there a politician with his nose in the trough whose exposure could take some heat off me?"

The other woman laughed. "I'll see what I can find."

They signed off and Vienna released a shuddering breath. For one second, her expression was both haunted and hunted. How had he seen her as shallow? She felt things very deeply. She was too damned sensitive for a marriage based on business. Had no one seen that? Why hadn't anyone tried to stop her? Why hadn't Hunter?

She glanced self-consciously at him, then straightened her face and shoulders and spine.

"Everything's under control," she assured him with a bland smile. "Can I help with dinner? It smells delicious."

"No, it's ready if you are."

The food was delicious, but Vienna could hardly swallow. The silence between them felt thick and heavy. Sticky as tar.

When she found the courage to lift her gaze, she found Jasper watching her over the tilt of his wineglass.

The lump of food in her throat turned to stone. She washed it down with her own wine.

"I can't imagine what you think of me," she said in a voice scored by the tang in the wine.

"I think you're someone who wants more for herself and I can't help admiring that you're going after it, despite what you're up against."

"Really?" She searched his flinty expression, finding it far easier to believe that he would look down on her than up. "I thought you'd be wishing you'd never met me." *Or touched me. Or held me.*

All they'd done rushed back into her thoughts, making her cheeks sting.

"Not at all. But I can't help wondering if you'll wish you hadn't met me, once the dust settles." Something shifted behind his eyes, too indefinable for her to properly catch. "I'm happy to be your port in a storm, but I don't want to take advantage of you during a vulnerable time."

Her heart took a leap and a dip.

"I'm not vulnerable." She reflexively rejected any

label that suggested she was weak. She couldn't afford to be. Ever.

His brows went up, skeptical. Was that slow blink of his patronizing? Pitying? The way he was focused on her gave her the sense he saw right through her. Almost as if he saw her more clearly than she saw herself. It was disconcerting.

"Vi. Can I call you that? I like it." He set his glass aside.

She nodded jerkily, even though it was a short form only people very close to her were allowed to use.

"I want you to be honest with me. I really do. But if you choose not to be, I can't stop you. Be honest with yourself, though."

She sucked in a breath, one that entered her chest like a blade. Inexplicably, fresh tears arrived behind her eyes.

"You told me today that you don't know who you are. Start by acknowledging what's true. You're not hiding here because you're a coward. You've made a really tough decision to leave the life you had, knowing you'd be attacked for it. You're *vulnerable*. If you can't acknowledge that, then I'm definitely taking advantage of you."

She was so disconcerted by his assessment she could have sobbed.

"I'm not allowed to be vulnerable," she said on a soft cry. "I'm not allowed to be anything." Didn't he realize that?

That was the crux of it, though, wasn't it? She had spent her life trying to be what she thought others wanted her to be, rarely letting her true self into the light. When she had, she'd been mocked for it.

"What if you don't like who I am?" she asked in a near

whisper. She couldn't take that kind of rejection. That was why she wore all these layers, so the scoffs and dismissals weren't really a rejection of *her*. She definitely couldn't take that depth of rejection from *him*.

She had already revealed a lot to him, though. Things no one else knew. And he was still here, saying that he wanted to be her port in a storm.

"I want…" Oh, it was hard to give voice to her desire. It was an even greater risk now than it had been a few hours ago, when she had still thought she could have a fling with him and keep possession of herself. That wasn't possible at all now. She knew that, but she still wanted to be with him. If he rebuffed her after she worked up the courage to say so, she'd be crushed.

She tried to swallow, but her throat was too dry.

"I'm really scared," she admitted. "All I could think about was getting out of the cage, not realizing how much protection those bars offered. If I were here alone right now, I would be drowning in bleak terror. Maybe I would have lost my nerve and not gone through with the divorce. But you're here and…and you're showing me what I can have if I believe I deserve it. I really want to keep sleeping together. If you do."

The blue in his eyes turned to the heart of a flame.

"I do. I very much do."

Jasper had never taken ayahuasca, but making love with Vienna had to be what a hallucinogenic trip felt like. His senses were acute, making each touch and moan and taste that much more intense.

Vienna was right here with him, the connection between them exactly that: a connection. They occupied a plane of synchronicity where she seemed to know that the swirl of her tongue exactly *there* was precisely what he needed. That the sweep of her hair across his stomach would both soothe and incite him. She knew when it was time to roll beneath him with exquisite welcome because he was going to die if he wasn't inside her.

This was life at its most basic. Everything made sense when he was thrusting into her, lost to the magnificent, addictive madness. Her orgasm was swift and sharp and so powerful, it could have been his own.

He dragged her fist from his hair and scraped his teeth on the heel of her palm, waiting for her eyes to flutter open before he sealed his mouth over hers again, all of him screaming at himself to capture and conquer and *keep*.

He couldn't. The sheer power of this desire for her told him they were a dangerous combo, but he couldn't get enough of her. Even as her lips softened and parted beneath his, he withdrew so he could feast on the banquet of her.

"Where are you going?" She clawed at him, grimly sweet in her panic.

"Here," he rasped, sliding down so he could worship her breasts. "Everywhere."

Soon she would leave and he wouldn't have this. The sense of a clock ticking made him urgent and greedy. Demanding. He ran his mouth everywhere on her trembling body, until she was once again making those helpless noises that sent pleasurable shivers down his back.

"I can't bear it…" she gasped.

"What's wrong?" he crooned, rising over her again,

cupping her cheek and pressing a tender kiss to the corner of her mouth.

"I need you inside me. So much." There was something chagrined in her pleading gaze.

"Take me, then."

Her hand slid between them, guiding him to sink back into her.

He shuddered with pleasure. His heart began to slam in his rib cage. He wanted to envelop her. Crush her. A flood of thick heat threatened to burst from him as he plunged into her molten core once more, now with more power. More need.

This isn't real, he insisted to himself.

Their response to each other was heightened by their isolation and their strange circumstances. They had been thrown into the same lifeboat and were clinging to each other out of desperation.

But when her nails curled against his skin and her breath broke, when her thighs clamped to his hips and she clenched around him like a fist, he reached the limit of his self-discipline. He abandoned control and thrust unevenly, taking her with him as he launched them both into oblivion.

Jasper swore, stiffening atop her even while Vienna was still enjoying the floaty afterglow.

They'd come back to bed after breakfast—or rather, she'd been admiring his physique while sketching him and he'd swooped the way a raptor snatches up a bunny. She still felt as though she was soaring.

He wasn't so mellow, though. He withdrew with less

than his usual tenderness, setting an apologetic touch on her thigh when she flinched.

"What's wrong?" she asked.

"The condom split."

"Really? How old are they?"

"I never checked. I should have." His expression was grim as he shifted to sit on the side of the bed while he discarded the broken latex.

He stayed there gripping his knees, profile forbidding.

"Jasper." She touched his spine. "I can't get pregnant," she reminded, not bothering to hide the anguished pang in her throat. He knew this about her, the longing and the disappointment. It was who she was. "I've had every test you can imagine. There's nothing for you to worry about unless...?"

"I had a physical before I went to Chile. I haven't been with anyone except you." He looked over his shoulder, brows lowered in consternation.

"Then it's not a problem. Is it?"

He didn't look reassured, but his hands relaxed slightly. He restlessly swept them up and down his thighs as he looked forward again. "No. I guess it's not."

A cool breath of premonition lifted the hairs on the back of her neck. She opened her mouth, not sure what she needed to ask, but he rose abruptly.

"I'm going to shower."

He didn't invite her to join him, she noted with a pang, so she didn't follow him. She went to her own room, pensive as she pulled on a sundress.

This affair was thrilling and wonderful and *temporary*, she reminded herself. It needed to remain a physical thing, not become an emotional relationship. Not deeply emotional, anyway. Jasper could easily take over her life if she let herself fall for him.

She probably would anyway, she realized with a wobbly sensation inside her. She was already wondering if he would ask her to come back here after she went to Germany. He hadn't said anything more about his plans for Orlin Caulfield and REM-Ex, but it was very clear that he would lie in wait as long as he had to. It bothered her that he was here all alone.

She wondered if there was anything she could do for him while she was away. She would have to ask him because people like Micah Gould and Remy Sylvain were as well-connected and powerful as Hunter. Maybe they could help.

A crunch of gravel outside had her dropping her hairbrush to peek out the window she had left open to let in the night air.

An SUV parked where the late morning light penetrated the trees and painted the driver in dappled spots as he stepped from behind the wheel.

Neal? What the hell!

She could hear the water still running in the en suite, but didn't yell to Jasper, not wanting Neal to hear her talking to anyone. She flew down the stairs, rushing out the front door to meet her ex on the walkway to the front doors.

Neal Briggs had the handsomeness of a man with wealth—not classically good-looking, but polished and tailored to highlight his assets, the primary one being his money. His gym membership went mostly unused, but he skied and golfed to keep his weight down. He saw his barber monthly, paid his dentist to keep his teeth white, and kept his jaw shaved clean. He bought a new suit every season, but today was dressed casually in knee-length shorts and a green polo shirt with a designer logo on the pocket.

"Hello, darling." He removed his aviator sunglasses in a move she was sure he'd been practicing since seeing his first action star do it, back when he was twelve.

"How did you find me?" she demanded.

"My heart led me to you, of course." He spoke through a grimly satisfied smile.

She had never been afraid of him. He was a man who got what he wanted by saying what he had to, but she faltered briefly as she realized he was incredibly angry.

"I'm serious." She stood taller. "I want to know how you found me. Did Steven tell you?" If so, Hunter's assistant was very freaking fired.

"Mr. Chow remains loyal to the crown, don't worry. No, I bought some handy little stickers last year. They help you keep track of things that are easily misplaced." Neal held up his phone.

"You *tracked* me?" She had removed a tile tag from her keychain before coming away, but it hadn't occurred to her to go through her luggage or purse looking for devices that Neal might have planted. Her brain exploded over how invasive this was. "That is stalker level awful, Neal."

"Relax," he scoffed. "I wouldn't have had to use them if you had told me where you were going, would I?"

"I don't have to tell you where I'm going! We are separated. *Divorcing.* Kindly get back in your car and drive out of my life or I'll call the police."

It was a bluff. Her thoughts immediately leaped to

Jasper. She couldn't actually call the police. That would risk exposing him.

Neal saw her falter and snorted, mistaking her hesitation for a lack of mettle.

"Nice try, but we are not divorcing, Vienna. We had a good thing going with living apart and I'm willing to continue that, after our very public reconciliation, of course. Let's go inside and talk about how this will play out." He crowded up to her, trying to scoop his arm behind her back to bring her with him toward the front door.

She shoved his hands off her, pushing away and coming up against the rail on the walkway. Her reaction only allowed him to slip right by her into the house.

"Get. Out," she demanded.

"Who rented this place for you?" He glanced at the desk where Jasper's laptop sat closed and charging. "Chow? Hunter? I couldn't find anything on your credit card statement."

"*My* card?" She had opened new ones and hadn't used their joint accounts in months. "How do you even have access to that?"

He sent her a pitying look over his shoulder. "I know your mother's maiden name and the first concert you attended."

Ugh. All those times when he'd actually seemed to be interested in her had just been a fishing expedition?

"I'll tell my lawyer about this." She was growing more revolted by the minute at how closely Neal had been monitoring her activities. She was also sickly aware of Jasper upstairs. What if he started rattling through drawers and Neal heard him?

Neal looked toward the kitchen and paused.

"That's two coffee mugs." He swiveled his gaze the other direction. "And a pair of really big shoes." Slowly he lifted his gaze to the top of the stairs. And went very still.

Vienna's insides congealed.

With horror, she watched Jasper's bare feet appear through the peekaboo stairs, unhurried as he descended into the cesspool that was her dissolving marriage.

CHAPTER SEVEN

As HE STEPPED from the shower, Jasper heard the chime of the front door opening. Voices. Vienna sounded angry. Distressed.

He stepped into a pair of shorts and yanked up the fly, hearing her cry, "You *tracked* me? That is stalker level awful, Neal."

Neal? A ball of hatred coalesced in his gut.

"I'll tell my lawyer about this." The shaken edge on Vienna's voice took him to the top of the stairs in time to see a crisply dressed man halt below and take note that she wasn't alone.

Jasper's plans for Orlin Caulfield and REM-Ex, delicate as a house of cards, flashed in his mind's eye as he met the affronted gaze of Vienna's ex.

"Who the hell are you?" Neal asked as Jasper descended the stairs, shirtless and shoeless and never breaking eye contact with this A-grade piece of garbage.

Was he infuriated that his plan for justice was suddenly in grave jeopardy? Oh, yes. But he wasn't going to leave Vienna to face this jackass alone.

"Everything all right, Vi?" Jasper paused on the bottom step.

"You didn't have to come down. Neal is leaving." She

was clinging to her elbows, cheekbones standing out like tent poles holding up the distressed hollows of her cheeks. Her pleading eyes said, *I'm sorry.*

"Wow." Neal shoved his hands in his pockets, looking between them while wearing a calculating expression. "I genuinely didn't think you had it in you, sweetheart. You do recall there's an adultery clause in our prenup? Big brother put that in."

"I remember." Vienna's chin came up. "I remember why, too."

"*I* have stayed faithful since our wedding." He set a hand on his chest as though insulted she would suggest otherwise. "You can take that to the bank. Actually, *I* will, since you haven't."

"You can't claim adultery when we're separated," she said crossly.

"We'll see if the courts agree."

"Oh, go ahead. Run up the lawyer bills!" She flung her hand in the air. "I don't care."

"But what will the *papers* say?" He was enjoying toying with her. Jasper could see it and wanted to punch that smug glee right off his face.

"She didn't leave you for me," Jasper said flatly. "She simply left. *You.*"

Neal didn't know what to make of that. His jaw worked as he held Jasper's stare, then his eyes narrowed. "I know you."

And there it was. Vienna had said he was in sales. People successful in that field tended to remember faces and names.

"You're Amelia's missing brother."

The pyramid of cards began to topple.

"That's going to play *really* well with the shareholders," Neal said to Vienna. "You left your husband for an affair with your brother-in-law? The one who's on the run for...what the hell is it you've done?"

Jasper stepped off the stair and would have stomped on Neal's foot if the other man hadn't stumbled backward in fear.

"Touch me and that's assault," Neal stammered.

"You came into this house uninvited. You're making threats against the occupants. I think it would be ruled self-defense. Would you like to find out?"

Neal curled his lip, but he had the heart of a coward. With fading bravado, he edged toward the door.

"I'll leave you lovebirds." He sent a smarmy smile at Vienna. "Buckle up, darling. It's going to be a bumpy ride."

As he walked past her, she spat two words that were not very ladylike, but under the circumstances, completely appropriate.

Shaken, Vienna watched to be sure the SUV left, then turned back to see Jasper wearing a thunderous expression.

Her stomach rolled sickly.

"He put trackers in my things." She couldn't even begin to imagine where all she would have to look. Luggage? Makeup? "That's criminal, isn't it?"

Knowing Neal, he would claim it had been a husbandly gesture, that he was tracking property, not her. She doubted it would go very far with law enforcement, but her skin was crawling.

"You didn't have to come down," she continued as

Jasper's forbidding silence plucked at her overwrought nerves. "Let him see you, I mean. I could have…" She didn't know what she could have done. Picked up her keys and left? What if Neal had walked through the house and met Jasper upstairs anyway?

She had been so confident last night when she'd told her team that Neal had no idea where she was! All that careful planning and, instead of avoiding a feeding frenzy in the press, she'd made it worse. For both of them.

"He'll dox me. He might be posting something right now. We can't stay here." She could have cried. An hour ago, they'd been making love. Happy. "I'm so sorry, Jasper."

"So am I," he said grimly.

It's not my fault, she wanted to cry. Wasn't it, though? If she had just stayed in her suffocating little box of a life, not reaching for more, she wouldn't have caused him to be discovered. She'd ruined his plans. His life could be in danger!

"I have to make some calls," she said, lurching into damage control by searching for her phone. If she hurried to clean up the mess she'd made, maybe Jasper wouldn't hate her so much. "I have to inform Hunter and my lawyer. I'll ask the B-team to make a statement right away. We only have one chance to get ahead of whatever Neal might say. We'll say he's making more of this than it is," she asserted, having played the spin game many times with her stepmother's antics. "Relatives are allowed to stay in the same holiday house. There's nothing more between us than casual acquaintance."

She'd left her phone outside on the deck.

When she came back in with it, Jasper hadn't moved.

He looked even more severe than he had when she'd first turned up here as his unwanted houseguest.

"I'm—" She had to clear a catch of dryness in the back of her throat. "I'll have my team arrange flights and security for us."

The adrenaline in her system ought to be making her feel stronger and faster. Fight. Flee! Instead, her arms and legs were growing sluggish and heavy. Her brain was turning to mush, sinking into a swampy darkness so she had to fight to keep breathing.

As Jasper stood there looking like he was cast in bronze, still and cold and hard, she heard her presumption in that word "us".

A tearing schism left her split and off-center. Her heart was on the floor as she hugged herself defensively.

Don't be needy, she scolded herself. She'd known they didn't have a future and this was why. She was a liability. The sex had been sex, nothing more.

"I feel responsible for breaking your cover," she said shakily. "I would like to mitigate the damage if I can. Tell me what you need and I'll have my team provide it."

His reply was a choked noise that could have been insult or lack of trust or sheer disbelief at how thoroughly she had compromised him.

She swallowed, but the hard lump in her throat remained.

"If you would prefer to do your own thing..." *Then I will feel like a discarded piece of trash.* She would *look* like trash, once Neal went public with his infidelity accusations.

Why did Jasper have to be her brother-in-law? It was *so* sordid. She wanted to curl up in a ball, but that was never an option. No, her dirty laundry always had to be on the line for all to see. Her only option was to walk forward through the gauntlet of shame. Again.

"Call Hunter," he said gruffly. "Make sure Amelia and the baby are protected. I'll call my father and make my own arrangements."

She didn't blame him for distancing himself, she really didn't, but she felt steeped in poison as his words filled her ears.

She nodded jerkily. "I'll leave as soon as possible."

She was gone thirty minutes later.

Jasper told himself that was good. His preference was to navigate this alone, as he had done for most of his adult life. It wasn't because he didn't want to involve himself in Vienna's divorce drama, although he didn't—yet he already had, he acknowledged grimly. Not that he had any regrets in how he'd handled Neal. If anything, he hadn't been hard enough on him. He should have scared him off for even glancing at Vienna ever again.

No, his far greater concern was that a public acknowledgement of their involvement could put her in the same jeopardy he and his family faced. He had already been thinking they should deny their relationship and part ways as quickly as possible when she had said, *There's nothing more between us than casual acquaintance.*

That had slid with unexpected abrasion across a very old wound, one that shouldn't still be so raw, but was.

In those seconds, as she offered to put her *team* at his disposal, as if he couldn't afford his own flight and security detail, he'd flashed back to a very well-dressed woman in a Lexus pulling up beside him as he was doing cart returns at the grocery store. She had introduced herself as his girlfriend's aunt and offered an upscale shopping bag with string handles. It had contained his hoodie, his favorite book on mineral identification, and the empty keychain that read *Sweet*, matching the fob on his own keys that read, *Heart*.

Your things, the woman had said. *Annalise is staying with me while she finishes school.*

But what about—?

His heart had thrust itself into his mouth.

She's seen the broader picture of her future. It doesn't include becoming a mother right now. Or you. Don't contact her.

Her body, her choice. Jasper had respected that. Given the still fresh loss of his mother and his crushing responsibilities to his father and sister, he'd been in a panic as to how he would also support a partner and a baby, but he felt no real comfort in having all of that yanked away. Especially not when the disdain in that woman's face left him feeling so inadequate and unworthy.

Her future doesn't include you.

Like he was some kind of war criminal. Annalise hadn't changed schools to avoid gossip. She hadn't wanted to see *him*.

And there was Vienna dismissing their relationship just as dispassionately, now that her association with him had consequences.

With bile sitting in the back of his throat, he had carried her bag to the garage and nodded curtly when she said goodbye.

He didn't dwell on her abrupt departure. He had his

own vehicle and his own crisis to manage, which was where he forced his thoughts to turn.

After a brief call to his father, warning him to take precautions, he called his lawyer to advise that he was moving his timeline up. He might not catch Orlin Caulfield in his net, but he could still snag a lot of slippery fish.

He packed as he made his next call, requesting his financial advisor reactivate all his accounts. Most of his holdings had been moved into trusts while he'd been missing. Amelia had been able to do that much, which had turned out to be a genius move, protecting his crypto balance when the rest of the world's had crashed.

He'd been using some of those funds to buy up REM-Ex shares under a shell company, but that was hardly the extent of his investments. Jasper had always had a leg up when it came to reading a feasibility study for a mining venture. He'd been growing his portfolio from his university days and could easily leverage what he held into whatever cash he might need for a flight. Or to purchase a private jet, if it came to that.

Vienna didn't know what kind of resources he had at his disposal because he hadn't told her. His father and sister probably didn't even know the extent of it. He preferred to live simply, rather than throw his money around, but he had plenty of it. That early experience of not being good enough had driven him to work hard and prove he *was* good enough.

Then Orlin Caulfield had cut short the life of his friend as if Saqui was unimportant. He'd tried to sacrifice Jasper in the same way, all to hang on to his own riches.

Jasper loathed that level of arrogance and kind of despised himself that he had felt so compelled to rise—

sink?—to the same affluent level. At least it meant he could make Orlin choke on his misapprehensions.

Or could have, if he'd been able to wait until Orlin was back. *Damn it.*

His last sweep of the house for his own belongings took him outside where fat raindrops had begun to plonk on Vienna's sketchpad.

Stand there, she had insisted this morning—had it only been this morning?

He'd watched the dreamy look that transformed her face as she moved her pencils, fluidly exchanging one color for another, bringing her gaze back to him again and again.

It had been erotic, standing there unmoving while her eyes traveled over him so thoroughly. When he was so hard he couldn't stand it, he'd stolen the pad from her hands and carried her up the stairs.

He was making more of their affair than it was, likening their lovemaking to a drug trip that had left him fundamentally altered. They'd come together at a time of heightened pressure. Releasing that pressure had felt inordinately good. *That's all.*

He studied her sketch. It was undeniably good, but unsettling. Revealing, even, which caused an itch behind his sternum. It was him, but it was an image of himself he didn't recognize. Had he really packed on that much muscle? He wasn't one to preen in front of a mirror, especially once he'd seen how wasted he'd been after a year of trading farm labor for meals and a bed.

He'd been eating three squares since arriving here and worked out downstairs every day, mostly to relieve tension and try to exhaust himself toward sleep. He hadn't noticed that his T-shirt was sitting so snugly against his skin, though.

The perspective against the rail, with the treetops below and behind him, made him seem bigger than he was. Her faint blocking lines gave him the suggestion of an invisible suit of armor, too, increasing the impression that he was strong. Powerful.

It was strange to see himself like that when he'd spent a year feeling like quarry, hamstrung and outgunned.

This was the ambitious man he'd been before he'd left for Chile, the one who had been confident in who he was, but it exposed how he'd also become harder. Hardened.

A splat of rain landed on the pensive line of his mouth, snapping him out of his introspection.

He took the pad and pencils into the house, thinking to leave them on the table, but when he carried his things out to the garage, the sketchpad was among them.

One week later, Jasper stood outside the REM-Ex boardroom, flicking through his phone while he waited for the board to assemble themselves.

"What you're seeing are the actions of a disgruntled ex," Vienna had said of Neal's accusations when she held a press conference shortly after she had left Tofino. "I can't and won't speak for Mr. Lindor except to confirm that he and I were staying in the same summer house for the same reason. We both wanted privacy during a difficult time."

Neal had then gone ahead and revealed Vienna's infertility. According to Amelia, Vienna had promptly lashed back by having Neal fired from Wave-Com for breaking a nondisclosure agreement regarding family privacy. He'd lost all his perks in one swoop, including his condo, company car, and cell phone.

Jasper was grimly proud of her for going full scorched earth on the bastard.

Now she was in Germany, where photos were emerging of her at a lavish wedding. It was held at some fancy palace hotel and every snapshot showed her smiling and beautiful. Different. She wasn't the woman who had padded barefoot through the house, hair in a low ponytail, face clean of makeup. She wore elegant gowns and diamonds in her ears. A man in a tuxedo—Remy Sylvain, the caption read—stood with his arm around her while they beamed at each other with unmistakable affection.

Not his business, Jasper assured himself, clicking off his phone and ignoring the churn of gravel in his gut.

Vienna had moved on. Fine. He had no quarrel with that. They'd made no promises to each other.

But it ate at him.

"Sir? Everyone is present," his new executive assistant informed him.

Not everyone. Orlin Caulfield, President of REM-Ex, was beaming in via video conference along with a handful of other board members. He scoffed the second Jasper was introduced.

"*You're* Keady Holdings?" Orlin said of the company Jasper had formed on his return to Canada. "I knew something was off when I couldn't find anything about the company that's been buying up our shares these last weeks. This is not an acquisition offer, gentlemen. It's an HR dispute. Meeting adjourned."

"This *is* an acquisition offer," Jasper said firmly, not

bothering to take a seat. "Since the board is legally required to consider all serious offers, stick around."

"How serious could you possibly be?" Orlin scoffed.

Jasper named a share price that had everyone sitting up and looking at one another.

"The shareholders will want to hear about that, won't they?" Jasper said knowingly. "I'm not attaching a lot of strings, either. My only condition is an environmental audit going back for the last five years. And an independent investigation into Saqui Melilla's death."

Figuring out who were the rats on this particular ship was as easy as watching which faces turned to stone. A couple of the remote screens went black.

"This is a stunt," Orlin charged. "You're about to find yourself in the middle of a very grave safety violation. One that could end in criminal charges."

"No, Orlin. You are." Jasper leaned on the table and looked at the ring of uncomfortable expressions around him. "I strongly suggest the board remove this liability from the helm. Immediately. If you don't, I will fire him the minute I'm in charge. I assume that those of you with nothing to hide will support my takeover and the ensuing investigations. As a one-time offer, I will allow anyone worried about what might crawl out from under a rock to quit the board, sell your shares to me, and flee to a country without extradition agreements. Those who want to fight me had better have the capital to back up the legal bills. I sure do."

He could see the bluster bleeding out of everyone as he spoke. They were all looking to each other and casting uncertain glances at the stony-faced Orlin.

"Do we need a special resolution?" Jasper pressed. "All

in favor of selling the company to Jasper Lindor, raise your hand. I think that's two thirds, isn't it?" He said to his assistant as they counted the votes. "Bring in the rest of my team. Let's close this deal."

CHAPTER EIGHT

VIENNA HAD BEEN home from Germany for more than two weeks, but couldn't seem to shake her jet lag.

She'd been going through a lot, she reminded herself. It was natural that she would have a hard case of the blues, but she had weathered bad press and bruised feelings before. This was different. She was heartsick over Jasper and the way things had ended between them.

He seemed to have landed on his feet. In a press conference he declared, "Given how my friend and interpreter, Saqui Melilla, was killed, I feared my own life was in danger. Now that I'm back in Canada, I'm looking forward to working with REM-Ex to find who was really responsible for Saqui's death and hold them accountable."

With that hand grenade thrown firmly back into REM-Ex's court, Jasper had proceeded to *buy the company* in a hostile takeover, forcing an independent investigation, the kind they should have performed in the first place. According to reports, he'd been an early adopter of cryptocurrency and had quietly made a fortune that he had rolled into mining investments through the years. The REM-Ex board approved his purchase and installation as president *because* he was revealed to be so successful in their field.

Orlin Caulfield was ousted without ceremony and was quoted as being "very concerned" and "cooperating fully." He was also still out of the country. Vienna knew it must gall Jasper that the man was literally getting away with murder.

And whose fault was that? *Hers.*

With a whimper, she threw her arm over her eyes where she lay on the couch.

The guilt was killing her, but it was exacerbated by the knowledge that Jasper would never forgive her for ruining his plan. If they had managed to keep their relationship under wraps, they could have at least parted as friends. Maybe, at some later time, they might have come together again, but that was never going to happen now. She doubted he would so much as give her the time of day.

She was so mortified and agonized over what she'd done, she couldn't even face him. Amelia had invited her to come visit and Vienna had demurred, making excuses because she knew Jasper was living in Vancouver. She didn't want to see him.

She didn't want to see his antipathy and blame up close where it would be undeniable and real.

It wasn't supposed to be like this! They had agreed to a harmless fling. Not something that would torture her to the depths of her soul forever.

The little she had read on relationships after divorce claimed they were often very intense and sexual and also that they stung like hell when they ended. She might have believed this was nothing more than a textbook case of rebound melancholy, but the way she felt went beyond the emotions that were forming a bleak aura around her.

She was exhausted. Anemic, maybe. Her stomach wasn't quite right, either.

She had tried to dismiss it as stress-related, but yesterday, her divorce had been finalized. She had signed the papers and Neal was out of her life for good. She ought to be over the moon.

Maybe she needed to see a doctor. Given her travel and stress, she had probably picked up a virus. Maybe she'd been bitten by a deer tick when she'd been hiking through the woods in Tofino. Maybe a mosquito had given her some new exotic fever.

Ugh. She hated the idea of doctors so much. The mere thought of making an appointment gave her trauma flashbacks to all those invasive procedures trying to address her fertility issues. The last thing she wanted was to get poked or prodded or patronized again.

Wait.

She sat up so fast, her head swam. Her stomach twisted in hope and dread before she had fully done the math on her last cycle.

She dropped her head into her hands, trying to think through her ricocheting thoughts.

Her last one had been before Tofino. Two weeks before. She clearly remembered having a horrific backache when she went to see her lawyer. That date had been one year on the dot from when she had begun living away from Neal, marking the required year of separation.

It's not possible, she reminded herself. Doctors had said so. More than one.

But it was—technically—possible. The condom had broken.

No. Being pregnant right now, by Jasper, would be a

disaster. He had been upset by the broken condom. He hadn't wanted the risk *before* she'd sent his plans off the rails. He wouldn't want a baby with her. No way.

Which was exactly the backhanded luck that convinced her to entertain the idea that maybe she could be pregnant.

Her heart began to flutter in an unfettered mix of excitement and trepidation.

Did she still have a test in the bathroom?

Her pulse slammed so hard that she was afraid to rise in case she fainted.

It's not possible. It's not possible.

After a few deep breaths, she rose to find out.

"Your divorce is final! That must be why you're glowing." Amelia swayed and patted Peyton's back while Vienna set out the clothes and teething toys she had bought for her niece in Germany.

Vienna didn't confess what was really lighting her up from the inside. The baby's father deserved to be the first to know—even if he was liable to be furious.

It didn't matter how he reacted, she assured herself. She was absolutely prepared to raise the baby alone. She was only telling him because their close alignment through family meant he would be aware of her baby and she didn't want him blindsided by any surprises in the future.

Of course, she might have dragged her feet a little if Amelia hadn't mentioned that Jasper was leaving for Santiago within the week.

"Oh? Do you have commitments with him before he leaves? I was thinking to finally take you up on a visit this weekend," Vienna had said, as if it was unrelated. "I want to hear all about Bora Bora and see my favorite niece."

"Bora Bora was all the *S*'s. Sun, sand, swim, sleep. Maybe that other *S* that goes along with a honeymoon." She winked through the camera. "I'll invite Jasper to come for dinner while you're here." Amelia's voice had dipped with curiosity. "I'm sure he'd like to say hello."

"If he's not too busy. I'd love to see him again." Vienna had fought to keep her voice at exactly the right balance of friendly without betraying anything more. *She* hadn't said anything more to Hunter and Amelia about her intimate relationship than her first report that Neal had misconstrued what he'd seen when he found them there together.

Neither had Jasper, apparently, because Amelia had only mentioned him in passing when Vienna arrived last night, saying he was very busy finalizing some things before his trip, but had agreed to come to dinner Saturday night.

Vienna had barely slept. Now she was on pins and needles, struggling to appear nonchalant while sneaking glances at the clock.

Peyton let out a robust burp.

"Is that how you thank Auntie when she's spoiling you?" Amelia wiped the chin of her grinning baby. "Give Auntie a proper hug." She tipped the baby into Vienna's lap, handing her the spit-up towel as well. "Just in case."

"Oh, sugarplum." Vienna hugged the warm little midge into her chest, enjoying the sensation of her toes digging into her thighs and not minding the pull of her hair in a tight fist.

It struck her that soon she would have her own small

and mighty love machine to give her gooey kisses and wobbly bounces on her lap.

The specialist she'd seen had confirmed her pregnancy and assured her there was no reason to fear pregnancy loss. Not any more than the average first-time pregnancy, but after so many disappointments in her journey to getting pregnant, Vienna couldn't help worrying that this miracle wouldn't stick.

Those misgivings were cast away in a sudden rush of anticipation, however, when she wondered if her baby would look like her cousin Peyton. How magical!

Her eyes welled with such joy that Amelia might have noticed, but the doorbell rang.

"That's Jasper." Amelia slipped away to let him in

Vienna hugged Peyton, trying to get hold of herself, but fresh nerves attacked. She was dying to see him, yet filled with trepidation. How would he react to her, let alone her news?

She heard them exchange a few words at the door. The timbre of his voice seemed to resound in her own ears, sending trickles of excitement down her shoulders and spine.

Amelia led him into the living room and a painful flash of nervous excitement struck Vienna, stealing her breath.

"Hunter's in his office," Amelia was saying. "Still playing catch-up from while we were away. I'll go down and tell him it's time to be sociable."

"No hurry," Jasper said, but Amelia was already trotting down the stairs, leaving a weighted silence behind her. "Vienna," Jasper said with a distant nod of greeting, staying by the windows instead of sitting down near her. "It's nice to see you again."

Not Vi. Vienna. Her mouth went dry.

Her whole being was reacting to him. He had a fresh haircut and had let his beard grow in, but wore it closely trimmed. His striped button shirt over suit trousers and polished shoes made her wonder if he'd come straight from the office, since these clothes seemed so much more formal than the ones she was used to seeing him wear.

Was it the clothes that made him appear so remote? He looked like the man she had felt so close to, the man she had longed to see again, but his flat mouth and lowered eyelids made him more inimical than ever. He struck her as even more guarded than he had been in the first moments when they had met.

His gaze flickered over her, his expression softening marginally when he looked at Peyton. That tiny, indulgent curl at the corner of his mouth gave her so much hope. It wrapped around her like a hug until his cool blue eyes lifted to hers again and sent a chill into her chest.

"It's good to see you, too." The pale platitudes sounded ridiculous, especially in her abraded voice. "I—" She looked over her shoulder, aware Amelia would be back with Hunter any second. "I need to tell you something."

He lifted inquiring brows.

She shifted forward and rose with Peyton still in her arms. As she took a few faltering steps toward him, she searched for the man who had shown her those brief moments of tenderness and understanding, but all she saw was enmity.

"This is hard to say." She glanced over her shoulder again. "I'm…"

Amelia and Hunter's voices were coming up the spiral staircase. The desire to put this off nearly overwhelmed her, but this was why she was here. To tell him. She needed him to know.

"I'm pregnant," she whispered.

"You're…" His brows flew upward and he rocked back on his heels, then held himself so still it was as if he had hardened to stone. Only the flare of his nostrils told her he was still breathing. "How? And why are you telling me? Are you saying *I'm*—" He jabbed the knife of his fingertips against his chest, then dropped his hand, cutting off his words as Amelia and Hunter appeared.

The other couple halted, sensing the wall of tension they'd walked into.

Vienna didn't know what to do except to look at Peyton. She was blissfully ignorant of these undercurrents. All she wanted to do was bounce and chew her own fist.

Vienna felt Jasper's outraged glare radiating against her cheek, though, and the bounce of her brother's attention striking her then Jasper and coming back to her.

"Jasper," Hunter said in a tone that held a bevel of warning. "You're also working on the weekend?"

"I was," Jasper said, shaking Hunter's hand in greeting.

"What can I get you to drink?" Hunter moved to the bar.

"It's so funny to me that you two already know each other," Amelia said, taking Peyton when the baby reached for her, but dividing her attention between Vienna and Jasper. "It's a dream come true for me to have you both here. Do you know that? Even when Jasper was missing, I would promise myself that one day he would join my new family for dinner and here we are." She beamed a huge, emotive smile at the pair of them.

"We can't stay," Jasper said flatly.

Amelia's face fell. "What? Jasper!"

"Jasper," Vienna urged softly.

"Vienna and I have things to talk about," Jasper said.

"What things?" Amelia demanded.

"Use my office." Hunter waved toward the stairs.

"No. We'll go to my place. Sorry, Melia." Jasper tried to kiss her cheek, but Amelia brushed him off.

"I made Mom's meatloaf. You *asked* me to," she said with annoyance.

"Good thing it freezes," he muttered. "Let's go." He jerked his head at Vienna.

"I'll have some later," Vienna promised. If she survived.

She veered her gaze from Amelia's shocked expression to her brother's grim, suspicious one before she followed Jasper out the door.

"We could have talked there," Vienna said beside him as Jasper drove toward his penthouse. "What are they going to think?"

"Who the hell cares what anyone thinks?"

She gasped as if he'd struck her. "That's really unfair, Jasper. I've never had the luxury of not caring what anyone thought about me."

"I guess you're right because I *thought* you couldn't get pregnant." He was still in shock. Feeling tricked. Behind that frontline anger was a closet loaded with emotions he had sealed a long time ago. The ones he was trying to keep at bay while he absorbed this news.

"I didn't lie to you! For heaven's sake, Neal—" She cut herself off, covering her eyes in anguish.

He swore silently. He knew what she was referring to. The way Neal had aired that particular detail about their marriage had been inordinately cruel, especially when Jasper had witnessed how devastated Vienna had been over her inability to conceive. He knew the lengths she'd gone to when it came to trying for a baby.

He was searching for the right words to apologize when she cried, "Would you *slow down*?" She clasped the handle above the door.

He grappled himself under control, easing up on the accelerator, but he took the shortcut with the illegal left turn so he arrived at his building sooner.

He parked and would have come around to her door, but she flung hers open and threw herself from the car, marching wordlessly across the underground parking lot toward the elevator.

She looked really good. That was what he'd been thinking since seeing her on his sister's sofa, hair loose, minimal makeup, smiling warmly at the baby. Now he took note of the way her blue jeans cupped her ass. He'd already admired the way her bohemian-style top hugged her breasts. On first look, he'd taken it as a comfortable shirt for the changeable temperatures of an early fall day, but now he saw how its loose drape down to her hips made it a subtle and trendy maternity blouse.

How was he supposed to process this?

For the last month, he'd immersed himself in work, finalizing his takeover of REM-Ex while pushing for the investigation that was needed into Saqui's death. Did he blame Vienna for the fact that Orlin had sailed off into the horizon without facing the consequences for his crimes? Not exactly. Neal had pulled a fast one and was the one who had exposed Jasper, not Vienna. Despite a last-minute scramble for a new plan, Jasper was still able to make headway on cleaning up REM-Ex. Now that he had full access to his finances, he had also ensured Saqui's family was as comfortable as possible.

What he did resent was how persistently Vienna stayed on his mind. She chased him into his sleepless nights and her name was attached to any headline about him. The trolls and bots had figured out they were a sure-fire combo when it came to clicks.

Even his sister insisted on dropping her name into his consciousness.

Vienna's home from Germany.

Vienna's arranging us tickets to an art show.

Vienna's divorce is final.

Vienna's coming to visit this weekend. Would you like to come for dinner?

He had agreed because it would be rude not to. To get it over with. Between him and Vienna, they had managed to convince Hunter and Amelia, and the world at large, that they had platonically shared a house for a couple of nights. Nothing untoward had happened.

Surely they could uphold that ruse for the duration of one meal? He was leaving for Santiago within the week, so they wouldn't cross paths again for a long while.

He had hoped this meeting would prove to himself that whatever had gripped them in Tofino had been a mirage. He should have known he was kidding himself when a twitchy restlessness had gripped him as he counted down the hours to seeing her. When he had walked into his sister's home, he'd felt Vienna's presence so clearly it was as if he'd scented her. Every part of him had reawakened in a way he hadn't felt since the day he'd met her.

Even as an expanding force had risen in him, he'd noticed she was wide-eyed with apprehension. She was bracing herself to face him, fearful of whatever he might say or do.

He'd done nothing. Or rather, he had tried to be as neutral as possible, but as his sister walked away and Vienna approached him, his abdomen had tightened with tension that had its roots in memory. In lust.

Nothing had prepared him for the blow she had delivered, though.

"This is lovely," she murmured as the elevator let them into his foyer.

It was an older building, but the endless views of Vancouver Harbor and Stanley Park had sold him the minute he'd walked in.

She spared a moment to admire the view, then froze as she saw what hung over the gas fireplace.

"Why did you frame it?" She walked across to the sketch she'd made of Peyton, now matted and framed behind a pane of glass.

"I like it." It felt telling that he'd gone to so much trouble, but he did like it and it was his niece. "What was I supposed to do? Tack it to the fridge with magnets? Do you want anything?" He went to the sideboard where he poured himself a whisky, neat.

"I didn't bring my purse or phone," she realized with a look at her empty hands. "But no. Thank you. I can't drink." She pointed at her middle, then folded her arms.

"And yes, you are the father." Her voice shook. "Why else would I tell you?"

He could think of a few hundred million reasons. It was astonishing how many women had begun throwing themselves at him now that he was revealed to be one of Canada's wealthiest bachelors.

"You were just hobnobbing around Europe. It's none of my business if you were with anyone, but it does create other possibilities where your pregnancy is concerned."

"Really?" she choked. "Okay. Unlike perhaps *you,* I haven't been with anyone else." A white ring appeared around her lips. Her cheeks went taut. "And it's none of my business if you have slept around," she continued facetiously. "Obviously. But it does create the possibility that you have other pregnancies out there. Do you?"

He supposed he deserved to have his words thrown back at him like that. They still rankled.

"I do not," he said flatly. He couldn't seem to forget about *her.* He took a deep gulp of the fiery alcohol. "Tell me how it happened."

She coughed out another humorless laugh.

The condom had split. He remembered. Vividly.

And this was exactly the situation—another unplanned pregnancy—that had risen in his mind like a cold specter when it had. She had reminded him she couldn't get pregnant and he'd dismissed the whole thing from his mind, not wanting to wade through any of those old, conflicted emotions.

He held a threatening onslaught of feelings at bay now, watching as she rubbed her arms and paced a few steps to look out the windows again.

"The specialist couldn't explain why it happened with

you and not with Neal," she said in a low, troubled voice. "Maybe the *lack* of stress? Once I was separated from him, I began eating better and sleeping better. I was happier. Or at least less unhappy. The doctor said that might have given my body a chance to level out, hormone-wise. Heal. She pointed out that the world is full of babies conceived after the mother was told she was sterile and decided to quit trying. Nature is mysterious. Sometimes it's a matter of taking the pressure off, she said. And different couples have different chemistry." Her cheeks went pink.

Yeah, they had a different level of chemistry all right. He could feel the pull of it even as he resisted fully accepting this news. It wasn't that he didn't want the baby. More like he didn't want to want it then discover she didn't.

"There's no real explanation for why I got pregnant, but I definitely am. It's definitely yours."

"Okay. And?" His ears were ringing, and he was straining so hard to hear what she hadn't yet said. He didn't want to ask in case the answer wasn't what he wanted to hear.

What *did* he want to hear?

The tendons in her neck flexed and she seemed to lose more color. She blinked fast and seemed to pull a cloak of dignity around her, standing taller as she did.

"I realize this isn't something you asked for." Her voice thickened and her eyes grew brighter. "I'm informing you because you have a right to know."

Know what? *Breathe*, he reminded himself, barely able to hear her voice through the rushing in his ears.

"I'm not trying to obligate you. I have all the resources I need to raise it alone," she continued.

"You're having it." He felt numb. As though he stood outside his body.

"Yes! Oh my God, yes. How could you even question that when you know how much I want a baby!" Her eyes were wet, her voice soaked in raw emotion. "I want this baby *so much*."

He knew he was still holding his drink in front of his lips, but his whole body was paralyzed. He hadn't realized how badly he had needed to hear those words. Hadn't realized how profoundly they would affect him. A wrench of emotion accosted him, crashing past the wall he'd reflexively erected because this was too big.

This was real now. He was becoming a father. *This* was the news that really took his feet out from under him. *Now* his life was fundamentally altered.

"I was hoping you would be happy." She dashed at her cheeks. "Or at least…not angry. I can't help that I cause so much trouble for you, Jasper. I don't mean to. I *swear*. That's why I'll raise it alone. You won't be involved at all. In fact, if you don't want to tell anyone you're the father, that's okay. I understa—"

"Like hell, Vi. If you're having this baby, then *we* are having a baby. This time, I'm one hundred percent involved."

CHAPTER NINE

"W-WHAT?" HER LIPS went numb. Her equilibrium wobbled from a tentative joy—that he seemed to want the baby—to deep confusion. "What do you mean, 'this time'?" Her tender stomach curdled.

Agony flexed across his expression and a muscle pulsed in his jaw.

"Oh my God." Realization struck with such a deep spear of jealousy she felt impaled by it. "Do you already have a child?" Even as her mind tried to fold that news into her current reality, she experienced a pang of anguish on his behalf, thinking he'd been shut out of his child's life in some way.

Neither reaction made sense because he wasn't hers to feel possessive or compassionate toward.

It was hitting her, however, that they were co-parents. The moment she had found out, she had wanted to tell him. She hadn't known how he would react. In her heart of hearts, she had hoped he would be the one person who might share her exuberant joy, but she'd also been prepared for a flat rejection.

She definitely hadn't begun to process how much of a role he would play in her child's life, not beyond offering him a choice as to whether he wanted to be involved.

It had never once occurred to her that he might already have a child.

"No," he muttered, draining his glass and setting it aside. "That other pregnancy was terminated."

"When?" she blurted, then, "I mean, I'd like to know what happened if you're willing to tell me. Obviously it's affecting how you're reacting to this baby." She lowered herself onto the sofa, dazed by this news and the charged emotions radiating off him.

"It is." He acknowledged tightly. "It happened right after we lost Mom." He took another sip, his gaze focused on the past. "Dad and Amelia were wrecked. My entire future had gone gray. My girlfriend and I had been using condoms, but—"

"That's why you were so upset that day," she realized. That was why he had shut down and shut her out even before Neal had turned up.

"We took one stupid chance," he muttered. "I swore I'd never be so careless again. I was going to say to you that day that I would get you one of those pills if you wanted. But you said you couldn't get pregnant and I knew how much that upset you. I couldn't bring myself to say anything more about it." He ran his hand down his face. "How the hell am I this lucky?"

His tone suggested he didn't feel very lucky at all. That hurt. She felt like she'd won the lottery. She had!

"Do you resent her for what she decided to do?" she asked carefully.

"No. I genuinely don't. Her body, her choice. I support that all the way. She was seventeen, same as me. I sure as hell didn't know how I would have shouldered even more responsibility at that time, so I completely understand how overwhelmed she felt." He squeezed the back of his neck. "There was a part of me that was relieved it wasn't my decision to make. I'll admit that. Maybe, if things had been different, we would have gone on to marry and have a family at a better time, when we were both equipped to handle it."

"You were in love with her." Long tentacles of jealousy lashed and stuck to her skin, worming their stinging chemicals deep into her organs, making her heart writhe in agony.

"As much as the average teenager could be." He shoved his hands into his pockets. "Our feelings might have matured as we matured ourselves, but we didn't get a chance to find out. She went to stay with her aunt. I thought—" He swore and turned his face away so she couldn't read what was in it. "She sent her aunt to tell me she'd decided to terminate. Maybe she thought I would be angry or blame her. That's always bothered me, that she felt she couldn't tell me herself. It makes me feel like I failed her in some way. But I think her aunt wanted to do it, to get her own point across."

"Which was?" Cold fingers trailed down her spine, raising goose bumps of dread all over her back and shoulders.

His flinty expression became conflicted and grim, revealing how much the experience continued to ravage him.

"She said Annalise had realized she would have better prospects in the future. She could do better, so she didn't want to tie herself to me." He finally looked at her, gaze flat, expression stony, but she knew how much those sorts of words hurt. She knew all too well.

"That's really awful, Jasper. You didn't deserve that."

Especially not when he was actually a very caring and conscientious and generous person.

"It *was* awful." He blue gaze narrowed to pierce into her.

"I wasn't trying to shut you out!" she insisted. "I'm still in shock that this has even happened. I wanted you to know because it felt like the right thing to do, but I had no idea how you would react. Given how I caused things to go sideways with your plans for REM-Ex, I couldn't expect anything from you."

She had only hoped, really hoped, that he would welcome this news the way she did. Maybe she had hoped for a welcome of another kind, too, for her, but that was definitely not something she had expected.

"*I* expect things from *myself,*" he asserted. "Of course I'm obligated to my child, exactly as much as you are. I'm obligated to the woman who carries my baby. You are both my responsibility, Vienna. Starting now. Your divorce is final, right?"

"Yes. But no." She held up a finger that trembled, her mind hung up on that dreadful word: *obligated.* "My divorce is final, yes, but it took me *years* to make that happen. I fought really hard to get to this point where I make my own choices. I won't give that up for anyone."

"I'm not 'anyone.' I'm the father of your baby. And you should go have a quick chat with Amelia because, guess what? Babies run your life for roughly twenty years."

"I know that!" She was prepared to make *those* sacrifices. "I'm not saying you can't be involved, Jasper." She pushed the heels of her hands into her eyes. "But you can't sweep in here and tell me how it's going to be the second I tell you I'm pregnant. I haven't had time to *think.*"

"What is there to think about? This isn't a case where

more information changes the decision. You want the baby. I want the baby. It's basic anthropology that we stick together and do everything we can to give our child their best start."

"How? What are you suggesting? A loveless marriage? Been there, done that and no. I can't, Jasper. I *can't*. And you can't make me believe it's what you would want, either. Not after what you just said." Her voice cracked and she had to look away.

Was he still in love with Annalise? A little? That thought ate clean through her soul.

His hands were knotted into fists in his pockets, his jaw hard as ironwood.

"Your marriage was absent of more than love. From everything you told me, it lacked basic respect. We have that much."

"Do we?" she asked wildly. "You just accused me of sleeping around and trying to pawn someone else's baby off onto you."

He sighed and pinched the bridge of his nose.

"This caught me off guard," he said tightly. "Frankly, I have trust issues after the people who hired me killed my friend and tried to frame me for it. That's not on you, though, so I apologize for what I said."

Oh, he absolutely destroyed her when he was fair and recognized his own missteps. She buried her face in her hands again, trying to think of a reason to keep her distance from him.

"We both want this baby, Vi."

"That doesn't mean we'll work as a couple."

"We work very well as a couple." His voice curled with dark irony. "Too well."

She scowled at him for playing dirty by reminding her. His low blow was a sensual pulse between her thighs. His heated gaze insisted she remember how they had conceived that baby, promising more of that pleasure. As much of it as she could stand.

Her throat grew hot.

"Marriage has worked out for Amelia and Hunter," he pointed out.

"Of course Hunter fell for Amelia," she scoffed. "Who can help loving her? She's perfect." *I'm not.* That was the sharp pang that struck deep in her heart. She wanted to be loved. She really did.

"It's true I don't possess my sister's capacity for affection and warmth. I've always preferred to live alone, but I'm not walking away from my child. We owe our baby an honest effort at raising it together. Did you really tell me expecting I wouldn't want anything to do with you or the baby?" She thought there was a ring of injury beneath his disbelief. "Then why tell me at all?"

Her chest tightened as he forced her to confront her true motive in coming here. She looked to the ceiling, acknowledging she could have waited months to tell him. She could have lied for years, claiming to anyone who asked that the father was someone in Europe or an IVF donor.

The real reason she had wanted to tell him was because she had wanted an excuse to see him. To see.

She had wanted to see if he still wanted her.

Maybe he did, sexually, but what he really wanted was the baby. *Not* her.

Even so, that was alluring to her. She didn't want to do this alone if she didn't have to.

"I do want you involved," she said tentatively. "I just don't know how much."

"Well, I'm telling you I'm all in, one thousand percent."

"Please think about what you're saying, Jasper. You don't know what my life is really like." She rose to pace with agitation. "You've had a taste of the Waverly drama. We're very messy." She was. "Ask your sister how she likes it." She flicked her hand toward his phone.

"Is that what has you worried? That I'm afraid the press will say something ugly about me?"

"I promise you they will," she said with the agony of experience.

"I genuinely don't care. This baby has become my highest priority."

"Just like that?" She shook her head and flung out a hand. "You only found out about it twenty minutes ago."

"How long did it take for you?" he challenged, gaze clashing into hers.

Not even that long. In fact, she was already distressed that the press might denigrate their baby because they weren't married.

"Things have happened so fast. Can we take a beat?" she pleaded. "There's actually a three-month rule— guideline, I guess—where you keep your pregnancy private in case..." She didn't even want to say it.

"Is that a concern? How are you feeling?" He came to stand in front of her, holding out one hand as if she might feel faint and he would have to catch her. "I should have asked already."

"Everything is fine." She laughed with bemusement at that hand, still offered for her to grasp, but there was a bleak fear behind her shaky smile that she couldn't completely disguise.

"What aren't you telling me?" He frowned.

"Nothing. I swear. It's me. The doctor said everything is normal." She absently rubbed at the cobalt blue polish staining her cuticle. "But I'm very aware that my body didn't cooperate with getting pregnant. I'm afraid to get too attached in case it lets me down again. I'm not being rational, I know that." She lifted her gaze, embarrassed at her irrational fears.

"Your caution is understandable. No part of this belongs online unless you choose to share it. If you want to keep this between us for now, I support that." He nodded. "What about physically? How do you feel?"

Her heart gave another swerve as he accepted her wishes without batting an eye.

"I feel okay." Her mouth didn't feel quite steady as she smiled wryly. "Normal for early pregnancy, I guess. I'm nauseous and tired. Some foods taste funny. Nothing I can't handle."

"Good." He nodded again, more thoughtful. "I don't mind waiting to announce things, and we can even keep this from family for now if that's what you prefer, but I want to operate on the assumption we'll be welcoming this baby together in…?"

"May," she provided, all of her beginning to tremble. This felt really monumental. She wasn't prepared for it.

"I was born in May." His harsh features eased into bemusement.

"Taurus. Stubborn."

"So I've been told. I refuse to believe it."

"Shocking."

They shared a faint moment of amusement, one that almost gave her a ray of optimism that they could at least go back to the companionable friendship they'd shared in Tofino.

"We'll go through this pregnancy together so anything that happens, happens to *us*. You won't have to face it alone," he said somberly.

Was he trying to make her cry?

"I think that's naive on your part, since it's *all* happening to me," she joked, but she understood what he was saying and she was deeply touched.

"I'm as invested in this baby as you are," he said, spelling it out.

She swallowed, blinking her hot eyes. His words were beyond heartening, especially given how alone she had felt through all her past disappointments.

"Besides, we should take advantage of this time to get to know each other before the baby changes everything."

"You want to live together? Here?" She glanced around the penthouse with fresh eyes, thinking she might like that, especially with Amelia and Hunter so close by.

"Eventually here. Initially, in Santiago."

"Wait. What?"

"Are you sure about this, Vi?" Hunter leaned in the doorway of the guest bedroom that she used when she visited him here in Vancouver. "Fealty to my wife demands I believe Jasper is as solid a person as was ever built, but you just got out of a rough marriage. You spent a couple of days with him a month ago and you're prepared to follow him to Santiago? How well do you know him?"

"That's kind of the point." She smiled blithely, refusing to show any of her misgivings.

They had come back for dinner last night and announced that Vienna would be accompany Jasper to Santiago; there had been no mention of the baby. Hunter and Amelia were surprised, but Amelia had recovered quickly, saying how thrilled she was that they were getting together.

"We might have got to know each other better in Tofino if we'd had the chance," Vienna told Hunter. "Since Jasper has to be in Santiago for a time, and I have flexibility, it makes sense for me to go with him. I'm looking forward to getting away from the attention here and checking out the art scene there. If things aren't working out, I'll come home."

Please let it work out. She folded her top and smoothed it down her front, wondering what "work out" would look like. Love. That's what. She couldn't settle for anything less. Not again, but she couldn't shake her nagging fear that she wasn't the sort of person anyone loved.

"Why was he so upset last night when you two left?" Hunter asked.

"I told you." She hated lying to him, but this was at least a partial truth. Jasper *had* been concerned when she had told him about her conversation in Germany. "When I was at the wedding, I mentioned to Micah and Remy that something fishy was going on with REM-Ex. I thought it was simple good manners to warn them if they happened to be invested there. Jasper pointed out that it doesn't look good on him if I started a whisper campaign while he was acquiring shares."

"Remy would never reveal his source."

"I don't think Micah will, either. Neither of them had shares anyway. Micah sold his ages ago."

"How was the wedding?" Hunter asked with mild interest.

"Beautiful." She couldn't help smiling as she remembered it. "Quinn and Micah seem very happy."

"And Eden?" A shadow of concern flickered across Hunter's expression.

"Also very happy." She set her blouse into the suitcase. "I'll apologize one last time for setting you up with her and promise *not* to pursue a career in matchmaking."

"Good thing. I'm pretty sure you'd starve," he teased. "Do you want me to carry that down?" He nodded at her suitcase as she closed it.

"Thanks. Are you really worried about my going to Chile with Jasper?" She chewed the corner of her lip.

"Not worried exactly." He hefted the case. "Disappointed. I prefer having you close by. I'll miss you if you're so far away."

"Toronto is 'close'?"

"Five hours is better than sixteen. At least I go to Toronto every few months."

"I like this sentimental softie you're turning into." She lightly poked his chest.

He responded by giving her hair a tug. "I want you to be happy, Vi. You're sure that this will do that for you?"

She wasn't, but… "There's only one way to find out."

He cocked his head in acceptance of her logic and took her case down to Jasper's car.

CHAPTER TEN

JASPER HAD PLANNED to fly commercial, but with Vienna coming along, he chartered a private jet and hired a maternity nurse to travel with them, one who would stay to provide prenatal care until Vienna found a doctor in Santiago.

The charter allowed them to fly earlier, which meant they would have a few days to get settled before he went into the office every day. He wanted to ensure Vienna was comfortable.

He was still trying to wrap his head around becoming a father. He'd always been of two minds on the idea. Growing up, he had assumed he would create a life like the one he had known—a stable, loving family with a wife and children.

Then he'd lost his mother, which had given him a front-row seat on his father's grief, and had been judged not worthy of being a husband and father. That had messed with his ability to see himself in the role. That was why he'd been so careful in the ensuing years, refusing to put himself in the position of a surprise pregnancy again.

Despite that, he wasn't the least bit conflicted on whether he wanted *this* baby. A persistent ache of impatience sat behind his sternum. He wanted to hold their baby *now*. Vienna's concerns were sobering, making him all the more protective and urgent to get through the pregnancy so he could be hands-on with looking after their baby. At that point, it really would be a team effort on ensuring their child thrived.

Were they a team? He didn't do group activities, and when he did, he led.

Pressing her to come with him, to try to form a family, was in their child's best interest. He stood by that. But he did have certain misgivings about their relationship. They came from very different worlds and all they really shared was a baby.

And the heat with which they'd conceived it.

He was trying not to dwell on that, even though it was definitely a factor in why he'd pushed her to come with him. Could she even have sex? He hadn't yet asked. He'd been focused on the immediate business of yanking her firmly back into his life while trying not to hold a grudge over what had happened with REM-Ex.

"Can I ask you something?" Vienna asked quietly. She dragged her eyes from where the nurse was watching a movie, her ears covered by noise-canceling headphones.

"Yes?" He lifted inquiring brows.

"Why—" She seemed briefly perplexed and a little self-deprecating. "I'm wondering how rich you are and why you didn't tell me? Which I know is rude, but I had the impression in Tofino that REM-Ex had much deeper pockets than you did. I was surprised when I heard you had bought them."

"I'm rich enough that we'll need a robust prenup if we decide to marry." It circled back to that moment in the grocery store parking lot and a burning need to prove himself to a woman who had forgotten him the moment she turned her car back onto the street.

"You're insulted. I shouldn't have asked." She wrinkled her nose.

"I'm offended that I was ever judged on what I have or didn't have. Orlin Caulfield made the same mistake, thinking I wasn't his equal."

"You're not."

He snapped a look at her.

"You're far more than he could ever hope to be, whether you own REM-Ex or not."

Those eyes of hers could drown him if he wasn't careful.

"What's going to happen to him?" she asked. "Is it dangerous for us to be in Santiago? I heard you talking to someone about upping security to include me."

"That's an abundance of caution. I asked a firm to shadow us for a few weeks, to confirm there's nothing to worry about. I wouldn't have brought you if I thought it was dangerous for you. No." He shook his head. "There was a rash of firings and resignations when I took over. The guilty ran for cover, but they're hoping to get away with their crimes, not come back on me for exposing them. Mostly my takeover has been greeted with enthusiasm because I'm cleaning house."

"And the investigation into Saqui's death?"

"I have an email that shows Orlin Caulfield ordered the landslide. I don't know if I'll ever find the person who set off the charge, but Orlin is the one behind all of this. The investigation has moved into calculating a settlement number for the Chilean authorities for the environmental damages, which I support. The REM-Ex lawyers are already filing a list of charges against Orlin for misrepresentation and other corruptions. There are liens on his Canadian assets pending the outcome, so he's definitely enjoying a taste of what he served me. He's unable to access his money and is stuck on his boat with few ports of call where he won't be arrested and extradited."

"Are you satisfied with that?"

"For now." He would never be satisfied. Not until Orlin was rotting behind bars.

"What I mean is, I don't want it between us that I ruined your plan to have him arrested."

"It's not."

Her mouth quirked to a skeptical angle as she searched his gaze.

They really did have a distance to go before they trusted one another. Fine. He went with brutal honesty.

"For Saqui's sake, I can't rest until Orlin is in jail, but it's not productive for me to keep it between us, so I'm doing my best to let it go," he said.

She flinched and looked away, nodding jerkily. "At least I know where I stand."

Sensitive, he remembered with a pinch of chagrin. She felt everything twice as hard as most people.

Grudges had always been his fuel, though. He didn't know how to operate without feeling that burn of rancor inside him.

What more did he need, though? What did he want to prove? To whom? Vienna?

You're far more than he could ever hope to be.

"I'm going to lie down in the stateroom," she said, unbuckling. Avoiding his gaze.

It was barely eight o'clock Vancouver time, but he nodded and watched her go.

* * *

They had left the drizzle of autumn in Vancouver for early spring in Chile. Snow on the Andes formed a backdrop to a fascinating city of contrasts. The green spaces had yet to green up, but thick vines and tall palms grew in abundance between old-world stone buildings and glass skyscrapers. The bright, sunny sky cast deep shadows into narrow streets where elderly women ran flower shops brimming with fragrant blossoms.

All of these things managed to distract Vienna from her concern that she and Jasper didn't really stand a chance, not if he continued to resent her.

He seemed to be genuinely trying to smooth things over, though.

After they checked into their penthouse suite in the hotel, they napped and freshened up from travel, then ambled through the downtown area to have lunch with a property agent.

The woman was excited by the idea of a generous commission and couldn't wait to get started.

"I was thinking to leave the house-hunting in your capable hands," Jasper said as they walked through a park on the way back to their hotel. "Would you feel comfortable if she took you around without me? The security detail would go with you."

"I don't mind doing it alone if you're too busy, but would you trust me?" They had talked with the agent about finding something they could call "home" at least part-time for the next several years—which felt very permanent when their relationship was still so delicate. Vienna was holding her breath, convinced any misstep on her part could wreck everything.

"Did you not agree with the direction I thought we should take?" He had told the agent they wanted several bedrooms so family could visit for extended periods, along with room for entertaining and accommodation for staff. He wanted grounds that offered a sense of privacy and a pool if possible. "In terms of style, I liked your place in Tofino."

"Hunter found that house."

"Yes, but we both liked it, so we have similar tastes. You'll have opinions about what might work as a studio, too."

That had been her contribution to the wish list, but, "What if I reject something you might think is perfect?"

"If you don't like it, how could I see it as perfect?"

She halted in the middle of the wide path. For a second, she could only stare at him.

"What?" His brows came together over the mirrored lenses of his sunglasses.

She started to dismiss her astonishment, then admitted with a flex of shame in her brow, "It still surprises me when you're so considerate. I'm not used to it."

His sighed out a subdued rumble of discontent and they continued walking.

"We both bring baggage into this relationship," he said with deliberate patience. "We're going to leave it out sometimes and the other one will trip over it. But I'd rather not be compared to your ex if you can help it."

"I don't. Believe me, there is no comparison on that front," she said with a husk of humorless laughter because it was so true. Jasper could tell her right now that he didn't think they would work after all and he would be miles ahead of Neal on the honesty and consideration scale. "Neal wasn't the only one who really didn't give a damn about what I wanted or needed, though."

She hated admitting that. There was always a lingering fear that maybe the way she'd been treated was her own fault because she genuinely didn't measure up. Maybe it was only a matter of time before Jasper saw it, too.

"Your stepmother?" he asked. "I thought she was… I don't know. A narcissist?"

"She was. And a sex addict, I think? She definitely had a troubling relationship with alcohol and drugs."

"Why did your father stay married to her?"

"I don't know. But his reason doesn't matter, only that he did. And the fact he took her side makes him just as bad as she was, in my opinion." She paused as they came up to the lip of a giant fountain filled with shiny coins. "It makes him worse, I think, because he should have protected me from her, but he sided with her instead."

"Where was Hunter all this time?"

"Being a child, too!" She would never hear a word against him. He ought to get used to that. "Hunter was dealing with the same thing I was—being belittled and humiliated at any sort of gathering because she refused to wear underwear and loved to dance on tables." Among thousands of other things. "Hunter did what he could, standing up for me and talking to Dad, but he started working at Wave-Com in high school. The board pressured him to rein her in, as if it was up to him to be responsible for two grown adults! I know he felt guilty, leaving me alone with them when he went to university, but it wasn't like I was in danger." Not physically, anyway.

"That's not the sort of father I intend to be," he said gravely.

"I know." She started walking again, offering a polite smile to a woman who walked by with her miniature schnauzer. "But they did leave me with horrible self-esteem issues." It was so lowering to admit that. She had grown up and moved past a lot of it, but that kind of baggage lingered and still ambushed her sometimes. "Everyone always asks me why I don't work at Wave-Com and the answer is that I asked Dad if I could, when I was fifteen. I wanted to job-shadow in the marketing department for a school assignment."

"Why would he refuse? Graphics. Art. That's right in your lane." He glanced at her again.

"Irina laughed so hard." Vienna could still hear the cruel ring of it. "She said I wasn't smart enough to work at the company. That I would only embarrass Dad by being there. Granted, my grades were very average, but—"

"It was a job-shadow. A *day*."

"He said no and I couldn't bring myself to ask again. Ever. I should have known better than to ask at the time. It didn't matter what I wanted to do, Irina would mock me for it. Puberty was absolute hell, when I was growing into my body. She always wanted to be the center of attention, even if that meant getting negative attention by insulting me in front of my friends or criticizing my sketches in an art competition. The online trolls loved what they saw as a feud between us, when it was really just her saying mean things about me. That's why I'm still such an easy target for them. She trained them."

"Where is she now?" Jasper asked in a falsely pleasant tone.

"Marrying Orlin Caulfield, if there's a god."

He barked out a laugh.

"The point is, she did a number on my belief that I can do anything right. It doesn't help that I'm human and actually do make mistakes. The marriage that was supposed to prove to my father that I was an asset to the company turned into a disaster. Then, when I filed for divorce and thought, *There, I'm putting that behind me and starting with a clean page...*"

They shared a wry look.

"I'm glad you told me this." He took her hand as they came out of the park and steered toward the pedestrian crossing to their hotel. "I'm going to guess she was jealous because you're actually very beautiful. I'm sure she felt threatened by that."

Vienna must have winced at that because he said, "Vienna," with a mix of gentle scold and astonishment. "Please tell me you know how beautiful you are."

"I know how to tick the boxes on what most people think is beautiful," she said helplessly as they moved into the portico of the hotel. "Blond streaks and shaped brows and..." She brushed at the stylish linen culottes she wore with a bralette and satin blazer. "Fooling people into thinking I'm beautiful isn't the same as being beautiful."

She released his hand to skip into the revolving door then crossed the lobby, trying to get away from that conversation, but Jasper brought it into the elevator with them.

He leaned on the wall, staring at her. "The most beautiful woman I have ever seen was wearing my T-shirt and no makeup. She didn't even have her hair brushed. It was all piled on her head with a crunchie—"

"Scrunchie," she corrected, laughing, but also blushing. She remembered that morning all too well.

"She told me to stand still and wasn't even looking at me, which drove me *crazy*. So all I could do was look at her."

"I *was* looking at you! I was drawing you."

"And you looked so happy doing it that I wanted to stand there forever." He launched himself across the elevator and caged her against the opposite wall. "But it was so freaking erotic I couldn't handle it. And you *didn't even notice.*"

"Buddy, I was drawing you." She tapped the middle of his chest. "Just because it was from the waist up doesn't mean I wasn't aware of what was going on below the edge of the page."

His hot gaze drifted to her mouth and he might have kissed her, but the bell pinged and the doors opened.

He straightened away and motioned to the German-speaking couple that the car was going up, not down. They were left alone again.

Vienna looked to him, expecting—hoping—he would come back to her, but he was facing straight ahead now, his cheeks hollow.

"It was a good drawing," he said, as if the flirtatious lunge hadn't happened. "I kept the sketchbook. It's in Vancouver. I meant to give it to you."

"I have dozens of sketchbooks and I'm not afraid to buy more." It was true. Some women had a shoe fetish. Hers was an eternal search for exactly the right tooth on the right size of ivory paper, bound in a way that pleased her.

They entered their spacious suite. It was tastefully decorated in whites and blues and silver. The drapes were pulled back on the wall of windows, offering gorgeous views of Santiago and the mountains. Through a pair of double doors, the king-size bed still showed the wrinkles from their nap when they had arrived.

Would they use it for anything more than sleeping?

Vienna glanced again at Jasper, wondering how to open that conversation when that, too, was baggage she still carried.

He was looking at her.

"What?" she asked, glancing down at her jacket to see if she'd spilled something at lunch.

"I've been thinking about asking the nurse something."

The nurse had her own room on a lower floor. Aside from checking in daily and responding to texts, she was mostly free to do her own thing.

"But it just occurred to me that it doesn't matter if she says you're allowed to have sex. The question is whether you want to. I understand if you have reservations, given how delicate—"

"Jasper," Vienna cut in with absolute astonishment. "Did you seriously bring me all this way believing we might not have sex?" Her cheeks began to sting. "I mean, I presumed we would, but..." She cleared her throat. "I mean, I didn't come all this way *not* to have sex."

"No?" He sauntered toward her. More like stalked.

Her pulse began to race and her body screamed an enthusiastic *Yes*. The rest of her was searching his features for signs this was more than sex for him.

Which wasn't realistic. She knew it wasn't. In reality, they'd only spent a few days in each other's company, but he had filled her thoughts for the month they'd been apart. She was starting to feel as though she knew him well enough to know that deeper feelings were only a short stumble away—for her, anyway.

She really wanted to believe he was coming right along with her, though.

"Don't worry, Vi." He misread her expression and gathered her close, smoothing her hair behind her ear. "I can go slow and gentle." He ran his tongue over his teeth. "Previous performance notwithstanding."

"I don't know if you noticed, but I didn't submit any complaints. In fact, I left you five stars."

"Was that you? I wasn't sure if TofinoBabe was you or— Ouch." He caught the hand pinching his stomach and the corner of his mouth kicked up in a very sexy grin, one that had her catching her breath at how handsome he was. "I don't kiss and tell, but of *course* you get all the stars. There aren't enough stars for how great sex with you feels."

Just sex, then. She grabbed at the heart that was tipping forward into the abyss, but it remained right on the edge as she stared into the banked hunger of his eyes.

"We can take our time, you know. We have lots." His finger was still tracing her ear, making fine hairs stand up at the back of her neck. "Tell me what you need."

She opened her mouth, but words wouldn't form. He was barely touching her and she wanted to melt right into him.

She set her hand on his chest, unable to resist trailing light fingers across the hard muscle of his pec, then finding the nipple that puckered beneath the crisp fabric.

His chest swelled and his head dipped, but his lips only

went into her neck. At first, all she felt was his breath. A hot swirl against sensitized skin, then the lightest nuzzle of his lip.

She whimpered, knees softening.

His arms around her tightened. "I haven't even kissed you yet."

She knew. The effect he had on her was magnificent in its devastation. It was terrifying. A loss of self every time, but she succumbed all the same.

He was determined to conquer her in his own time, though. It was a small frustration when she wanted the heat and the blindness. She wanted to know he was as affected by her as she was by him, but he refused to be rushed. He slid his hands in slow circles all over her back and hips, brushing his lips in those kisses that made her hurt inside because they were so tender.

"Jasper," she whispered in a small plea.

"Let me learn," he chided, his voice just as soft while his hands skimmed the satin of her jacket, rubbing it against her skin. He released the button at her navel and pressed the lapels open.

"This has been driving me crazy," he growled, bracketing her waist with his palms and sliding his thumb along the scalloped band beneath her breasts. "Is this a bra? Are you wearing one under it? No," he answered himself as his thumbs climbed higher, discovering her nipples.

"Careful." She sucked in a breath. "They're sensitive."

He made a crooning noise and his touch gentled. His mouth skimmed her brow and the point of her cheek before his teeth caught her earlobe.

"Every night, I think about touching you again," he confessed. "I think about the stairs and our kiss in the woods when I wanted to have you against that tree. It wasn't enough. None of it. I wanted this. More time. More."

A strangled noise broke from her throat. Her hands were sliding over him, pulling his shirt from his trousers, seeking hot skin, but even though he groaned and his whole body flexed, he kept to the slow slide of his hands and the unhurried brush of his lips along her jaw toward her mouth.

With a noise of frustration, she cupped his head and caught at his lips with her own, pressing her tongue past the seam of his lips.

He grunted, but dragged his hands up to her hair and threaded his fingers into the length. The weight of his hands pulled her head back so her mouth was tilted up for his and he lifted away so he was fully in control, barely touching her with the teasing graze of his lips against hers.

"Kiss me," she demanded.

"I am," he assured her, pressing soft, soft kisses against her upper lip, then her chin, her throat. Sensual lips found their way down her breastbone before his teeth opened over the cup of her bra.

She didn't know how to process this many sensations, this much attention and care. She ran her fingers through his hair and shaped the base of his skull, sliding her touch beneath his collar before seeking the line where his shaved throat met the stubble of his thickening beard.

"You scare me," she admitted as he released the zip on her culottes and they started to slide off her hips.

He paused. "Stop?"

"No. Keep going. *Please* keep going." Her voice was jagged.

But leave me something. He was stealing every inch of her soul, one kiss and caress at a time.

"What scares you?" His mouth was on her collarbone, his clever fingers tracing the satin and lace of her underwear.

"How you make me feel…it's too much." But yet also not enough.

She couldn't bear the anticipation. While her flesh cried out for the caress of his, she yanked at his belt and opened his fly, then slid her hand inside his briefs. Velvet over steel met her questing touch. Hot, fierce arousal and a tender tip that made his breath hiss when she caressed him.

He yanked up his head to reveal the way lust had shattered his vision before he crushed her mouth with his. His arm around her held her tight as he rocked his mouth across hers while one fingertip quested beneath satin.

When he found the moisture, he spread it around, sliding his touch upward, parting her, lifting his head to watch desire diffuse her vision. His tongue licked flagrantly along her bottom lip while he caressed her in the most blatant ways.

"How close are you? Let me watch," he rasped. One finger invaded, two. The heel of his palm pressed against the knot of nerves at the top of her sex, making her shake. Making her rock her hips in craving.

She clung one arm around his neck. The other squeezed him in a fist while her hips lifted into his touch. She couldn't help herself. She *needed* this.

"Softly, softly," he whispered, but this was too profound to be soft. Her body clamped onto his intruding fingers and her hips rolled, trying to catch the wave that would take her to the top. That one…? That one? Oh, yes, *this* one.

With a tortured groan, she gave herself up to the rapture.

She's here. She's not going anywhere, he kept telling himself, trying to dull his greed, but the wolf in him was hungry, so damned hungry and horny and howling.

The clothes between them were an affront. He dealt with them while she was still limp on the bed, catching her breath.

Oh, he liked being responsible for that flush on her skin and the glassy haze in her eyes. When he stretched out atop her, the only thing that kept him lucid was her slight flinch as his arm brushed the side of her breast.

He had to be careful with her. He knew that. Not because her pregnancy was delicate, but because she was. She was sensitive, her heart easily bruised. She was so damned good at hiding it that he forgot at times, but she was an artist in her soul, feeling everything.

A ferocious rush of tenderness and a need to protect overcame over him, the kind that felt so juvenile he instinctually shied from letting it fully envelop him. He had to protect himself, too, right?

Yet, as her legs brushed his and her fingertips stroked his shoulder and neck and her abdomen quivered under the weight of his splayed hand, he knew she was already in possession of more of him than he was comfortable giving up.

He wanted to devour her. Fill himself up with her. But when he set his mouth on her trembling lips, he lingered, drawing out the kiss, taking his time to deepen it and slowing each of his caresses. He was putting off the moment when he would lose himself in her while stealing more of her, drinking in the way her arms curled around him.

He needed these signs that her defenses were utterly vanquished. It was the only way he could let down his own shields. He reveled in the way she opened her legs, inviting him, while her mouth pressed damp, desperate kisses across his chest. She set her teeth against his biceps and rolled her tongue across his nipple and her nails grazed his buttocks in helpless urging for him to press inside her.

Condom, he thought once. But they didn't need one.

He shifted her beneath him. She was more than ready. He slid deep in one thrust.

It felt too naked. Too profound. A harsh groan left him at the delicious, melted heat of her, but he was stripped to the very essence of his being. Elemental.

His arms shook when he braced himself over her, trying to physically hold himself apart, but she threw her head back, throat exposed, skin damp and glowing. His. All his.

He fought to keep it slow. He surged into her with careful power, luxuriating in the sheer perfection of her, enjoying the way she writhed beneath him and released throaty noises of anguished joy with each thrust.

This was what he had been craving in the weeks since they'd parted, this evidence that she was as powerless against this desire as he was.

And powerless he was. Despite taking it slow, despite his focus on driving her inexorably toward culmination, his grasp on control grew slippery and weak. Electrified tingles worked their way down his spine. It took everything he had to hold on and wait for her.

This gentle lovemaking should have resulted in a gentle release, but when she twisted beneath him, and her mouth opened in a silent scream, he felt the intensity of her climax in her convulsive squeezes.

Her pleasure triggered his. An orgasm crashed through him with cataclysmic force, brutal in its strength and unrelenting in its duration.

He was lost, utterly lost to her, but in those euphoric moments he didn't give a single damn.

CHAPTER ELEVEN

IT WAS AS good as she remembered. That was what Vienna was thinking after several days of near constant lovemaking. Sex with Jasper was actually better than she remembered because they were both getting to know each other's bodies, learning how to truly drive the other past their endurance of pleasure. This morning, she had joined him in the shower and blew his mind, leaving him sagged against the tiled wall, catching his breath and promising sensual retribution when he got home later.

She had never felt so confident in her sexuality. If this relationship failed and she walked away with a shattered heart, she still wouldn't regret being with him because he had given her a belief in her desirability.

Sex wasn't enough to build a future on, though. Was she being greedy or impatient to want a signal that he felt more for her?

She was ruminating on that, struggling to pay attention to the agent as she showed her yet another house, when her phone dinged with a text from him.

Saqui's parents are here, meeting lawyers. Dinner with them tonight?

Of course, she replied back.

Vienna wasn't sure what to expect from the dinner, but Jasper was withdrawn when he came back to the hotel to change and collect her. Usually their hello kiss turned into more, but he only pecked her cheek and asked how her day had gone.

"No luck today, but the agent said she's getting a better sense of what we're looking for. She'll have more to show me later in the week."

"Good." He was so distracted that it bordered on hurtful, but she was pretty sure his mood wasn't about her. This must be a difficult and emotional meeting for him.

She slipped on a scoop-necked blue dress and gathered her hair in a chignon, not talking until they were ready to leave.

"You look very nice," she told him as she made a tiny adjustment to his tiepin.

"So do you." He was still brisk, but he paused to study her, then took her hand and wove their fingers together as they walked down to the waiting car.

Saqui's parents were already at the restaurant when they were shown to a table in an al fresco courtyard. An accordion player's notes floated on the soft air while strings of light gave it a soothing, magical atmosphere.

The Melillas were warm and welcoming, hugging Jasper and cupping his face while smiling widely. They were delighted he had brought his *novia* to meet them.

Vienna was still working on her Spanish, and thought that might mean bride or fiancée, but Jasper wasn't hiding that they were involved romantically. He touched her often through the meal, squeezing her hand or knee or setting his arm on her chairback and grazing her shoulder with his fingertips.

"Artista excepcional," he told them at one point and took out his phone, proceeding to show them her sketches of Peyton.

That prompted Saqui's mother to ask teasingly, *"Cuándo tendrás un bebé propio?"*

Vienna caught "when" and "baby." A hot blush of exposure rose in her throat, but Jasper took her hand and caressed her palm.

"That's something we would both welcome, wouldn't we?" he said, looking at her with so much tenderness she blushed even harder.

She nodded shakily as he repeated the comment in Spanish and the other couple wished a big family for them.

When they said their goodbyes, Mrs. Melilla hugged her and said in Spanish, "It's good to see him happy."

Vienna wanted to believe he was, but he was very quiet on the way back to their hotel.

"That was really hard for you," she noted when they were in their room, changing into something more comfortable.

"It was," he agreed, yanking at his tie. "They don't blame me. They said so, but I feel so damned responsible anyway."

"What was Saqui like? Funny, like his dad?" Mr. Melilla had cracked her up a few times, leaning over with a silly aside.

"So funny. And smart. Unafraid. Grounded. I liked that about him a lot. He was ambitious, but he wasn't materialistic. He wanted a good job so he could support a wife and have a big family. Family was so important to him. If I could at least—"

He cut himself off, but she knew what he was going to say. If he could only put Orlin Caulfield behind bars, he might not feel so awful about moving forward with his own life.

"I'm not throwing that on you again," he clarified into the silence that had fallen between them. "I'm frustrated there isn't more I could do for them, to ease their loss."

And his own?

"I know," she murmured, recognizing his reticence with her for what it was: survivor guilt. If one little thing had been different, Saqui might have lived. "I'm really sorry you lost your friend." She moved closer and slid her arms around his waist. "He sounds like a really good person."

Jasper turned to stone as she touched him, but now he took a shaken breath.

"He was." His arms closed convulsively around her. "He really was."

They stood like that a long time.

Jasper had thought living with Vienna would be an adjustment, maybe even claustrophobic at times. Surprisingly, he liked the domestic routine they fell into, especially once they moved into their new home.

Vienna had found a stunning house situated at the foot of Manquehue Hill in the upscale Vitacura neighborhood. It was not unlike the Tofino house in its terraced architecture. The tree-lined property and the hill rising behind the house gave the impression they were the only house for miles. Abundant windows looked to the lawn, the gazebo next to the pool, and views of the city lights in the distance.

Here in the primary bedroom, no expense had been spared. The palatial suite had its own sitting area, the dressing room where he currently stood, and a massive bathroom awash in luxurious touches. On its private terrace, there was an outdoor shower and a claw-foot tub open to the elements where Vienna liked to soak in fragrant bubbles.

Any of the other three bedrooms on this level would be perfect for a nursery, but when Jasper had glanced at her while touring the house, she had pointed to the room closest to where they slept. They were still keeping the pregnancy news quiet so decorators hadn't yet been hired, but he glanced in there every time he came upstairs, picturing it occupied.

On the main level, there was both a formal living room and a casual family room. The dining room table sat twelve, but they tended to eat on the terrace or on the breakfast patio off the long, narrow kitchen. It was full of stainless steel appliances, managing to be both functional and welcoming.

The bottom floor had a wine cellar, which was overkill for their needs, as was the cinema room with a bar. They were converting that into a guest suite with a kitchenette so family would be comfortable staying for long periods.

Finally, the home gym had already been emptied so Vienna could use it as a studio. Its high band of windows allowed natural light to pour in and its private courtyard with mature trees and flowerpots was the meditative atmosphere she liked to work alongside.

Thinking of her studio reminded him to take a closer

look at his shirt. Rainbow-colored fingerprints occasionally showed up when he interrupted her work with a questing kiss.

He shifted while he finished buttoning his shirt so he could see her in the mirror where she was sleeping off their early morning lovemaking.

The sex only got more amazing, which obviously contributed to his satisfaction with their living together, but they had enough outside interests that their relationship wasn't all one note. He was still restructuring at REM-Ex, hiring and meeting with officials and implementing new procedures. She had reached out to some of her clients back in Canada, telling them about various artists she she had found here in Chile, continuing the curating work she'd been doing back home.

Vienna insisted art was a wise investment and had also begun a collection for him that had earned appropriate compliments when they had held a housewarming party last weekend.

That had been a game changer for Jasper. He still felt very middle-class, but given his ownership of an international mining firm, he felt obliged to entertain executives and dignitaries. Vienna had said the housewarming was a perfect excuse. He hadn't looked forward to it at all, but she had made all the arrangements and it had been a tremendous success. Everyone had raved about how *encantadora*—charming—his "wife" was.

He hadn't corrected anyone, but the more he thought about it, the more he wanted to call her that. His wife.

It was strange to feel so compelled when he had carried a resistance to the institution of marriage for so long. After witnessing his father's agony on losing his spouse, and suffering his own rejection, Jasper had avoided thoughts of marriage. He still felt enormous guilt that Saqui couldn't carry on with life the way he was, but this would be for their child.

And Vienna, obviously. It was vitally important to him that she be looked after in the best possible way. Marriage to him would ensure she and their child had the absolute strongest foundation and rights to all he possessed.

It made sense and, armed with that rationale, he was impatient to close the deal, but she had made clear that she had certain reservations about planning for the future. She wanted to feel sure about the baby before she could feel secure in anything else. He was trying to respect that, but his mind drifted to buying a ring anyway.

Tomorrow. He was tied up today, but tomorrow he would shop for a ring. A day studying gemstones was pretty much his idea of Christmas and birthday combined so he was already looking forward to it.

"You're up early," she murmured, rolling over in the reflection of the bed behind him.

"Meetings with the Environment Superintendency today." He finished knotting his tie and centered it.

"What time?"

"All day. We're flying out to the site, but I'll be home at my regular time."

"Oh. I thought…" She sat up. "Well, that's important, obviously."

It was. He'd been trying to meet with this branch of government since he and Vienna had arrived six weeks ago. Until he had them on his side, his efforts to restart mining were dead in the water.

She looked crestfallen, though.

"What's wrong?" He turned.

"Nothing." She rearranged her features, obviously not realizing he'd seen her disappointment in the mirror. "I have my first scan today. I thought you wanted to come."

"That's tomorrow." How had he got that wrong? He reached for his phone and there it was in their shared calendar. His attendance was marked "optional," so he had accepted his own day being blocked for the other commitment, not reading this one closely enough.

He swore. "I'll see what I can do."

"I'm sure everything will be fine." She was doing that thing where she acted unbothered, sitting taller and manufacturing a pleasant smile. "I'll text you after."

"You're sure?" What if No. He refused to borrow trouble.

"It will be fine," she insisted. "But I have a video chat with one of my clients before I leave for the clinic. I should get in the shower." She rose and slipped into the bathroom.

Vienna was petrified.

She had no reason to be. She knew she was being illogical, but she had this unrelenting fear that something would go wrong with her pregnancy. If it did, she told herself as she entered the clinic with clammy hands and an upset stomach, it was better that Jasper wasn't here to watch her fall apart.

It would mean, however, that she and Jasper had lost their linchpin. Without this baby holding them together, what else would they have? That was what she was really afraid of.

They had grown a little closer over the last weeks as

they began to intertwine their lives more fully. Dare she say, they were becoming friends? They flirted and made bad jokes and, if they happened to disagree on something, managed to work through it without tearing the other down.

It wasn't strong enough to withstand a loss, though.

"Vienna? *Hola*, Mami." The technician was very warm and chatty as she confirmed Vienna's information and asked her how many weeks along she was.

"Twelve yesterday." If she counted the two weeks before she and Jasper had even met, which the doctors seemed to think was important.

"You're nervous?" the woman asked with a shrewd look at Vienna's apprehensive face. "It can be uncomfortable, but it won't hurt."

"I've been waiting to tell people until I know this scan shows everything is well," she admitted, watching closely as the woman smeared cold jelly on her abdomen. She searched the woman's cheerful expression for clues, as if the technician had X-ray vision and could tell anything just from looking at her.

The instrument was about to touch her skin when there was a knock on the door.

"I'm sorry to interrupt." A woman cracked the door, poking her head in. "Mr. Lindor is here. May he join you?"

"What?" Vienna lifted her head. "Yes," she hurried to say.

"Is that Papi?" the technician asked. "Come, come. You can stand over there."

Jasper looked every bit as powerfully handsome as he had this morning when he'd shrugged on that light gray suit jacket and kissed her goodbye. The pale glow from the ultrasound screen made his expression difficult to read, but the kiss on her brow was tender enough to leaving a lingering tingle.

"I thought you were busy?" She was floored that he had made this a priority.

"I told them to fly to site without me. If I can't trust my team, why did I hire them?" He picked up her hand and squeezed gently. "Is everything okay?"

"We're just starting." The technician pressed a dull, hard instrument against Vienna's abdomen.

Vienna gritted her teeth against the discomfort of her full bladder, waiting for—

"Here's your baby's heart." The woman pointed to a fluttering glow on the screen.

"Oh," Vienna sighed with relief. Tears came into her eyes.

Jasper wove his fingers with hers. In a very visceral way, she felt each of those flutters traveling through both of them, fusing them together.

"And already posing for selfies," the technician teased, clicking when the baby's profile came into focus. "You can use that for your announcement," she told Vienna.

"We can tell people?" Jasper asked, voice not quite steady. He looked to Vienna. "No more worries?"

Logically, she knew the twelve-week mark was not a clear line that guaranteed anything. It only meant it was less likely that loss could happen, but emotionally it was a tremendous milestone for her. It was one that choked her up with joy at the miracle she was finally letting herself believe could come true.

"Vi," Jasper asked in a hushed voice, caressing her wet cheek. "What's wrong?"

"Nothing. Nothing is wrong and that makes me really, really happy."

"Me, too." He pressed his smile to hers.

Jasper had rushed back to his office for the afternoon, but he came home early, surprising Vienna where she was cooling off in the pool, still metaphorically floating after seeing the evidence of their growing baby. It was real!

"Oh. Hello," she said when he appeared in his swimsuit. It was a low-waist, snug black band that underlined his six-pack abs and stretched across his flat hips, barely containing his gear. He didn't say anything, only dove straight in, not surfacing until he was beside her in the shallow end where she sat on the stairs.

"Honey, I'm home," he said when he popped up. He kissed her, beard and lips wet as he lingered with his greeting. When he drew back, she was as breathless as if she had swum the length of the pool underwater.

"So you are." She was insubstantial as he gathered her in his arms and stole her seat on the stairs, guiding her into his lap. "How was the rest of your day?" she asked.

"Good. We passed muster and can move to next steps."

"That's good news!"

"It is."

"Not least of which is that we get to continue spending winters here, where it's summer. I'm officially a snowbird," she said, referring to the Canadians who flew south in October. "Why do they even call them that when they're trying to escape the snow?"

"Right? Team sunfish. The more time I get to see you in a bikini, the better."

"This is probably my last day in a bikini for a while," she said ruefully, patting the distinct roundness that was starting to show in her middle.

"Don't get self-conscious on my account." His hand was on her hip and his thumb stroked toward her navel. "I think you're cute as hell." He shifted her so her bottom was more firmly in the cradle of his thighs. "Did you talk to anyone at home?"

"I wanted to wait for you." She played her fingers over his ear and the back of his neck. "I kind of want to do it in person, but also, I can't wait until spring. What do you think of going home for Christmas?"

"Amelia asked me the other day what our plans were. I said I'd check with you. I think we should go home. When we do, we could…" He tipped her slightly and his hand worked under her thigh.

"You're usually better at this," she said blithely, while hanging on around his neck so she didn't fall into the water.

"I have something in my trunks."

"I'm familiar with the contents of your trunks. I'm pretty sure you're off the mark there, too."

"You think you're so funny." Amusement was glinting in his eyes. "There's a pocket in them."

"Where? And for *what*? If you have your phone in there, I will be very impressed." She wiggled, trying to see, but whatever he wanted was in his fist.

"When we go home, let's make this official." He opened his hand to show her a ring with a vivid blue stone that flashed purple in the light. The platinum setting was elegant in its simplicity.

"Jasper! That's beautiful. Sapphire?"

"Blue diamond. They're very rare. This one is ethically sourced. I checked. I thought it suited a woman who is the diamond of diamonds."

"Flatterer," she accused, but she was genuinely moved by his words. "You've already given me the most precious thing I could ever want, though." She meant their baby.

"I'm being sincere." He cupped her cheek, waiting for her eyes to meet his. "You are very special, Vienna Waverly. Remarkable. Not just for this beautiful miracle you're creating, but for the very specific sparkle you bring to my life. I'm in awe of you every day—as an artist and as a woman who is starting a new life on her own terms. I already know you'll be an amazing mother to our child. Will you marry me?"

How could she say no? It wasn't a declaration of love, but he was making a point of telling her this wasn't just about their baby. For the first time in her life, she felt as though someone really saw her and valued her and *wanted* her. That meant everything.

Her throat closed up with emotion so she could only whisper, "Yes." She held out her hand for him to thread the ring onto her finger.

As he did, an old wives' tale came to her, something her grandmother had told her as a child. She had said the wedding ring went on the left ring finger because there was a direct vein from that finger up her arm and into her heart.

It certainly felt that way as Jasper slid the ring into place. A sweet sensation arrowed into her chest and, even though she had never felt anything like it, she knew what it was: love. True love. The kind she had always wished for.

The words hovered in a glow around her heart, glittering and fragile in their newness.

His mouth covered hers before she could say them aloud, which was okay. She wasn't ready yet and, pretty soon, she forgot about anything except where her bikini had gone and what else he had in his trunks.

CHAPTER TWELVE

VIENNA USED HER connections at home—Jasper was still trying to get her friends straight, but he was pretty sure she called the one Hunter had jilted—to squeeze the only available date out of a boutique hotel in Toronto. It had been converted from a nineteenth-century bank and they were booked solid for the busy holiday season, but they'd had a last-minute midweek cancellation.

They sent out invites, but kept the baby news to themselves. After a busy month of making arrangements from afar, they landed mere days before their nuptials, into a typical snowy, blustery Ontario storm.

Jasper didn't mind the weather. It gave them an excuse to stay in while Vienna slept off her jet lag. He did relent and allow his sister and her family to invade the first afternoon they were back. Truthfully, he was excited to see Amelia's reaction to the baby news and she did not disappoint. She screamed.

Peyton was so startled that she cried and needed a cuddle with Mommy to calm down, but the adults were laughing and Amelia said, "I'm going to cry for days. I'm so happy for you both. For all of us." She kept hugging each of them, even Hunter and Peyton, unable to contain her elation.

"Vi." Hunter was quieter in his reaction.

Jasper tensed, not caring what Hunter might say to him, but he was damned protective of Vienna's feelings. If her brother was the least bit offside, they would have a very serious conversation.

But Hunter's eyes were damp when he said, "This is really great news. Congratulations. Both of you." He shook Jasper's hand with genuine warmth.

Jasper tried not to let the sentiment get to him, but the way Vienna looked so incandescent humbled him. It was a moment of pure shared happiness. Moments like this were as rare as that blue diamond she wore and as close to perfection as anything could get.

Guilt speared into him even as he basked in it, smearing a streak of darkness across the day. If only Orlin Caulfield wasn't also enjoying life to the fullest. The last report had placed him somewhere in the South Pacific, still evading any sort of law enforcement or consequences for his actions.

"What's wrong?" Vienna asked, touching his arm. She was always tuned in to his moods.

"Nothing." Jasper shook off his grim thoughts. He wouldn't ruin this for her. Or Amelia.

But even as he held his niece and imagined holding his own baby soon, all he could think about was Saqui, and the fact he would never get to experience this at all.

Jasper seemed remote over the next few days. Vienna put it down to how busy they were.

They drove to see his father, so they could share the baby news in person. Tobias was delighted and promised to see them again soon. He was bringing a date, Ola, to their wedding, but they wouldn't arrive until the morning of the ceremony.

Once all the family had been informed, they made a public announcement confirming that Vienna Waverly was newly engaged, and yes, she was pregnant, and yes, she was marrying Jasper Lindor at a downtown hotel a week before Christmas.

Paparazzi were soon braving the sleeting weather and thick holiday traffic to photograph them as they left her apartment to run a few errands.

"That's another thing I love about Santiago," Vienna mused in the car. "No one cares who I am there."

It wasn't the most profound statement, but Jasper didn't respond, seeming distracted.

"Is everything all right?" she asked. "I'm sorry about the party tonight, but people expect to see me there."

"My sister expects me to be there," he pointed out dryly.

"True." It was more of an obligation to Hunter, though. Her brother had always been efficient with his socializing. He hosted two or three huge parties throughout the year, inviting all the celebrities and business contacts who expected it. Vienna had often played hostess in the past, so she knew practically everyone who was invited. "I could be indisposed if you prefer to stay home."

"I don't mind. I still feel like the blue-collar boy from Goderich, but you always make these things very easy to bear."

"That's funny. You're the one who makes it easy for me." They had hosted several of their own parties full of high-profile strangers in Santiago. Vienna still suffered a certain tension, expecting a drunken spectacle like her stepmother used to provide, but Jasper made a good wingman. He knew how to talk *fútbol* and business opportunities while she leaned into arts and culture.

They were turning into quite the power couple, she thought with amusement as they parted. She had a fitting for her wedding gown, but was also picking up the dress she would wear to tonight's party.

Jasper was out when she returned, which made her wonder where he'd gone, but he was home by the time she rose from a brief nap. The party was black tie, so he dressed in a tuxedo, one tailored to accentuate his shoulders and wedged frame. His beard had been trimmed and his hair was professionally tousled.

"You look amazing."

"So do you." His gaze nearly incinerated the blue sequined gown right off her body. His attention flowed down her abundant cleavage to where her little bump was proudly front and center. "You don't need any adornments, but when you said you were wearing blue, I thought these would go with your dress. Maybe not." He showed her a pair of earrings. "Tourmalines. They're from Brazil."

They were a startling neon blue with icy diamonds surrounding them.

"I love them!" she gasped. "I'm definitely wearing them." She removed the simple diamond studs she had put in her lobes. "We'll call it an early Christmas present."

"Actually, I have something else for under the tree." He scratched beneath his beard.

"Wedding gift?"

"Same."

"Jasper. Do you buy these for me? Or for yourself?" she

asked with teasing suspicion. He had told her once that he was single because he had a small obsession with rocks. He seemed to take a lot of pleasure in finding rare and beautiful gemstonés for her, not that she minded in the least.

"Little of both," he admitted ruefully. "I get to look at them when you wear them, so that's definitely a win for me. Did you know there's something called a push present?"

"You're incorrigible," she chuckled.

For a moment, he seemed to have shed whatever heavy mood he'd been wearing. They were smiling and lost in each other's eyes and the words were right there. *I love you.*

The doorman buzzed.

"That will be the car," he said and crooked his arm in invitation. "Come on. I want to show you off."

"Me, or these earrings?"

"You," he insisted, lifting her spirits even more.

The party was a crush, filled with pro-athletes, Canadian film and music stars, and executives from various corporations.

For the first time in memory, Vienna was completely relaxed as she circulated with Jasper. She felt as though she had rewritten her life with a far better ending. She was in love with her fiancé, expecting his baby. In two days they would marry. Everything was finally going right for her.

As the party reached its height, Hunter gave a toast. First, he thanked his guests for coming, and thanked Amelia for putting together such a wonderful bash. They shared a look of naked adoration that had Vienna swallowing a lump of emotion.

"Finally, I'd like to offer a toast to my brother-in-law, Jasper, who is soon to be my brother-in-law." Hunter cleared his throat and waited for the chuckles to sub-side. "And my sister, Vienna, who kept me sane through some very rough years. I'm so proud of you for going after the love and happiness you so rightly deserve. To Jasper and Vienna."

Vienna felt Jasper's arm come around her as he raised his champagne and she lifted her sparkling cranberry juice. His lips touched her temple and she made herself smile, but Hunter's words were echoing in her ears like a death knell.

The love and happiness you so rightly deserve...

Did she have that, though?

Vienna was still trying to shake off her doubts the next afternoon. She and Jasper had a great relationship, one that built her confidence and gave her the other things she had so wanted in her life—art, a baby.

But the other vital thing she had wanted was love.

Jasper went out for the morning, joining college friends for coffee since they couldn't make the wedding, but he wanted to see them while he was in town.

Vienna had needed a quiet morning anyway. She woke feeling headachy and vaguely nauseous, which she put down to the late night at Hunter's party and grazing all that rich and sugary food. Maybe she had picked up a bug from travel. Her cheeks felt hot while the rest of her was chilled, but she told herself her pregnant body was having trouble adjusting to the switch from summer warmth to subzero winter and relentless central heat. A quick text to her maternity nurse, who had returned to Vancouver for the holidays, told Vienna she could have an over-the-counter headache tablet if she wanted one.

Vienna took one and it seemed to help. She felt less

touchy when Jasper returned and they left for the hotel. They were having their final meeting with the wedding planner and touring the rooms where the wedding ceremony and reception would be held. Soon, the wedding party would arrive for the rehearsal, then they would all have dinner.

Due to the short notice, their guest list was only three hundred, but they had spared no expense, starting with booking this venue. It was stunning. The Renaissance architecture featured arched windows and high, ornate ceilings, imposing columns, and polished brass rails. They would marry in a gallery where a bower had been set up against heavy wooden doors. After the vows, while they were having their photos taken in the vault turned wine cellar, the guests would enter the main hall where they would be entertained by bartenders who spun and juggled bottles while serving cocktails at the long bar.

The reception ballroom was decorated in a winter theme with frosted red roses in tall crystal vases standing like icicles in circles of holly. Tartan throw blankets were draped over the backs of chairs as gifts for the guests. Handwritten calligraphy place cards were propped up in pine cones, and sparkling snowflakes hung from the ceiling. Candles in lanterns were waiting to be lit.

"I'll leave you to enjoy this while I check on the gift bags. I know everything arrived, but staff may still be assembling them. This is genius, by the way. I will be stealing this idea for future guests." The specialist touched a button on her way out the door, lowering the lights.

A projection of the night sky appeared on the ceiling with the aurora borealis flickering in streaks of green and purple dancing across it.

"Wow." Jasper tilted back his head so Vienna couldn't see his expression, but he sounded awed. "You made all of this happen in a few weeks?"

"I wanted it to be perfect."

"It is. You are." He reached for her.

She nudged up against him, both of them watching the ceiling a moment longer.

"Jasper." She had to know.

"Yes?" He looked down on her with tenderness and cupped her cheek. "Oh. You're nice and warm."

"I love you," she said, heart in her throat as she searched his eyes.

She saw the shift in his gaze to caution and it stole the floor right out from under her. She was falling into an abyss all by herself.

Oh, God.

"You don't love me," she realized in horror while old voices asked, *Why would he?*

"Vi. I care about you very much. You know that." His hands firmed on her, as if he sensed her slipping away and was trying to hold on to her.

She pressed until he released her, all of her going hot and cold as her profound mistake crashed over her in churning waves.

"I'm doing it again," she realized with horror. A terrible burn seared up from the pit of her belly into the back of her throat. "I'm getting caught up in creating the appearance of perfection, but that's not what this is."

"There is no such thing as perfection. You know that." His tone hardened. "What we have is very, very good, though."

"I thought we were falling in love, Jasper! I thought if

I gave you time…" How long had she waited last time? *Years*. She felt so stupid. *Again*. "*Can* you love me? *Will* you?" Oh, she felt pathetic asking that, but she had to know. Had to.

"I can't see into the future, Vi. What I can promise is to always be honest with you."

She recoiled from that.

"But you haven't *been* honest. You've made me think…" Had he, though? Or was she the one who had interpreted every gesture as burgeoning love? She had seen what she wanted to see, mistaking kindness and decency for something more than that. That was how little she'd had of those things!

The stupid lights were making her sick, so she impatiently moved to the door.

"Vienna!" he shouted behind her.

She smacked the switches to put on the main lights, washing out the romantic sky with cold, clinical white.

For a moment they stared at each other across the sea of colorless crystal and faux snow and unlit candles.

Jasper's jaw was clenched tight, his chest rising in agitated breaths. "You're acting as if a couple of words would change what we have."

"They do!" she cried. "I just said them and you didn't. That changes *everything*."

"It does not," he asserted firmly. "We're still getting married, we're still having a baby, we're still building a life together."

"On what?" She flung up helpless hands. "On me feeling *again* like I'm giving everything while my husband offers me nothing?"

"It's hardly nothing, Vi," he shot back darkly.

"Of *yourself.* You are asking me to wake up every morning knowing I'm in love with you while you don't love me. That's even worse than neither of us feeling any love! I can't do it. I won't."

What was she saying? She covered her mouth, already seeing the canceled wedding and another huge scandal.

She grasped onto the wall, so nauseated she was dizzy with it.

"Vienna," he growled. "Don't make threats you're not prepared to back up."

"Do you really want to marry someone you don't love?" she asked him with anguish. "Take it from me, Jasper, it's not great." She was shaking, her whole body chilled, but sweaty. "I think I'm going to throw up."

"This is cold feet. Let's sit down—" He yanked out a chair. "Let's talk this out."

"No. I'm literally…" Her stomach was curdling. The chill on her skin deepened. She hurried away, rushing to where she'd seen the door to the ladies' room earlier.

Jasper started after her, but decided they could use a minute to cool off.

He looked around and saw…

He swore and rubbed his eyes.

He saw how much care she'd put into this wedding. How much it meant to her. He saw love.

He also saw a culmination of everything he'd been seeing and hearing since their return to Canada. Just this morning, he'd heard it again from one of his old college buddies.

"You've really got it all, eh? You're living the dream."

He was. He was at the top of his professional game,

had a beautiful fiancée, a wedding planned and a baby on the way. What more did anyone need?

Love. Of course Vi wanted love.

He could barely accept it from her, though, let alone offer it. Which would crush her if he dared to say it, but all of this was so much more than he deserved. Not when—

"What kind of wife do you want?" Saqui had asked him one day while they were hiking into a valley.

"Are you placing an order?" Jasper asked dryly.

"Online," Saqui said with a swish of his finger to indicate swiping. "But they keep sending the wrong one." He grinned his mischievous grin.

"Yeah?" Jasper chuckled, expecting Saqui was working up to a tall tale on his dating antics. "What are you looking for, then?"

Saqui took him seriously, pressing his bottom lip with thought.

"Someone who thinks about things. Pretty would be nice, but she has to be kind. And she has to like dogs. I want her to make me laugh. She had better cook," he decided with a grimace.

That made Jasper chuckle again because they had established that Saqui was a terrible cook.

"Why are you so eager to marry?" Jasper had to ask. "Are you saving yourself for your wife?"

"No," Saqui chuckled. "But I want to hurry up and meet her. This…" He scanned the hillside they were scaling. "What we're doing is interesting, but it doesn't mean anything. This isn't my life. *She* will be."

Whenever Jasper thought about that conversation, he thought about the poor girl out there somewhere who would never get to meet the man who had been so anxious to find her.

"Where's Vienna?" Amelia asked, yanking Jasper out of his agonizing memories.

Amelia and Hunter were Vienna's matron of honor and escort down the aisle. Jasper's father, Tobias, would stand up for him as best man and two of Jasper's cousins were coming in with his father in the morning to be groomsmen.

Would the wedding even go ahead? Jasper's heart lurched.

"She went to the ladies' room. Would you check on her for me?" He was starting to suspect she'd left altogether.

He pinched the bridge of his nose, unable to look at Hunter when Hunter asked gravely, "Is everything all right?"

"We had an argument," Jasper admitted.

"About?"

Cold feet, he wanted to say, but that wasn't true at all.

He didn't get a chance to reply. Someone else arrived.

"Hunter."

"Remy." Hunter shook the man's hand with the familiarity of long friendship. There was ruefulness in his tone when he greeted Remy's partner, briefly kissing her cheek. "Eden. Good to see you. You look wonderful. Congratulations." He nodded at the baby bump she revealed as she unbuttoned her coat.

Vienna had worriedly asked Amelia how she felt about her inviting Eden, the bride Hunter had thrown over for Amelia, to be her bridesmaid along with someone named Quinn. Amelia had said it was time she properly met everyone.

"It's good to see you, too," Eden said to Hunter, seeming sincere if sheepish and amused by her equal rush to the altar with someone else.

"Quinn, Micah. Have you all met Vienna's groom?" Hunter introduced the second pair as they came in.

Jasper wanted nothing less in the world than to meet new people right now. He gave everyone distracted handshakes, looking past them for his bride.

This isn't my life. She *will be.*

Something hard was lodged in his throat, making it hard to breathe.

"Where are Vi and Amelia?" Remy looked around.

"I'm wondering that myself," Jasper said tightly and started for the door.

At that moment, Amelia rushed back in. She was pale, eyes wide with alarm.

"I've called an ambulance. Jasper..." The look on her face sent a sword straight through his heart. "Vienna is having stomach pains. She can't walk."

"Vi." Jasper burst into the ladies' room and dropped to the floor in front of where Vienna had curled up on an upholstered bench.

"She has a fever," the hotel's first aid attendant was saying as he read the instrument he had just aimed at her forehead. He relayed the number into the phone.

Jasper cupped her cheek and tried to dry the tear tracking from her eye onto her nose.

She couldn't take the look of anguish on his face and closed her eyes against it.

"No bleeding. How many weeks?" the attendant asked.

"Seventeen and a half," Jasper said. "Can you check the heartbeat?"

"Not with a stethoscope. Too early in the pregnancy."
The attendant offered a tight look of apology.

Jasper tried to take her hand, but she drew it away,
wanting to keep it on the side of her bump. She was certain she had felt a flutter there. Did she, though? Or was
that more wishful thinking?

The stabbing pain was relentless, sitting there angry
and horrific, making her sick. She just wanted to be left
alone with her agony, but people kept asking her stupid
questions about when it had started and what she had
eaten and what sorts of medications she was on.

Now the first responders were here, making her shift
onto the bed, touching her and—

"Let me do it," Jasper snarled, then ever so gently
stroked her hair. "Okay, Vi? Can you hold on to my neck?
I'm going to move you onto the stretcher."

He gathered her as carefully as he could, but she was
still biting her lips as he moved her, moaning with protest. It hurt *so much*.

They covered her with a blanket and hurried to roll
the stretcher outside where snowflakes melted against
her hot face. Jasper climbed into the ambulance with her,
taking her hand in two of his while the attendant poked
something into the back of her other hand and asked her
to help him time how quickly the pains were coming.

"It's one long pain," she said for the thousandth time,
clenching her wet eyes. "Even my own baby doesn't
want me."

"Vi." Jasper had never felt so helpless in his life. He
would do anything, *anything*, to stop this from happening. He was agonized at the thought of losing their baby.

It would kill him, but he *could not bear* what it would do to Vienna.

How could he have been so stupid earlier, when he had felt guilty for "having it all." He should have been on his knees with gratitude. He *knew* how fragile life was, but he had still taken his good fortune for granted. This incredible woman had told him she loved him and he hadn't wanted to hear it because it was more good on top of good. Too much good. He hadn't felt entitled to that much happiness.

He had met the woman who would be his life, but he hadn't wanted to fully embrace her and all that he felt for her because of guilt. Guilt that he held up like a shield so he wouldn't have to suffer the grief that waited behind it.

"Vienna, listen to me." He had to consciously keep himself from crushing her hand. "I love you. Do you hear me? No matter what happens, I love you and I want you to marry me. *You.*"

"You don't have to say that." Her lips quivered.

"I do have to say it," he said grimly. "I should have said it an hour ago, but—" He swore under his breath. "An hour ago, I was afraid to let myself need you, as if it hadn't already happened. How would I cope if I lost you?" He pressed the back of her hand to his cheek, only becoming aware tears were leaking from his eyes when she caught her breath and shifted her finger against his wet skin.

"I didn't know fear an hour ago. Not this kind. Now I do. I love you. You are everything to me. Whatever happens, you are not alone right now. I'm right here beside you and I will stay beside you. Okay?"

She blinked her matted lashes, choking, "It's just s-so unfair."

"It is." He leaned over her and stroked her brow. "But let's be thankful this baby came into our lives and brought us together. Right now, we're still all three together, hmm?"

She nodded and clung to his hand, not saying anything more until they arrived at the hospital where she was wheeled into the emergency room and quickly assessed.

"The fetal heart rate is elevated," the doctor said as the instruments were hooked up.

They both looked to each other with tentative hope.

"There's a heartbeat," Jasper confirmed, squeezing that news into Vienna's arm.

She nodded through her tears of distress while the doctor ordered an ultrasound and promised to give her something for the pain.

A few minutes later, she was wheeled into a similar imaging room to the one that had made them so happy in Santiago. This time, the technician was somber, but she quicky identified the baby's heartbeat. The baby was moving, too.

"Are you having contractions?" the technician asked.

"I don't know what this pain is. It's constant."

The technician continued to torture her, pressing into a spot that made Vienna nearly scream. She stuck her fingernails into the back of Jasper's hand.

"Be careful," Jasper growled at the woman.

The technician nodded with concern and the doctor was brought in.

"You're not miscarrying," the doctor said after consulting the screen. "You have appendicitis. You need surgery. Tonight."

Jasper's heart fell as quickly as it had lifted.

"But—what about the baby?" Vienna asked, mouth trembling.

"We do it laparoscopically. The risk to your pregnancy is low. We'll begin prepping you immediately."

She looked to Jasper, openly afraid.

He swallowed down his helplessness. He couldn't bear it. He cupped the side of her face, looking deeply into her eyes.

"I love you. Whatever happens, *I love you.* I'm not going anywhere," he swore.

Jasper was allowed to stay with her until they took her to the OR. When he walked into the waiting room, Amelia and Hunter were there, both pale with concern.

"Appendicitis," Jasper said, running his hand through his hair. "It doesn't seem to have burst, so that's a silver lining. They said surgery will take an hour."

"Surgery," Hunter repeated in a hollow voice. His gaze went to the doors where Jasper had come through. He looked as though he wanted to go find his sister and see for himself.

"What about the baby?" Amelia asked anxiously.

"Okay for now." Jasper sat down, knees no longer able to hold him, quietly begging his friend to do what he could to give him a second chance.

I'll get it right this time, Saqui. I promise.

Amelia moved to sit beside him and wordlessly hugged his arm, leaving her head tilted against her shoulder. Then she reached out her hand to Hunter, beckoning him to sit on her other side so she could hold his hand, too.

How could Vienna have ever worried her brother would disown her? Hunter was as wrecked by this as Jasper was. If Amelia wasn't between them, they would be clinging to each other.

Hunter shifted once, taking out his phone and replying to a text, murmuring, "Remy," but otherwise they sat like that the whole time, wordless, holding on to each other while they waited for news.

Finally, a nurse came in to say, "She's in recovery. Everything went well. The baby's vitals are strong, too. You can see her shortly," she said to Jasper. "Only one visitor, I'm afraid."

"I'll call Dad," Amelia said with a shaken sigh. She rose when Jasper did and hugged him. "It's going to be okay now."

He sure as hell hoped so.

Amelia placed the call and moved into a corner while Hunter pushed his hands into his pockets and studied him. Jasper realized he had never told him what his argument with Vienna was about.

"I'll call off the wedding," Hunter said.

"No," Jasper asserted. "I said some stupid things to her, but I love her and told her so. She loves me, too. No one is ever going to work harder than I will at making her happy. We're getting married."

"I'm pleased to hear it," Hunter said with a trace of amusement coming in at the edges of his somber expression. "Vienna made choices years ago that I had to respect, but I knew she was shortchanging herself. I've always hated myself for not trying harder to dissuade her. I need to know she's marrying someone who sees how incredible she is. I *want* you to marry her. God knows, that will make my wife happy and that's all *I* want. But I don't think Vienna is going to make it to the ceremony tomorrow."

Jasper swore and shut his eyes.

"I meant that I'll deal with informing the hotel and the guests." Hunter was definitely laughing at him. "Based on experience, I suggest letting the guests eat the food and drink you've paid for. It goes a long way toward smoothing everything over."

"Thanks. Have a great time," Jasper said wryly. "Take photos so we know what we missed."

Jasper wouldn't miss anything except the vows. He needed that formal connection to her more than ever now.

The nurse came to get him as Amelia finished her call to their father. "Dad will still come tomorrow. He wants to see all of us and make sure Vienna is okay."

Jasper nodded.

"Do you want us to wait and take you back to the hotel?" Hunter offered.

"No, I'll stay with her as long as they'll let me."

"Give her our love," Hunter said.

"I will." Jasper hurried to Vienna's side.

Every time Vienna woke over the next two days, Jasper was there. Each time, he reassured her that the baby was doing well, that she was recovering nicely, and that he loved her.

"The wedding," she said plaintively when she got enough of her faculties back to remember it.

"The cocktail show was a big hit, as was the improvised snowball fight," he said dryly.

"Oh? Did Amelia go? I love Eden and Quinn, but I was so worried she would feel awkward with them."

"She said she spent a lot of the night chatting with them. She thinks they're great."

"Oh, that makes me happy. Did you go?"

His frown scolded her for even suggesting it. "When I go to *our* wedding, you'll be there." He brought her palm to his lips, pressing a kiss there. "You will marry me, won't you?"

A latent misgiving struck. "Maybe I was putting too much pressure on our relationship." She could see now that the pageantry of the wedding had been one of her old coping strategies, where she had projected the grand romance she had longed for.

"That's not true at all." He hitched his hip on the bed and pressed her hand to his thigh. "I couldn't take being this happy, Vi. It was hard to accept your love when Saqui will never have what we have, but he would be the first to say, *Love her, you fool.* He knew how rare and special it is to find the person you want to spend your life with. He would be angry with me for wasting a single minute of our time. So would my father, for that matter. Love is scary. Loss hurts."

His mouth flattened and he continued to iron her hand to his thigh.

"I was using my guilt and anger over Saqui's death to buffer my grief, so I didn't have to face it and feel it. Rather than dealing with the pain, I put it between us. On you. I won't do that again. I promise."

"You miss him a lot." She turned her hand so she was holding his.

"I do." His brow flexed. "But I have to accept that he's

gone. Putting Orlin Caulfield in jail won't bring Saqui back, so I won't obsess over that anymore. It's important to me that he be caught and brought to trial, but I'll let the authorities handle it. That isn't my life. You are. Both of you." He released her hand to set his palm on the top of her bump. "I'm so glad you and the baby are going to be all right. I don't know what I would have done without you, I really don't."

She covered his knuckles, so moved by his naked honesty she could hardly speak.

"I let my own ghosts come between us when I said you don't give me anything." She felt so remorseful for saying that. "You give me everything. My life with you is the one I always wanted. I would be honored to marry you, Jasper."

They married a few days after she was discharged, on the morning of Christmas Eve. Vienna was still moving slowly, but feeling much better. She put on her wedding dress, which was a classic ivory silk with a crossover top and a satin sash. Since she thought they were simply meeting the wedding officiant at the hotel for a private ceremony, she didn't bother with the tiara and veil or even a bouquet.

She was greeted with a miniature version of their wedding decor in an intimate lounge. The arbor was in place before a marble fireplace where a fire crackled merrily.

Vienna gasped as she took that in along with the dozen smiling faces.

"My cousins are home with their families, but these guys were happy to step in."

He meant Eden and Remy, and Quinn and Micah, who

were standing with Tobias and Ola. Hunter held Peyton, who was in layers of silk and tule. Amelia was trying to put a band of silk flowers on her head, but Peyton pulled it right off.

The baby smiled when she saw Vienna. Everyone did.

"I can't believe this!" she said to Jasper, touched to the bottoms of her feet.

"We wanted to come," Eden said.

"Yeah. You scared us the other day," Remy said, coming forward to give her a gentle hug.

"You came all the way to Germany for our wedding," Quinn said.

"We weren't going to miss yours," Micah agreed.

"Shall we get started?" the officiant said in a gentle nudge.

The women arranged themselves to the left of the arbor, the men on the right. Ola took Peyton to lead Vienna and Hunter down the short stretch of carpet that formed the aisle.

"He really loves you, you know. We all do. *I* do," Hunter said in a quiet, sincere undertone as he offered his arm to her.

"I know." She hugged his arm. "But thank you. I like hearing it. I love you, too."

They started to walk. Her pulse tripped with enchantment, taking in everything from the soft notes of an unseen harp to the light shining from her groom's eyes.

Jasper was profoundly handsome in his morning suit. He took both her hands as she joined him. His eyes were damp with joyous emotion. So were hers.

They spoke their simple vows in strong, confident voices and, when they kissed, they were both smiling.

The spark of passion was always there, though, keeping her lips clinging to his as he tenderly brushed at the happy tear on her cheek.

"I never imagined I could feel this way about anyone," he told her, right there in front of all their witnesses. "I love you with everything in me."

She hadn't known she could feel this much love, either. Or that she could let it spring out of her, confident that Jasper would catch it and hold it with such tender care.

"I love you, too." She had never felt so truly loved, so surrounded by love, in her life.

EPILOGUE

Almost one year later

"I PROMISE YOU, son, that if you let yourself sleep, the whole world becomes a brighter place," Jasper told Finley Tobias Saqui Lindor.

The infant interrupted his own overtired cry to give a big yawn that showed his four tiny front teeth. He scrubbed his fist into his eye and started to cry again.

His first nap of the day had been interrupted by workmen downstairs, but he was a little too much like his father, pushing himself when he wanted something. Today, he wanted to not relax and nod off.

He wasn't hungry, having almost fallen asleep while Vienna had fed him a few minutes ago. Jasper had then brought him up here, thinking he would fall right asleep, but no. He had decided to get some things off his chest first.

Jasper didn't mind an excuse to pace the room that was decorated with yellow ducks between the green stripes in the wallpaper, rubbing the back of his grouchy son. He knew what a privilege this was.

"I thought we had a gentlemen's agreement about this, though," he chided softly. "We're both working on better sleep habits. I will if you will."

Jasper's insomnia meant that he'd been hands-on from the earliest days—and nights—with their newborn. They were both getting better at sleeping longer stretches, though. The turning point for Jasper had been when Orlin Caulfield had stopped at Rapa Nui for provisions. He'd been apprehended and was now in the custody of Chilean authorities.

"What's holding you back? Hmm?" Jasper asked his son. "Are you angry Mommy's working so much? She's getting ready for her show. If you knew how many of her sketches were of you, you might not be so put out."

Fin finally took the pacifier and quieted. His eyes drifted closed and his small body relaxed into sleep.

Jasper very carefully eased him into his crib, taking an extra minute to absorb those miniature echoes of his wife in Fin's features. The peak in his barely-there brow and the shape of his ear and the color of his fine hair.

As he turned to the door, he found Vienna waiting there, watching them, her face wearing the serene love that filled him with such humble gratitude.

He touched his lips and joined her outside the room, bringing the baby monitor and gently closing the door behind himself.

"You didn't have to come up. He's asleep."

"The workmen left, so hopefully he'll get a full nap this time," she said, smiling at the screen.

Fin was a ball of energy who kept them firmly on their toes, then this—a cherub who mesmerized until he woke and burst into chortles and bounces and squirms all over again. He had already started to crawl, much to their terrified delight. His near daily swim was his absolute favorite time of day, so a plexiglass fence was being installed around the pool tomorrow, long before they really needed it, but Peyton would be here soon and she *ran*.

Hunter and Amelia were bringing Tobias and Ola for Christmas. They were arriving Friday and staying through the holidays. Then, since Micah and Quinn were joining Remy and Eden in the Caribbean, the foursome had proposed coming to Santiago to celebrate New Year's Eve with them. They were both looking forward to a fun, lively time with friends and family.

"Are you going back to work?" he asked her as she stayed here with him beside the baby's door.

"I thought we might take advantage of a quiet house before it gets very noisy and busy again." She slid her arms around his waist, pressing her curves up against him in a way that always lit his fire.

"I like how you think." He slid his hand down her hair, catching the scrunchie and releasing it from its ponytail.

"I like how you make me feel." She took his hand and led him to their bedroom.

"How's that?" His mind was already tracking down the sensual paths he planned to explore with her.

"Loved," she said simply.

His heart swelled in his chest as he pressed her to the bed beneath him. He could definitely keep doing that.

* * * * *

COMING SOON!

We really hope you enjoyed reading this book. If you're looking for more romance be sure to head to the shops when new books are available on

Thursday 25th May

MILLS & BOON®

Coming next month

WHAT HER SICILIAN HUSBAND DESIRES
Caitlin Crews

"Truly," he said, in that low voice of his that wound around and around inside her, "you are a thing of beauty, Chloe."

"So are you, Lao," she said softly, then found herself smiling when he looked surprised she should compliment him in return.

It made her wonder if he was so overwhelming, so wildly intense, and so astronomically remote in every way that mattered, that no one bothered to offer him compliments. But any such thoughts splintered, because he carried her hand to his lips and pressed a courtly sort of kiss to her knuckles.

It should have felt silly and old-fashioned, but it didn't. Not in an ancient castle, perched here above an island so steeped in history.

And not when the faint brush of his lips across the back of her hand made everything inside her seem to curl up tight, then begin to boil.

"Welcome, little one," he murmured, the heat in his gaze making everything inside her take notice, especially the tender flesh between her legs. And that heart of hers that would not stop its wild thundering. "To our wedding night. At last."

Continue reading
WHAT HER SICILIAN HUSBAND DESIRES
Caitlin Crews

Available next month
www.millsandboon.co.uk

LET'S TALK

Romance

For exclusive extracts, competitions and special offers, find us online:

- **f** facebook.com/millsandboon
- **𝕏** @MillsandBoon
- **⊙** @MillsandBoonUK
- **♪** @MillsandBoonUK

Get in touch on 01413 063 232

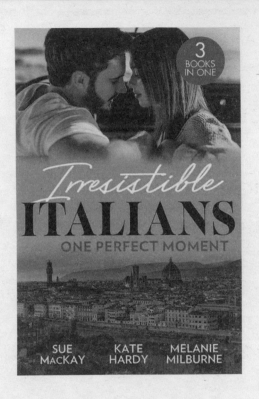

MILLS & BOON

THE HEART OF ROMANCE

A ROMANCE FOR EVERY READER

MODERN

Prepare to be swept off your feet by sophisticated, sexy and seductive heroes, in some of the world's most glamourous and romantic locations, where power and passion collide.

HISTORICAL

Escape with historical heroes from time gone by. Whether your passion is for wicked Regency Rakes, muscled Vikings or rugged Highlanders, awaken the romance of the past.

MEDICAL

Set your pulse racing with dedicated, delectable doctors in the high-pressure world of medicine, where emotions run high and passion, comfort and love are the best medicine.

True Love

Celebrate true love with tender stories of heartfelt romance, from the rush of falling in love to the joy a new baby can bring, and a focus on the emotional heart of a relationship.

Desire

Indulge in secrets and scandal, intense drama and sizzling hot action with heroes who have it all: wealth, status, good looks…everything but the right woman.

HEROES

The excitement of a gripping thriller, with intense romance at its heart. Resourceful, true-to-life women and strong, fearless men face danger and desire - a killer combination!

To see which titles are coming soon, please visit

millsandboon.co.uk/nextmonth

JOIN US ON SOCIAL MEDIA!

Stay up to date with our latest releases, author news and gossip, special offers and discounts, and all the behind-the-scenes action from Mills & Boon...

 @millsandboon

 @millsandboonuk

 facebook.com/millsandboon

 @millsandboonuk

It might just be true love...

GET YOUR ROMANCE FIX!

Get the latest romance news, exclusive author interviews, story extracts and much more!

blog.millsandboon.co.uk